JONATHAN BUCKLEY lives in Brighton. He is the author of *The Biography of Thomas Lang* (1997), *Xerxes* (1999), *Invisible* (2004) and *So He Takes the Dog* (2006).

Visit www.AuthorTracker.co.uk for exclusive information on your favourite HarperCollins authors.

From the reviews of *Ghost MacIndoe*:

'Remarkable . . . Elegiac, beautifully written and compelling, Buckley's novel is a fine achievement'   *The Times*

'Deceptively powerful . . . it is as a meditation on the nature of memory itself that it makes its most lasting impression'
                                                            Sunday Times

'Impressive and melancholy . . . The work of a writer of considerable talent'   *Daily Telegraph*

'Full of quietly effective writing' D.J. TAYLOR, *Independent*

'The quality of attention that Jonathan Buckley brings to his material deserves to be called poetic . . . His story makes a good deal of other contemporary fiction look empty and a bit foolish'   *TLS*

By the same author:

So He Takes the Dog
Invisible
Xerxes
The Biography of Thomas Lang

JONATHAN BUCKLEY

Ghost MacIndoe

HARPER PERENNIAL
London, New York, Toronto and Sydney

Harper Perennial
An imprint of HarperCollins*Publishers*
77–85 Fulham Palace Road
Hammersmith
London W6 8JB

www.harperperennial.co.uk

This special Waterstone's edition published by Harper Perennial 2006
1

First published in Great Britain by Fourth Estate in 2001
First published in paperback by Fourth Estate in 2002

Copyright © Jonathan Buckley 2001

Jonathan Buckley asserts the moral right to
be identified as the author of this work

A catalogue record for this book
is available from the British Library

ISBN-13 978-0-00-724004-3
ISBN-10 0-00-724004-X

This novel is entirely a work of fiction. The names,
characters and incidents portrayed in it are the work of the
author's imagination. Any resemblance to actual persons,
living or dead, events or localities is entirely coincidental.

Set in Ehrhardt by Rowland Phototypesetting Ltd, Bury St Edmunds, Suffolk

Printed and bound in Great Britain by Clays Ltd, St Ives plc

All rights reserved. No part of this publication may be
reproduced, stored in a retrieval system, or transmitted,
in any form or by any means, electronic, mechanical,
photocopying, recording or otherwise, without the prior
permission of the publishers.

This book is sold subject to the condition that it shall not,
by way of trade or otherwise, be lent, re-sold, hired out or
otherwise circulated without the publisher's prior consent
in any form of binding or cover other than that in which it
is published and without a similar condition including this
condition being imposed on the subsequent purchaser.

for Susanne Hillen

Ghost MacIndoe

1. Our Lady of Fatima

The postman was sitting on the doorstep of a shop halfway down the hill, with his empty bag like a cat on his lap, but he stood up when Alexander MacIndoe and his mother stopped, as if he had been waiting for them. There was dust all over his moustache, Alexander noticed, and on his eyelashes. The postman tipped his helmet to Alexander's mother. 'Morning, Mrs Mac,' he smiled, showing teeth that were the colour of pencil wood. 'Very elegant today, I must say.'

'Too kind, Mr Durrant,' she replied, with a serious face. She adjusted Alexander's cap and tucked the trailing end of his scarf into the breast of his coat.

Mr Durrant knocked the cap skew-whiff again, then straightened it. 'Hello, Master Mac, how are we this morning?' he asked.

Alexander said nothing. He looked from the postman's grey jacket to the clouds behind him, which were a different grey, and then to the balloons that wagged above him, which were another different grey and were bent like sad old dogs on their long, long leads. And when, in his fifty-eighth year, Alexander MacIndoe came to assemble the chronology of his life, this would be the oldest memory of which he could be certain. He would see a postman in a grey jacket, with grey barrage balloons above him, on a cold yellow morning in February, in 1944.

'A bad night, Mrs Mac,' said Mr Durrant.

'It was that,' she agreed, shifting the canvas bag that she had put in the seat of Alexander's pushchair.

'A grim one,' mused Mr Durrant. 'Your place come through all right?'

'Thank you, yes. All's well.'

'Count our blessings, eh?'

'Indeed we must.'

Alexander turned for a moment to watch a dray-horse haul a van out of Wemyss Road, and Mr Durrant moved a step closer to his mother. 'Copped it down there they did,' the postman told her, jabbing a thumb over his shoulder. He smiled sympathetically at Alexander, who saw that his eyes had tears in them. 'Would the wee man like something?' asked Mr Durrant. And here Alexander MacIndoe's earliest true memory would recommence, with a postcard sliding upwards from a flap and a picture of the Virgin Mary, her white-shrouded head at the centre of the swirling rays of an orange sun, against a sky that was bluer than any he had ever seen. Mr Durrant turned the card and traced the words he then displayed with a finger that was creased like a worn sock. 'The Thompson Family, 13 Shooters Hill Road, London, England.' He worked the card between Alexander's fingers and left it in the boy's grip.

'He can't take that,' said his mother.

'Well, I can't deliver it, Mrs MacIndoe,' Mr Durrant replied. 'Nobody of that name at that address for as long as I've been around.' Gently he extracted the postcard from the boy's grip and turned its reverse to her. 'No message anyhow, see? People, eh? Forget their own names, some of them would.' He posted the card back into Alexander's hands and patted him on the head.

'Say thank you, Alexander,' his mother instructed him. Without a sound he mouthed the words.

'We'll meet again, young fellow-me-lad,' said Mr Durrant, pinching a cheek. 'Take care, Mrs Mac. Take care, tiny man.'

His mother took him along a street that was not the way to Mrs Kiernan's. Her curls bobbed quickly as she hurried, steering the pushchair with her fingertips; Alexander, holding the cold steel handle, had to skip along to keep up. She began to sing to him the song she sang every morning on the way to Mrs Kiernan's house. 'She's the girl that makes the thing that drills the hole that holds the spring, that drives the rod that turns the knob, that works the thingumebob,' she sang, stroking his nose with a fingertip at the end of the verse. The pavement became gritty, and soon there was water running down the road, water that was plaited like his father's belt. He saw Mrs Murrell, Mrs Beckwith, Mrs Darling and Mrs Evans, standing side by side in the middle of the street, looking away from them. The women glanced back and parted to allow Alexander and his mother into the line. There were branches all over the ground and an ambulance parked by a stump of a tree, and behind it was a hill of bricks and broken boards, over which some men were walking. To the side of the hill was a wall with a chimney on it, and pink-striped wallpaper on the upper part, above patches of blue stripes. On one blue-striped patch hung a mirror on a thin chain.

'Terrible business, Irene,' said Mrs Evans, the first of the women to speak.

'It is, it is,' his mother agreed. 'There but for the grace,' she added, a phrase her son would often, in the following weeks, repeat silently to himself, reassured of his mother's wisdom by his inability to understand what she had meant.

'The Fitchies,' said Mrs Darling. She sniffed loudly, jerking her head back as though she had been struck on the forehead. The doors of the ambulance opened and two men stepped out of it, carrying two long poles between them, with a sling of canvas between the poles.

His mother seized his hand. He watched the two men picking a path across the bricks, past a bread tin and a whole glass bottle that stood between the legs of a chair with a snapped back. A mauve eiderdown, speared on a broken windowframe, was the only thing on the hill that was not the colour of cement. At the back of a gully in the rubble, an empty doorway stood upright still, and Mr Nesbit, from the ironmonger's shop, stood in its frame, looking at something he had placed in the bowl of a white tin helmet. Alexander watched Mrs Murrell fold a handkerchief then drop it into her handbag, which fastened with a click of the two brass berries on the clasp.

The women talked in whispers to his mother. 'They found Moira. Donald's in there as well, almost definitely,' he heard Mrs Murrell say, a moment before Mr Nesbit lost his footing and tumbled out of sight.

'Mind how you go, Douggie,' said Mrs Darling, not loudly.

All the women, even Alexander's mother, made a brief laughing sound, but none of them smiled.

'All right your way, Irene?' asked Mrs Beckwith.

His mother nodded, watching Mr Nesbit as he clambered back up towards the doorway.

'Ruby's son-in-law, too. Out on patrol in East India Docks,' said

Mrs Murrell. 'Couldn't have seen the parachute. God knows how he missed it. Lovely lad,' she said, and shook her head. 'Shame it is. Bloody shame.'

'Rita,' said Mrs Evans.

'Siemens caught it and all, I heard,' said Mrs Darling.

'Not what I heard,' Mrs Murrell told her. 'And a bloody shame is what it is. A bloody damned shame.'

'Rita,' insisted Mrs Evans. 'The boy.'

'Oh Christ,' Mrs Beckwith winced. 'Irene,' she said, and then his mother's hands closed over his face. He could not breathe properly, so he pulled at her hands. She turned his face into her coat, but Alexander strained his eyes to peer through a gap in her fingers, and what he saw was the two men coming down off the ruins of the house, and a pair of feet sticking up from the sling, one with a brown sock on it and the other bare and yellowish, like a pig's trotter in the butcher's. One of the men opened the ambulance door and climbed in. The feet waggled like ducks on a pond.

'We're not doing any good here, girls,' said Mrs Darling, which made Mrs Murrell, Mrs Beckwith and Mrs Evans turn and form a circle around Alexander and the pushchair. Alexander put out a hand to bat a coat aside; the ambulance doors were closed.

Mrs Evans stooped down to Alexander and touched the postcard. 'What have you got there, Allie?' she asked him, squeezing his chin lightly.

He bowed his head and with the nose of a shoe scuffed a circle in the rough powder that lay over the pavement.

'Be polite, Alexander,' said his mother.

Mrs Murrell crouched beside Mrs Evans. There were grains like sugar, but finer, amid the fine pale hairs of her cheeks, and in her hat was a pin in the shape of a swan, with wings of red stones.

Alexander raised the postcard to hide himself behind it.

'Same colour as I'm wearing,' said Mrs Murrell, holding her overcoat open to reveal a pleat of her radiant blue dress.

Mrs Darling hitched up her coat and came down so her face was level with Alexander's. Her lips glistened with wet red lipstick; her breath had a smell he would later know was the smell of cherries. 'That's nice. Where did you get that?' she asked him. Alexander Mac-

Indoe shrugged and looked to his mother. 'Who is it?' coaxed Mrs Darling.

'The bomb lady,' said Alexander.

Mrs Murrell laughed and touched his cheek as if to wipe a bit of dirt away. All together the three women stood up straight. Mrs Evans tapped the arm of his mother and spoke to her in a voice that sounded like gas flowing into a mantle. He felt something settle on his head; it was Mrs Beckwith's hand. She teased his hair as his mother sometimes did at night when he could not sleep.

Mr Nesbit, raising a plank upright, called out and waved his hands. The other men all went towards him, kicking half-bricks down the hill.

'Must get his highness delivered,' his mother said, swivelling the pushchair around.

'We'll all be late at this rate,' answered Mrs Murrell. 'See you in the slave quarters, Irene.'

Mrs Evans squeezed his hand before he could reach the handle of the pushchair. 'You're a funny little mite,' she said to him with a smile up at his mother, and she pressed his fingers softly in her soft, cool palm.

Alexander would remember clutching his postcard on a corner where the smell of burned paint was strong, and the clanging of a fire engine as his mother said goodbye, then being put on the draining board of the kitchen sink for his evening wash. He was there when his father returned.

His mother slapped the wrung flannel onto the sink between the taps before kissing his father, who flipped back the shiny steel bar of his briefcase and took out a thing that was like a dirty handkerchief stiffened with frost. He placed it on the table and gave it a nudge; it rattled on the wood. 'Look at that,' he said to them. 'You know what they are?' Alexander shook his head. 'Letters, that's what. Written on stuff called vellum, which is an old kind of paper. A fire shrivelled them up. Nobody will be reading those again, will they?' he said to Alexander. His coat had brought the atmosphere of the street indoors; the perfume of smoke rose from his collar in a draught of coolness.

Touching the baked object, his mother shivered. 'Like having someone's shinbone on the table.'

5

'Something odd to amuse our child,' his father said. 'It's going back tomorrow anyway. If you knew the risks I've taken to bring it here.' He turned up the collar of his coat and squinted shiftily at his son. 'Mr MacIndoe, Undercover Operations Man,' he croaked.

'Mr MacIndoe, daft man,' Alexander's mother sighed. She raised the jug above the boy's head to trickle the lukewarm water over him.

Alexander watched his father squirm free of his coat, then settle in his chair and close his eyes. A moment later his father yawned, took off his spectacles, placed them on the round table, and lifted the newspaper so close to his face that Alexander could see nothing of him except his hands and legs. Over the top of the paper was the top of the door, which had been on the tilt, his mother said, since the day after he was born, when the Thousand Pounder fell in the next street. The crockery had flown across the room and scratched a shape like the letter A in the table, which is why he had been called Alexander.

Briskly his mother rubbed his chest with the thick green towel, humming as she buffed his skin. His cheek rested on the flesh of her upper arm, which was smooth as soap and smelled of lavender. Wrapped in the towel, he was carried to the fireplace and into his mother's lap, on the chair beside the round table. She scoured his hair and combed it and parted it, then placed him on her knee and held him towards her husband.

'We are beautiful, aren't we?' she asked and then pressed her open lips to Alexander's ear.

The newspaper came down a few inches. Slowly his father put on his spectacles again, and peeped over the edge of the drooping page. 'We are,' he said.

'We both?' replied his mother.

His father flapped the newspaper open wide. 'Fish, fish, fish,' he said, and turned a page.

'Daddy will take you to bed,' his mother told him, slicking his hair with her hand.

'In a minute,' said his father from behind the page. 'The home front can wait a minute longer.'

Pursing her lips, Alexander's mother looked towards the window. Underneath the reflection of the ceiling moved a cloud that was the colour of tea. 'Where's Mr Fitchie?' Alexander asked.

She turned him to face her and regarded him as if she were not certain that it had been Alexander who had spoken. 'Where's who?' she said.

'Mr Fitchie. Where's he gone?'

She tucked the towel more tightly around his shoulders. 'He's not here any more,' she said.

'I saw him.'

'Saw who?' his mother asked. He would remember the shape of her eyes as she asked him this, narrowed as if straining to see in the dark.

'Mr Fitchie.'

'When did you see him?'

'Today. I saw him. Where's he gone?'

'Away, Alexander.'

'Where to?'

His mother smoothed his hair again. 'Graham,' she pleaded.

'I like Mr Fitchie,' he told his mother.

'So did I,' said his mother.

'He's nice.'

'Graham,' she repeated.

'Where's he gone?' asked Alexander.

'He's with Jesus, Alexander. Mr Fitchie's gone to live with Jesus.'

'Might have,' his father joined in. 'But then again –'

'Graham. Please.'

Alexander closed his eyes once more, and in his head he saw the ambulance door and waggling feet. His father picked him up and carried him to his bed in the shelter.

From this night and from other nights Alexander would remember the top of the cellar steps, where the mud-coloured boards of the hallway ended at two shallow troughs of pale, splintery wood. The material of his father's jacket scratched at his face when his father hunched over to duck through the gate of the cage in the cellar. He would recall his mattress in the corner of the cage, and the toy truck that was wedged into the folds of the blankets. He recalled gripping the wires in a span of his hand as his father climbed back up the steps, and testing his tongue against the metal, getting a taste that was tart.

Unequivocally from this February night he remembered waking in the darkness to hear first the grinding in the sky, and then his mother's breathing. Her hand touched his forehead and its dampness made him shudder. 'It's all right,' she said. 'They'll soon be gone. We'll be all right.' He pressed his face against his mother's arms, waiting for the ack-acks on the Heath and the woof of the big guns. Upstairs someone knocked on the door and he heard the clang of his father's helmet against the wall as he left.

'You were born on a night like this,' his mother told him. 'Nothing bad is going to happen to you, or to any of us.' She sang to him quietly. 'The cats and dogs will dance in the heather,' she sang, and soon he could not hear the planes, but only his mother's voice and her heartbeat, and Alexander slid into sleep, imagining tiny aeroplanes flying out from under a big blue gown like the flies around the bins at the end of the road, and the men on Shooters Hill firing their guns while the big balloons grazed in the clouds above them, and a factory full of seamen, and Mr Fitchie. Mr Fitchie was in a black suit that shone like a crow's feathers and he was staring across a road at Alexander as if Alexander was floating past in a boat. Mr Fitchie was not happy but he was not sad either. He looked across the road with his head at an angle, and his hands in his pockets. His eyes blinked quickly three or four times, in the shadow of the brim of his hat, the way the geese blink at you through the railings around the lake in the park.

2. Gisbert

He was in the street with Jimmy Murrell, as Alexander was to recall in his fifty-eighth year, and they were taking it in turns to throw a ball against the kerbstone for the straw-coloured stray to catch. The ball was black and almost as hard as a cricket ball, and each time they took it from the dog's mouth it left crumbs of rubber mixed with dog spit on their hands. Jimmy Murrell had a thick white gap in one eyebrow where he'd fallen from a rock and cracked his head in the farmyard at Exmouth, the town he soon went to live in, with his mother and father and his sisters.

To confuse the dog, Jimmy chucked a handful of air towards the kerb and the dog was twenty yards up the street before it heard the ball hit the tarmac down the slope. Its claws made a noise like a sewing machine as it ran, and its head went up and down in time with the bouncing ball. In Exmouth, Jimmy Murrell said, it was warmer than in London. With all the other children Jimmy used to go to a beach that was bigger than the Heath. Again he described the house at the back of the dunes, the only house for miles, with a fence of white boards around it and big nets hanging from the boards. The walls of the house were white wood, and right in the centre was a red door that looked like a pillarbox stuck in the sand. Thousands of pools were left on the sand when the tide went out, said Jimmy, with shreds of seaweed in them and sometimes a small green crab-shell. The tide went out so far that it was farther than walking from his house to the shops, and at night if the tide was low you couldn't even hear the sea. But if the tide was high at night, you could see the waves glowing, as if there were torches under the water.

The dog, too tired to drop the ball, sat down beside Alexander. Its tongue was bent behind the ball and drooped sideways out of its mouth, dripping big dark circles onto the paving stones.

'Bigger than all the houses,' Jimmy Murrell said. 'Higher and longer,' and with a swing of his arm he made Alexander see the marvellous dunes.

Alexander would remember in his later years that Jimmy Murrell was waving his arms and speaking to him when he heard his mother's voice. She was calling his name and she was running alongside the privet hedges with her arms straight up in the air in a gesture that frightened him.

'Boys!' she yelled, and then she did a couple of skips just like Jimmy's sisters when they played on the path. 'Boys! Come here!' she shouted, though she was running so fast she was with them before they could get to their feet. She picked up Alexander and hugged him to her chest. It remained in Alexander's memory that she was wearing the pale blue blouse with the daisies on it, and that the second button of her blouse was in the top buttonhole. Then she put him down and hugged Jimmy Murrell where he stood, squashing his face against her legs. She put out a hand and ruffled Alexander's hair, and it was then he realised that nothing bad had happened.

'It's over,' she said. 'It's over, it's over, it's over,' she sang and she clapped her hands as she looked down on them, as though they had done something that had delighted her. 'Your daddy will be back soon,' she told Jimmy Murrell.

'How soon?' asked Jimmy.

'Very soon,' she said. With her left hand she took hold of Jimmy's right and she gave the other to her son and whirled them both around her skirt. 'Home we go,' she declared, then hand in hand they walked back up the road, with the dog behind them.

The kitchen was full of women when they arrived. By the radio sat Mrs Murrell, her cheek close to the front of it, as if it was telling her something no one else was meant to hear, while Mrs Evans was at the sink, rinsing and wiping the tea cups. Other women stood around the table, and on the garden step was a woman Alexander knew worked at his mother's factory, but he did not know her name; she was smoking a cigarette, and she turned as he came into the room and breathed out a cloud of smoke that covered her face for a moment. There was hardly any space for him to stand in.

'Jimmy with you, Alexander?' Mrs Murrell asked, then Jimmy stepped in from the hall. She did not get up, but held her arms wide open for her son to walk into, and pinched his cheeks so his lips stretched like a rubber band.

Setting the tray on the table, Mrs Evans remarked – 'It'll all be different now.'

'It will that, Iris,' said Irene MacIndoe. 'Everything will change now.'

'Different world,' agreed Mrs Murrell.

Lying on the lawn beside his friend, Alexander stared at the sky and wondered in what way the sky would be a different sky. He imagined planes that were different planes, shaped like starfish or painted green. Rockets meandered over the horizon and nosed among the chimneys like curious dogs, then meandered off again. He thought he might live in a house by the sea, and he saw on the inside of his eyelids a beach as long as the river, and a house with a red door. He saw Mr Fitchie walking along a beach towards a red door that was on its own, and felt as if he were floating up off the grass into the warm high sky. A cheering came from the kitchen, and then church bells were ringing like on a Sunday, but they did not stop; the bells kept on for hours.

The following day his parents took him out of the house at an hour when normally he would already have been in bed, and they went to call for Mrs Beckwith. There were more people on the street that night than he had ever seen in the day. Their heads bobbed like apples in a bowl, and the noise of their voices and feet blended into one loud rumble. On the Heath there were hundreds and hundreds of people, moving towards a fire that rose in a single pinnacle of flame over their heads. Alexander and his parents and Mrs Beckwith joined the crowd, falling in with the purposeful pace. The people pressed more tightly on Alexander with every step; the bit of the sky that he could see was no larger than his father's head; he looked down at the grass, and seeing it flattened and ripped by the thousands of feet he suddenly cried out, and was in an instant hoisted onto his father's shoulders.

'What can you see?' his father asked. The fire glinted on his spectacles as he bent his head back to speak to him.

'Nothing,' Alexander reported.

'You must see something, Alexander,' said his mother.

'I can see the top of the fire,' he replied. 'And lots of people,' he added, scanning the Heath. Every road was full of marching people.

11

'All of England must be here,' said his mother.

'Not quite,' said Mrs Beckwith.

Alexander saw his mother touch Mrs Beckwith's shoulder. He was impatient to discover what it was they had come to see.

They came across three soldiers in berets, sitting on a settee beside a track, and drinking from a bottle which one of them jiggled at Mrs Beckwith as they passed. Alexander saw a woman he thought at first was the woman who worked in Mr Prentice's shop; a man's bandaged hand was resting on her waist, and she had a little trumpet in her mouth. They were near enough to the fire for him to glimpse two shrieking faces on the other side of the flames when a split appeared in the crowd and what looked for a second like a galloping bull rushed through the gap. It was two men carrying a park bench between them; on the bench was stretched a man made out of an old jumper and trousers, with newspaper hands and feet and a football for a head. The two men seized the dummy, held it up for everyone to see, then hurled it onto the fire. The people around all cheered, and they cheered again when the two men rocked the bench backwards and forwards and let it go into the flames.

They stayed by the fire for half an hour or so, then his father led them off the Heath, past the Nissen huts. It was late, but they did not go straight home. They walked down the hill with Mrs Beckwith, who held Alexander's hand but seemed dejected. His father and mother went in front, her head resting on his shoulder as they walked. At the railway bridge they stopped. A train was at the station below the road; above the grumbling of its engine he heard Mrs Beckwith say: 'It'll be a time yet, Irene.' His mother put a hand on Mrs Beckwith's shoulder again and nodded at his father, who lifted him to look over the parapet as the train pulled out.

Inside the carriages every seat was filled. Men were standing between the seats, clinging to the racks, while women were sitting on the laps of other women, and the pale blue light in the carriages made all the faces inside look as pale as peeled potatoes. A window clacked open and a man yelled up something that Alexander could not hear. Mrs Beckwith waved at the train without looking at it.

'They're going up to town,' his father told him.

'Tough work,' said Mrs Beckwith, 'but someone's got to do it.'

'Not for the likes of us, young man,' said his father sternly, but smiling.

'It's bed for us,' his mother confirmed, and Alexander watched the red light at the back of the train disappear into the darkness of the cutting on its way into town, a place he saw as an arrangement of perfectly regular streets and buildings with thousands of windows, all undamaged because town was somewhere that was always there, outside the war. It seemed to him that the passengers he had seen on the train were on a night-time mission of some sort, a mission that was to do with making things change.

His mother was always at home now, and throughout that summer he went to the shops with her most mornings, and queued beside her patiently, while the other children larked on the pavement outside. In the afternoon he would play with Jimmy Murrell or with other boys whose names he was to lose from his memory in his twenties and thirties, or he would walk through Greenwich Park with his mother, sometimes continuing right down to the river, where they might go into the tunnel beneath the water, to see the long walls that were curved and covered in tiles like frozen milk. Often, when they walked through the park, she would take him to the statue of Wolfe and sit on the slope below the bronze general, making an armchair for him from her arms and legs, and he would lie back against her chest while she sang an American song for him under her breath. Once she pointed across the river and said something about St Paul's, something that made him think the church had somehow fought off the bombers, a scene he pictured as the dome swivelling and sending out some sort of beam to bring the enemy down.

It was an image he would always retain, though within a few years it had slipped from its mooring in the weeks between the victory days. What Alexander would recall unerringly from that interval, throughout his life, was the sight of his mother dabbing her eyes as she made his bed one morning, and on a different day dusting the sideboard as if in a daze, her eyes fixed on the wallpaper in front of her, and another day standing in the hallway with the mop planted upright in its bucket, gazing through the open door and down the front path as if she were waiting for someone, though it was several hours before his father would finish work. Many times he would stand silently beside her when she was doing her housework, as he did when they queued in the shops. And once, he remembered more completely than anything from that period, she put the mop aside and framed his face in her hands to stare into his eyes. 'My God, you do look like an angel,' she said, but she said it as if it were some illness that he had. She gathered both his hands in one of hers and kissed them. 'My black-eyed angel,' she murmured, and looked over his shoulder through the narrow window beside the door, at the pavement along which nobody was passing.

This was a short time before a Saturday on which he went with his father to the church hall to collect a pair of trestles which they put in the garden of Mrs Darling's house, alongside a stack of planks. Later that day he made flags with his mother, holding the scissors for her as she pulled the old sheets through the open blades, so they ripped with a thrilling squeal. They cut out triangles of material and stewed them in pots of red and blue water, then pegged them out to dry on the line, and when that was done they made letters of black card which they pasted on a placard out the front, spelling the words 'Welcome Home George'. When Mr Evans came over with Mrs Evans to see the placard, Alexander looked down from his bedroom and saw Mrs Evans begin crying as soon as she had read the word 'Welcome' aloud; Mr Evans steered her back through the gate, his enormous hand spread right across her back, and his shoes made sparks on the paving stones.

At the start of the party Jimmy Murrell handed out conical paper hats and Alexander was tucked into a place at the end of the table by Mrs Beckwith, facing the stage that the men from the pub had built. The air smelled special, of marzipan and hair oil and washing powder, and the sunlight made the raspberry jelly glow so beautifully that he felt sad when one of the adults spooned a divot from it and tipped it on his plate. The owner of the pub played the piano on the stage while everyone ate, and then Mr Evans made a speech and all the adults banged their cups up and down. 'Irene, if you will,' said Mr Evans, holding out a hand in mid-air. Alexander watched his mother climb the steps at the side of the stage. She went over to the piano and stood beside it, with one hand resting on the top of it. He waited for her to call him. The pianist played a few notes and stopped. Alexander leaned forward to find his father, but could not see where he was. His mother

14

was looking at her shoes. Mrs Beckwith stood up and moved a couple of steps away from him, towards the stage. The pianist played the same tune again, and this time Alexander's mother began to sing. It was the song about the bluebirds that she sang, and she sang it in a voice that was not like the voice with which she used to sing at home. Her eyes were closed as if she were singing for herself alone, but her voice was stronger than he had ever heard it, so strong that all the people around began to sing with her one by one, and when the chorus came he could barely hear her above their shouting. The pianist took one hand off the keyboard and made a scooping motion; all the adults who had been sitting rose in front of Alexander, excluding his mother from view. Hands went threading under elbows; backs swayed against backs.

Unnoticed, Alexander eased his seat back from the table. The stray was lying close by, under a tail of tablecloth. Crumbling a piece of cake on the road to entice the dog, Alexander wandered off, in the opposite direction from the stage. There was another chorus, even louder than the first, and when it was finished everyone sang it again. And as the first line began again, Alexander glanced up from the dog to see a man sitting with his back against the shelter at the top of the road. He was a thin man, doubled over as if he were made of folded card, and he had hair that was the colour of the dog's hair. The man was looking at Alexander but he was not singing. He had eyes like the sky and a big thin nose.

Stretching his long legs into the gutter, the man put his hands on the sides of the dog's head and looked at its face as if it was a cup that was cracked. 'He is yours?' he asked, in a voice that was peculiar, and sounded as though he was telling him something rather than asking. His jacket was inky blue and made of stuff like the felt Alexander's mother put on the sideboard to stop the vase from scratching. 'Not yours?' the man asked, to which Alexander shook his head. 'What is his name?'

'He doesn't have a name.'

'But you have a name,' the man responded, but Alexander did not reply. 'My name is Gisbert,' said the man. 'My name is Gisbert. G-I-S-B-E-R-T,' he recited. At the bottom of the street the piano made a booming sound and everybody laughed. 'Now you tell me your name.'

'Alexander.'

'Alexander what?' asked Gisbert.

'Alexander MacIndoe.' His name sounded strange when he spoke it to this stranger, as if he had been labelled like a bottle in the kitchen.

'Where do you live, Alexander?'

He pointed to the placard. 'The house with the writing,' he said.

'Welcome Home, George,' Gisbert read, but he said the last word so it sounded like 'judge'.

'Where do you live?' asked Alexander.

The man stood up; he was much taller than Alexander's father, and the cuffs of his jacket did not cover his wrists. A bony forefinger indicated the rooftops. 'Today I live on the Shooters Hill,' he explained. 'But my home is a longer way.'

'Over the hill?' asked Alexander.

'Yes. A long way over the hill. A long way.' Gisbert made his brow wrinkle, and scratched the side of his nose. 'I will go there soon. Tomorrow perhaps. Next week perhaps.' Then he smiled so widely that the gums showed above his back teeth.

'Is it like here?'

'No, not like here,' said Gisbert, and he petted the dog as though the dog had asked the question. 'There are big mountains, big forests, big lakes. Everything green. Not like here.'

Alexander would always remember Gisbert's name, the fabric of his jacket, his chilly eyes, and these words that conjured for him a scene in which Gisbert walked over the rise of Shooters Hill and down a long slope to a vast green forest, a forest he imagined as being just beyond his sight when, some five months later, his father and mother took him past the crest of the hill for the first time.

'Here is something for you, Alexander MacIndoe,' said Gisbert as he reached into his jacket. He extracted a button, breathed on it and rubbed it on his sleeve. Alexander extended a palm to receive the gift. Raised on the button was a wonderful and mysterious sign, a pair of wings with no body. Holding it by the little loop of metal on the other side, Alexander breathed on the button too, and slipped it into his pocket. 'Thank you,' he said.

'You are welcome,' said Gisbert. 'But I think you must leave, Alexander,' he added, in the same moment as Alexander heard Mrs Beckwith's voice.

'Away, Alex,' she shouted. 'Come here. Come away. Here.' She tugged him towards her and bent over to get close to his face. 'You mustn't talk to him,' she said. Alexander looked back to see Gisbert shrug his shoulders at him and raise his left hand. Mrs Beckwith tapped the boy's chin to make him turn.

'Why not?' he asked.

'Because I say so.'

'Why?'

'Because you shouldn't be talking to him, that's why. He's not one of us,' she said.

'Who?'

'Don't be contrary, Alex,' Mrs Beckwith told him.

'One of who?' Alexander persisted.

'Us, Alex. You and me and your parents and your friends,' she stated. 'He shouldn't be here.'

At the table she pushed the chair into the backs of his knees. His mother was moving towards him, cradling a dish of custard. Alexander craned his neck to see if he could see Gisbert, but he had gone back to the hill. He repeated inwardly the letters of Gisbert's name, the first name he ever made an effort to remember.

Five hours more the party lasted, but only one moment from those hours was to endure in Alexander's mind as long as Gisbert's name and Gisbert's forest. It was at the end of the night, and he alone was left sitting at the table. He was inhaling the tangy smoke from the candles that his mother and Mrs Beckwith had blown out, when he heard the sound of a footfall he recognised as his father's. A firework slid up the sky with a shush and sprayed new stars on the sky. His father leaned over him to pick him up. 'Little Lord Weary,' his father said to his mother. Alexander watched a red dot of burning tobacco chase around the rim of his father's cigar. He looked at the fire below the flower of grey ash and then he saw his father kiss his mother on her mouth, which he had never seen him do before.

3. Nan Burnett

The hedge at the front of his grandmother's house was so high that even his father could not see over it, and instead of a front gate she had a proper door of dark wood, around which the leaves grew in a solid arch. The metal numbers on the door – 122 – were held in place by screws that had gone furry with rust. A spoon-shaped thumb-pad protruded through the keyhole on the right side of the door, and when it was pressed the catch always screeched. Inside there was a slab of greenish concrete on which the underside of the door would scrape, then three steps made of red bricks that had crumbled into a shape like a half-filled sack. From the steps a path of crazy paving zigzagged across the grass, passing a rose bush that grew so few flowers it looked like a ball of wire on which the shreds of a small pink scarf had snagged. Down the length of the garden ran a washing-line held high by a stick of dirty-looking wood, which was planted in the grass near the hollow that had once been a pond. All of this Alexander would remember, and the white rhododendron overhanging the hollow, under which he would find a frog sometimes, and kneel on the soggy ground to watch the panicky pulse in the animal's side until it sprang away, falling into the dandelions with the quietest of crashes.

An ivy, rooted under the bay of the front room, swerved under the sills and then spread outwards, covering most of the bathroom window and part of the bedroom's bay, spilling down over the porch and flowing inwards to the door. Once a month, on a Sunday, Alexander and his parents would visit Nan Burnett, and if the weather was fine his father would be certain, at some point in the afternoon, to lean aside and look down the hallway from the kitchen, remarking: 'Things a bit wild out front, aren't they, Nan?' or 'Had problems locating the entrance recently?' or 'Found any Japs this week?' And whatever the joke, Nan Burnett would pat the back of his father's hand and call him a treasure, and his father, standing behind a chair to grasp the topmost rung of its back like the handrail of a captain's bridge, would order all MacIndoe hands on deck. 'Action stations!' he commanded, opening the door from the kitchen to the backyard, which was nothing but a small rectangle of glazed grey bricks, with a tiny shed where Nan Burnett stored the stepladders and the shears, and a gate opening onto an alley that had a crest of grass down the middle and lumps of black glassy rock on its verges.

Alexander would follow his father back through the house, bearing the shears blade-downwards past the coat-stand and the oval mirror and the line of Nan Burnett's shoes, with their toe caps turned up like heads, watching the goings-on in the hall. When his father had rolled his sleeves up above his elbows and loosened his tie, Alexander would present the shears and then stand back in attendance, while his father sliced long cords of ivy from the wall and lopped hanks of foliage off the hedge that separated the garden from the street.

'Remove please, toot sweet,' his father said, glancing back over his shoulder first at his son and then at the tangle of cuttings, which Alexander scooped into his arms and carried out to the yard, where his father would burn them. If ever he was left alone to keep an eye on the smouldering leaves, Alexander would step into the blue, stripy smoke that streamed from the fire, so that his clothes that evening would be soaked with a smell that had come from Nan Burnett's garden.

On days when Alexander's mother had to go up to town or do something else that she had to do without him, she would usually take him to Nan Burnett's house, and often another visitor would arrive while he was there. Sometimes it was Dot, whose surname he never knew; she lived somewhere further down the street, past the newsagent's shop, and from time to time she would hand him a twist of paper in which four or five boiled sweets were wrapped. Or it might be Mrs Solomon, Nan Burnett's neighbour, who brought one of her cats with her in a wicker basket, and had a hairy mole in the centre of her cheek. On a Wednesday it was likeliest to be Beryl Stringer, a woman of his mother's age, whom he was to remember only for her turquoise woollen bonnet. If he were at Nan Burnett's on a Saturday he might see Nurse Reilly, who had violet hair and thick legs that had no ankles, and always brought two things with her: a paper bag full of wool and knitting needles, and a small bale of magazines, tied up with rough yellow twine. Always Nan Burnett would place the magazines on a stool beneath the table before taking her own piece of knitting from the basket on the shelf above the oven, and then the two women would sit on opposite sides of the table and the only sounds would be the ticking of the big clock beside the hall door and the jittery clicking of the needles. And once in a while the caller would be Miss Blake, whose name perplexed Alexander, as Miss Blake was no younger than Nan Burnett. Neither her name nor any feature of her appearance lasted long in Alexander's mind, but one image of her presence did persist, in a scene in which Nan Burnett and another old lady were seated at the kitchen table, each with one elbow on the tabletop, each facing the window that looked onto the yard. There was a pot of tea between them, under a knitted tea-cosy, and they were listening to a tennis match on the radio. Alexander was listening too, but intermittently, for what engrossed him was the intentness and pleasure of the two old women, whose eyes flickered back and forth as they listened, as if the game were visible to them on the glass of the kitchen window.

But the visitor whom Alexander was to remember most fully was the one whose heavy tread down the hallway made the boards creak in the front room, where Alexander was, and whose laugh – a laugh so like a scream that momentarily he thought Nan had scalded herself – raised his curiosity to a pitch that forced him out to see who this person was. It was a short fat woman, and she was sitting in the chair that Nan Burnett normally sat in. She was dressed all in black but for a band of shiny white material above her eyes, below the black scarf that covered her hair. Her skirt was made of stuff that was like a tablecloth and it came down to the laces of her highly polished shoes, which were men's shoes and also black. Instead of a blouse or a cardigan she wore a sort of cape that hung from her shoulders down to her waist. Her arms, tightly covered in black fabric, rose from the folds of the cape as she gave Alexander her hand.

'So this will be Alexander MacIndoe?' she said. Her fingernails were so perfectly trimmed and so white and so clean they made him feel queasy. 'Alexander the tiny, is it?' she laughed, clapping her palms on her knees.

'Don't be shy, Alexander,' said Nan Burnett. 'Say hello to Sister Martha.'

He did not speak. He looked at Sister Martha's faintly creased pink cheeks; they reminded him of marshmallows.

'Let's take a view of you,' said Sister Martha, resting her hands on his shoulders. 'You're a fine young specimen of a boy, I must say,' she said. 'A handsome young man. You watch out for the ladies now,' she warned him, and when she laughed her cheeks bunched into little globes right under her eyes. 'Are you at school yet?' asked Sister Martha, and Alexander replied that he was.

'And are there other Alexanders at your school?' she asked.

'I don't think so.'

'Do you like your name, Alexander?'

'Yes,' he replied, beginning to be troubled by the idea that his name bore some significance of which he was unaware.

'And so you should, young fellow. It's a distinguished name,' said Sister Martha. 'A very distinguished name. Lots of great men have been called Alexander. Alexander the Great, he goes without saying. There have been Russian kings and Scottish kings called Alexander, too. Mr Alexander Fleming, he's a great man. There was Alexander Pope the poet, though I'm not so sure about him. And there have been many Alexander popes as well, of course,' she chuckled.

Alexander looked at Nan Burnett, who winked at him and passed him a sandwich she had made. The sliver of brown meat lay between slices of bread that were as grey as her hair.

'There have been many popes called Alexander,' Sister Martha said. 'There was Mister Borgia, who was from Spain and a very bad man, it must be admitted. Not a great one at all. But then there was Mr Chigi, who was Italian and a good man, though he was very rich. And a long time before him there was a young Pope Alexander, who was made a martyr in Rome on the third of May.' Sister Martha wiggled her eyebrows at him. 'You look astonished. Your birthday wouldn't be the third of May, would it, by any chance?'

'No,' said Alexander, lifting the sandwich to his mouth.

'No. That would have been a strange thing,' Sister Martha told him. Putting her fists on her hips she looked up at the ceiling and said to it: 'And we mustn't overlook another young Pope Alexander, one of the seven sons of Felicitas.' Her attention returned to the boy. 'Another saint,' she smiled, as if to encourage him. 'Also made a martyr in Rome.'

When he was alone again, in the front room, he repeated to himself the mystifying phrase. 'Made a martyr in Rome,' he muttered, imagining something that was like being knighted, but more important, and very pleasing to the people who saw it happen.

He enjoyed sitting on the kitchen floor and scanning the pictures in the magazines that Nurse Reilly had brought. He might pass an hour bowling a ball at a line of milk bottles in the alley out the back, or shunting his Dinky van around the streets defined by the cracks between the bricks in the yard. Most of all, however, he enjoyed being in the front room of Nan Burnett's house. The room had a rich and sleepy smell, a smell of varnished wood and old rugs, a smell that no other room had and was always the same. There were pictures in every corner of the room, hanging on nails midway up the walls, attached to the picture rail by slender brass chains, displayed in cardboard frames that stood on the sideboard, on the china cabinet and the mantelpiece above the fireplace, which had not been lit in years. To the left of the fireplace the miracles were gathered: The Loaves and the Fishes, The Bath at Bethesda, The Wedding at Cana, The Woman of Samaria, all in shades of cream and brown. To the right was Moses, tipping a dog-sized calf off its pedestal, standing aghast before a burning bush, dividing a sea that curled back onto itself like drying leaves. The pictures on the cabinet were photographs of his mother's father and two other men, all in tones of brown and cream but with a chalky finish that made it seem as if everything in the pictures – the men's skin, their jackets, the walls behind them – were made of the same stuff. Alexander once asked Nan Burnett who the other men were, expecting to hear that they were relatives, but they were friends of her husband, who had died with Stanley Burnett at a place Alexander never forgot because Nan Burnett swore when she said it. 'Wipers,' he would repeat as he regarded the dead men. 'That bloody place,' he would whisper, echoing his grandmother's curse, and sometimes he would take the red glass stopper from the perfume bottle that Nan Burnett kept with the china and put it over one eye while he looked at them. And having looked at them, he would draw the thick brown curtains all the way across the window, then take the wide cushions from the brown velvet armchairs and lay them in front of the fireplace. Lying in the silence that seemed to come out of the walls of Nan

22

Burnett's front room, Alexander would close his eyes and see the handsome women balancing the pitchers on their heads, the men with smooth beards and the children in striped gowns, walking down roads that were strewn with stones shaped not like real stones but more like miniature boxes. As clearly as if his eyes were open he would see The Last Supper, with the figure of Jesus looking straight at him, and the picture of the nameless woman holding her chest on a crumpled bed, her head thrown back as if she felt sick, and the rigid faces of Stanley Burnett and his two dead friends.

'What on earth do you do in there all day?' he would recall his mother asking him, as he rubbed his eyes in the hall.

'The boy just likes to be quiet,' Nan Burnett answered for him.

'Odd thing for a boy,' said his mother.

'Don't fuss, Irene. He's a happy lad. Aren't you, Alexander?' Nan Burnett asked.

'Yes,' he said, blushing, because he did not know if he was telling the truth.

Nan Burnett would never call him from the front room until his mother returned, but sometimes she called him from the yard to run an errand for her. He was on an errand when Megan arrived.

'Take this round to Mrs Solomon, will you, pet,' said Nan Burnett. She gave him a piece of paper full of numbers, with a drawing of a pullover on one side.

Mrs Solomon was putting a saucer of milk at the top of the stairs; one of her cats sprinted between Alexander's legs and the banisters; he stroked the cat a few times, handed over the pattern, and no more than five minutes after leaving he was back in the hall of Nan Burnett's house, his hand outstretched to open the door of the front room. Startled to hear his mother call his name, he jumped and looked to his left, and saw Megan for the first time.

His mother and Mrs Beckwith were advancing towards him down the hall, pushing the girl before them. Her eyes were the same colour as Gisbert's had been, but they were wider and brighter, like marbles, and her hair was red, exactly the red of the stain under the tap in Nan Burnett's bathroom. More than fifty years later, Alexander would be able to describe to Megan the outfit she was wearing: the white cotton blouse with the scallops around the neck; the blue-checked pinafore;

the sandals with the pattern of petals cut over the toes. His mother said: 'Alexander, this is Megan. She will be living with Mrs Beckwith now.'

The girl looked at him as if she was the one who lived in the house and Alexander was the one who had never been there before.

'You'll be friends, Alexander. That'll be nice, won't it?' said his mother.

Megan held out her right hand like a man. 'Hello, Alexander,' she said.

'Come on, say hello,' said his mother.

Alexander stared at the girl. Silently he repeated her name. The word had a taste and a texture, a bit like toffee.

'Pleased to meet you,' said Megan, jerking her hand as if she were already holding his.

'Come on, Alexander,' his mother chivvied, but still Alexander stared. 'Buck up, boy. Show some manners.' Over his mother's shoulder, Nan Burnett made a mock frown at him; she wagged a finger and mouthed the words 'bad boy'. And then Alexander kissed the girl, who took a step back and put a hand to the place where his mouth had touched her. 'You're an impossible child,' said his mother, taking hold of an arm.

A few minutes later Alexander and his mother were at the door, ready to leave. 'Next week,' she said as she reached for the handle. Alexander took one last look down the hall. Nan Burnett was standing in the kitchen with her hands on Megan's shoulders and smiling as if the girl's arrival were a treat she had arranged for him.

That was the face Alexander saw on the day on which, three years and five months after this one, he came back to Number 122 with his parents, to say goodbye to the house. His mother and father went upstairs, up the bare staircase, past the three white rectangles on the wall. He heard their feet on the floor above him, and when they moved into the room that had been Nan Burnett's bedroom he pushed open the door of the front room. As the door gave way to his touch, he heard his mother's voice in the hall say 'Alexander' softly, and he saw his grandmother in her kitchen, alone, but smiling as she had smiled when she had stood on that spot with Megan in front of her. A cold terror doused his body; he flinched and sucked in a breath without meaning to, and she was no longer there. And then it was like putting a finger in water and expecting it to be very cold and feeling it very cold when in fact it is warm, as it quickly becomes. He was not frightened, he realised. He had the sensation of being absolutely alone in a pleasant place, like a big garden that everyone else has left.

His mother saw a tear on his cheek. 'Are you all right, Alexander?' she asked him. 'We are a pair,' she said, and she put her handkerchief to the corners of her eyes and then to his.

'You're all right, aren't you?' asked his father.

'Yes,' said Alexander honestly, but he knew he must not mention what he had seen.

4. Eck

A nightlight, set on a saucer which had a crack across its pattern of blue willow leaves, burned on the stool between Alexander's bed and the window, casting the hilly shadow of his body across the wall. The short yellow flame, batted by the draught, nodded on the surface of the molten wax, in which tiny tadpoles of cinder swam about in circles, drifting close to flame, darting away to the edge of the pool, drifting back. Sometimes he would pluck a hair from his head and feed it into the flame to watch it become a wisp of smoke before it could enter the body of the fire, or hold his hand over the candle until the heat felt like a nail driven through his palm. Then he would lie motionless again, his arms folded on his chest, his face to the ceiling, watching the steam of his breath roll off into the room. At last he heard his mother's footsteps on the stairs, and the creak of the floorboards as she came to the landing. Downstairs the doors were being shut, always in the same order, ending with the clunk of the kitchen door and the rattle of its tall pane. His father's slower tread followed, becoming even slower as he reached the top of the stairs, making a louder creak. And on the nights when the electricity was off he would twice see the candlelight rise and fade under his door as first his mother and then his father went by, and then the door of his parents' room would close with a small thump and the light was gone. He lay listening to the rustling of the gardens and the dwindling grumble of his father's voice, keeping his eyes open until only the sounds of the wind remained.

In the mornings the glass was caked with ice on the inside, and often the night's fall of snow sloped high up the pane. When he opened the curtains the walls of his room were the tone of chicken flesh, and clammy as the disc of white wax that the nightlight had become. On the back of the chair beside the door a clean white shirt hung in the shadowless light like a big strip of cold fat. The tin bomber that was parked on the chest of drawers looked wet, like a car in fog. Rather than get out of bed, he would often daydream of Nan Burnett's garden,

26

where the snow was so deep he could tunnel through it, crawling on his hands and knees into the hollow that had once been the pond, and lying down under the radiant white roof, with no idea which way the house was, and then digging on until the floor of the tunnel changed from grass to bare earth, when he would leap upright, diving up into the world again. And sometimes, lying like an effigy on a tomb, he would send himself on an imaginary walk across the ceiling of his room, around and around the twisting stalk of the lightbulb's flex, over the bulge of plaster that looked as if it should yield like a pillow, and then stepping over the dam below the door to gaze up at the stairwell, which he could see so clearly it was as if his door were not closed.

When his mother called from the foot of the stairs he dressed and went down. 'Rip Van MacIndoe, awake at last,' she often said, and this was how she greeted him on the one morning that he would always be able to recall from this winter.

The smell of the previous evening's fish was still in the room. Every windowpane was streaming, and strings of water lay in the cracks of the windowframes between the sashes. Frozen clothes were stacked against the wall at an angle of forty-five degrees, the stiff cuffs and shirt-tails resting on the floor. He picked up a shirt and bent it across his knee; it cracked softly, like the rending of a dead branch.

'Where's your tumbler?' his mother asked him. She was holding the ribbed glass bottle of rose-hip syrup in one hand, while the other formed the shape of the missing glass. 'Have you left it in your room?'

'No,' he replied, and his mother laughed.

'Look at that stupid animal,' she said, pointing out of the window.

A black cat was stalking across the garden's perfect snow, pausing after every step and lowering its head for a moment; a robin watched it from the fence then flew away before the cat was close. Alexander looked at the track that the cat's belly had smudged across the snow, and it made him think of the snowball fight in the street two days before, when Mrs Beckwith and Megan had passed by. 'Go on,' Mrs Beckwith had said, and Megan had gone over to a car that was parked nearby and wiped a handful of snow from its bonnet. She raised her arm, but before she could throw it he threw a ball that hit her on the buttons of her coat. She dusted the snow off, and turned to walk back to Mrs Beckwith, and she did not stop when another snowball fell apart on her back. He called her name, but she did not look round. 'It's all right, Alexander,' Mrs Beckwith had called to him, as she patted the snow from Megan's back.

'Is Mrs Beckwith Megan's mother?' he asked.

'No, Alexander,' his mother replied. 'She's her auntie.'

It was a word that Alexander had never heard Megan use. 'So where is Megan's mother?' he asked. His mother placed the bottle on the draining board and drew a chair from the table for him to sit on. Putting her hands on his legs, she looked into his eyes.

'She doesn't have a mother any more,' she said.

'What about her father?'

'Megan doesn't have a father any more, either,' said his mother. Her fingers went tight on his legs. 'It is very sad, Alexander, and we mustn't ever say anything about it. Not to her and not to anybody. Do you understand?'

'Why doesn't she have a mother and father?' he persisted. 'Were they killed?'

'No, they weren't killed.'

'So where are they?'

'They're not here any longer, Alexander. That's all we need to know. We mustn't talk about it. It won't do any good.' She fastened the top button of his cardigan, as if to signify that the subject was at a close. 'It would upset Megan and Mrs Beckwith and everybody. Now, let's find that glass.'

Alexander followed his mother to the pantry, where her slippers made a sticky sound on the painted floor. She reached for a tin from the shelf below the perforated panel of zinc, on which the dots of sky always looked white, whatever kind of day it was.

'Will we be friends?' he asked.

'Who?'

'Me and Megan.'

'Of course you'll be friends. Don't you like her?'

'I don't know,' Alexander replied. 'Why doesn't she come here?'

'She will do. She's a bit shy, that's all,' his mother explained, but he thought of the way Megan looked at him when he said hello in the corridor at school, as if she had heard some story that had made her think she should stay away from him, and he remembered her walking across the playground with her teacher and talking to her as she would have talked to Mrs Beckwith, and she did not seem shy at all.

'I don't think she is,' he said.

'Yes, she is, Alexander,' his mother assured him. 'Give it time. Just wait.'

Through the spring of that year Alexander waited, even when he saw Megan ahead of him as they came out of school, walking on her own. She never looked back, and he could not speak to her, because there were things about Megan that nobody could speak about, and he was afraid that by accident he might say something that would make her unhappy.

'Hello, Alexander, how are you?' she said to him once, by the door of the assembly room, and it seemed she was pretending to be older to prevent him from talking to her, and he smiled at her and left her alone.

And so it continued until May, and the Saturday morning that would begin in Alexander's memory outside the shoe repairer's, from which he and his mother had emerged to find that the rain had stopped. His mother suggested they go to the park for an hour, and a short way beyond the gates, on the path to the Ranger's House, they met Gladys Watts, who had also worked at the plating factory when the war was on. Too big to bend, Gladys tickled the side of Alexander's face with her black cotton gloves.

'I'll be lucky if he's sweet as this one,' she said. 'We've met before, young lad. At your house. Remember?'

Alexander glanced at his mother. 'Go on, then,' she said to him. 'Not far, mind. Not out of sight.' She unbuttoned the black and white cardigan that Nan Burnett had knitted for him.

'One word from us and they do as they like,' said Gladys Watts, who gave him a smile as if he had said something clever, though he had not said a word.

His mother folded the cardigan and threaded it through the handles of her shopping bag. 'Wouldn't say that,' she remarked. 'Would you, Alexander?'

He would not be able to recall, even five years later, to whom his mother had been talking in the park that Saturday morning, five minutes before he first saw Mr Beckwith, but he would remember to the end of his life what happened then.

He was standing close to the roses, and a squirrel was fretting at a nut by the foot of a chestnut tree, not a yard from where Alexander stood. A bandy-legged Jack Russell hurried after its owner with a peculiar skipping motion of its hind legs. To his right, walking along a tarmac path towards one of the gates, was Megan, two steps in front of a man who looked like no person Alexander had ever seen. The skin of his face and arms and hands was the colour of the wall behind him, but it shone like it had oil all over it. The man was both old and not old. His hair was dark and thick and he kept his back very straight as he walked, like Alexander's father did, yet he had the face of an old man. Down his cheeks ran lines like the grain on floorboards, and the lines beside his mouth were so deep it was as if his jaw had two slots cut into it. He wore no tie but the collar of his shirt was fastened and looped slackly around his dark brown neck. The trousers that he was wearing did not seem to belong to him. They hung like curtains around his legs and were bunched around his waist with a narrow leather belt, the end of which dangled down past his pocket. His arms dangled too, lifelessly, from his rolled-up sleeves, as if they were attached to his body on hooks, and although he held his head up and was looking straight ahead, he did not seem to be seeing what was around him. The Jack Russell scampered across the path, kicking up clumps of cut grass, but he did not look down. A pigeon flew low past his head; he appeared not to notice it. Staying two steps behind Megan, saying nothing, the man might have been playing a game in which she was the adult and he the child.

Alexander followed them for a minute, keeping to the grass beside the path. 'Megan?' he said, when he was about ten feet from them. She looked up and quickly turned her face, as if she did not know who he was. Her left hand went back towards the man, and for a moment he touched her fingers as she led him to the gate. The man followed Megan out into the street, not even glancing at Alexander and his mother, who was now beside him, on her own. Preventing him from following, his mother's hand came over his shoulder and pressed in the centre of his chest.

'Who's that with Megan?' he asked, and she told him it was Mrs Beckwith's husband.

'Why wouldn't they stop?' he asked.

'It's nothing to concern yourself over, Alexander. Sometimes when we're together we don't want other people barging in. Isn't that so? Even if they are friends. Some things are private.'

'But they weren't talking to each other,' Alexander observed.

'You don't know that.'

'I do. I was watching them. They didn't say anything.'

'Well, you shouldn't be so nosy, Alexander,' said his mother, refolding his cardigan. She looked towards the gate through which Megan and Mr Beckwith had departed. 'The thing is, Alexander,' she went on, 'that Mr Beckwith is poorly, and you don't really want to talk much when you're poorly, do you?'

Alexander looked at the gate, where the trace of the brown-skinned man appeared in a dark flash, in the way a shape of light would appear inside his eyes after he had glanced at the sun.

'What's the matter with him?' he asked.

'It doesn't matter. He needs to be left alone for a while, that's all. He'll be well again soon.'

Several times that summer Alexander saw Megan and her uncle, and Mr Beckwith never seemed to be well. The next time he saw them was at All Saints church. From the parade of shops he watched Megan walking down the path from the church door, as if testing an icy track for Mr Beckwith, who walked two steps behind her, with his arms as loose as lengths of rope. Then on Vanbrugh Hill he saw her standing on the kerb and beckoning across the road to Mr Beckwith, who lifted his head and looked at her and squinted as if she were too far away to make out clearly who she was. Megan crossed over and took his hand to lead him to the pavement, where she let it go and his arm swung back onto his leg as if it had gone dead. Once he saw them crossing the Heath, on the horizon of the hill, as if pretending to be Indian scouts in file. And once again, allowed to roam away from his mother for a while, Alexander saw Mr Beckwith and Megan in the park, and followed them again, but from a greater distance than before. For a quarter of an hour he followed them, down the broad path past the hollow oak tree, back up the slope, on the grass. Now

31

and then Mr Beckwith would stop and stare up into the branches of a tree, or stop and look down at his feet, like a clockwork toy that had wound down, and Megan would crouch at his knees and gaze up at him, and brush his hand to make him walk after her again. Mr Beckwith never spoke, nor did he look at Megan, except for a moment, when, standing underneath a plane tree in a spread of light that turned his white shirt the colour of lime juice, he threw aside his cigarette and touched her on the back of the head, and Alexander saw her smile as broadly as she had smiled in the hallway of Nan Burnett's house. Fascinated by the strangeness of it, Alexander stood wondering, until Megan came hurrying towards him, leaving Mr Beckwith to continue his walk without her.

She held out her hands as though pushing something invisible. A couple of yards from Alexander she stopped and pointed a finger like a gun. 'Don't stare at him,' she demanded.

'I'm sorry,' he said.

'You always stare.'

'I'm sorry,' Alexander repeated.

'You always stare. Do you think nobody can see you? Standing there gawping. Don't stare at him.' She pushed her hair out of her eyes and glared at him before turning back.

'I'm sorry,' he said again.

'You're so stupid,' she shouted over her shoulder.

When she and her uncle had gone from sight he returned disconsolately to his mother, pausing on his way under the plane tree, where he retrieved the stub of Mr Beckwith's cigarette.

This was the last occasion that Alexander spoke to Megan Beckwith that summer, and it was not until one morning in late September that he spoke to her again. He was sitting on the step that had sparkling bits of mica in it, watching the cricket game, when Megan came clambering over the wall from the girls' playground. She pushed him on the shoulder to move him along, sat down beside him and asked directly: 'What are you thinking about?'

He would always remember what he was thinking about. The night before, listening from the top of the stairs on his way to bed, he had overheard his father talking to his mother. He had heard the words 'Marshall aid' and something of an explanation, from which he had arrived at a picture of men like military cowboys, patrolling the towns of Europe and handing out money to the grateful people.

'It's nothing to do with that,' said Megan, circling her knees with her arms. 'It's a man's name. He's an American,' she stated firmly. 'My mum says that America is the country of the future,' she said. 'It's amazing what they have there. In America they've seen UFOs. That stands for Unidentified Flying Objects.'

Megan peered up into the sky, wrinkling her nose; Alexander mimicked her gaze. She looked at him and sighed an adult sigh. 'It's all right,' she said, in a tone that sounded like his mother's. 'About my father. It's all right. Mum talked to me.'

A teacher appeared in the doorway and called out: 'Megan Beckwith. Come here. This instant.'

'Caught,' she muttered, and she shook his hand. 'I'm sorry I was angry with you, Eck,' she said, using for the first time the name she was always to use.

The teacher, after shepherding Megan into the corridor, asked him: 'Exempt from exercise are we, Alexander?'

'No, miss,' he said, but he returned to the step as soon as she had gone, to sit where Megan had sat.

5. The Doodlebug House

His mother would take his hand to cross the road and, pointing towards the shops, begin gaily: 'Now what do we see?'

And he would quickly respond: 'We see a queue.'

'So what do we do?'

'We join it.'

'And when do we join it?'

'Straight away.'

'We join it now, without delay,' his mother agreed, concluding the singsong exchange that she and Mrs Evans had made up as the three of them walked along the same street on another Saturday morning.

There were always five or six women outside the shop, whichever one they stopped at, and another woman halfway through the doorway, with her foot against the bottom of the door, and a dozen more inside, packed tightly like on the bus. 'What's today's special, girls?' Mrs Evans might ask as they took their place at the back, and sometimes she would answer herself: 'Whatever it is, it'll be worth the wait.' Once, however, a woman in a black coat with huge buttons turned round and said sharply, 'I don't know what you're so cheerful about. The war's not over yet.' Then another woman said, 'You're right about that,' and thus Alexander conceived a dread of the day when the bombers would come back, a fear he kept to himself until the day, five weeks later, on which a dormant mine, excited by the tremors of a nearby demolition, exploded in the garden of a house two streets from where he lived. That night he told his mother what he thought about every night, and he would always remember standing beside the bath that evening, gazing at the ebbing bathwater as his mother explained that he had misunderstood, while rubbing the towel on his hair as if to scrub off his foolishness.

An hour or more they sometimes queued, but Alexander's patience was constant, because no pleasure could exceed the pleasure of at last

34

entering the shop. Nestled amid coats and skirts, he would breathe in greedily to take hold of the scents that came from the women. An elusive aroma of lemons arose whenever one particular woman stepped forward, a woman with soft white arms and bracelets that clinked when she handed her money over. There was a woman who sometimes had a thin black line down the centre of her bare calves, whose clothes gave off a perfume that was like roses when they begin to wilt. Often she was with a friend called Alice, who had beautiful fingers and a perfume that remained mysterious until the day his father brought home a pomegranate in a stained paper bag.

Every sense was satisfied in these crowded shops, and a dense residue of memories was left in Alexander's mind by the mornings he spent in them. Forty years later, looking at the maritime souvenirs that filled the window of what had been the grocer's, he could hear above the traffic's growl the crunch and chime of the ancient cash till, and he saw again the brass plate on the front of the till, and the comical bulbous faces mirrored in its embossed lettering. He saw the counter of the chemist's shop, with the dimpled metal strip on its front edge that looked like a frozen waterfall. His fingers touched the window as he remembered how he would stroke the old wooden drawers by the chemist's counter, sweeping his fingertips slowly across the varnished scars that looked like the script of an unknown language. The scurf of stinking pink sawdust in the butcher's shop returned to him, and the sun shining off the slanted glass that covered the white trays of kidneys in their little puddles of brown blood. And standing before the *Cutty Sark*, gazing up through its spars at the coalsack-coloured October sky, he sensed the elation that arose instantly in him one morning, when he arrived at the head of the queue to see, displayed in a wicker basket, a heap of fat oranges that had come from Spain.

Only if his friends took him off to play would Alexander leave his place. 'Bad news I'm afraid, Mrs MacIndoe,' Eric Mullins joked, twirling the horns of a phantom moustache as he brought his heels smartly together. 'We need your son.' The company behind him – Lionel Griffiths and Gareth Jones and Davy Hennessy, whose leather-trimmed beret would last far longer than any other aspect of his appearance in Alexander's memory – nodded their regretful confirmation that this was so. 'Beastly business,' said Eric, jamming his spectacles tight to the bridge of his nose with a forefinger. 'Sorry and all that.'

'Very well. Dismissed,' his mother replied solemnly, lowering her chin, and they ran around the corner to Mr Mullins' pub.

Entering by the door marked 'Private', below the white plaster unicorn with its scarlet crown, they bounded up the back stairs to the empty top floor, where each of the rooms had no furniture nor any curtains or carpets, but had a washbasin with taps that did not work. The rooms were connected by a corridor that curved like the tunnel under the river, and up and down its lino they would smack a tin of snoek wrapped in a sock, using cricket bats for hockey sticks and aiming for the swing doors that led to the stairs. Or in their stockinged feet they would skate along the lino rink, and their feet would make a hissing noise that Alexander, looking down the corridor at the two blind eyes of the windows in the doors, once imagined as the building's breathing, an idea that so absorbed and unsettled him that he was startled when Lionel Griffiths, slithering to a stop behind him, shouted in his ear: 'Wake up, Alex. Park time.'

In the park, at the side of one of the hills, there was a miniature valley in which the grass grew long between untrimmed bushes, and there they would stalk each other, descending the slopes on their bellies. When the others had gone home Alexander would stay for a while in the overgrown gully, and lie unseen within earshot of the path and listen to the talk of the people trudging up the hill towards the Heath. And when there was time he would then go to the place he called the Doodlebug House and continued to call the Doodlebug House even after his father told him it was not a doodlebug that had wrecked it but incendiaries and a broken gas main, many months before the flying bombs arrived.

A flap of corrugated iron, daubed with *Danger – Keep Out* in wrinkled red paint, was the door to the ruin. The four outer walls still stood to the height of the gutter, framing a square of sky, and within the walls were piles of debris, embedded with fractured joists and floorboards and laths that were like the ribs of a scavenged carcass. Against one of the walls leaned a huge tent of roof tiles, protecting a mantelpiece that had not been damaged at all. A perpetual stink of damp plaster dust and cats and scorched wood filled the Doodlebug

House, and silvery ash was in every cranny. Low on the walls were stuck little rags of ash that vanished when he touched them. A book with leaves of ash trembled under the block of the toppled chimney. A skin of ash, pitted by raindrops, covered the door that lay flat in the middle of the house. Lumps of ash like mushrooms lay around the sheltered cradle of broken boards in which Alexander would recline and watch his portion of sky, hearing in his head the doodlebug's misfiring snarl and then the thrilling moment of silence before it plummeted, a silence that excited him like the moment before he let himself drop from the empty window into the pool of torn bedding and sodden clothes at the back of the Doodlebug House.

Ash as slippery as sleet coated the joist by which Alexander would climb to the window at the side of the house, to sit between the battens that had been hammered crosswise into the empty frame. There, hidden from view, he would watch the people in the street pass by, or take out his *Tales from the Bible*, and read the story of the walls of Jericho or the Tower of Babel. Every time he came to the Doodlebug House he would go up to the window, until the day that Mrs Darling walked by and, without raising her head, called out 'Be careful up there, Alexander' and waved her hand behind her as if fixing a headscarf that had become unknotted. In later years he would often recall his lookout in the Doodlebug House, but most frequently he would revisit the part of the building that had once been the kitchen. Beached on a hummock that bristled with fractured pipes, there was a bathtub in which he sometimes dozed, and ten feet or so from the bath, wedged into the stump of the stairs, there was a wardrobe door that had a mirror fixed to it. The mirror was cracked from top to bottom, and the door was set at such an angle that, as Alexander neared the top of the hummock, he would find a place from which the mirror showed the wreckage to his left and to his right, but did not show any image of himself. Perched on a raft of wallpapered plywood, his arms held out like a tightrope walker, he stared in fascination at the reflection of the ruin, experiencing the smells and sights and sounds of the Doodlebug House, while apparently invisible. And he remembered that as he squatted on a beam and surveyed the rubble, a sadness seemed to flow through his body, a sadness that seemed to strengthen and purify him, to raise him out of his childhood for as long as it lasted. He was the guardian of the house's relics, and such was his care for them that fifty years later he could draw a plan of the craters and barrows of the Doodlebug House, mapping the resting place of every item. Behind the bath there lay a washboard with barley-sugar glass rods that had not even been chipped by the blast; beside it was the brown canvas camera case that had been chewed by mice, and the cookery book with the spine that was a strip of bandage clogged with brittle glue. Closer to the wall there was the black iron mincer with its heavy crank attached, and the mangle with hard blue rubber rollers, and the soggy cartons of bandages and rusting nails. Some days he would touch one of the relics or raise it on his open palms and close his eyes, and Mr Fitchie would sometimes appear and look at him, as if across a river.

Neither would he forget the only time he ever took anyone to the Doodlebug House. Mrs Evans was with them, wearing the big silver brooch in the shape of a sleeping cat, and her green felt hat with a pheasant's feather tucked under its band. They were at the butcher's shop, and Mrs Evans made up another rhyme: 'What a peculiar thing to do, to spend all day in the butcher's queue, and all for a sausage, or sometimes two.' When a man behind them started swearing, Mrs Evans cupped her fingers over Alexander's ears. 'For what we're about to buggering well receive may the buggering Lord make us buggering grateful,' said the man, and from the sly way Mrs Evans looked at Alexander he could not be sure if she had not meant him to hear. Then Mrs Beckwith turned up with Megan, who was holding the shopping bag in front of her, gripping its handles in both fists as if carrying the bag was a serious undertaking.

'Why don't you two go to the park?' said Mrs Beckwith.

'We'll come for you in an hour,' said his mother. 'Shall we see you by the pond?'

Megan submitted the bag to her mother without saying anything, and the idea occurred to Alexander that he should take her to the Doodlebug House. 'It's wonderful,' he told her as they entered the park. 'It's like being in a big well, or a castle. The walls are as high as that tree, on all four sides, and there's nothing in the middle of them.'

'How far is it?' Megan asked.

'Can't tell you,' said Alexander. 'But we won't be late back. Promise.'

38

Megan looked at the tree to which Alexander had pointed. She made her mouth and eyes slightly smaller, as though she doubted what he said, but then she followed him to the Doodlebug House.

'No one except me has ever been in here,' he told her. He pulled up a corner of the corrugated iron sheet so that she could crawl in. 'You mustn't tell anyone,' he said.

Megan stood on a small rectangle of clear floor in the hallway, swatting the dust from her dress. Rising behind her, the walls seemed higher than ever, and the movement of the clouds that were edging over the Doodlebug House made the bricks seem to teeter. Alexander began to climb the joist to his window, but was stopped by Megan's voice. 'This is a pile of rubbish, Eck,' she said, looking about her as if someone who had annoyed her was hiding in the ruin. 'It's nothing like a castle.'

He could not think what to say. He rested one foot on the fringe of floor that stuck out from the wall and held out a hand, though she was a long way below him. 'Look from up here,' he said.

'Don't be stupid, Eck,' Megan told him. 'It's dangerous. I'm going.' She licked a finger and turned her attention to a mark on her dress.

Despondent and resentful, he followed her away from the Doodlebug House. 'You won't tell anyone?' he pleaded, when they were back in the park.

'Of course not,' she said.

'Promise?' he persisted.

'God, Eck,' she snapped. 'Don't be so boring. Why would I tell anyone? There's nothing to tell.'

Alexander returned to the Doodlebug House many times afterwards, and the echo of Megan's voice was always there. He could no more rid the atmosphere of her irritation than he could get rid of the smell of cats. With his arms crossed he would sit on the lip of the bath and scan the shell of the building, as if waiting with diminishing hope for a friend to answer an accusation. 'A pile of rubbish,' he heard her say, and he could no longer bring himself to see it differently. Finally there came the day on which he found that he was in a place that felt like a copy of the Doodlebug House, and he resolved that he would never visit it again.

He would always remember something of the evening of the day on which he left the Doodlebug House. Sitting on the grass in the garden, he closed his eyes and brought to mind the things that he had abandoned. He could see the slivers of grime between the rods of the washboard and the lustrous disc of white porcelain on top of the bath's single tap. He could see the rake of shadows on the wall above the upstairs fireplace and the stiff blisters of paint on the back door. He could even taste the bitter air of the Doodlebug House. It was as if he were lying on his cradle of boards, and the Doodlebug House was again a place that belonged only to him.

When Alexander came out of his daydream a red admiral was closing its wings on a dandelion beside him. He remembered this, and his father looking at him from the kitchen door. The light through the branches of the tree in next door's garden made his father's face vanish under a pattern of brilliant ovals. His mother's voice came from very far away inside the house, saying something he could not hear, and his father went to her.

One morning towards the end of 1951, not long after Churchill's election, Alexander heard that the Doodlebug House was being demolished. In the afternoon he watched the wrecking ball sink into the wall below his lookout window. The wall gave way like a hand making a catch, he would always remember.

6. The Winslow Boy

Alexander was sitting in the corner of the garden where the bindweed came over the fence and the fat tongues of dock leaves stuck out from under the nettles. Holding the stalk as he had seen his mother hold the stem of a glass, Alexander turned the white trumpet of a flower half a circle one way, half a circle back.

'He's a contented wee soul,' he heard Mrs Beckwith remark. 'If you ask me, he's got a real talent for calmness.'

'You think so?' asked his mother, standing alongside her.

'I don't see what you're fussing about, Irene. I'd be grateful if I were you. Not a minute's peace with Megan.'

'Nothing but peace with this one,' said his mother, and she looked at him as if he were a mystifying but precious-looking object they had unearthed from the lawn. 'Not like the others, are we, my love?' With the toe of her sandals she dug gently at his ribs, he would remember. 'Not a boisterous boy, are we?' She threaded a hand under Mrs Beckwith's elbow. 'You wouldn't credit how long this one can go without moving a muscle,' she said. 'Meditating MacIndoe we should have called him.'

'A genius at hide and seek, I'll bet,' said Mrs Beckwith, and she kissed him on the top of his head.

A week later he was taken to see Dr Levine, in a room that he would remember for its smell of cold rubber and for its chairs, which were made of metal pipes and had red seats that glued to his skin. Dr Levine was a short, stout man with silver hair and a silver moustache that was striped with two yellow stains below his nostrils. His eyes were small and pale brown, and he looked at Alexander over the lenses of his half-moon glasses.

'What exactly is the difficulty, Mrs MacIndoe?' he asked.

'It's not a difficulty, as such,' she replied.

'Not a difficulty, as such,' the doctor responded, as though repeating a sentence in a foreign language.

41

'No.'

'Then what precisely would it be?'

'A feeling that something's not quite right,' she tentatively explained.

'Could you be more specific, Mrs MacIndoe?' asked the doctor. 'Could we pin this something down?'

'He doesn't seem to have much energy, for a boy,' she stated.

'For a boy?' smiled Dr Levine, putting down the gold-hooped black pen with which he had been toying.

'For a child.'

'He eats well? Sleeps well?' asked Dr Levine.

'Yes. I think so.'

Dr Levine rose from his chair and leaned on the edge of his desk, gazing down at Alexander. 'Do you eat well, Alexander?' he asked, and narrowed his eyes as if there was some trick to the question. 'Do you sleep well?' he added, before Alexander could speak.

'Perfectly,' said Alexander.

'Perfectly,' repeated Dr Levine, and he smiled at the floor as he placed a hand on Alexander's brow. His skin was cold and very soft, like a balloon that has lost some air. 'Give me your hands,' he said. He put the tips of his fingers under the boy's and bent forward to inspect the fingernails. 'Look up,' he said. He prodded the flesh around Alexander's eyes, then took hold of his lashes and tugged at his eyelids. 'Nothing to worry ourselves about so far,' commented Dr Levine, reaching behind his back and lifting a small, flat stick.

'I'm not worried.'

'I'm glad to hear it,' replied Dr Levine, and he pressed his lips together, making his moustache bulge outwards. He placed the smooth dry wood on Alexander's tongue and peered along it; the whites of the doctor's eyes, Alexander noted, were the colour of the wax of his nightlight in the morning.

'There's nothing wrong with him that I can see,' declared Dr Levine eventually. 'Do you feel there's anything wrong with you, Master MacIndoe?'

'No, sir.'

'Well, neither do I.' Dr Levine yawned, removed his glasses and bent his fingers to grind at his eyes with his knuckles.

'He looked like a big squirrel,' Alexander told Megan that afternoon, and he copied the way the doctor's mouth had grimaced and his cheeks puffed out as he rubbed his eyes. 'Nothing wrong with him,' he repeated with a superior sniff, twiddling his thumbs pompously on his stomach. 'Are you a fool, Mrs MacIndoe?'

It was not the first time he had heard Megan laugh, but that is how he was to recall it, with Megan standing on the opposite side of the road from Mrs Beckwith's house, and stamping her foot as though the shock of her laughter had travelled right through her body. 'So you're not ill then?' she asked.

'No, I'm not ill.'

'You're just odd. That's all there is to it,' she said, walking backwards across the street.

'That's all there is to it,' he parroted.

'Odd Eck,' said Megan as a goodbye.

'Odd Eck, odd Eck; odd Eck, odd Eck,' he repeated for her, to the tune of two chiming bells.

There was a place at the turn of the stairs where the grain of the wood had come through the varnish to form sand-coloured terraces that he would magnify in his imagination to the dimensions of the cliffs and bays that Jimmy Murrell had described. At the foot of the banister that rose from this step he had found a globule of varnish that was not absolutely hard, from which his thumbnail could detach a black sliver that had an aroma that was something like the tobacco that was left in the bowl when his father's pipe went out. The morning after the visit to Dr Levine, he was sitting at the turn of the stairs, his face against the cool wood of the banister. His mother came up, carrying the laundry basket, and as she sidled past him he asked her: 'Do you think I'm odd?' The smile that he saw, immediately before she put her arms around him and kissed him, convinced him that she did.

'You do, don't you?' he called up to her.

'I don't at all,' she said, and she dropped over the banister a handkerchief that fell over his face.

She was as worried after the visit to the doctor as she had been before. He would be sitting on the threshold of the house, watching the traffic or the sky, and she would rush to him and urge him out into the street to play. 'Come on, Alexander, look lively,' she would almost shout, clapping her hands to recruit him for some chore about the house. 'Watching the grass grow?' she would ask, or 'Saving shoe leather?' or 'Holding the floor down?' And once, when he was in the garden, he heard her say to his father, 'Our son's turning into a tree, Graham.'

One afternoon in April she strode down the hall, lifted him up, and said: 'What would you say if I said we were going up to town? To see the lights come on.'

'That'd be nice,' he replied.

'Once more, with feeling?' she requested.

'That'd be very nice,' he said, loudly enough to earn an embrace.

They left the house in the dusk, and it was dark when they reached Nelson's Column. His mother pointed down the wide road that stretched off to Buckingham Palace. 'Do you want to go down there?' she asked. She did not seem interested by the idea.

'Don't mind,' he said.

'Fine. What about down there? Do you want to go and see the Houses of Parliament?' she asked, and it seemed she would be disappointed if he did.

He looked down Whitehall. The buildings were all the same colour and all the people were walking with their heads down, as if they didn't want to see anyone. 'We saw them from the train, didn't we?' he replied.

'Let's go and see the lights then,' she proposed.

The lights were in Leicester Square, where the Empire was presenting *Easter Parade* with Judy Garland and Fred Astaire. For a few minutes they stood in the drizzle, while his mother marvelled at the signs for the shows. 'Magnificent, isn't it?' she said, gesturing at a building on which huge grey shadows floated like the spirits of the dead in the picture of heaven in Nan Burnett's front room. 'We'll take a walk through theatreland,' said his mother, and bareheaded in the rain they went up Haymarket and down St Martin's Lane and across Covent Garden, where the pavements smelled of dustbins. Facing the Theatre Royal she took his hand and said to him, as if telling him something he must not tell anyone else: 'This is a very famous place. A very special place. *The Desert Song*, *Show Boat*, *Oklahoma!* – they were all performed here.' Under the theatre's colonnade she sang a whole song for him, and she sang a few lines as they strolled back along the Strand, and on the journey home. But before the train reached Blackheath station she turned away from him and rested her forehead on the dark glass. From what felt like a great distance, Alexander regarded her, wondering what they had done that had made her unhappy.

Within twenty years the walk through theatreland would dwindle to the memory of the rain-slicked cars in Leicester Square and the sign for *Easter Parade*. The train journey home would vanish, but for the image of the tree of steam that rose from the funnel of a waiting engine, and of the railway lines rushing in like streams between the platforms of London Bridge station. The face of Dr Levine would vanish, as would the conversation on the stairs, and his mother's conversation with Mrs Beckwith in the garden. All this he would forget, but he would remember acutely and at length the Saturday, in July of that year, on which he followed his mother.

Early on a Saturday afternoon he would sometimes go to Mr Prentice's shop, for no reason except that it was a pleasant place to be. For as long as ten minutes he would stand behind the potato sacks, where he was not in anybody's way. Breathing in the bountiful smells of the shop, he watched the brass cylinders flying over the heads of the customers, shuttling along the wires that ran between the counters and the cashier's turret, where an old woman with a hairnet unscrewed the lids from the cylinders and scooped out the money and the chits, like a cat hooking food from a bowl. To his left were ranged the glazed grey flagons of ginger ale, lemonade and dandelion and burdock, and to the right were the greasy pink hams and wheels of cheese, and the slicing machine with the blade that spun quickly under its shiny steel cowl and made a ringing sound when its edge came out of the meat. Opposite was the door to the back room, where Mr Prentice worked.

Sometimes Mr Prentice would turn round from his desk and call out to him: 'All in order, MacIndoe?' To which Alexander's response, copied from his father, was: 'Aye aye, Mr P,' and a soldier's salute. And in reply Mr Prentice would brush his brow with his forefinger; and then, having hitched up the metal bands that held his shirtsleeves to his upper arms, he would return to his letters and bills. On this particular afternoon, Mr Prentice gave his one-fingered salute, glanced over Alexander's shoulder and said, pointing: 'Wasn't that your mum going past?'

Through the gaps in the whitewash prices on the window Alexander watched his mother hurrying along the pavement. She was wearing her long chequered skirt and her chequered jacket, and the dark blue hat that he had seen on top of her wardrobe but never seen her wear.

Alexander looked at Mr Prentice, but Mr Prentice was leaning forward in his chair and looking out at the street, though there was no longer anyone to see there. 'Better hurry home,' he said.

'Suppose,' responded Alexander. He stepped out under the awning and saw his mother go straight across the road at which she would have turned right had she been going home. From a distance he pursued her, dashing from doorway to doorway, watching for a few seconds before following, excited by the adventure but agitated by a sense of his own deceitfulness. When he saw a man stop to look at her as, waiting on a kerb, she glanced at a window and altered the angle of her hat, Alexander's anxiety became so strong that he almost turned back. He saw his mother pull at her cuff to check her watch, then quicken her stride; he followed again, his heartbeat seeming to increase with the speed of her footsteps. She crossed another road and then, beyond her, a bus drew out from its stop, uncovering *The Winslow Boy* in white boxy letters, and his limbs became hollow with the relief of knowing where his mother was going.

From behind a lamppost he watched her slide a coin under the grille of the booth and receive her ticket. She smiled at the woman in the booth, and she was smiling as she pushed at the curving brass door-handle and crossed the deep red carpet of the foyer. A commissionaire with golden bands around his cuffs held open the inner door, and eased it shut once she had passed through, as if it were the heavy steel door of a strongroom.

Alexander sat on the pavement, his back against the lamppost, and waited for a while. When three men arrived and bought tickets he stood up to watch the commissionaire open his door, thinking that perhaps she would come out as they went in. He walked around the block, stopped to watch the commissionaire's fingers drumming on the ashtray on the wall, and walked around the block again. He crossed the street. In a padlocked glass cabinet to the side of the outer doors there were advertisements for the new films: a photograph of Orson Welles in a shadowy doorway, and a picture of Alec Guinness in a dress and one of John Wayne on a horse. It was when he noticed that the woman in the ticket booth was watching him out of the corner of her eye that Alexander was spurred into making up his mind.

Two buildings along from the cinema there was a blind alley which Eric Mullins had once taken him down. The alley made a right-angled turn twenty yards from the street, and on this angle there was a flat, handleless door which led, Eric said, to the cinema. 'It's not locked,' he said. 'They can't lock it, because then it wouldn't be an escape, would it? You can get it open with a knife.' Alexander inserted a penny into the crack of the door and levered it out a quarter-inch. He grappled his fingers onto the strip of door and worked it open far enough to slip through.

On the other side was a corridor of bare brick with a floor of rough, ridged concrete; a single bare lightbulb burned in a socket above a door at the far end, through which came the sound of indistinct voices talking loudly. Another door, halfway down the corridor, opened with a judder and a woman came out, fiddling with a button on her blouse. She smiled and looked at him as if she were trying to work out who he was. 'Hello, mischief,' she said. The light from the bulb made her hair gauzy. She opened the door and pushed aside a velvet curtain. 'You coming or aren't you?' she whispered.

He went inside. The cinema was so large and dark it seemed to have no boundary. Like a drift of scum on a river, a stream of smoke flowed upwards through the beam of light, which swelled and shrank and twitched incessantly. Dozens of faces tilted upwards underneath the beam, all of them with the same expression of expectation, or so it appeared initially. Alexander wrapped himself in the folds of the curtain, which smelt like curtains in Mr Mullins's pub. Unable to understand what the people on the screen were doing, he looked again at the people who were watching them. A few sat open-mouthed, as if waiting to be fed. Some were chewing, while some sucked on cigarettes, making scarlet bugs appear in the darkness. One woman seemed to be joining in with the words that the actors were speaking. Under the lip of the balcony, a man kissed the woman in the seat beside him; in

47

front of them a man had his eyes closed, next to a woman who was frowning as if she disagreed with everything she was hearing.

Alexander's gaze travelled to the end of the row in which the frowning woman sat, and travelled gradually back, to halt at a face he had already passed over once, and realised now was his mother's. It went dark for a moment and then the light flashed on her skin, but she remained motionless, like a woman balancing a book on her head. Voices were raised in the film. The frowning woman shook her head and the sleeping man woke up, and then his mother's eyes widened in amazement, though nothing had happened, that Alexander could see, to make her react in this way, and her lips formed an expression as if someone he could not see was in the seat beside her and telling her something she could scarcely believe. She smiled to herself, curling a strand of hair around her finger.

Alexander smiled too, yet her lonely pleasure made him sorrowful. He was ashamed, and he told himself that he should not have left Mr Prentice's shop. He picked a cancelled ticket from the carpet and turned it repeatedly in his fingers to keep his eyes from his mother.

'This is where we came in,' said a man somewhere in the shadows under the balcony. Three men and a woman came down the slope, making the floor boom under their tread. Alexander rolled under the curtain and reached the end of the corridor before the door behind him opened. He returned to his post at the end of the side street, and waited. Half an hour passed, and still his mother did not come out. He counted the buses that drove by. Ten buses passed, and in that time he saw many people leave, but not his mother. The sun was resting on the roofs when he decided to go home.

Alexander would remember the pursuit of his mother, and the apparition of her face amid the other shadowed faces. And from the evening of that day he would remember his father putting his elbows on the dinner table and drawing on his pipe so strongly the liquid rattled in its stem, and saying to him: 'Anything wrong?'

Alexander stirred his spoon around the empty soup bowl as his mother gathered the rest of the cutlery and crockery. 'Nothing,' he said.

'There is, I think,' his mother teased.

'Come on, what's up?' asked his father, taking off his glasses.

'No, nothing,' he repeated. 'There's nothing wrong with me,' he grinned, holding his spoon upright like a sceptre. 'Dr Levine said so.'

'Comedian,' said his mother. She stacked the plates and went off to the kitchen.

'Come on,' his father said. 'Let's go and help your mother in the galley.'

Alexander followed his father down the hall, twisting the ticket in his pocket as he walked.

In the kitchen his mother was reading a newspaper she had spread out on the draining board. Her head was posed like one of the women in the glass cabinet at the cinema, but she was even prettier. Alexander stood in the doorway and looked at her in the way the man in the street had looked at her, with his head angled slightly to one side and both hands in his pockets.

'Can I have a picture of you?' he asked her.

His mother looked sideways at him. 'What do you need a picture for?' she asked.

'For my room.'

'Don't be silly,' she told him. 'You've got the real thing. You don't need a picture.'

'Please.'

'No,' she said. 'You're being silly.'

'Please.'

'Alexander, stop it,' she said, and he ran out of the kitchen because he felt he might cry.

7. The Bovis stove

The afternoon was so hot that Alexander's father took a chair from the kitchen and carried it out into the garden, where Alexander, propped on his elbows in the middle of the lawn, was turning the pages of the old atlas.

'Would I be disturbing you, son and heir?' his father enquired, in the butler's voice he often used when he was joking. 'I would not? Well and good. We shall study together,' he replied to Alexander's smile, and he placed the chair on the patch of concrete to the side of the kitchen door, under the honeysuckle that grew across the wall that year. He went back inside and emerged again with a sheaf of square-ruled paper and the big tin tray, which he laid across the arms of the chair to make a desk. 'This is very agreeable,' he remarked, examining the point of a pencil approvingly. He unbuttoned his collar and slipped his feet out of his broad-strapped sandals.

Askance Alexander watched his father working, drawing graphs and reckoning figures across the gridded paper, placing the completed sheets neatly upon the pile underneath the chair. His mother brought a pitcher of lemonade and poured a glass for each of them; his father kissed her fingers and his mother made a curtsy, holding out the hem of her dress so the shape of a leg showed through the red and white checks, as Alexander would remember.

'Alexander, come inside when you've finished your drink,' she said.

'He's fine, Irene,' said his father. 'Quiet as a monk, aren't you?'

So Alexander continued to roam the pink expanses of the maps, measuring the distances between names that seemed to have been invented for their melody, tracing systems of rivers that looked like roots. From time to time he turned to the first page of the atlas, where his great-grandfather's name was written in a script that resembled blades of grass, with ink that was chestnut brown and gave the book an aura which the name of Duncan Manus MacIndoe deepened with its ancient, clannish sound. With a forefinger he stroked the loops and limbs of the writing, as if to encourage a visible presence to rise like a genie from the paper.

Occasionally his father broke the silence, stopping his pencil and enquiring quietly, without looking up: 'Eight times thirteen?' or 'Twenty-two nines?' or some other sum. Alexander would give his answer, and whenever the answer was correct his father would say, with pretended briskness and still without looking at him, 'Carry on,' then get back to his work.

Late in the afternoon the clouds began to cluster on the city side of the sky. Alexander watched the sun fall behind them, turning parts of them to tangerine foam as it sank. The white shirts on the neighbours' washing line, hanging with arms raised in the breezeless air, took on the tint of skin. As if soaking a dye from the horizon, the clouds became tangerine right through, a colour that brought to Alexander a sensation that seemed a foretaste of the pleasure he would have at the funfair that evening. It was a sensation so strong that for many years this quality of sunlight in a cumulus sky would elicit a moment of anticipatory happiness, and sometimes he would glimpse the tomato-red metal panels of the merry-go-rounds under loops of electric bulbs, and hear the jubilant, malicious music of the steam organ above the hum of the generators.

Following his father, he passed between the caravans that formed a wall around the fair, and stepped onto grass that had been mashed into arrowhead tracks and heel shapes. Beside the Hall of Mirrors there was a coconut shy, where his father handed his jacket to Alexander before hurling three wooden balls into the netting behind the coconuts, and close by was a stall at which his mother threw two black rubber rings at hooks on a wall that was painted with red fish, then handed the third ring to Alexander, whose throw struck a hook and bounced off. They bought toffee apples from a man with blurred tattoos of a dagger and a red snake on his right arm. Standing by the test-your-strength machine, Alexander raised his half-eaten apple in the direction of the Big Wheel.

'Can we go on that?' he asked.

'You're not getting me on that, I can tell you that right now,' said his mother to his father.

'Can I go?' Alexander asked his father.

'You wouldn't like it,' his father told him.

'Have you been on one?'

'No.'

'Then how do you know I wouldn't like it?'

'I know.'

'How?'

'Don't be contrary, Alexander,' said his mother.

'No, he's right,' said his father, raising one forefinger in judgement. 'But don't say you weren't warned. You'll get no sympathy from me if you get up there and find it's too high. Do you want me to go on with you?' his father asked, in a tone that Alexander took as a challenge.

'Not if you don't want to,' Alexander replied, and his father pressed a couple of coins into his hand, as if he were handing over an important message for him to deliver.

A woman with curlers in her hair took the money. 'Just for you, lover?' she asked, letting the coins slide down her hip into the pouch that was slung across her dress. Alexander looked at his mother, who looked at his father, who was studying the wheel. 'Shouldn't really, you being a little 'un,' said the woman; then, after a teasing pause, 'but go on.' She touched his cheek with her inky fingertips as he crossed the steel ramp to the empty car. 'Hold tight,' she told him, pressing his hands onto the iron bar that she fastened across his belly, and then she turned towards the man in the sentrybox at the foot of the ramp and cried 'Up and away,' letting her voice trail off like someone falling a long distance.

With a jolt he rose backwards and in a second he was above the stalls and then pitching down towards them, through air that smelled of onions and hot sugar. His parents appeared and receded, and he looked over his shoulder, down on the tarpaulin roofs, which glowed like multicoloured lampshades. He saw the gigantic shadows of the stallkeepers quivering on the tents as he swooped towards his parents. At the top he looked across the fairground, and was fascinated to see how orderly it appeared from this height, but the wheel was now gathering speed. A wind was whirring in his ears. Becoming frightened, he closed his eyes. The car swung as it was flung over the apex, and swung again at the end of its fall. A woman in a car behind him let out a gleeful yell, urging the wheel to turn faster. Alexander screwed his eyes so tightly shut that he could no longer sense the fairground lights. He heard his mother's voice say his father's name. 'Make it stop. Please make it stop,' he prayed, and then it did stop.

The car rocked, suspended at the start of its descent. On the rim of the footplate a line of red lightbulbs bobbed like fishing floats, then came to rest. Under him something metallic clanged against another piece of metal. The wheel juddered forward an inch, another inch, another inch, and stopped again. 'Alexander!' his mother cried out. She ran into his sight, waving her arms; miniature black cars circled behind her, on a roundabout for small children. 'Keep calm,' she called. 'Alexander. Can you hear me? They'll get it going in a minute. Stay calm, Alexander. Stay calm,' she kept repeating, but there was no need, for he was no longer upset, not in the slightest. He gazed over the Heath, where the blades of grass seemed to stand to attention in the headlights of the cars, and then he surveyed the fairground, carefully, as if it were an interesting picture spread out below him. Here and there stood groups of people who were looking in his direction; new groups were forming on every path, and from the farther parts of the fairground they were coming nearer. The hats and headscarves moved between the stalls like leaves flowing on water towards a drain. Over the wall of the park he could see the paths that ran under the black foliage of the trees. Wings clattered somewhere among the leaves, but no birds appeared; he imagined the grass alive with nocturnal animals, foraging on the slopes where people cycled in the day. The park was transformed into an enclave of forest, but he understood that he could only observe this forest and never be in it, because it would cease to be a forest if anybody was in it. He told himself that he would be happy to stay all night where he was, and see the sun come up over the houses, and the park become a park again.

He realised that the steam organ had fallen silent. The horses had ceased prancing on the biggest of the merry-go-rounds, but a girl remained seated on one of them, pointing straight at him and laughing. Alexander waved to her, and leaned forward to wave to the people gathered around the booth below. His mother had one hand to her mouth and with the other was waving to him with her fingers, while his father was chatting to the woman with the hair-curlers as if he were simply talking to an acquaintance in a shop.

'Sit back,' his mother called, making the motion of pushing at a door. His father glanced up and appeared to nod commendingly to him before resuming his conversation with the woman, who turned away briefly to shout 'Hurry it up, for God's sake,' to someone hidden from view by the floor of the car. 'Sit back, Alexander,' his mother called, and it was then he noticed that a man with a panama hat was standing to her side, watching her as she gestured. Alexander watched the man follow her line of sight upward. 'Alexander, please sit back,' his mother cried. The man's eyes were trained on Alexander's face for a few seconds, then traced the track of his mother's gaze back down to her face. 'Alexander! Now!' his mother demanded, unaware that she was being watched. Alexander lay down on the bench. He regarded the stars for a while, and fell asleep in the mild summer night's air.

He awoke with a spasm of the machinery and found that he was slowly returning to the ground. The woman with the hair-curlers took him by the hand and passed him to his mother as though he had gone missing and she had discovered him. 'You'll be the death of me, young man,' said his mother, sandwiching his head between her hands. 'I told you it was dangerous, and then you make it worse. Messing around like that.'

'I wasn't messing around,' he replied.

'Give me patience,' said his mother to nobody. She held him tightly against her side and sniffed. Under her arm he saw the man in the panama giving a small white card to his father.

'We'll consider it,' his father was saying. The man raised his hat as they shook hands.

'Hello, Alexander,' said the man, bracing his hands on his knees to greet him. His eyebrows bounced up and down as he smiled. 'You handled that situation with aplomb, I must say,' he remarked, narrowing his eyes admiringly. With a thumb he scratched the bristles in the hollow beneath his lower lip. 'Not to be flattered, eh? I like that in a chap,' said the man. Obtaining no response, he straightened his back and turned down the brim of his hat. 'Extraordinary,' he muttered. 'Thank you for your time, Mr MacIndoe, Mrs MacIndoe,' said the man, making a bow to each of them. 'An extraordinary child,' he remarked. He wriggled his neck to settle the fit of his collar and strode away across the fairground as if he were going to greet someone, but

54

he walked past the tombola stall and kept going, through the wall of caravans, across the road and onto the Heath.

'Who was that?' Alexander asked.

'Nobody in particular,' replied his father, interrupting his mother before she could utter anything more than the first syllable of his name. 'Someone who fancied a yatter, that's all.'

The following Friday evening, at bedtime, Alexander's mother told him that the next day they were going up to town, just the two of them. 'A sort of adventure,' she said. Tantalisingly she flourished the small white card, which had something written on the side that was not printed. 'We'll have a bit of a laugh.' In the morning she made him wash his hair, and she washed her own as soon as he was out of the bathroom. When she came downstairs her lips were made up the way Mrs Darling did hers. They were going to see the man in the panama hat, Alexander knew, and this made him feel uneasy and vaguely ashamed of his mother. On the platform of the Underground station he noticed her surreptitiously checking the handwritten words on the card. 'Where are we going?' he shouted over the roar of the arriving train.

'You'll see,' she replied, wincing at the noise and the gritty air. 'It'll be fun,' she assured him, but she fussed at his hair as if she were taking him to an examination.

They came back above ground in a place that was not like the streets around his house. There were more cars here, and fewer shops. The paving stones were perfectly level, and the houses were taller and had rows of bell-pushes beside the entrance. Some of the houses were made of bricks that were dark red and smooth.

'Which way's the river from here?' Alexander asked, and he would remember the way his mother put her hand on the pillar of the Belisha beacon as she looked one way up the street and then the other way, like an explorer taking her bearings in a jungle clearing.

'Your guess is as good as mine,' she said. 'Which way is it to Timbuktu?' she asked him.

It was as though she had known what he had been thinking as she stood beside the beacon, and instantly Alexander was cheerful for the first time that morning. 'I'd really like it if you'd tell me where we're going,' he said, sensing that this time she would tell him.

'We're going to have our picture taken,' she replied, and the next moment she stopped walking. They were at an open door, beside a clothes shop. She consulted the card again. 'We're here,' she announced, reaching for a hand.

At the end of a corridor that smelled of paste there was a flight of stairs, and at the top of the stairs there was a door of ribbed glass through which Alexander could see something pink and conical. 'Please enter' he read from a card that was attached to a sucker on the wall. His mother let him turn the handle, and as the door opened he saw a fat little girl in a pink frilly dress, holding the hand of a woman with a fierce fat face. A very short man with wide braces over his dirty white shirt was writing something in one of the squares of a calendar that hung above a filing cabinet. That he was not the man in the panama hat both relieved and confused Alexander.

'Goodbye, Elizabeth. Mrs Gordon,' said the short man.

'Thank you, Mr Stevens,' replied the woman rapidly, and she pushed past Alexander without acknowledging him or his mother.

'Mrs MacIndoe and Alexander,' said the man, looking at them appreciatively, with his hands on his hips. 'Ha ha,' he exclaimed. 'Sounds like a music-hall act, doesn't it?' His eyes were perfectly circular and his brow wrinkled, which made him look as if he'd just heard something that had surprised him pleasantly. Flakes of white skin, like the fraying skin of a mushroom, stuck to the sides of his nose. 'Harold Stevens,' he said, and smiled widely. Not one of his teeth was at the same angle as any other. 'Alexander?' he enquired, with the look of a delivery man estimating a parcel's weight. 'Who else could it be?' Mr Stevens answered himself. 'This won't take much of your time, Mrs MacIndoe. All has been arranged, has it not? The quid pro quo, as it were?'

'It has,' said Alexander's mother.

'Excellent,' said Mr Stevens. 'Follow me, if you'd be so good.'

Sunlight sparkled on the floor of the inner room, most intensely in front of the platform that was built against the wall on their right. On the platform, in front of a placard of plain black paper, there was a brand new stove with a smooth yellow door that looked like a huge half-melted slab of butter and had the word '*Bovis*' in sloping silver letters above the handle. At the far end of the room stood a big black camera on a tripod, its concertina lens pointing towards a young man who was hurling plump blue cushions onto a settee. 'Colin, my assistant,' said Mr Stevens, gesturing at the young man. Like a cymbals player Colin banged two cushions together, raising a smoulder of dust from each. Mr Stevens aimed his hand at a door beyond the platform. 'Colin will get you ready, Alexander. Colin, if you'd be so good? I am grateful. Mrs MacIndoe, if you'd follow Colin too?'

'Your things are behind there, Mrs MacIndoe,' said Colin when they were in the other room, indicating a folding cloth screen with willows painted on it. 'And this is your kit,' he told Alexander, lifting a towel from a pile of school clothes that lay folded on the seat of a chair. The uniform had never been worn before: the cuffs of the shirt were as hard as tea cups, and the toe caps of the shoes had not a single dent in them. Colin aligned the knot of Alexander's tie then slung an empty leather satchel over his shoulder.

'The model schoolboy,' his mother remarked as she came out from behind the screen. 'Perhaps Colin should get you ready every day.' She had a different dress on, and a starched white apron over it.

'You'll be needing this,' said Colin, and he thrust a wooden spoon into her hand. 'The master awaits,' he told them, in a voice that dragged with the dreariness of his duties. He held the door open and waved them through like a traffic policeman.

In the main room Mr Stevens was straightening the skirt of black material that hung from the back of the camera, and another man was entering from the office, combing his hair as he walked.

'This is Mr Darby,' said Mr Stevens. 'Mr Darby will be completing our – ensemble.'

Mr Darby had a face as smooth and symmetrical as a shopwindow dummy's, and like a dummy's outfit his white shirt and grey suit had no creases. He combed back his oily forelock, so it stood up like a little grille, and said 'Hi,' instead of 'Hello'.

'Pleased to meet you, Mr Darby,' said Alexander's mother.

'Call me Geoff,' he replied with a smile that went up as if pulled by wires. 'Irene, right?'

'And Alexander,' said his mother.

Mr Darby peered at Alexander over his mother's shoulder; he might have been looking over a wall at a guard dog. 'Hi, kid. Things OK?'

he asked, turning straight away to Mr Stevens. 'Come on, Harry, let's go. *Tempus fugit.*' Mr Darby leaped onto the podium and took up a position behind the stove, jerking the sleeves of his jacket and then his cuffs.

Mr Stevens manoeuvred Alexander and his mother into their places around the stove, on which Colin set a big copper pot and a snow-white saucepan. Mr Darby put his hand on Irene MacIndoe's shoulder and looked into the copper pot. 'Yum yum,' he said heavily, 'that does look so good. Get that spoon in there, girl, and give it a stir.'

A muffled voice came out of the head of the one-eyed, five-legged creature that was watching Alexander and his mother and Mr Darby. 'Mrs MacIndoe, could you raise your right hand a bit, and keep your left by your side? That's good. And look as if you've found fifty pounds in among the carrots. The imaginary carrots. That's good, Mrs MacIndoe.' Like a monstrous spider a hand crept out from the pleats of the cloth and advanced to the front of the camera, where it writhed around the lens and then retreated. 'Come on, Geoff, look keen,' said the voice. 'This blasted stove is the best thing that's happened to you since I don't know what.'

'The weekend?' suggested Mr Darby. He made a movement with his lips as if dislodging something from between his teeth.

The skirt of the camera bulged and out slipped Mr Stevens' head. 'Alexander, could you move in a bit closer?' he requested. 'And look at the pot, not the camera. Try to forget I'm here.' He raised the cloth, drew a deep breath like a diver, and ducked under. 'Nearly there, Alexander, nearly there. Left foot forward a bit. Perhaps tiptoes? And not quite so glum?'

'Smile at me, Alexander,' said his mother, and this was the moment of the day that he would remember most clearly: her damp red lips smiling into the vacant copper pot, while the fingers of her left hand shook against her thigh.

'The quid pro quo,' Alexander repeated quietly to himself, and the comical words made his face adjust itself to Mr Stevens' satisfaction.

'Excellent,' said Mr Stevens. 'Excellent. Don't move.' There was a flash into which everything vanished, and then the room seemed to assemble itself quickly out of the white air, wobbling for a second before standing firm. Alexander blinked. He saw a room that was colourless and stood like a ghost in front of the real room. He blinked again and the phantom room was fainter, and smaller, as if it were retreating. 'One more, everyone,' Mr Stevens called. Again everything disappeared and rushed back, and Alexander blinked to see the ghostly room.

'Thank you, Alexander. Very professional,' said Mr Stevens, satisfied at last, and then he dropped a spent flashbulb into Alexander's hand. Waiting for his mother to change out of the borrowed clothes, Alexander rolled the warm bulb on his palm. In the pock-marked glass he saw the grey of railway lines in the rain, the grey of the silted riverbank below the power station in Greenwich, the grey of the ash in the Doodlebug House. This he would remember too, and he would remember looking up to see his mother in the doorway to the back room, where Mr Darby stood in her way and said something to her. She lowered her eyes, then after ten seconds or so she smiled at Mr Darby as if he had said something amusing, though it appeared he had said nothing. She reached into Mr Darby's pocket, drew out his comb, snapped it in half and dropped the halves on the floor. Having wiped her fingers on the door jamb, she hurried across the shining floor, her heels hammering on the tiles.

'A pleasure to make your acquaintance, Mr Stevens,' she said, and snatched Alexander's hand in passing.

'And vice versa,' replied Mr Stevens to her back. 'Goodbye, Alexander.'

As the door to the office closed, Alexander turned to see Mr Stevens laughing with Mr Darby, who was fanning his hand in front of his mouth, miming an endless yawn.

'What happened?' Alexander asked his mother on the stairs.

'A very rude man,' she said, placing the back of a hand on her reddened cheeks. 'A very disagreeable person.'

'I didn't like him,' said Alexander.

'Quite right,' she told him.

'Smarmy.'

'Smarmy,' she agreed, but she was making them walk so fast they could not talk, and on the train she sat in silence, glaring at the window as if her reflected face were Mr Darby's.

The advertisement appeared in *Every Woman* magazine near the end of the year, next to a knitting pattern and opposite an advertisement in which a boy of Alexander's age was striding along a road in a countryside of wheat fields and sheep and thatched cottages, with a spiral of steam rising from a mug in the foreground, above the slogan '*It's The Only Way To Start The Day!*' The road and fields and cottages were painted, not real, and the vista of cupboards and shelves behind his mother and Mr Darby was unreal as well, like a pencil tracing rather than a photograph

His father leaned back in his chair and brought the page close to his face. 'A peculiar scene all right, son,' he said. 'Looks like no kitchen I've ever been in. And as for Mr Handsome, the cuckoo in the nest.' He shook his head in histrionic sorrow.

'Your idea as well as mine,' said Alexander's mother, turning her embroidery frame. 'We got a good deal.'

'Imagine, son. Your poor old dad not wanted on voyage. Insufficient juttiness of jaw. The humiliation of it.' He put down the magazine and picked up his newspaper, but as soon as they were left alone he turned to Alexander and whispered behind his hand, like a classmate playing a prank: 'Borrow your pencil?'

Alexander sat on the arm of the chair and watched his father draw a goatee moustache and glasses on the man, and then a speech bubble from Alexander's mouth. 'Who the hell are you?' he wrote in the bubble.

Their laughter brought Alexander's mother back. 'What's funny?' she asked, drying her hands on a tea-towel, and Alexander displayed the advertisement. 'Which one of you two infants did that, then?' she demanded, not smiling.

'He did,' said Alexander's father, handcuffing his son with his fingers.

'Idiot.'

'Vanity of vanities, saith the Preacher, vanity of vanities; all is vanity,' his father replied, for which he received a swat on the back of the head with the newspaper. 'I'll get you another one,' he laughed.

'You will indeed,' said Alexander's mother.

'Dog house for me,' said his father. He took the newspaper from her hand and unrolled it. 'Mind you, we'll all be done for at this rate,' he added, looking into the open pages as if he were staring into a pit.

Alexander would remember the words '38th Parallel' in the headline, and his pang of perplexity at the notion that something was happening in which peril and geometry were in some way combined. And he would remember looking at the advertisement his father had defaced, at his mother stirring the empty pot, at the simpering boy who was more like the boy on the painted road than he was like himself, and at the unpleasant Mr Darby, who seemed to be smirking at him, as if he knew that Alexander wanted him to go away.

8. Tollund Man

It was raining as the train went over Hungerford Bridge, and Alexander looked to his left at the roof of the Dome of Discovery, which was like a pavement of silver.

'That's called the Skylon,' said his mother, pointing to the rocket-shaped thing that balanced on tightropes beside the river. A boy across the aisle leaned forward to see, and slapped his bare knees with excitement. On the far bank, the big tower of the Houses of Parliament was wrapped in a cocoon of scaffolding.

'An hour till rendezvous,' said his father as they jostled down the steps off the bridge. 'Let's follow our noses for a while.'

First they went to look at the section on British wildlife, where Alexander, willing the time to pass, entranced himself with a picture of a Scottish wild cat cringing into the hollow of a tree trunk. People buffeted his back as he stood his ground, staring at the cat's gaping mouth. 'Come along, daydream,' said his mother, touching his neck. 'There's lots more to see. We can't spend all day looking at a moggy.'

'How much longer till they arrive?' Alexander asked.

His father did not even check his watch. 'Good grief,' he said. 'Patience, boy. About one hour minus five minutes.'

They went to a pavilion in which there were large straw figures of a lion and a unicorn. 'The twin symbols of the Briton's character,' his father read.

'Twin symbols?' said Alexander.

'Yes. Of the Britons,' said his father. 'All the people who are British. Me, you. All of us. What don't you understand?'

'Why two?'

'The lion is like the lion on the flags,' his father explained. 'Like the British Lions. Richard the Lionheart. Lion-hearted Britons in general – Francis Drake, Henry the Fifth, Winston Churchill, Randolph Turpin.'

'So not all of us?'

'Deep down, all of us, yes. But it's more obvious with some than with others, I grant you. Noël Coward, for instance. You have to dig pretty deep to find the lion there.'

'I thought it was the British bulldog.'

'It can be that too, yes,' his mother said. 'But the lion's more noble, more regal. And more ancient. There's history with the lion.'

'And a damned great straw bulldog would look pretty silly,' said his father, and he blew some dirt off his glasses.

'What's a unicorn got to do with it?' asked Alexander. 'They never existed, did they?'

His father pressed a thumb to the furrow between his eyebrows; he drew a long breath and let it go. 'No, that's right. They never existed.'

'The unicorn is for fantasy, Alexander,' said his mother. 'Imagination, playfulness, that sort of thing.'

'Think of Denis Compton,' said his father, and with an imaginary bat he clipped an imaginary ball up to the ceiling. 'Éclat, élan, vim, panache, et cetera, et cetera.'

'What?'

'Or Noël Coward,' said his mother.

Alexander trailed his parents out of the pavilion, ruminating on the mythical Briton, whose qualities were combined in nobody he knew. Sheltering under the eaves of the Dome, he watched the row of fountains in front of the Skylon as they wriggled like a squad of restless giants.

'This is definitely the right place?' his father asked his mother, hooking his cuff clear of his wrist.

'Well, how many domes can you see, Graham?' replied his mother. 'The dome at eleven,' she assured him, and no sooner had she said the words than Megan and Mrs Beckwith arrived, under a big black umbrella.

'We late, Irene?' asked Mrs Beckwith, picking at the net that held her hair bunched at the back of her head. 'Problems choosing young madam's wardrobe. Us girls always have to look our best, you know. A lesson you'll learn soon enough, Alexander,' she said, and she kissed him on his forehead.

Megan stood behind her, twirling her pleated tartan skirt. Her hair was held back above her ears by plastic clips that matched her eyes.

'Hello, Mrs MacIndoe,' said Megan, stepping out to the side. 'Hello, Mr MacIndoe. Hello, Eck. What are we going to do?'

'I don't know,' said Alexander, and he looked to his mother.

'Can I decide then?' Megan asked.

'Bossy child,' said Mrs Beckwith, and she nudged Megan towards Alexander.

Megan looked over his shoulder at the Skylon. 'It's beautiful, isn't it?' she said to Alexander. Her eyes followed the tower's curve up into space.

'No visible means of support,' observed his father. 'Just like the country.'

'Cynicism is inappropriate here, Graham,' chided his mother. 'For domestic consumption only.'

Tapping a cigarette on the lid of the steel case she had taken from her handbag, Mrs Beckwith nodded in the direction of the river. Two boys were kicking each other's shins underneath the Skylon. 'The male of the species,' she commented drily, then accepted the match that Alexander's father held out to her.

'Boys will be boys,' agreed his mother.

Megan's fingers appeared on Alexander's sleeve, and she said the only words that he would always be able to retrieve from his memory of that morning. 'But you're different, Eck,' she said, as if placating him. 'You're almost a girl.'

'Beg pardon?' exclaimed Mrs Beckwith.

'Whatever do you mean, young lady?' his father asked Megan, putting his hands on her shoulders from behind and looking down onto her face.

'I was being nice, Mr MacIndoe, that's all. Eck's gentle, like a girl, that's all I meant.'

Alexander's father frowned at Megan but he was more amused by her than he ever was by him, it seemed to Alexander, and it seemed throughout that morning that he preferred her company to his son's. 'That's called the regulator,' his father said to her, putting a finger close to a photograph in which a trio of iron spheres whirled on thick iron arms above a huge steam engine. Crouching between Alexander and Megan, he explained how the apparatus worked, but it was to Megan that he was speaking. 'They rise up, and the steam escapes here, and so the pressure drops and they fall again,' he said.

'Ingenious,' Megan commented, as if Alexander's father were the inventor and she was congratulating him.

'Ingenious indeed,' his father agreed, smiling to himself.

'Too technical for us,' commented his mother, pulling a face for Alexander, though he understood the machine well enough. She put a hand out to steer him to the next exhibit; he shrugged his shoulder away and followed his father.

'Now this,' said his father, in front of another photograph, 'was invented by a man who used to live not very far from here. Sir Henry Bessemer. He lived in Herne Hill. Do you know where Herne Hill is?'

'No,' said Megan, before Alexander could say 'Near Camberwell.'

'Between Camberwell and Dulwich,' his father said.

Side by side the three of them looked at the picture of a huge bucket from which a burning liquid flowed.

'What is it?' Megan asked, and his father explained how steel was manufactured.

At every picture they stopped and listened as his father talked to them like a schoolteacher. They were standing in front of a photograph of a shipyard when Alexander heard Mrs Beckwith, standing a couple of yards behind him, say to his mother: 'Sun's coming out, Irene.' Through a window Alexander saw a glow rise quickly on a wet concrete wall, turning it to the colour of chalk. The last raindrops of the exhausted shower sparkled against the dark gaberdine raincoat of a woman who stood with her back to him, her hand on the catch of her half-lowered umbrella.

'Shame to squander it,' said his mother, raising her voice slightly.

'Right enough,' agreed Mrs Beckwith.

'We can't leave yet,' moaned Megan. 'We haven't seen half of it.'

'You can't see everything here,' said Mrs Beckwith.

'Why not?' Megan demanded, with an eagerness that seemed overdone to Alexander and annoyed him.

'Well, let's work it out,' said Alexander's father. 'How long have we been looking at this one?'

'Half a minute,' replied Megan.

'More than that,' Alexander interjected.

'Let's say half a minute,' said his father, ticking off the first stage of the calculation on a little finger for Megan's benefit. 'There are twenty-five thousand photos here, it says. That's twelve and a half thousand minutes. That's more than two hundred hours. That's more than a week. And we have less than one day.'

Disgruntled by this proof, Megan appealed to her aunt. 'A bit longer?'

Mrs Beckwith looked at his father; his father smiled at Megan and rubbed his palms together as if limbering up for a tug-of-war.

'The wives are playing truant, then,' said his mother. 'Outside in an hour?'

Megan and his father walked away, and Alexander followed his mother and Mrs Beckwith, who were not aware that he had decided to go with them. Arm in arm the women walked, like grown-up sisters, perfectly in step with each other, their foreheads almost touching as they talked. 'Come on, Joan, tell me,' Alexander heard his mother say, and he stopped on the carpet that ran to the door, to avoid eavesdropping on Mrs Beckwith's reply. He would remember looking at the sharp tendons of their ankles as they moved away from him, and then looking at his mother's face, which now was in perfect profile. She laughed and her eyes became huge with astonishment as her mouth formed a word like 'No'. The vivacity of her expression was of a kind that Alexander had never previously seen in her face; it was mischievous and very young, more like Megan than his mother. With a vertiginous lurch he felt that he was seeing a moment from the life she had led before he existed, or her life as it would have been had he not been born, and he understood in that instant that she loved him out of choice. A curl of hair fell across her ear. He wanted to rush to her, but his legs were like iron. She turned, as if she had become conscious of the empty space behind her, and then noticed him standing on his own. 'Catch up, Alexander,' she called. He trudged to the door, encumbered by sadness. 'Slowcoach,' his mother said, with a look that told him she knew there was something on his mind but was not going to ask what it was.

'You have a run about, so we can gossip,' said Mrs Beckwith outside. 'We'll all go for something to eat soon.'

Alexander walked around the train that was parked on a short length of track nearby. He sat down on the pavement on the far side of the train, so that he could see his mother and Mrs Beckwith through the gap between the undercarriage and the track. Where the sun hit the rails there were red and blue grains in the steel. Tufts of grease glistened on the bolts of the rails; they were the colour of the jelly in a pork pie. Alexander touched a finger to one of them, and the smell of it made him close his eyes. He saw the fire station and remembered how, when he was younger, his mother used to lift him so that he could see through the panes in the folding red wooden doors. Pressing his palms to his temples he willed into sight the scarlet metal of the fire engines and the black gleam of their tyres, like varnished charcoal, and the firemen's jackets and tall boots arranged around the walls like vestments. Across his eyelids flooded a red so profound it brought a taste to the air in his mouth, a sweet and elusive taste he could name only as the flavour of redness. Again he brought the greasy fingertip to his nose. Water sprang into his mouth as if out of hunger.

'Are you all right?' someone was asking.

Alexander opened his eyes, and saw that a tall elderly man with a white moustache was looking at him quizzically. The waxed tips of the man's moustache stuck out of the bristles like prongs of chicken bone; these repulsive miniature horns would still be in his memory more than forty years later, though the face to which they had belonged would not, nor the place where he had seen that face.

'Yes, I'm fine, thank you,' said Alexander, and he peered under the train. His mother and Mrs Beckwith, arm in arm, were approaching. 'I'm waiting for my mother. She's coming now,' he said, pointing.

'Jolly good,' said the man, and he doffed his hat to Mrs Beckwith and Alexander's mother.

'Not easy, pet, I'll tell you that much,' concluded Mrs Beckwith, and she blinked one eye at the sting of the smoke from her raised cigarette. She looked at Alexander and it was clear that she knew he had heard. Her dress tightened across her ribs and creased as she sighed.

They all ate in the Regatta Restaurant, where the door handles were shaped like hands, and the plates were thicker and heavier and whiter than the plates at home, and they were served by a woman who said 'Oh yes' after every order, as if she had guessed perfectly what each of them was going to say.

'What did you do, Eck?' Megan asked as she chopped at her food.

'Just wandered,' Alexander replied.

'So what did you find out?'

Alexander glanced at Mrs Beckwith, who was comparing the contents of her plate with his father's. 'This and that,' he said.

Megan fidgeted dismissively. 'Mr MacIndoe explained such a lot of things,' she said to his mother. 'We're going back to the Dome after this.'

'Are we now?' his mother asked his father.

'It would appear so,' he said. 'Alexander, are you a member of the expedition?'

Megan was fiddling with one of her hair clips. 'These are a nuisance,' she complained. 'Help me out, Eck.'

The clip jumped like a cricket into Alexander's hand. 'Are we all going?' he asked.

His mother said they were, but before they left the restaurant she changed her mind. 'We'll join you in a bit,' she said to his father as she stood up. Alexander took hold of Mrs Beckwith's arm.

'Latching on to us, are we?' teased Mrs Beckwith.

'You don't want to listen to our chatter, Alexander,' said his mother.

'I won't listen,' he said. 'I'll walk behind.'

'In front, so we can keep an eye on you,' Mrs Beckwith ordered, and the three of them went one way while his father and Megan went the other.

Alexander led his mother and Mrs Beckwith from pavilion to pavilion, through rooms of new furniture and electric machines and wallpaper that was covered with patterns of crystals, and all the time he was holding the hairclip tightly in his palm. He was still holding it when Megan and Mrs Beckwith left, but the following day he decided to take it back, having convinced himself that it would not be wrong to go to Megan's house, now that she and Mrs Beckwith had spent a day with him and his parents.

Because his parents did not know John Halloran's parents, he made out that he was going to John's house. It began to rain, and he ran to the Beckwiths' house, where he paused at the gate to inspect the building. It appeared that nobody was in. He swung the gate back and advanced, cautiously, halfway up the path. Through the living room window he could see a newspaper lying in damp light on the arm of an empty settee. Alexander took the clip from his pocket and eased the letterbox open like a trap. He looked into the hallway; every door inside was closed. He was about to drop the clip when a sound to his left made him jump and the steel flap clacked shut. Mr Beckwith was standing at the end of the path that went down the side of the house. He was holding a trowel in one hand and something black in the other fist, and his white cotton shirt was clinging to his ribs, which showed like gills through the fabric. His bony knees looked like hammer-heads under the wet cloth of his trousers.

Alexander had seen Mr Beckwith many times in the previous year, always alone, always walking steadily with his peculiar padding gait, facing straight ahead. He had never seen him speak to anyone, nor even exchange a greeting with anyone, nor stop at any shop. Mr Beckwith was always moving, and now he looked at Alexander as if the boy had brought him to a standstill and he did not know what to do.

'Hello, Mr Beckwith,' said Alexander timidly.

Mr Beckwith looked meaninglessly at him, and his jaw moved rapidly up and down in a silent stammering.

'I didn't mean to disturb anybody,' Alexander apologised.

Mr Beckwith looked at the front door as if it were a third person waiting for him to speak. 'No one in, lad,' he said. His voice was very low, like the voice of a fat man, and the words seemed to buzz in his throat.

'I was only going to give this back,' said Alexander, unfurling his fingers from the clip.

Mr Beckwith gazed uncomprehendingly at the piece of plastic. 'Oh,' he said, as if rebuking himself.

'Is that all right?' asked Alexander, but Mr Beckwith appeared to hear nothing. 'Is that all right?' he repeated. 'If I put it through?'

'Put it through,' said Mr Beckwith, and with the trowel he made a posting action. Black water was dripping from the underside of his left hand. 'Are you Alexander?' he asked, stretching his narrow neck as if looking through murk.

'Yes, sir,' Alexander replied. 'Alexander MacIndoe.'

Mr Beckwith considered what Alexander had said. 'At school with Megan, are you?'

'Yes, sir.'

'Yes,' echoed Mr Beckwith. Seeming to have nothing more to say, he watched a car go past the house. His head swung back to face Alexander. 'My name's Harold,' he remarked at last, and he transferred the trowel to a windowsill so that he could offer a hand. 'Pleased to meet you,' he said. His fingers were cold, and rolled in Alexander's hand like a sheaf of short sticks. 'It's raining. Do you want to shelter inside for a while?'

'I should go home,' said Alexander.

Mr Beckwith looked at the sky. 'No,' he told him with a grave shake of his head. 'It'll get worse before it gets better. Come with me,' he said, and he picked up the trowel and turned back down the side path.

Ignoring the door to the kitchen, Mr Beckwith led Alexander into the garden. It was as neat as a garden in a magazine, and there were more colours in it than in any garden Alexander had ever seen. The lawn was an oval, not a rectangle like at his own house and every other house he knew, and close to its centre was an oval bed, in which only white flowers grew. In one part of the garden was a bed of yellow flowers; in another part every bloom was a shade of purple; at the end of the garden stood a wooden shed, with a row of red flowers along its wall. Every plant and bush seemed perfect in its shape, as if a smoothing hand had moulded the body of the foliage in one long caress, and there was not so much as a single stray petal to mar the darkness of the soil beneath the leaves.

Mr Beckwith opened the shed door, and they stepped into air that was warmer than the air outside and smelled of creosote and grass and newly cut wood. Their tread made the floor bend and croak. A rack of seed packets hung on one wall, above a tower of yellow newspapers. In a corner stood a stack of clay pots, next to a tool box and below a saw and a pair of shears that hung from the same nail. By the window was a high bench that was cross-hatched with blade marks, with a vice bolted to one end.

'Look at this,' said Mr Beckwith. He put his left hand on the bench and opened his fingers to expose the ball of wet soil that he had been

70

carrying. 'Blackleg,' he stated. 'See?' He turned his wrist, revealing the limp stem of a flower drooping from one side of the clod. He stuck the point of the trowel into the dark stringy pulp at its base. 'There's nothing you can do about this. Incurable, blackleg. You have to burn it and go back to square one.' With a foot he dragged a bucket out from under the bench. 'Look at that,' said Mr Beckwith. Half a dozen flowers lay on a bed of sludge in the bottom of the bucket. 'All of them ruined with it,' Mr Beckwith said. His teeth were as long as a dog's, Alexander noticed, and the skin of his cheeks seemed as thin as a leaf. Mr Beckwith looked at Alexander abruptly, as if he had asked him a question. 'Do you know what this flower is?' he asked. Alexander shook his head. 'No? Not to worry. It's a geranium. They're all geraniums.' Mr Beckwith lowered the clod and its diseased stem into the bucket, as if it were a small sleeping animal. 'Got a garden, have you?' he demanded suddenly.

'Yes, sir.'

'Nice one, is it?'

'Yes, sir. But not as nice as this.'

Gazing out of the window, Mr Beckwith lowered his head towards Alexander. 'Say that again,' he said. 'Hearing a bit dicky.'

'Not as nice as your garden, sir.'

'Thank you,' said Mr Beckwith. 'I didn't eat enough for a long time, you see. That's what did my ears. Do you eat properly?'

'Yes, sir.'

'Look like you do.' A sound that was like the first part of a laugh made his chest shudder, yet he did not smile. 'So you've got a garden?'

'Yes, sir.'

'Don't need the sir, lad. I'm not your teacher.' Mr Beckwith's face wore a vague and thoughtful look, a look that made it seem as if he were being reminded that there was something he should be doing but could not for the moment recall what it was. 'Megan's a good girl,' he declared.

'Yes, sir.'

'Don't need the sir, lad. Any good at woodwork?' He lifted from the bench two blocks of pale wood that had been fixed together in a mortice and tenon joint.

71

'Not really, Mr Beckwith,' replied Alexander, wondering what use the wooden object might serve.

'Neither am I,' said Mr Beckwith seriously. 'What about gardening?'

'Not really. My dad does the garden. Mum sometimes helps. I do a bit, too. Not much, though.'

Mr Beckwith raised his chin and turned his eyes to a blank portion of the wooden wall, as if allowing Alexander's words to trickle into his mind. Gradually he turned his head to look out of the window again. 'Rain's easing off,' he observed. 'Give it a minute or two. Sit yourself down.' He waved a hand at the pile of newspapers, and he turned his attention to cleaning the trowel and the other tools he had been using. Streaks of dark skin appeared through Mr Beckwith's shirt as he worked, and the sinews at the back of his neck stood out like the muscles of his forearm.

The stack swayed as Alexander sat on it, and when he spread his feet to steady himself his left foot slipped on a magazine. Alexander lifted his foot from a photograph that seemed to be of an old woman asleep on a mattress, with an old-fashioned night-cap on her head. He bent over the picture and realised that the person was not an old woman and was not asleep. What he had thought was a nightdress was in fact skin, which clung to the dead man's bones like a collapsed tent of soft leather. Fleshless fingers, sickle-shaped, hung from the wrists. A shaft of bare bone ended in a strong plump foot. Alexander picked up the magazine to read the caption. 'Who's Tollund Man, Mr Beckwith?' he asked.

Unwinding a length from a ball of twine, Mr Beckwith looked over his shoulder at Alexander. 'I'm sorry, lad. What did you say?'

'Who's Tollund Man?' Alexander repeated, holding the page outwards.

Mr Beckwith put his face close to the magazine. He pulled back a bit, then looked closely again. 'Danish chap,' he said at last. 'Hundreds of years old. From the Iron Age. They found him in a bog. All the water in the peat kept him fresh. He was hanged. See?' His finger touched the cord around Tollund Man's throat.

Alexander gazed at the ancient man, curled on his platform of peat. The leathery face seemed to be wincing away from the photographer. It should be terrible, this image of a murdered man, and yet Alexander could not feel what he knew it was proper for him to feel. Waiting for an urgent emotion to seize him, he gazed at Tollund Man, at the body and the peat that seemed all of one piece, like a pouring of dark metal.

'Fresh as a flower,' commented Mr Beckwith. 'Do you want it?' To please Mr Beckwith, Alexander said that he did. With three swift passes of his rigid fingers, Mr Beckwith tore the picture cleanly out. 'It's stopped now,' Mr Beckwith said, scratching a cheek that was as soft and dark as Tollund Man's. 'Shall we go?'

Together they walked a circuit of the garden, Mr Beckwith naming his plants as if introducing them, Alexander repeating the names and striving to embed them in his mind. Holding the picture of Tollund Man lightly in both hands, like a prayer book, he concentrated on the soft white flowerheads to which the word Viburnum belonged. The fragrant pink roses were called Penelope; the artificial-looking flowers that clung to the wall, like purple and white targets fringed with coronets of white petals, had two names, Passiflora and Passion Flower.

Clockwise Mr Beckwith and Alexander processed around the garden, then anti-clockwise they circled back. Mr Beckwith paused before a sheaf of pink flowers in a bed that was shaded by the neighbour's house, and gestured as if offering them to Alexander.

'Hydrangea?' Alexander volunteered.

'Exactly,' said Mr Beckwith. He took a step into the sun. 'And these?' he asked, by some yellow button-like flowers. 'No matter. It's Lavender Cotton, or Santolina.'

Five minutes later the rain recommenced, and Alexander's first conversation with Mr Beckwith was over. He would always remember how they parted. 'Hurry home,' said Mr Beckwith, and Alexander walked down the path at the side of the house, dodging the water that dripped from a crack in the guttering. He was by the back door when Mr Beckwith called his name.

'Mr Beckwith?' Alexander replied.

Standing in the slot of light between the two houses, Mr Beckwith held out a flat hand. 'Whatever it was you were bringing back?'

Alexander placed the clip on Mr Beckwith's muddy skin. Mr Beckwith looked at it, rocking his hand a fraction of an inch this way

73

and that, as if playing with a drop of water, and his eyes became kindly. 'Goodbye, Alexander,' he said. He looked at Alexander and seemed to be contemplating whether he should tell him something. 'Goodbye,' he said again, and went back into his garden.

9. Praa

They were standing at the end of a gravel driveway that ran between high walls of fresh brick. 'There's a five-a-side pitch out the back,' John Halloran said to Alexander, looking avariciously at the long clapboard hut that stood at the end of the driveway. 'They play football after every session,' he went on. 'Sometimes they do a manhunt round the streets. You get a five-minute start and you have to make chalk marks on the walls as you go, and the rest of them come after you.'

'It looks like an army camp,' Alexander observed. The severed neck of a milk bottle, like a crown of jagged glass, lay on the kerbstone. This detail Alexander would always remember, and that John kicked it away to make him listen.

'It's not like the army at all. You're not going to end up dead, for one thing, and you don't have to sign up if you don't want to. Come on, Al. Don't be wet. If we don't like it we won't join.'

'We don't have to join right away?'

'Definitely don't. You can muck around for months before making your mind up. That's what Pete did.'

'You sure?' asked Alexander, and he took a few steps up the drive, as if a nearer view of the building might dissipate his doubts. The hut occupied its quiet yard like a boat in a backwater dock. There was something appealing about its solitariness, and about the fleur-de-lys badge that gleamed on the door like an occult symbol.

'It'll be a giggle,' John urged. 'Give it a go, Al.'

So that evening they were collected from John Halloran's house by Peter Nichols, who was standing stiffly on the path when they opened the door, his arms straight against his sides. 'At ease,' John shouted, but their classmate's punctilious expression did not change.

Placing first one foot and then the other on the doorstep, Peter Nichols corrected the garters of his thick grey socks, and then he tapped the peak of his cap, to make the point that his uniform was the token of his seniority. 'You'd better button your shirt up,' he told John.

'You're kidding,' John replied.

'No,' said Peter Nichols.

'But it's not school.'

'It's not school, but if you're not smart you won't go far,' Peter Nichols told them. 'Better get used to it now,' he said, and he escorted them to the scout hut at a quick march, barely speaking to them.

When they entered the hut Peter Nichols crossed the floor to talk to a group of uniformed boys at the back of the room. Some of the boys Alexander recognised from school, but none of them took any notice of him or John. All were behaving like Peter Nichols, as if to make it clear that this place was governed by rules that superseded mere friendship. One boy even shook hands with Peter and folded his arms across his chest to listen to him, like a middle-aged man at a business meeting.

'Grim,' John commented. 'This is very grim. Not what I expected, I'll admit.' His doleful gaze moved down the rows of pennants and flags that were pinned to the rafters. At the end of the hall, under a large photograph of the king, one of the senior scouts was energetically buffing his shoes with a duster. 'We've come to a Nuremberg rally, mate,' said John.

The scout master, Mr Gardiner, introduced himself to them. His shorts were as wide as a skirt and his whiskerless white skin was as delicate as Mrs Beckwith's. 'Peter told me about you,' he said, looking at them as though they were items in an auction room. 'So what has kindled your interest in scouting?' he asked, with a whimsical lilt to his voice.

'All the things that Peter has told us, sir,' John replied. 'Making ourselves better members of society, helping each other, that kind of thing.'

Mr Gardiner made a concurring squint. 'Yes,' he said. 'That's what it's about. And you think it's the kind of thing for you, do you?'

'We think so, sir,' said John.

'Jolly good. Jolly good,' said Mr Gardiner, and he checked the time on his wristwatch. 'You two can join Peewit patrol for now. Peter will show you what to do.'

'Peewit patrol, eh?' John remarked to Peter Nichols once Mr Gardiner had left them.

'Yes. That's my patrol,' Peter Nichols replied.

'That's nice.'

'What's nice?'

'Peewit patrol.'

'What do you mean, it's nice?'

'It's a nice name.'

'It's not meant to be nice,' said Peter Nichols primly.

'No, but it's nice anyway. Nice sound to it. Peter's Peewit patrol.' John scowled at the floorboards and then at Alexander. 'But what's a peewit when it's at home?'

'Search me,' said Alexander.

'Another name for the lapwing,' Peter Nichols interrupted.

'Lapwing?'

'A type of bird, obviously. Now get in line. Stand like me,' he told them, sliding his left foot away from his right and stiffening his shoulders.

Mr Gardiner positioned himself proudly in front of the king and locked his hands in the small of his back. A thin, tall boy with a very narrow head took his place beside Mr Gardiner; with a hand placed over his heart he recited an oath, accompanied by a mumbling from the two parallel ranks of scouts.

'Jesus,' John groaned.

'It's not going well,' Alexander agreed, though he was intrigued and amused by the proceedings. The appearance of the skinny scout, like a small boy made big by stretching, seemed to Alexander wholly appropriate to this comical ritual.

'Sorry, Al,' John murmured.

'Quiet!' ordered Mr Gardiner, so ferociously that both John and Alexander blushed. The skinny scout was saluting the picture of the king with a rake-like hand.

'When's the football, Pete?' John enquired as the two ranks broke up, but Peter Nichols, drawing back the bolt on a black tin chest, ignored him.

'A few basics,' said Peter Nichols. 'What's this?' he asked, letting a bolt of cloth drop open from his outstretched hands.

'The Union Jack,' Alexander replied.

'Wrong. It's the Union Flag. The Union Jack is flown from a ship. On land it's the Union Flag.'

'What's the difference?' asked John.

'I told you the difference. The Union Jack is flown from a ship. On land it's the Union Flag.'

'But it's the same flag?'

'Yes. But it's wrong to call this the Union Jack, and there's a right and a wrong way to fly it.' Peter Nichols demonstrated the right way, and then they studied a chart of national flags and signalling flags, and then the skinny scout stood by the door to send semaphore messages to Mr Gardiner, who flapped his two small flags in reply, from in front of the king.

'SOS!' Mr Gardiner cried, and his rigid arms flew up and down in a sequence of electrocuted spasms. 'Once again!' cried Mr Gardiner, and the flags went up and down with a cracking sound.

'Why do they need the flags when they can holler at each other?' John asked Peter Nichols.

'That wouldn't do any good, would it?'

'Why not?'

'It's obvious.'

'Not to me.'

'You couldn't be heard in a storm, could you? It's obvious,' said Peter Nichols, with a contemptuous look. 'Use your head.'

'Ah,' said John, relieved to have at last been given access to understanding. 'This'll be handy, I'm sure. One day. Lost in a storm on the Thames, miles from dry land.'

'If you're going to be flippant, Halloran,' said Peter Nichols angrily, 'there's little point in your being here.'

'Quite true, mein kapitan,' John replied, but he and Alexander did return the following week and for several weeks after that. Under the tutelage of Peter Nichols they learned how to make a fire without matches, clean their teeth without a toothbrush, identify badger tracks and the tracks of foxes, otters, goats and sheep. They learned never to shelter under an oak tree in a thunderstorm, because the rainwater coursing through the grooved bark would conduct the lethal lightning bolt. They were required to memorise nonsense syllables that were said to represent the songs of birds they would never find in London. Doggedly Peter Nichols tied and untied knots of pointless complexity, until Alexander could form them unaided.

By then it required effort for John Halloran to dissemble his discontent. 'Only deer we're going to see are in the zoo,' he grumbled, as Peter Nichols, his hand obscuring the captions, held up a page of hoofprints. 'What about doing makes of cars instead?' he suggested, when presented with the silhouettes of various wings. 'Any chance of football, Pete?' he would ask at some point in every evening, and 'Not until you've got this right,' became Peter Nichols' customary reply. But only once did they go out to the yard for a game, and that was for no more than ten minutes, and then one evening Alexander called at John Halloran's house and was told that he would have to go on his own.

'Kicked out before I could walk out,' John explained. 'Himmler put in a call to the ma. It'll be your turn next if you don't put your name on the dotted line. Why don't you tell them to stuff it?'

'I think I will,' said Alexander. 'Soon.'

'It's so boring,' said John. 'Making a bivouac out of lettuce leaves and all that.'

Alexander did soon leave, but not because he was bored by the peculiar skills he was being taught. He was never bored, though he could rarely think of any use for what he was learning. He enjoyed making cross-sections from contoured maps of London, plotting the altitudes on a graph and bringing out the shape of the land beneath the houses and roads of his neighbourhood. There was pleasure in becoming able to shorten a length of rope with a sheepshank without looking at what his hands were doing, and to read the coming weather from the clouds. Had it not been for Mr Gardiner, he would have stayed longer. 'You have an enthusiasm,' said Mr Gardiner, but in a way that made enthusiasm sound like something Alexander did not want to have. The blue skin under his eyes, Alexander noticed, was like the skin that covered the bulging eyes of the dead fledgling he had found one evening below the gutter of the scouts' hall. Mr Gardiner sat so close that his feet jammed against Alexander's underneath the bench. 'Johnny was a disruptive influence. You have the makings of a good scout,' he said. 'I'll keep my eye on you,' Mr Gardiner smiled, and an odour of sour milk escaped from his mouth. It was that evening, in the week that the last London tram broke down on its final journey to New Cross, that Alexander told his parents he did not want to go back.

'Why on earth not?' asked his father, folding the map that had been spread open on his lap.

'It's dull,' said Alexander.

'Dull,' echoed his father dully.

'Really dull.'

'It'll do you good if you stick at it.'

'But it's so boring.'

'Any training's boring sometimes.'

'This isn't training for anything, and it's boring all the time.'

'So it wasn't boring when John Halloran was with you, but now it's boring all the time?'

'Yes.'

'Sounds to me as if you weren't there for the right reason in the first place.'

'And we'll have to get him the uniform soon, if he keeps going,' said Alexander's mother. 'The uniform's expensive, Graham.'

'We've discovered that today, have we?' his father rejoined.

'No. Alexander has discovered that it's not for him. That's what we've discovered.'

'There would seem to be little purpose in continuing this discussion,' said his father, raising the map. He was still reading it, as if it were a device to preserve his annoyance, when Alexander came downstairs to say goodnight.

'What's the map for, Mum?' Alexander asked.

'A graphic representation of the land, for the purposes of comprehension and navigation,' replied his father. His left hand let go of the map, stirred the spoon in his mug of cocoa, and took hold of the map again.

'Graham,' said his mother. She closed the fashion magazine in her lap and stared at the map, waiting for it to be lowered. 'Graham,' she said again, and his father made busy humming noises. His mother made a loudhailer from the magazine and directed it at Alexander. 'He's planning our holiday,' she whispered loudly. 'A proper holiday.'

'Possibly,' responded his father.

'Two whole weeks,' said his mother, making delighted eyes.

'Possibly. If the piggy bank has put on enough weight.'

'In sunny Cornwall.'

'Don't count your chickens.'

'Next month.'

'Possibly,' his father repeated, but there was now a sardonic inflection to his gruffness.

'Graham,' said his mother. 'Come on, Graham. Don't be a grump.'

'A grump?' said his father, feigning bafflement. 'A grump? Come,' he called, and when Alexander came around to the side of his chair his father reached out to fold down the collars of his dressing gown and pyjamas, feigning displeasure at Alexander's disarray. 'X marks the spot,' he said, scribbling with the mouthpiece of his pipe on a long stroke of yellow ink. 'Praa,' he read. 'Possibly Praa.'

Alexander looked at the bite-shaped bays and the roads that ended short of the coast, like wires that had been cut. 'Next month?' he asked his father.

'I should think so,' his father said. 'Let's see.'

Every night until the day they left Alexander lay in bed at night, recalling the enormous dunes that Jimmy Murrell had seen, and the glowing sea, and repeating the strange bleat of a word, 'Praa, Praa.' He tacked the map to the back of his door, and drew a bull's eye around the beach. He would always remember staring at the pencilled ring, as if into the entrance to a tunnel that led to a place that was unlike any he had seen before, and he would remember standing at the window of the train carriage and asking his father to name a distant town that came into view as the trees fell away from the railway line, and being pleased that his father could not name it, because this meant they had reached a region that was mysterious to all of them. He would remember the trees becoming stunted and the fields bigger, and his expectation that every vague, flat vista would come into focus as the sea, and his disappointment when one far-off field did indeed become the ocean, making its appearance as though by subterfuge. He would remember that the windows of the bus they boarded in Penzance were greasy with sea-spray, and that when his father asked for three tickets to Germoe, the conductor said something that his father could not understand, which made his mother hold Alexander so tightly he could feel her ribs vibrating with pent-up laughter. And he would remember the bus doors smacking open, and there were the houses of Germoe, all low and white, as if salt had caked every one of them.

In Mrs Pardoe's dining room they ate mackerel that Mrs Pardoe's son had caught, and then they walked down to the beach in the last minutes of dusk. They passed a castle and a lorry carrying steel churns as big as pillarboxes. Flowers of a sort that Alexander had never seen before overflowed from a barrel. The vinegary smell of the beach grew stronger, and the road began to go under a skim of sand that had cigarette butts and lollipop sticks in it. Taking one hand each, his parents swung him over a long bolster of sand and he sprinted away, down to the water. Though the dunes were smaller than he had imagined they would be, he was thrilled by what he saw. This was not a sea like the sea near London: here was the ocean, a wilderness of immeasurable dark water. Looking towards the black horizon, he imagined that the night was not falling but was rising from the sea. Low in the sky a single yellow star could be seen, above a boat that seemed to dissolve into the clouds as he watched. All he could hear was the ceaseless gasping of the surf, and when he breathed deeply the air from the sea made a column he could feel in his throat. In his exhilaration he gathered a handful of soft dry sand and threw it onto the breeze.

His mother's hand, cooler than the air, made a band around his brow. 'We've a surprise, Alexander,' she said, and she turned him to face her.

'Yes, we're going straight back to London,' said his father with a straight face, buttoning his jacket.

'Mr and Mrs Beckwith are here, and Megan as well,' his mother told him. 'Two weeks they'll be here, same as us.'

A man and a woman were coming onto the beach; Alexander watched them approach until it was clear that they were not the Beckwiths. 'They're here already?' he asked his mother warily.

'Yes. They arrived yesterday.'

'We thought you might be pleased,' said his father in such a tone as to make it seem that the Beckwiths' presence was a gift that it was in his power to revoke.

'No, I am, I am,' said Alexander. 'Where are they?' he asked.

His mother pointed up the hill. 'Over there somewhere.'

'Hendra,' confirmed his father. 'A place called Hendra.'

The white walls had turned the colour of mackerel in the thickening darkness, and here and there a lighted window shone, tantalizing as the windows of an Advent calendar. A car's headlights tilted down from the top of the hill and brushed along the houses, as if inviting Alexander to guess which one was home to the Beckwiths.

'We'll see them tomorrow,' said his mother. 'Next thing you know we'll all be together.'

In the back bedroom of Mrs Pardoe's house Alexander slept with his window open, listening to the sea at its nocturnal work, imagining that Megan was listening to it too, in her room somewhere up the hill, in a village with a name like a girl's name. And in the morning, after Mrs Pardoe had knocked on the door to rouse him, he sat on his bed for a few minutes, looking over the rooftops towards Hendra and listening for the sea through the racket of the gulls and the clink of the cutlery in the dining room. His mother opened the door, and a smell of smoked fish gusted into the room. 'Let's be having you,' she said. 'We haven't come all this way for you to hibernate.' Alexander listened for the sea and did not hear it, but there were grains of sand on the pillow case, and these were sign enough that a day unlike any other had begun.

After breakfast they walked in procession down to the beach, fifty paces behind a woman with a blue towel held under her arm like a pet dog. His mother bought some food and his father bought a newspaper in a shop that sold sandals and rubber balls as well as bread and sweets and cigarettes. At a chart of the tides his father stopped again, as if he had forgotten that the Beckwiths were waiting. 'Should be fine today,' he announced. A luring breeze swirled over Alexander's skin. At the end of the road the surf was rushing up as though to meet them, then scampering away.

Cubicles of striped canvas had been raised on the beach. Alexander and his parents walked past them all, searching for the Beckwiths. They walked towards the cliffs on their right, checking every hunched and supine figure. A woman in a turquoise swimsuit looked like Mrs Beckwith from afar, but was not Mrs Beckwith. They turned round and retraced the footsteps they had left. As they reached the end of their trail Alexander looked up at the dune and saw that a woman wearing a dark blue dress and dark glasses was waving as if wiping an invisible window.

Mr Beckwith stood up on the crest of the dune and came down the slope to shake hands with them all, including Alexander. 'Graham,' said Mrs Beckwith to his father, shaking his hand. 'Irene,' she said to his mother, and kissed her once on each cheek. To Alexander she said nothing, but looked at him with her hands on her hips as if debating with herself what was to be done with him. At last she smiled concedingly: 'Megan's with the other loonies,' she said.

'There,' explained Mr Beckwith, raising a rigid arm to point across the beach. 'The woman in the red cap's keeping an eye on her.'

Without changing into his swimming trunks Alexander leapt down the dune and ran out to the sea. The woman in the red cap was standing in hip-high water, watching a girl who was dog-paddling along with her head held up and her eyes wide open, as if peeping over a tiny wall. Beyond her was Megan, her brick-coloured hair making snakes on the surface of the sea. She stood up and ducked her head into a breaking wave.

Alexander cupped his hands and shouted to her. She looked the wrong way, then noticed him. Her mouth spat out a gobbet of seawater and made a shape that might have been the shape of his name. With the flats of her hands she beat on her belly. 'Eck?' she yelled, and Alexander realised then that his parents and the Beckwiths had plotted together to bring about this moment for himself and Megan.

'Didn't you know?' he called, as Megan strode towards him, raising frills of water from her foam-white legs.

'Top of the class, Eck.' Her laugh became a cough as she stumbled out of the shallow water. 'No, of course I didn't know. Did you?'

'Not till last night,' Alexander replied.

'You're staying here?' she asked. He told her about Mrs Pardoe's, and she trampled the soggy sand while he was speaking. 'This is terrific, Eck,' she said, poking him in the midriff with a forefinger.

'You getting out now?' asked Alexander. 'It's really warm up on the dunes.' Megan looked landward and then seaward. Her eyes were bloodshot and a violet line was spreading from the centre of her upper lip. 'Come on,' Alexander urged, touching her stippled forearm. 'You're freezing.'

'I've only been in a couple of minutes, Eck. Why don't you get changed and come in?' she cajoled. 'Go on. Go and get changed.'

Alexander removed his shoes and socks and extended a foot into the rinse of an expiring wave. 'You've got to get right in,' said Megan, walking backwards into the water, 'otherwise it's cold. Once it's over your chest you start to warm up. Believe me,' she said, kicking with her heels. 'A city boy,' she commented to the woman in the red cap, and she sprawled into the surf and swam away. Alexander turned to wave at the dune, though now there were so many people on it that he could not be certain where his parents and the Beckwiths were.

Every day they all shared a picnic in a trough of sand on the grassy dune. Alexander and Megan would watch for the signal from Mrs Beckwith's polka-dot scarf, and their return was in turn a signal to Mr Beckwith, who would come down from the crest of the dune where he sat like a sentinel through most of the morning, his face directed at the horizon.

On the third afternoon, once the sandwiches were finished, Mr Beckwith stood up, shook the sand and crumbs from the lap of his trousers, and then, instead of climbing back up to his lookout, placed a hand on Alexander's shoulderblades and said to him: 'I'll show you something, young Alexander.'

At the back of the dune Mr Beckwith stopped, his feet bracketing a tussock of pink flowers. 'Do you know what this is?' he asked.

'I don't,' replied Alexander, promptly, as Mr Beckwith required.

'It's thrift,' said Mr Beckwith. 'It's called thrift because its leaves retain its water thriftily. Do you recognise it? You've seen it before.' Mr Beckwith looked at Alexander with an expression that was as stern as the one with which he faced the sea, but his voice was soft and coaxing.

'Have I?'

'Yes, you have,' said Mr Beckwith. 'You've seen it on the back of a threepenny bit,' he said, displaying a coin on the tip of a middle finger. 'You see: thrift on a coin. It makes sense. It's also known as sea-pink or ladies' cushions, and that makes sense as well.' Turning slowly, he looked around the dune. 'And that,' he said, not indicating

85

what he meant, 'is lady's bedstraw.' Alexander followed him to a spume of tiny yellow flowers. 'Put your nose on that,' Mr Beckwith told him. 'What does it smell of?'

'Honey,' replied Alexander.

'Used to be put in mattresses to make them smell nice. And that over there, that's henbane by the look of it,' he said, walking over to a stunted bush on which grew clusters of watery yellow flowers. 'Henbane all right. Take a look, but don't touch it.'

Alexander crouched by Mr Beckwith's feet. Thin purple lines made webs on the petals and the leaves were hairy as caterpillars.

'A type of nightshade this is. Can make you very ill indeed. Worse than ill, in fact. Dr Crippen – you've heard of Dr Crippen?' Alexander shook his head. 'No matter. A nasty piece of work was Dr Crippen. Poisoned his wife he did, and this is what he poisoned her with.' The face of Dr Crippen appeared to Alexander as a version of Mr Gardiner's, sallow as henbane flowers, with hard little veins under his eyes.

From then on, Alexander spent part of every afternoon with Mr Beckwith. When the picnic was over, and the others spread out the towels to sunbathe or went down the slope to look for shells, Mr Beckwith would unhurriedly survey the sky and the sea and the beach, and quietly propose: 'Shall we take a stroll?' Over the dune and onto the roads they would walk, not strolling but striding, as if Mr Beckwith were taking him to an important appointment. From village to village they strode along the empty lanes, beyond the reach of the sea's rustle, and sometimes the only sound was the ripping of the soles of their sandals on the hot tarmac. Looking to right and left in regular alternation, as if to ensure that nothing could happen on the other side of the hedgerows without his noticing it, Mr Beckwith would suddenly remark 'Look at this,' and drop a hand onto Alexander's shoulder to steer him towards a verge. 'Look,' he would say, kneeling on the turf to hold aside a stand of grass, revealing a flower with petals like shavings of frozen cream, or moths' wings, or tiny bits of sky-blue silk.

As if they were the words of a vow between himself and Mr Beckwith, Alexander would never forget the names of the villages and hamlets through which he walked with him: through Rinsey Croft and Colvorry and Trewithick they went, through Pentreath, through

Kenneggy and on to the path above Kenneggy Sands, through Penhale Jakes and Trevena and then up the hill at Tresoweshill, and through Hendra, past the wooden bungalow in which the Beckwiths were staying, with its porch of white-painted wood and the whitewashed stones beside the path to the door. And after more than forty years he would still be able to recall every plant that Mr Beckwith named for him during the walk of one particular afternoon. 'Common mallow,' he said, crouching at the roadside to cradle in his palm one of the dark pink flowers that hid behind the dust-covered leaves. 'Marsh-mallows are related to these. You make the sweets from its roots.' The road curved in the shadow of a slender elm, and where the road straightened a company of tall yellow flowers stood on the verge. 'Now this is a kind of St John's-wort,' Mr Beckwith explained. 'If you snap the stem a juice comes out that's red as blood.' He put a finger on the translucent speckles of a leaf. 'Because of that, and because these look like holes, people used to think it was a cure for wounds. But they're not holes. They're like sweat glands. Smell,' said Mr Beckwith, and Alexander squatted next to the flowers to inhale a smell of dog fur. On a wall near the sign for Germoe they saw navelwort. 'Known as coolers,' said Mr Beckwith. 'Used to be put on burns, to cool them.' He took Alexander's hand and turned it over to press the dimpled leaves to Alexander's skin. On the church at Germoe there was saffron-coloured lichen and red valerian. 'Called kiss-me-quick, or drunkards,' said Mr Beckwith, smiling as a breeze made the deep red flowers bob drunkenly for them.

A tractor was snarling up the hill, out of sight, when they sat down on a tussock to look at a pat of bird's-foot trefoil, a flower as gorgeous as yolks. 'Known as eggs and bacon, ham and eggs, butter and eggs, hen and chickens,' said Mr Beckwith. 'Sometimes called Dutchman's clogs,' he added. He hooked a little finger under a flower and made it move, as if tickling it.

'Day,' said the driver of the tractor, eyeing them dourly.

'Good afternoon,' replied Mr Beckwith to the driver's back. 'Cheerful soul,' he commented to Alexander, and he released the tiny flowers. 'The others will wonder what's become of us,' he said wearily. 'We should get going. Lead the way.'

On the way back Mr Beckwith walked a pace behind Alexander, as he used to do with Megan, and did not speak until they came to the top of the cliff, where they sat together cross-legged on the closely cropped grass, overlooking the beach. A black and white collie coursed across the sand; a man in voluminous swimming trunks swung a bat, and the impact of the ball sounded faintly at the cliff-top, like the click of a pen-cap. A trawler on the horizon was overtaken by the sky's solitary bulbous cloud. 'There's our girl,' said Mr Beckwith, raising an arm. 'Off you go,' he said, as though he thought Alexander had been waiting for permission to leave him.

Megan was walking with stiff, long strides and her head down, seeming to count her steps, and then she stopped and looked back towards the cliff, as if aware that he was following her. Putting her hand out like a relay runner receiving the baton, she continued her walk, smacking her feet onto the sand. She let him take her hand, but there was no pressure to her touch. It was as if her hand were something she was allowing him to carry.

'You must have gone miles,' she said.

'We did.'

'I'm going to the rock pools,' Megan told him. 'Mum's asleep but your dad said it was all right.'

The tide was low and the sand they were treading was rippled like the soles of feet that have been in a bath too long. Megan released his hand and bent down to uproot an open razor clam. She scooped the runny sand from the shell into her palm and held it chest-high between them. 'It makes you feel frightened when you think about what this is, doesn't it?' she said. 'Look at those cliffs. All this sand has come from them, and one day they'll be nothing but sand. Isn't that frightening?' Alexander regarded the pat of damp grains. 'Like looking at the stars,' said Megan. 'You must do that sometimes?'

'Yes.'

'And what does it make you think? Doesn't it make you frightened? You must think something.'

'Makes me wish there were no clouds in the way.'

'That isn't a proper thought, Eck,' said Megan sharply, and she shook the sand from her hand. 'Some of them are millions and millions and millions of miles away. So many millions that what you're looking at isn't there any longer. The light is like a parcel sent by somebody who's died before it reaches you. Isn't that horrible?' She watched Alexander as he inspected the sky. 'The stars are there now, but we can't see them because the sun's out. Or did you think they all went off somewhere for the day?'

'Of course not.'

'But doesn't it make you feel giddy?'

'Doesn't what?'

'That a long time ago all this wasn't here, and a long time from now it won't be here any more.'

'No,' said Alexander. 'It's here now. We're here now. I don't think anything about the beach. It just is.'

'Don't be daft, Eck. Nothing just is.'

'Well, you just are. I just am.'

'No you're not. You're the son of your parents. You're part of them.'

'No I'm not.'

'You are, Eck. Where do you think you came from?'

'I know where I came from. I'm not thick.'

'Well then. You look like your mum. Exactly like her. It's not a coincidence. A part of you is her.'

'No,' protested Alexander. 'All of me is me.'

'Same with your dad,' continued Megan.

'I'm nothing like him.'

'Your dad's a bit serious and a bit scatty.'

'He's not. He's not at all scatty.'

'Yes, he is. He's always larking about.'

'I don't lark about,' Alexander complained.

'Yes you do. You do silly voices.'

'No I don't.'

'Eck, you do,' said Megan emphatically. 'You do other people's voices.'

'But that's not silly voices.'

'Yes, it is.'

'What's the point of this?' he asked. 'Why do you want to argue?'

'I don't, Eck. But you're so sweet, I can't help it,' Megan told him, and she took his hand as they picked a route through the fallen stones.

89

They were on their own below Hoe Point, where Megan found a pool that was as smooth and long as a bathtub, with a fringe of spinach-coloured seaweed at one end, where she rested her head as she lay down. Water from the breaking waves frisked along the channels of the rocks and leaped into the pool. The water lapped at Megan's goosefleshed thighs. Alexander would always remember this, and her hair twisted into unravelled plaits by the saltwater, and the freckles of dried salt that were mixed with the freckles of her cheeks.

Alexander watched the gulls wheeling out from the cliff where he had sat with Mr Beckwith. The birds made no noise now, and evening was beginning. The white flecks on the sea were like flowers that nobody would ever be able to pick.

'You haven't blinked for a minute,' said Megan. 'What are you thinking about?'

'Not again,' he moaned. 'I'm just looking, Meg.'

'Looking without thinking anything. I don't believe you. It's not possible.'

'There's a lot to look at.'

She looked at him as if pretending to be baffled. 'Faraway Eck,' she said, and she put her arms around his shoulders as a sister might have done.

'Odd Eck,' he responded. Creamy water hurried up through the gullies and touched his toes.

And he would remember the pyramid of towels packed onto a saddle of sand between two clumps of grass, and his father handing Mr Beckwith his Brownie camera. His father and mother and Mrs Beckwith stood at the back, their arms folded as if they were footballers in a team photograph. Alexander knelt in the sand by a mat of black seaweed that was baked as stiff as wicker, and Megan looped her arm through his. He looked back to see his mother picking a windblown strand of hair from her face. 'Come on, Harry,' said Mrs Beckwith. 'The tide'll wash us away before you press that blasted shutter.' Mr Beckwith's smile appeared at the side of the camera. Drifts of dry sand were moving down to the sea, flexing like snakes in their sidelong flight. A dog came running through the marram grass and Alexander wanted someone to ask him if he was happy because he wanted an excuse to say it, because he had realised that he had never been happier than he was at that moment, looking over Mr Beckwith's shoulder and seeing the colour that the setting sun was painting on the rocks of Rinsey Head and the engine house of the Wheal Prosper mine.

10. Monty

Mr Owen had been at the school for no more than a month when, one morning after assembly, he stopped Alexander in the corridor, outside Mr Darrow's room, and said to him in an aggrieved tone of voice: 'Montgomery is an hero, is he not?'

'Sir,' Alexander agreed, after a hesitation, having heard 'Anne Eero'.

'Field Marshal Bernard Montgomery, commander of the Eighth Army and victor of El Alamein, is an hero.' Mr Owen shifted his feet as if adjusting his balance on a moving deck, and his plimsolls squealed on the stone floor. 'He is a man who has achieved things. Stupendous things. He is a leader of men,' said Mr Owen.

'Yes, sir.'

'A leader of men you are not.'

'No, sir,' Alexander replied, puzzled as to what he might have done to offend Mr Owen. His classmates were passing behind Mr Owen, filing in for the English lesson. John Halloran glanced at Alexander and grimaced in sympathy.

'So?' demanded Mr Owen. He wiped a hand over the crown of his head, as if to quell his exasperation.

'Sir?'

'What is the connection, MacIndoe? Where is the relevance?'

Still having no notion what Mr Owen was talking about, Alexander assumed a posture of contrition, fixing his gaze on the books he was holding to his waist.

'Simple question, lad. It's not an algebra problem. All I want to know is what's the connection?'

At the window of Mr Darrow's room appeared a sheet of paper on which the word 'MAD' was crayoned in capital letters. Lionel Griffiths' head rose into view beside it, with a finger tapping at his temple. All of a sudden Alexander understood. 'Not that Monty, sir,' he said.

'I beg your pardon?' queried Mr Owen, his lip crumpling into a sneer.

'It's not that Monty, sir.'

'What do you mean, MacIndoe? "Not that Monty"? There is only one Monty.'

'No, sir, there's another one. It's the other one, sir. Montgomery Clift.'

'Montgomery Clift?' Mr Owen repeated in an outraged shriek.

'The actor, sir. *The Search. Red River. A Place in the Sun.*'

'Yes, yes. I am not an ignoramus, MacIndoe.' Momentarily deflated, Mr Owen looked without interest at Alexander's books, and then he looked Alexander in the eye and instantly rediscovered his indignation. 'Montgomery Clift? The gooey American?'

'Sir.'

'That long lump of unbaked dough?'

'Yes, sir. They think I look like him. Some of them do.'

'Is that so?' Mr Owen rejoined, and the delayed repercussions of a thought spread across his features, like a gust of wind rippling the grass on a hill. The sneer subsided, to be succeeded by a look of placid distaste. 'Nothing like him, if you ask me,' he said.

'I don't see it either, sir,' Alexander replied.

'Whatever could they be thinking of, eh?' Mr Owen rubbed the toe of one plimsoll with the toe of the other, then looked at Alexander's face as if it were a tepidly amusing drawing that a child had done. 'Off you go, MacIndoe.'

The gymnasium was beyond a pair of storage rooms and a padlocked classroom that he was never to see open, at the end of a corridor that smelled of stale canvas and rubber and skin and coconut matting. The way in was through the changing rooms, where in the morning the dairy-white tiles gleamed in the light that came in through the gymnasium door. From the playground the pointed high windows of the gymnasium and the terracotta plaques on the wall gave it the look of a chapel, and there was something church-like in its appearance in the morning, before it had been used. Some mornings Alexander would arrive at school early and enter the corridor by the door that led to the playground, and if nobody was around he would creep between the steel mesh clothes-racks, and go into the quiet, high-ceilinged hall. The painted white lines on the parquet he could see as the patterns on the floor of an aisle, and he could see the vaulting horse, standing against the end wall behind a painted semicircle, as an altar of sorts, capped with its pad of blood-red leather. Between the windows on both sides the wall-bars were arrayed like tiers of memorials. Looped over the bars, the ropes made curves like stone vaulting, rising to the rings by which they were attached to the rafters. Until five minutes before the bell was due to ring he would sit under a window, listening to the voices growing louder outside, fortifying himself with the emptiness of the gymnasium before crossing the playground to his classroom.

Mr Owen's lessons always began the same way. They would await his arrival in a line across the centre of the gymnasium, facing the changing-room door, through which the squeak of Mr Owen's plimsolls would be heard and then, a few seconds before he appeared, his command: 'To attention!' Swivelling on his heels, he closed the door, leaving his hand on the knob for a moment, an action that signified that he was not merely shutting a door but imprisoning them for his thirty minutes. 'All here?' he would ask, before squeaking towards them, reciting a selection from his roster of nicknames. 'Hercules Halloran here; Goliath Griffiths here; Tiny Tim Pottinger here,' he would call out, while Alexander concentrated on the great volume of air above their heads. 'The Mighty Pickering here; Girly MacIndoe here; Fat Boy Radford here,' Mr Owen would call out, smiling to himself.

'One day, one day,' Mick Radford once muttered as he retrieved a medicine ball that Mr Owen had thrown at him, and the phrase became the class's refrain. 'One day, one day,' repeated John Halloran, peeling a handkerchief from his bleeding shin. 'One day, one day,' promised Timothy Pottinger, running cold water over a rope burn, before writing 'One' on the underside of the tongue of his left plimsoll, and 'Day' on the tongue of the right.

That day arrived at the end of an unseasonably cold week, near the end of term. It was a dark morning, as Alexander would remember, and it became darker and colder during the walk to school. Hail started to fall during assembly, and pools of melting ice were forming in the playground as they crossed to the gymnasium.

Alexander took his place in the line, underneath the basketball hoop. Locking and unlocking his fingers as Mr Owen would do when watching them exercise, he leaned forward to look at John Halloran. He licked his palm and swiped it across his hair from brow to nape, and blinked as if unable to credit the evidence of his eyes. 'Oh dear, oh dear, oh dear,' he said. 'What an abomination. Yes. You. An Johnny Weissmuller you are not, Halloran.' He put his hands behind his back and flexed his knees, like Mr Owen did, and mimicked Mr Owen's dry, mirthless laugh: 'uck, uck, uck'. Roy Pickering bit his lip to prevent a smile. 'I don't know what you find so funny, Pickering. You are an fairy, are you not?' Roy Pickering's lip was turning white under the pressure of his teeth, and it was then that Alexander saw that Mr Owen had come soundlessly into the gymnasium, and was closing the door.

'You're dead, Monty,' whispered Mick Radford. 'I'll bring the wreath.'

But Mr Owen did not appear to have heard Alexander. 'Come on. Jump to it! In line!' he ordered, looking at nobody in particular. 'Right then, girls,' he shouted in his usual exultant voice. 'Ten sit-ups, ten squats, ten press-ups. Spread out. Now. Get to it.' As he did every day, he wandered among them, ordering one to stand and explain the state of his singlet, another to account for the hole in his shoes. 'Sloppy, Pickering, sloppy. Parents got no pride?' Grinding the keys in the pocket of his tracksuit, he stood over David Kingsley. 'Oh come on, Kingsley. This is pathetic. My grandmother could do better.' He spun round to shout at Roy Pickering: 'You seem to think you could do better, Pickering. Ten extra press-ups. Yes. You. Now. Get to it.'

Mr Owen wiped his hair; the flesh above his mouth flinched as if he had toothache. 'Right, then,' he said, in the doom-laden tone that always signified the same thing. 'Your favourite game. Captains Allerton and Fletcher. Come here.' Neil Allerton swaggered to his place on Mr Owen's right hand, rotating his arms as if swinging Indian clubs; Dennis Fletcher stood on his left, regarding his classmates with a compromised look. 'Allerton first,' said Mr Owen, and so Allerton and Fletcher took turns to choose the members of their teams. Only Lionel Griffiths and John Halloran were left after Alexander had been selected for Allerton's squad.

Mr Owen had left the gymnasium while the captains made their choices, and now he returned, cajoling a football along the floor with dainty taps of his instep. He inspected the teams. 'No, no,' he decided. 'Too many weeds in this brigade. MacIndoe, go to Fletcher. You too, Malinowski. I'll join Allerton's mob. Form up.'

They adopted their skittle formations at opposite ends of the hall. Mr Owen nudged the ball towards Fletcher's team, then pushed his way into the midst of Allerton's. 'Fletcher, your man,' said Mr Owen.

Paul Malinowski, from his place at the point of the triangle, chipped the ball softly into the midst of the opposition. The boy whom the ball had first struck stepped out of the formation, taking care that his gratitude was not apparent. 'Ten squats, ten press-ups, ten sit-ups,' Mr Owen ordered. The boy withdrew to the sector of the gymnasium where the eliminated players did their penance, while Malinowski went back to his position.

Allerton's front player kicked the ball hard and low into Fletcher's formation, dislodging Malinowski. A member of Fletcher's front line retaliated with a powerful strike, and thus the game proceeded until Alexander, the last survivor of his row, faced Mr Owen. Alexander would remember the way Mr Owen put the ball softly on the circle of blue paint in the middle of the floor, then turned it two or three times, as if locking a manhole cover. He would remember seeing the wet leaves swabbing the glass of the windows to Mr Owen's left, and noticing for the first time the pelt of dust on top of the rafter closest to the door, while in the periphery of his vision Mr Owen took a pace backwards. Then he realised that Mr Owen was taking more than a single pace. He saw Mr Owen look at the ball, at him, at the ball, again at him, and dash forward, his face still up.

There was no pain to the blow immediately, just a sound like the sizzle of lard in a hot pan, and a warm dribble over his lips. His head felt too heavy on the floor. A long way away, Mr Owen's feet were splayed like a penguin's; there were other feet close by, rocking from heel to toe. No one approached him. The ball was at rest against his arm; he placed his hand on it, and felt the texture of the matt leather, the rib-like laces and the yielding rubber nipple between them. With no thought of what he was doing, he scooped the ball into his lap and lifted it. He stood up dizzily, and then he dropped the ball and kicked it on the half-volley. Indifferently he saw Mr Owen double over. He could feel the air congeal about him.

Mr Owen unfolded himself and looked pensively around the gymnasium. He contemplated the cages that protected the light bulbs on the walls; his gaze skimmed over the boys' faces, and his head nodded in agreement with himself. When at last he spoke, his voice was precise and low, and pleasant. 'Right,' he said. 'Continue this game without me. Then the same teams for an end-to-end relay. Then out on the field for a few laps. Allerton, keep order.' He fetched the ball from the corner of the room and handed it to Allerton. 'MacIndoe. You come with me.'

Mr Owen led him through the changing rooms and out into the corridor, where he opened the outside door. 'Please,' he said, ushering Alexander into the rain. 'If you'd oblige,' Mr Owen requested, indicating that Alexander should move farther away. Alexander took a backwards step, into the puddle that was spreading from the drain; the cold water flowed over the tops of his plimsolls. From the shelter of the doorway Mr Owen looked at Alexander with the expression of someone trying to understand why the shivering boy had chosen to stand in ankle-deep water. 'Now, Monty,' began Mr Owen solicitously. 'We have a choice. We could proceed forthwith to the headmaster's office. It is my belief that a measure of corporal punishment would ensue from this course of action. A report to your parents might follow. To be frank, Monty, I would stake my job on such an outcome. In fact, not to beat about the bush, I would make damned sure of it.' He stooped forward to inspect the sky and made a snort of satisfaction. 'Or we could resolve this matter now and have done with it. What do you say, Monty? The choice is yours.'

Water dripped from Alexander's fingertips; blood dripped from his chin. Watching Mr Owen's hands squirming in his tracksuit pockets, he realised that he could hold an adult in contempt, and the chill of his flesh seemed to increase his exhilaration at his discovery. It was his intention to say nothing, so he was taken aback to hear himself say: 'I don't mind, sir.'

One of Mr Owen's feet made a movement as if crushing a cigarette. 'I suggest the latter course of action,' he said.

'Whatever you say, sir,' Alexander replied.

For half a minute Mr Owen blankly regarded Alexander, and then, like a man preparing for an arduous task, he pulled the hood of his tracksuit slowly over his head. 'We shall proceed to the playing field. On the double. Now.'

On the slope above the cricket nets Mr Owen overtook him and stopped him with a straight arm. 'Give me those shoes,' he demanded, and he cracked the soles against the back of Alexander's legs six times. 'Now you'll run around that field until I tell you to stop. Do you understand? And if you ever do anything like that again, ever, ever,' he repeated, with the tendons of his neck straining, 'I'll have you running on roads in your bare feet until the bones come through. Do you understand?'

'Yes, sir,' said Alexander.

'Do you understand?'

'Yes, sir. I'm sorry, sir.'

The pain of Alexander's beaten skin seemed to dissolve into his body, and as it weakened he experienced a clenching of his mind against Mr Owen. It was not a hatred he felt now, but an adamant exclusion, and the pain in his ribcage enclosed him perfectly. Armoured by his discomfort he ran over the cold, clutching grass; the rain tingled on his tongue.

'Don't slacken, MacIndoe,' shouted Mr Owen from the embankment, flapping a plimsoll.

'No, sir,' Alexander replied, assuming for Mr Owen's benefit a rictus of agony.

Alexander's classmates were appearing on the path above the playing field. 'Right, MacIndoe,' called Mr Owen when Alexander came back on to the straight. 'Back to the gym with you. A dozen more press-ups, I think.' He lobbed the sodden plimsolls towards him, so they landed short, in the waterlogged long-jump pit. 'Eyes right!' ordered Mr Owen as Alexander neared his approaching friends. They all looked away from him, and he from them, but as he trudged down the line Alexander heard them chanting quietly: 'One day. One day. One day.'

Before the day was over Alexander MacIndoe understood that he had been transformed into a new character. Mick Radford, who had often thrown a punch at him whenever they had met in a place where there was no teacher to observe them, ambushed him in an empty corridor. The fingers of Mick Radford's right hand furled into a fist, then opened out again as he cackled. 'An hero, Monty,' he said. 'Proud of you, pal.'

Mr Owen did not return after the summer holiday, and by many of the boys it was taken as a fact that his departure was due to his punishment of Alexander MacIndoe. 'That's what made the boss twig he was a loony,' said Lionel Griffiths on their first day back. 'It's obvious.' A note in Paul Malinowski's handwriting was glued to the underside of his desk's lid: 'By his sacrifice we were redeemed.' Throughout the winter term and into the spring, boys to whom he had never spoken would acknowledge him with the password of his name. 'MacIndoe,' they hailed him, clenching a fist and raising it to shoulder height. He was being acclaimed for something he had not intended to do, but which had become a story, he told himself, a story like a garment that had been put over him. 'MacIndoe,' the boys pronounced defiantly, and he would be obliged to act in a manner befitting the figure he had become, nodding like an officer to his off-duty men.

11. The girls' party

The Gattings moved into their house before Coronation Day. Of this Alexander would always be certain, because he would remember the way the street looked for the party: the bunting slung so low that he could touch it when he stood on his chair, and the house in which the new family lived standing out from the others in the terrace, with its windowframes freshly painted white and the front door a blue-grey colour that was like a pigeon's plumage. He would remember helping to set the trestle tables down the centre of the road, as they had done for the VJ party, and the paper plates coloured red, white and blue. He would remember that he had tried to picture the makeshift stage on which his mother had sung eight years before, and had succeeded in hearing her voice for an instant, like the voice of someone trapped. This he would recall, and the car – a black Jowett, with one front wheel removed – that was parked exactly where Gisbert had sat. He would not remember, however, that it was over Liz Gatting's bent back that he had looked to see where Gisbert had been. Alexander would have no recollection of Liz Gatting that preceded a birthday party the following year, a week after Roger Bannister broke the four-minute mile.

It was because he was a friend of Megan's that he was invited, but he walked to the house on his own, and she took no notice of him when he arrived. Sitting on one of the rugs that had been spread on the lawn, she was taking a plate of sandwiches from the mother of the girl whose birthday it was. 'Feeding time,' the mother called out, and each of the girls who were sitting in a ring around Megan reached over to grab from the plate.

The mother carried a plate to a second group of girls sitting on another rug, in front of a juniper bush. Her husband came out of the kitchen, bearing a pie in a fish-shaped dish. Balls of sweat were threaded onto the hair at his temples, and ovals of pale skin were disclosed between the buttons of his straining shirt. 'A gooseberry are you, son?'

he remarked to Alexander in passing, as he swivelled the dish high above his head. Only then did Alexander realise that, apart from himself, there were just two boys in the garden.

'Find yourself a place,' said the mother. 'This lot'll eat every last crumb in five minutes.'

A tortoiseshell cat with matted fur butted its head on Alexander's shins. Turning away from the girls, he knelt on the grass to rub the animal's throat. A pair of crepe-soled sandals appeared beside the cat. Crumpled white cotton protruded through the gaps between the straps, like peaks of mashed potato, Alexander thought, and he almost laughed.

'That's Nelly's cat,' said a girl's voice. 'His name's Willow, but her dad calls him Zeppelin. I'm Liz. Who are you?'

'I'm Alexander,' he said. 'Megan's friend.'

'Only got one, has she?' Liz replied. The gap where a tooth had come out at the side of her mouth increased the jollity of her smile, and there was something amusing, too, about the way her hair was done, in ringlets that bent on her shoulders, like the hair of a much younger girl. The collar of her blouse was sticking up, as if she had pulled it over her head. Awaiting Alexander's answer, she tucked her thumbs behind the big rectangular buckle of her belt. Her missing tooth and this buckle, covered with grass-green hessian, would be what Alexander would continue to remember of her appearance that afternoon.

'She's got a lot of friends, I think,' said Alexander.

'You think?'

'No, she does,' said Alexander. 'Don't you?' he asked Megan, who had left her group and was coming towards him.

'Don't I what?' Megan asked.

'Have lots of friends.'

'What are you talking about, Eck?' said Megan. She gave the cat's head a quick scratch then looked impatiently at Alexander. 'Come over here if you want anything to eat,' she told him, hauling him by a shirt-sleeve.

When the food was finished they all went indoors to play games. In the hall Liz Gatting jabbed him in the small of his back and demanded: 'We too boring for you, then?'

A girl in a pink cardigan rested her chin on Liz's shoulder to stare

101

at him. 'Yes. More fun with your Megan, is it?' asked the girl.

'Stick with his Megan,' said Liz to her companion, smugly.

'Alexander's Megan's friend,' said the girl in the pink cardigan, putting on a haughty face.

'Goodbye, Megan's friend,' taunted Liz.

The two girls went into the living room, but Alexander stayed in the hall until Megan joined him.

'You know Liz?' he asked.

'Yes.'

'Don't you get on with her?'

'Sort of,' said Megan.

'So you don't?'

'So I do.'

'So why are they being like that?'

'Like what?' she asked, and Alexander repeated what they had said. Megan looked at him for a moment, searching for something in his face. 'You don't know?'

'No. If I knew I wouldn't ask you.'

Water filled the inner corners of Megan's eyes; she put her right hand firmly on his shoulder. 'Eck, sometimes you really are slow, you know that?'

'What do you mean?' Alexander asked.

'I mean, there is a mirror in your house somewhere, isn't there?'

'Of course there is.'

'Well?'

'Well what?'

'Good grief, Eck. It's perfectly simple. She wanted you to sit with them, not with me.' She raised her hands to her face in mockery of his surprise.

'I don't think so,' said Alexander.

'No, Eck. "I don't think." That's what you should say.'

'She doesn't even know who I am,' he protested.

Megan pulled her socks up tight to her knees. 'What a nit,' she said to her shoes, and she left him in the hall.

For an hour or so they played charades. Embarrassed by the perpetual blush that he could feel on his skin, Alexander sat on the floor in a corner of the room, trying to hide behind the other two boys,

102

who sat upright on adjacent straight-backed chairs. 'One of the boys should have a go,' the mother decreed, and the two on the chairs simultaneously looked back at Alexander, as if passing the blame for something.

Encircled by the girls, Alexander could think of nothing except his awkwardness. Megan was sitting under the keyboard of the piano, her chin on her knees, waiting for him. 'Do _The Cruel Sea_,' the mother told him. Alexander ground his teeth on the mouthpiece of an imaginary pipe and made a visor with his palm. Heroically he scanned the room's horizon, facing the terrible waves. Decisive as Jack Hawkins, he gave wordless orders to his men and directed their efforts. Nobody guessed what he was doing.

'That's not how you do it, you nit,' said Megan after he had given them the answer. With a mad grin she flailed at the carpet, then serenely made wave shapes with a fluttering hand. 'That's how you do _The Cruel Sea_. You do "cruel" and then you do "sea".' She smiled at him for a long time, however, and it was Megan who took the satin scarf to blindfold him for the last game of the party, and spun him around three times. 'Behind you, behind you,' she murmured. 'Behind you, behind you.' Shoeless feet made a constant shuffling all around him, and the springs of the armchairs groaned as they were trampled. Alexander's fingers fell into the pleats of a puffed sleeve. He could distinguish the pitch of this girl's breathing and the minty smell of her. As Liz Gatting's hip touched his a girl shrieked, 'Sandy MacIndoe, beware!'

'Oh, shut up,' said Liz. Her eyes were levelled at his when he slipped the scarf off. 'Take no notice,' she said, and she touched his hand as he pulled the knotted blindfold over her hair.

'That's right,' said Megan, 'take no notice.' She sat down on the edge of the settee, where she remained, with her arms crossed, while Liz Gatting fumbled along the curtains and groped broadly at the air. 'Over here,' instructed Megan, and then she walked on her toes to the door, stealthily pushed its handle down, and closed it silently behind her, as if this were part of the game. She had left the house before Alexander could think of an excuse to follow her.

Three days later he went to visit Mr Beckwith, hoping to see Megan. He went to the back of the house without knocking on the front door.

Mr Beckwith was not in the garden and the padlock was clasped on the shed. The lilies Alexander had planted with Mr Beckwith were in bloom. He picked a snail shell from the soil of the flowerbed and lobbed it over the shed, but his throw was too weak and the shell bounced on the roof and fell back on the lawn.

Until he heard Mrs Beckwith's voice he had not seen that the French windows were open. 'Who's that?' she called from somewhere inside the back room. 'Is that you, Megan?'

'It's me, Mrs Beckwith.'

'Alex?' she responded in a strange voice, as if he were someone who had been away for years.

'Yes, Mrs Beckwith.' Alexander stood on the edge of the grass, stranded.

'He's asleep, if it's Harry you're after.'

Alexander approached the windows. The curtains were three-quarters drawn, obscuring everything except one end of the table and a rectangle of wallpaper to which was attached a calendar and a clock in the form of a ship's wheel. 'Sorry to have disturbed you, Mrs Beckwith,' said Alexander, speaking into this segment of the room.

'And Megan's down the shops,' she said, as though conversing with someone right beside her.

'Oh well,' Alexander replied. 'I'll be going.' He had moved closer and was standing on the crescent of irregular paving stones in front of the French windows. Still he could not see where Mrs Beckwith was.

'She'll be back in a little while. Come in and wait for her.' Alexander placed one foot on the metal strip at the threshold.

'It was Mr Beckwith I came to see really. In case I could help out, that's all. It's not important.'

'Well, you're here now. Come on in,' said Mrs Beckwith. She was sitting in an armchair, facing the empty grate and brushing at a lapel of her navy blue dress. A sliver of sunlight cut across the arm of the chair, on which Mrs Beckwith's hand was curved around a glass of clear liquid with a cube of ice in it.

'How are you, Alex?' she asked, pushing herself up on her elbows to look at him. Her mouth was darkened with lipstick and she was wearing ruby-coloured studs in her ears, as if she were about to go out.

'I'm well, Mrs Beckwith, thank you,' Alexander responded.

'Sit down, why don't you?' said Mrs Beckwith, pointing at the armchair beside the chimney breast.

Next to the chair in which Alexander sat was a cabinet with sliding glass doors and a tea service on the lowest of its three shelves, below two rows of books. Aware that Mrs Beckwith was watching him, he began to read the spines. '*The Day of the Triffids,*' he said, at the first title he recognised.

'Megan's the reader in this household,' said Mrs Beckwith.

'My dad's the reader in ours. I think he's read that one.' Mrs Beckwith stirred the ice with a little finger and did not speak. Alexander completed his reading of the higher row; upstairs a toilet flushed. 'I'm in your way,' said Alexander. 'There wasn't anything special.'

'No, Alex, wait for her,' said Mrs Beckwith softly. 'She'll be glad to see you. We're always glad to see you.'

Eking it out for as long as he could, Alexander read the lower titles; the churning of the water pipes was the only sound.

'How's school?' Mrs Beckwith asked.

'It's OK, Mrs Beckwith.'

'Do you like school?'

'Not much.'

'Neither did I,' said Mrs Beckwith, with a rueful smile at the grate.

In the room above them Mr Beckwith coughed; a thrush sprang across the piece of paving that Alexander could see from where he sat. He twisted in his chair so that Mrs Beckwith could see him look at the ship's-wheel clock. 'I should be going, Mrs Beckwith. My mother will be expecting me back soon.'

'Your mother and I,' said Mrs Beckwith, and she paused for so long that Alexander thought she had finished her sentence and he had misheard. 'We were at school together. You knew that?'

'Mum said, yes,' he replied.

'She was gorgeous. A stunner she was. We used to go out together. To the cinema. Very popular with the boys was your mother. I was the invisible girl when I was with her.'

The talk of his mother's schooldays made Alexander uncomfortable, and from the way Mrs Beckwith took a sip from her drink he sensed that if he stayed he would hear something he should not know. He cleared his throat, but she looked at him and spoke before he could get to his feet.

'She could have been a singer, I reckon. A professional singer. On stage. Had the looks, had the voice. You've heard her sing?'

'Yes.'

'Of course you have. Silly question. Wonderful voice. It's a waste, Alex.'

'I don't know, Mrs Beckwith,' replied Alexander.

'Not the worst waste in the world, I grant you,' said Mrs Beckwith, but suddenly her eyes became lustreless. 'My brother went somewhere in France and never came back and his wife has gone looking for him and won't ever come back now.' She scratched at the lapel of her dress as if something were stuck to it. 'Harry gets taken into some godforsaken jungle halfway round the world and comes back half-starved and half-cracked,' she said, forcing a laugh.

'Mr Beckwith doesn't seem cracked to me, Mrs Beckwith.'

'You're sweet, Alex,' she said. 'Half-cracked, not cracked all the way.' She took another sip. 'Harry's very fond of you. You know that?'

'I like him a lot.'

'So do I,' she smiled, turning to look at him. 'He thinks you're like him. You've got patience, he says.'

'That's kind of him.'

'And respect. A respectful young man, Harry calls you.'

'Thank you.'

'Not many young ones have that. Respect and patience, either of them.'

'No, Mrs Beckwith,' Alexander replied.

Mrs Beckwith took a final sip of her drink. 'He was a handsome one, too.' She put the empty glass on the floor and stood up for a moment, before sitting back on the arm of her chair, facing him.

'I should be going, Mrs Beckwith,' he told her.

'Megan will be here any second,' she said. She folded her arms on her stomach and, bending forward, looked at him as though to press the anxiety out of his mind with her gaze. 'You're such a beautiful boy, Alex. One day my girl will fall in love with you, I wouldn't mind betting.' The fabric of her dress hung away from her skin in a hammock shape, exposing to Alexander the swell of her breast.

'She thinks I'm stupid,' he said.

'She thinks we're all stupid sometimes, Alex.'

Alexander meshed his hands together and clenched his fingers on his knuckles.

'You're a fearful lad, aren't you? Don't be. You don't want to have lots of regrets when you're older. They eat you up, regrets.'

'I don't think I'm fearful, Mrs Beckwith.'

'Don't be. Because nothing lasts, Alex. The whites of my eyes, look at them. They've gone all mucky now. But they used to be like yours once. Look here,' she instructed, and she pinched up a ridge of skin on the back of her hand and watched it subside. 'I was a slender girl. A slip of a thing, my mother used to say. But nothing lasts,' and she leaned over him. She kissed him lightly on the lips. Her lipstick pulled at his skin and he caught the sweet fume of her breath. Sitting on the arm of the chair once more, she breathed out as if exhaling smoke and gave him a look as if he had done something foolish but endearing. A key rattled angrily in the lock of the front door. 'The princess returns,' said Mrs Beckwith. 'That you, Megan?' she called out.

'Who else?' asked Megan from behind the opening door. 'Hello, Eck,' she said upon seeing him, and then she went out of the room, closing the door.

'Sorry, Alex,' said Mrs Beckwith after a minute. 'Megan's in a mood, it looks like.'

'I'll go then.'

'Yes, OK,' agreed Mrs Beckwith cheerfully, as if what had happened had been instantly forgotten.

12. The Diet of Augsburg

Alexander's mother was painting the skirting boards in the kitchen and she had set the record-player on top of the stove so she could listen to her LPs while she worked. Spread on the lid were half a dozen record sleeves, illustrated with islands of uniformly green palm trees, and the Manhattan skyline against a cornflower sky, and vast fields of custard-yellow wheat. A record lay on the table, inside its paper inner sleeve. Alexander picked it up and slipped the disc into his palm.

'You be careful with that,' she told him, looking at him over the table's edge as she tightened the maroon scarf that was knotted on the top of her head. She went back to her painting. Singing softly, she dragged the brush along the beading of the skirting board with an elegant bending of her wrist, as if trailing a piece of fine fabric across the wood.

'Is there a spare brush somewhere?' he asked. 'I could help.'

'Nearly done,' she said, jabbing the bristles into the angle by the pantry door. 'But thank you for the thought.'

Alexander gazed down onto the surface of the record. Something of the richness of America was implied by the deep wet blackness of it and by the rays of rainbow colour that swung across the oily plastic. 'Do you want to see my report?' he asked, rolling the disc back into its sleeve.

'After your father,' she replied. She pressed a hand into the small of her back, and released a long breath.

'Shall I make you a cup of tea?'

'Later. It'd only taste of paint right now,' she said. 'Shouldn't you be doing your homework? Better get it done before your dad gets back.'

From the window of his bedroom Alexander saw his father turn into the road, and he was at the top of the stairs before the front door opened. In the hall his father dropped his briefcase and whisked his fingers against each other. 'The stains of filthy lucre,' he said, showing his hands. He draped his jacket on the finial of the banisters and tugged at its lapels as if correcting someone's attire. 'Ah, well. Puts bread on the table, doesn't it? Your mother in the galley?'

His father returned a minute later, balancing the report book on his fingertips like a salver. 'Come before the throne of Solomon,' he intoned, leading the way to the living room with a portentous tread. Gravely he eased himself into his armchair and pointed to the seat that Alexander was to occupy. His reading glasses were on the round table, with his pipe and tobacco and a bottle of Zubes Cough Mixture which was stuck to the front page of a newspaper. He opened the book and scanned the page rapidly through one lens, and neither approval nor displeasure was legible on his face. '"Biology",' he read, putting his glasses on properly. '"A subject for which Alexander seems to possess little talent and less interest." Rather severe. Remind me who this chap is again.'

'Mr Porterfield.'

'A reasonable man, is he?'

Reluctant to prolong his interrogation, Alexander shrugged, studying the chrysanthemum pattern in the carpet.

'Would you agree? About the interest?'

'I suppose so,' Alexander conceded. 'It's all fruit-flies and frogs.'

'Flute fries and flogs, eh?' responded his father.

Alexander raised his eyes; his father was neither smiling nor looking at him, but Alexander could tell he was waiting for him to smile, and he realised in that moment that his father's disappointment in him was becoming habitual. Staring at his feet, Alexander made a laughing sound. 'Mr Porterfield once told me I was outstandingly average,' he joked.

His father did not appear to be listening. '"Chemistry – Average"', he read. 'Could be better. And could be worse. "English – Average". This is Mr Darrow, isn't it?'

Alexander confirmed with a nod, and there appeared in his mind the sight of Mr Darrow tripping on a paving stone by Mr Mullins' pub. A car's headlight illuminated Mr Darrow's face at the moment he comprehended, raising himself to a crouch, that Alexander was standing in front of him. 'Mum's the word, MacIndoe,' said Mr

Darrow, sealing his own lips with a finger that left a sooty exclamation mark on his chin. 'You are one of my favourite pupils. You know that? One of my favourites.' He settled his disarrayed quiff and belched demurely into his hand. 'I like you because you have no imagination. Keep it that way, MacIndoe.' Mr Darrow winked and turned his back. 'A fine English virtue,' he concluded, addressing the wall.

'"Geography – Average",' his father recited. 'Not doing too badly. But here's an interesting one,' he went on, in a rising tone. '"Mathematics – An indolent but personable boy." I think it's indolent. Couldn't be insolent. You wouldn't be insolent. Wouldn't be like you at all, would it?' Alexander would have answered, but from the kitchen came a crescendo of his mother's voice, in duet with a quieter tenor. 'But are you indolent?' resumed his father with a quizzical frown. 'It means lazy.'

'I don't think I am,' he replied.

'Mr Smythe is of the opinion that you are.'

'I just don't understand the subject, Dad, that's all. I try.' There was another crescendo, and Alexander thought of Mr Smythe. He saw his crew-cut hair and the gold-rimmed lenses that magnified his eyes, and then he saw him standing with his arms braced against the window-sill, gazing out at the street.

'Then try harder, Alexander,' advised his father. 'If you want to be somebody you've got to make an effort. We can all be good at something, if we try.'

'I try as hard as I can.'

'Then perhaps you should make more of an effort to let people know that you're making an effort,' his father replied.

Mr Smythe's hands stayed on the sill as he turned his head. 'I have thought long and hard about this, Halloran,' he said. 'And I have arrived at the opinion, after much consideration, that you are a rhino.' There was ragged, uncertain laughter from the other boys. 'Really here in name only,' Mr Smythe elucidated. The laughter was louder and more concerted. And then Mr Smythe smacked his hands on the sill and said through clenched teeth: 'And that goes for you too, Allerton. And you, MacIndoe. Really here in name only, all three of you.'

'Alexander?' his father was enquiring. 'Alexander? Who's your history teacher?'

'Mr Barrington.'

'Barrington?'

'He's new.'

'Chinese is he?'

'Really here in name only,' Alexander heard again, waiting for his father to explain.

'Seems to write in Chinese,' said his father. He turned the page towards Alexander. 'What's this say?' he asked. 'It looks like a steam-roller's gone over it.' His forefinger covered all but two words in the box next to Mr Barrington's signature.

'"Dark horse",' Alexander read, unsure whether this was a compliment.

'And this?' The finger slid away, uncovering the rest of the line.

'"Alexander has an excellent head for facts, but he must learn what to do with them."'

'And not all facts, it would appear,' commented his father. 'Numbers are facts too, Alexander. I think we should aim to impress our Mr Smythe next term. But this is good, son. This is good,' he repeated, putting the report aside. Briefly his fingers rested on its pale blue cardboard cover and a look of mild perturbation appeared on his face, as if his fingertips were detecting something that might be meaningful, but which eluded his interpretation. He picked up the pipe and tobacco together, while his other hand burrowed in a trouser pocket. With his silver penknife he dug at the crystallized tar in the bowl of his pipe, while Alexander prepared to ask if he could return to his room, having said nothing in response to his father's praise.

It was Mr Barrington's custom to install himself in the embrasure of the window as the boys processed into his classroom. Looking up from the book which his hands supported like a lectern, Mr Barrington might favour one or two with a glance that acknowledged that the chosen pupil was entering the class in the due spirit of solemn receptivity. When the last boy was at his desk Mr Barrington would cross the room, still reading his page, and push the book against the door to close it slowly. He then would sigh as he turned to face his class, or close the book so slowly it was as though its cover were resisting strongly the pressure of his hands, or watch the corridor until the room became absolutely silent. 'Good day, form,' he would invariably begin.

111

'And good day to you, sir,' they responded.

'Any absentees?'

'Radford,' said Timothy Pottinger on this particular day.

'He, of all people, cannot afford to absent himself,' commented Mr Barrington, raising and lowering his arms as though requesting Pottinger to reconsider his reply. The sleeves of his gown, so deeply ingrained with chalk that they were the colour of elephant hide, gave off a thin smoke of dust. 'Do we know if Mrs Radford has vouchsafed any reason for the indisposition of her firstborn?'

'Haven't heard, sir,' Paul Malinowski apologised.

'AWOL yet again, we must assume.' Mr Barrington bent forward, as if to ease the ache of indigestion, and the grimy lenses of his spectacles, moving into a belt of sunlight, became instantly opaque. His white and bumpy skin shone through the ladder of hair that crossed his head. 'Onward,' said Mr Barrington, shoving himself upright from his desk. 'The weather is somewhat oppressive, I think we would all agree? Inconducive to study, perhaps. Things we would all rather be doing. But thus will it often be. I am here to get you through your examinations, and that I shall do.' He wrestled the gown from his shoulders, rolled it up, and hurled it into the corner, behind the green steel wastepaper bin. 'Some dictation first,' announced Mr Barrington.

It was something to do with Pitt the Younger that he read to them, as Alexander would remember. Rocking his right foot on a loose brick of the parquet floor, Mr Barrington recounted a debate in Parliament, deepening his voice to quote the sententious speeches. Mid-speech he raised his eyes and asked of the class in general, as if asking to be reminded of a fact that had slipped from his mind: 'The Diet of Augsburg. When was it?'

'Sir?' replied Lionel Griffiths, his pen arrested on the rim of the inkwell.

'Don't be querulous, Griffiths,' said Mr Barrington. 'The Diet of Augsburg is not, I grant you, germane to the career of William Pitt. It is, however, a subject on which you may one day be examined, and it is, furthermore, an event we have previously discussed, in this very room. So, anyone?'

Every boy busied himself with correcting the punctuation and spelling of the dictated paragraphs.

'For crying out loud, one of you must know?' Mr Barrington picked up a stub of chalk from the gutter of his desk. 'Are my labours to be in vain? Tell me it is not so, in God's name,' he cried, with actorly anguish. Propelled by Mr Barrington's thumb, the chalk stub hit Alexander's sleeve, leaving a white tick above the braiding of his cuff. 'MacIndoe? Any prospect of an answer? Even a lunatic guess might mollify me.'

Alexander had never yet volunteered an answer in Mr Barrington's class. He studied the mark on his cuff for five seconds or so; he looked at Mr Barrington, who folded his arms in expectation of Alexander's admission of defeat; he looked at the blackboard's broad smears of half-erased writing, which struck him as an apt representation of the condition of his mind. His gaze lingered within a broad looping track of white dust, and his hearing seemed to fail. He had a vision of the thick walls of masonry and fantastical turrets he had imagined when he first heard the name of Augsburg, and the Diet again evoked a gathering of austere men whose vowels sounded like barks, and he saw a texture and a colour that were of limestone in the last moments of daylight. He felt an answer rise onto his tongue like a ball of sputum. Without a thought he let it out: '1530, sir.'

Mr Barrington blinked away his surprise. 'Good, MacIndoe. Very good. I thank you.' He looked at the clock above the door. 'The Peace of Cateau-Cambrésis?'

Alexander saw a cabal of slender Frenchmen in ruffs and stockings, and a castle by a river, and poplars swaying in a breeze. A number budded in his mouth, and he raised his hand swiftly.

'MacIndoe, again? This is bold of you. Speak.'

'1559, sir,' said Alexander.

'Fortune favours the brave. Indeed it was 1559. Good.' Mr Barrington inspected the clock once more. 'The Diet of Worms,' he proposed, and again, a few seconds later, Alexander alone raised a hand. 'Is nobody else prepared to venture an answer? No? Very well. MacIndoe?'

'1521, sir.'

'Were I wearing one, I should take my cap off to you, MacIndoe. And when was the great heresiarch born? Luther. Born. When?'

Alexander saw a diagram of a fat man in the shape of a number,

113

and another number that was the first number cut in half, like a fat face in profile. '1483,' he stated.

'And the year of his decease?'

'1546.'

'Astonishing,' remarked Mr Barrington, looking at the boy in a way that made him feel as if he were suspected of having played some sort of trick on the class. 'An example to you all,' he said. 'We shall have another catechism next week. I hope I'll see some evidence that MacIndoe is not the only one who has been paying attention to the proceedings. Now, where were we? Can anyone remember?'

The following week, while dictating an explanation of the Corn Laws, Mr Barrington pressed a finger onto the page as if pressing a button to set a machine going, and asked: 'The Council of Trent. Year of commencement?' Ignoring Alexander's hand, his gaze progressed down the left file of desks, then the centre file. 'Your colleagues would appear to have capitulated, MacIndoe. And your answer is?'

'1545, sir.'

'Another bull's eye. I congratulate you.' He looked at Alexander questioningly, and then at the book on his desk. 'And ended? Some-body other than MacIndoe, if that would not be asking too much?'

'1565,' John Halloran offered, twirling his pencil aloft as if he had impaled the answer on it.

The date sounded like a discord in Alexander's head. '1563,' he intervened, before Mr Barrington could ask for a correction.

'Of course,' said Mr Barrington. 'Edict of Nantes?' he requested, evoking in Alexander's mind associations of probity and a prospect of silk pennants on a cobbled harbourside in a clear summer light.

'1598, sir,' Alexander responded.

The puzzled twist of Mr Barrington's mouth began to soften into a half-smile. 'Issued by whom?' he asked, directly to Alexander.

'Henry IV, sir. Henry of Navarre.'

'Revocation of same?'

Alexander saw enormous wigs and a secretive chamber in which there was the sound of scratching quills and rain. '1685,' he said.

'Bravo. Another innings of Bradman-like consistency, MacIndoe.'

A routine was soon established, in which Mr Barrington would randomly punctuate his readings with 'Date, MacIndoe?', and Alex-

114

ander would immediately reply. Rarely did Mr Barrington look at him, and even more rarely did he remark on his response. It was like a circus turn, thought Alexander, the way the names and dates passed back and forth between them, yet Mr Barrington was the only teacher for whom he had affection, an affection that grew, however, not from these history lessons but from Mr Barrington's performances in his religious education class.

Mr Barrington taught religious education in a different classroom. It had once been a chemistry room and its air still smelled like bitter almonds and tasted metallic, though no chemicals were left there, except for a single jar of copper sulphate that had remained on the bottom shelf of the glass-fronted cabinet. The high benches at which they sat were scarred with shallow acid burns that had been varnished over so they looked like divoted peat. The teacher's desk, occupying the prow of a dais in front of the worn-out blackboard, had two porcelain basins sunk into it, and two taps that curved like swan's necks to left and right. Into one of the basins Mr Barrington would deposit the books he would consult in the latter half of his lesson, and then he would prop his Bible against one of the taps and begin to read. His voice was not the same as the voice with which he read from his history books: it was slower and more sonorous, with plentiful pauses and repetitions. He asked no questions that required a reply, and only when he had to turn a page did he look at the class. 'You are following, I trust,' he might say, or 'There's something for you to think about,' and then he would resume, continuing until twenty minutes had passed. Precisely at the lesson's midway point he would close the Bible, take a book from the pile in the basin, and begin to talk to them, ironically, sometimes mockingly, about the history of the church, the lives of the saints, witch-hunts, the complexities of doctrine and the multitudinous species of heresy, a word he pronounced in a way that seemed to allude to the illicit pleasures of adulthood.

'Let us hear what the greatest of all books has to say,' Alexander would remember Mr Barrington often saying, as he hoisted from the basin a heavy volume that was pierced by dozens of bookmarks. 'Edward Gibbon,' he would declare, flourishing the book like a smash-and-grab robber's brick. For many years Alexander would remember Mr Barrington pounding his chest with the book and turning his woeful eyes to the ceiling, in emulation of the self-flagellating Jerome. And similarly he recalled Mr Barrington with his cheeks sucked in, to emulate the holy starvation of Simeon Stylites, and swaying on the lip of the dais like Simeon atop his pillar, giddily surveying the desert in which the demented hermits swarmed.

More substantial than any of these, however, would be Alexander's memory of a gusty morning in spring, and all the windows open, and Mr Barrington wearing a tomato-red tie. With no preamble at all, Mr Barrington declaimed: ' "In the beginning was the Word, and the Word was with God, and the Word was God. The same was in the beginning with God. All things were made by him; and without him was not any thing made that was made." ' Pieces of apple blossom fell onto Alexander's bench while Mr Barrington read. From the street came the sound of a wooden crate full of bottles being loaded onto a van, as Mr Barrington turned back through the book. ' "These are the generations of the heavens and of the earth when they were created, in the day that the Lord God made the earth and the heavens," ' he read. Alexander looked around the room: John Halloran, his fingers pressed to his brow, was feigning concentration and was perhaps asleep; Mick Radford had a copy of the *Eagle* folded inside his Bible; only Paul Malinowski appeared to be listening

When he was done with Genesis, Mr Barrington stepped down from the desk and sauntered along the gangway between the windows and the benches, his copy of Gibbon held behind his back. 'To recap. Last week, as I fear few of you will recall, we grappled with the mystery of the incarnation of the Son. We were entertained by the quaint simplicity of the Docetes, who maintained that the conception and birth of our saviour were to be thought of as phantasms, that the figure who suffered flagellation and crucifixion was but the image of a man conjured by the Almighty. In the opposite corner we had Cerintus of Asia, who contended that Christ was a real, physical man who became the vessel of the Holy Spirit. Somewhere between these two extremes lies the subtle Nestorian heresy. Here the humanity of Christ is seen as a sort of overcoat that is thrown over his divinity. We spent some time in the company of other, more abstruse doctrines, and we came to have some sympathy, did we not, for those early theologians of whom the blessed Gibbon writes' – he brought the book to his face –

116

'"as soon as they beheld the twilight of sense and heresy, they started, measured back their steps, and were again involved in the gloom of impenetrable orthodoxy."' Mr Barrington clapped the book shut.

'The Incarnation is a difficult one, no question of that,' said Mr Barrington, and he rolled his eyes in comical bewilderment. 'A bona fide head-breaker. But today's mystery is the trickiest poser of them all. The Trinity,' he proclaimed with a throw of an arm, as if unveiling a statue of that name. 'Let me sketch a map of the terrain we are about to cross. The creed as we know it was formulated in AD 325 at the first Council of Nicaea. The Nicene Creed, we should more properly call it. The Council of Nicaea, convened in the place where the Turkish city of Iznik now stands, devoted much time and effort to the refutation of three great heresies concerning the Trinity. The first of these was Arianism, which maintained, crudely speaking, that God the Father was the creator of all things, even of God the Son. The Father preceded the Son by an interval too infinitesimal for the human mind to comprehend, but precede Him He did, so the Arians insisted, and of course in doing so they denied the eternal perfection of the Trinity. Tritheism, the second heresy, posited a sort of committee of three equal beings who comprise the Divine Essence. Sabellianism, a more abstract version of the preceding, posited the notion that the three component divinities of the Trinity were attributes rather than beings – a Trinity of abstractions, if you will.' Mr Barrington stopped beside Alexander and rubbed his troubled brow. 'The Council of Nicaea rejected these and many other abominable philosophies and asserted the absolute consubstantiality of the Father and Son. The Father and the Son, in other words, are somehow one and the same substance, for all eternity. As we shall now discover, this idea is difficult to contemplate for any length of time without falling, unwittingly, into heresy – which is precisely what the bishops did at the Council of Rimini, a mere thirty-five years later. Athanasius, esteemed by Gibbon as the wisest of theologians, confessed that the more he thought about the Creator of the universe, the less he understood. We might take some consolation from this.'

Little of this and little of what followed made any sense to Alexander, and barely one word of it would be left in his memory the next day. But he would remember that, as Mr Barrington expounded the errors and inadvertent blasphemies of the ancient bishops, the infinite formulations of the Trinity became an incantation that cast a mood of rapturous passivity over him. A flag of sunlight wafted across the room, making the benches shine like new bronze. Sunlight slithered into the jar of copper sulphate, illuminating oceanic depths of perfect colour. He could feel the pressure of the air on his skin.

Mr Barrington was concluding the lesson: 'A venerable hermit by the name of Abbas Pambo, upon being asked to give guidance to a visitor, memorably replied: "If he is not edified by my silence, he will not be edified by my words." Five minutes of our period remain to us. Let us spend it in instructive silence. Close your eyes, gentlemen. Consider the matter of today's lesson.'

Alexander imagined a hall of white stone with white stone benches around the wall and glassless windows that gave a view of an aquamarine sky and a sea as blue as copper sulphate. He heard the sweep of feet on a sandy floor and the murmuring of men in deep and pleasurable perplexity. He opened one eye, and saw that Mr Barrington was smiling at the apple tree, but with a smile that seemed veiled, as if what he was smiling at was not the petals that the tree was shedding by the hundred, but the memory of those petals.

13. The great McIndoe

'But I have to say, I believe our friend Nasser will get the better of it,' Mr Greening ruminated, accepting another slice of beef from Alexander's mother.

'You do?' said Alexander's father, eliciting Mr Greening's further thoughts rather than doubting his foresight.

'I do,' Mr Greening affirmed. From Alexander's father he accepted another measure of wine, which he held above the new tablecloth and gazed into for a moment, as if to read the omens in it.

Still looking at Mr Greening, Alexander's father replaced the wine bottle softly on its coaster.

'In the long run, I do,' confessed Mr Greening, with a sombre shake of his head. 'There will be mighty ructions. Damned mess there'll be. But when the situation settles down Mr Nasser will still be there, you wait and see. And we'll have made enemies of people we need on our side.' He raised a flap of meat towards his mouth. 'And then we'll have to look out,' he added, lowering his fork again.

'We shall,' said Alexander's father.

'A bad business,' said Alexander's mother.

With his knife Mr Greening pushed a tide of gravy across his wedge of beef. 'Oil,' he said. 'Oil is the key to everything. The engine of the globe runs on oil, and we should never forget it. Mr Nasser and his ilk are the chaps who have it, not our chums in Israel. We're making a rod for our own backs if we carry on like this.'

'We are,' agreed Alexander's father, and then for a moment everyone at the table was busy with their food.

Alexander glanced at Mr Greening, who was working his knife into the meat as if he were teaching it a lesson, while the champing of his jaws made wrinkles appear around the base of his ears and on the sides of his soft naked scalp. Mr Greening looked up and met his gaze. 'Madmen and buffoons on all sides, eh?' he said. 'Madmen and buffoons.'

'Yes, sir,' Alexander concurred, conscious that his father's hands had ceased moving over his plate.

'Still, not all gloom and doom in the world, is it?' resumed Mr Greening. 'Let's be grateful for Jim Laker, eh?'

'A remarkable exploit,' said Alexander's father.

'If we had more men like Laker we'd all be better off,' Mr Greening told Alexander. 'Fewer men like Eden. More men like Jim Laker, and more like your father,' he went on, sagely regarding his glass of wine. 'You're a sporting chap aren't you, Alexander?'

'I'm not very good at cricket,' Alexander replied, becoming aware that the collar of his shirt, starched that morning by his mother, was making his skin sore.

'A passable fielder,' said his father.

'But you follow the game?' demanded Mr Greening. 'Read the papers, listen to the wireless?'

'Yes, sir,' Alexander replied.

'Never trust a chap who doesn't know his cricket,' said Mr Greening. 'Diligence, dependability, application, a sense of history, sense of team spirit.' Mr Greening watched his own hand rotate the glass through ninety degrees. 'Your father, now. I knew he was a good egg from the moment I set eyes on him. I dropped by at lunchtime, out of the blue, and what do I find? What is your father doing? He's at his desk, statements of account on one side, Test report on the other, corned beef sandwich and a glass of water in the middle. Good egg, I thought to myself. And I was right.'

'Thank you, Mr Greening,' said Alexander's mother.

'Something of Stafford Cripps about that glass of water, I thought,' said Mr Greening to Alexander's father, and then he turned to Alexander again. 'What of your future path, young man?' he enquired, and lifted a potato to his mouth.

'We're undecided, aren't we?' Alexander's father replied.

'My advice,' Mr Greening commenced, before Alexander could think of an acceptable response, 'is that you should consider following in your father's footsteps. Give it serious consideration, young man. It's a good career, and a dependable one. People will always need a safe place for their money. And they will always need a bit more than they have. A position of responsibility, of trust,' said Mr Greening, but of what he went on to say Alexander would remember only the word 'profit', expelled repeatedly from his lips as if the excitement of the idea had set off a little explosion in his mouth. He would remember also Mr Greening's paisley silk cravat, and the way his parents sat like members of a preacher's congregation while Mr Greening was speaking, and that they used the dinner service that had once been Nan Burnett's and which was kept in a brass-cornered box beside the sideboard in the dining room. And he would remember that when Sidney Dixon came round, no more than one month later, they used the ordinary plates, and his father drew the box out onto the rug to let Sidney Dixon see the special plates.

'May I?' asked Sidney Dixon. 'It's very nice, very nice,' he slurred, turning a tureen in his white-gloved hands. 'About 1890? Worth a pretty penny. Don't ever sell it, though,' he said to Alexander's father. 'Not even to me,' he added, and his thickened purple lips opened in a smile. Careful as a bomb disposal man, he lowered the tureen into the box. He stood up, then walked across the room to the window and back to the sideboard, raising his foot to flex his knees after each step. In the mirror above the mantelpiece Alexander looked at Sidney Dixon's head, at the nose that was like a stub of melted candle on one side, at the ginger hair that sprouted in clumps on his mottled scalp. The reflection of Sidney Dixon's eyes, set deeply behind tight circles of skin as if peering through a torn sheet, met Alexander's in the mirror, and seemed to excuse him for his rudeness.

Alexander's mother left the room to fetch the dishes and when she came back they arranged themselves as they had sat for Mr Greening's dinner, with the guest at the head of the table and Alexander and his parents on opposite sides. Sidney Dixon watched the movements of her hands as she apportioned the food. 'Not so much for me, Mrs MacIndoe, if you wouldn't mind,' he said, making a narrowing gesture with his raised hands. At each syllable the struggling skin around his mouth tightened into minuscule pleats. 'A small portion only. A small portion for a guinea pig,' he said, glancing at Alexander's father, who smiled in return.

'Sidney's a guinea pig,' said Alexander's father, turning to his son, who smiled bemusedly. 'You explain, Sidney.'

'Your dad's right. I'm a guinea pig. A McIndoe Guinea Pig, second

121

class.' Sidney Dixon again exchanged a look with Alexander's father.

'Explain, go on,' said Alexander's father.

Alexander saw his mother fiddle with the roses in the bowl that she had put in the centre of the table, but his father's attention did not leave the face of their guest.

'Well,' Sidney Dixon began, 'as you can see, I got a bit mucked up. Frazzled I was, in the Blitz. Sort of in the Blitz, but that's another story.' He wriggled his hands over the edge of the table, like glove-puppets. 'Hands got fried, and the face, and other bits. In a bad way, I was. But it would have been worse if I hadn't gone to Archibald McIndoe. A lot worse. Wouldn't have made it, probably. Loads of us wouldn't have made it without him, or have come out looking like rashers of bacon.'

'What did he do?' Alexander asked, and it occurred to him that he had not made a single unprompted remark to Mr Greening.

'You wouldn't want the details of it,' said Sidney Dixon, looking quickly at Alexander's mother, who continued to stare at her plate. 'But he was a burns man, and he did things that nobody else could do.'

'And they worked,' said Alexander's father.

'They worked,' said Sidney Dixon, nodding. 'Dozens of airmen there were. Hurricane and Spitfire pilots, then bomber crews. They were the real McIndoe Guinea Pigs. Still stay in touch, a lot of them. Get together every year, down in East Grinstead. I'm an affiliated Guinea Pig, being a civilian.' He made a fist of his right hand and beat gently on the table, singing quietly: ' "We are McIndoe's army, We are his Guinea Pigs, With dermatomes and pedicles, Glass eyes, false teeth and wigs." That's our anthem. The bit that's suited to polite society,' he said, making a bow, unacknowledged, to Alexander's mother. 'Owe him everything, we do. He fixed us up in more ways than one. He fixed our skin and he loaned us money if we needed it. I couldn't go back to my old trade. Used to be a mechanic, but I'd keep dropping things now. Sir Archibald's money kept me going for a while, then I became a back-room boy in my old factory, ordering parts and all that. Deadly dull,' he said, shaking his head.

'Sidney is not cut out to be a pen-pusher,' said Alexander's father. 'Some of us are, but not Sid Dixon. And now the day of liberty is at hand.'

'My second stroke of luck,' Sidney Dixon told Alexander, without irony. 'I decided I had to set up on my own.'

'Swelling the ranks of the nation of shopkeepers,' Alexander's father interrupted.

'Needed a few quid more, and I wandered into your father's place. Saw his name on the door and I thought: this is fate. Same name. Spelt slightly different, but the same name. This is my man, I said to myself.'

'Yes, but this MacIndoe charges interest,' said Alexander's father, pursing his lips into a smirk of cupidity.

'What are you going to sell, Mr Dixon?' Alexander asked.

'Antiques is what I aim to do. Real antiques. Good quality stuff, like those plates. But it'll be bric-à-brac for the time being, most likely. And some of my pictures. Bung them in old frames to make them look better.'

'Your pictures, Mr Dixon?' asked Alexander's mother.

'A bit of an artist on the quiet,' said Alexander's father.

'I daub a little, Mrs MacIndoe. Watercolours. Something I did after I came out of the Victoria. Good exercise for the hands, and it keeps the spirits up.'

'And what do you paint?' asked Alexander's mother, at last looking at Sidney Dixon, focusing on his eyes fixedly, as if afraid of the consequences of allowing her gaze to wander.

'Anything that takes my fancy,' Sidney Dixon replied. 'I go up to town on a Sunday, and walk around for a while until a scene catches me. Something always turns up.'

'Sidney's a great walker,' Alexander's father observed to his son, as if Alexander and Mr Dixon were boys of the same age, whom he was hoping to make friends. 'Never takes a bus if he can help it, do you?'

'Hardly ever. Might frighten the children.'

With the side of her hand Alexander's mother brushed a microscopic crumb from the tablecloth. 'Alexander likes to walk,' she said. 'He can't wait till the holiday. Walks miles when we go away, don't you? Up hill and down dale.'

'Keeps you limber,' agreed Sidney Dixon. 'Not a country boy myself, though. Prefer the countryside, do you, Alexander?' he asked, and seemed intrigued that this might be so.

'Sometimes,' Alexander replied. 'I like the sound of the sea more than the sound of cars, I think.'

'Wouldn't call yourself a real Londoner, then?'

'Suppose not.'

'Couldn't live anywhere but London, me. Go mad with nothing but trees to look at. Give me noise and crowds any day. What about you, Mrs MacIndoe?'

'Our friends are here,' she said. 'Most of them. And Graham's job.'

'And a certain person's girlfriend,' Alexander's father joined in.

'She's not my girlfriend,' said Alexander.

'Companion of honour, then.'

'She's not my girlfriend.'

'Friend number one.'

'Like her mother is my friend number one,' Alexander's mother told Sidney Dixon.

'Precisely,' said Alexander's father.

Sidney Dixon's mouth convulsed into a smile, but his face was turned to Alexander and there appeared in his sunken eyes a look that seemed to Alexander a confession of desolation. And in the hallway, as Alexander's father held up Sidney Dixon's coat for him, Sidney looked at Alexander and smiled at his own clumsiness, and the same expression was momentarily in his eyes again. 'Perhaps your mother would appreciate a picture, for her hospitality? Custom made. What do you think?'

'No need,' said Alexander's father. 'The pleasure was ours.'

'But I'd like to. Perhaps you'd come along with me on Sunday, Alexander? You can choose the scene for her.'

So on the following Sunday morning, shortly before noon, Alexander met Sidney Dixon at Charing Cross and together they strolled around the West End until, an hour later, they arrived at the back of the Theatre Royal on Drury Lane, and Alexander chose the colonnade as the subject of the picture.

'Fate again, Alexander. Uncanny,' commented Sidney Dixon. 'Help us down, will you?' He raised his left arm like a wing, so that Alexander could take his elbow and ease him into a sitting position, with his back against the wall. 'You believe in fate? You look like a deep sort of lad. Think things are fated to happen?'

'Don't know,' Alexander replied. 'I don't think I've seen any proof.'

'Well, this is pretty close.' Sidney Dixon took a small bottle of water from one pocket of his greatcoat, and an enamelled tin of watercolours from another, and a pad of rough paper from an inside pocket, in which he also carried his sheaf of brushes, held together with a rubber band. 'You bring us here, and down the road there, fifty yards away, that's all –' he gesticulated towards the Strand – 'that's where I lost my face.' His teeth closed on the middle finger of his right-hand glove, and pulled it off. The skin on the back of his hand was like tissue paper that had been soaked and had then dried into hundreds of hard wrinkles. The fourth and middle fingers were fused by skin that was like a thin line of water. He clamped a brush into the crook of his thumb and forefinger and began to mix a colour on the lid of the tin. 'Puttering along on my motorbike, happy as Larry, I was. Still a week of leave left. Sun is coming up. All glittery on the river. Beautiful it was. Bombs been coming down all night, but lovely and peaceful now. This look right to you?'

Alexander compared the theatre's wall with the colour that Sidney Dixon had conjured from the tiny cakes of pigment. 'Looks perfect.'

'Nearly Christmas it was. Bloody freezing. Freeze the tits off a polar bear it would. Pardon the language. No telling tales, now. You won't squeal on me, will you?'

'No,' replied Alexander. 'Of course not.'

'No, you're not a squealer. I can tell. Not the snitching type. Sometimes you've got to call a spade a spade.'

'Or a tit a tit.'

'Exactly, Alex.' He touched the brush to the paper swiftly, and the colour of brick blossomed on the page. 'So the road's all ripped up, and I'm weaving round the pot-holes and all this debris. Then out of nowhere this bugger explodes. Too dark, do you think?' He angled the book towards Alexander.

'Just right.'

'If the sun comes out we're in trouble, but we're OK for ṛ charged the brush again, and dabbed it half a dozen times page. 'Clouds are what you need in this line of work. clouds and shadows. That's why the English are good

We invented clouds.' He looked at the wall then grimaced at the marks he had made. 'Where was I?'

'The bugger explodes.'

'Yes.' He rinsed the brush before stirring a lighter brown smear on the tin. 'All sort of happened backwards, it did. I saw this wall fall down in front of me. Sort of swooned, it did. Fell down like a fainting lady. And then I heard the bang, afterwards, and then there's all these black bricks flying across the road, like bloody great bats, all coming at me. Get clouted on the head I do, a right whack, and next thing I know I'm under the bike, pinned. Petrol's spilling all over the place. Engine's hot, you see? Might even have been running still. Can't remember.' Delicately he wiped a veil of ochre over the top of the page. Two teenage girls were coming towards them from Drury Lane. 'So it all goes up. Big pair of mitts on, I had. Big fat woolly things. Soaked right through, they are. There's a flash, and my hands are like matches, and I'm smacking myself with them, making it worse. Legs are getting roasted, hair's gone on fire and all, and all I can hear is this noise like a wind rushing, and some woman screaming.' The girls stopped; one of them opened her handbag, while the other looked at Sidney Dixon and Alexander. 'Then some bloke wraps me in his coat,' Sidney continued, 'and the next thing I know I'm on the Yellow Brick Road to East Grinstead and the great McIndoe.'

The girls crossed the road; at the junction, underneath the colonnade, they looked back with squirming faces, and turned down the side street. 'There's usually one big problem with doing this kind of thing,' remarked Sidney. 'There's always some nosy bugger wants to have a look at what you're doing. Unless you look like me. That's where I've got an advantage, normally. They leave me alone. Liked the look of you, though, didn't they?' he laughed.

'Sorry,' said Alexander.

'Nothing to be sorry about. You can't help it and I can't help it.' The brush's metal collar rattled on the mouth of the bottle. 'God, what a pair we make, eh?' he laughed again, and Alexander heard this as a request, and knew that he would be spending other Sundays with Sidney Dixon.

He would remember a frosty Sunday morning on which they walked n a Soho street where 'Don't Be Cruel' was coming from three different windows, and talking one afternoon to a broken-nosed police-man who stood in a doorway with a lit cigarette reversed in his concave palm, and the afternoon a boat collided with a pier of Southwark Bridge. Strongest of all, however, was to be the memory that began with the windows of the Old Curiosity Shop and recommenced with the grass in Lincoln's Inn Fields, under the leaves of a young silver birch. In the undergrowth there was a pigeon with deformed scarlet feet, and there was a shroud of moss on the trunk of a plane tree close to where they sat. 'I paint the buggers but I don't know what I'm painting,' Sidney cursed. 'What's that one?'

'Sycamore,' said Alexander.

'I think I'll do the building instead.' He pointed his brush at the columns on the front of the College of Surgeons. 'For a cack-handed painter there's nothing so nice as a line of cylinders.'

Alexander regarded the scrolls of the capitals; they were like the eyes of some monstrous crustacean. He watched Sidney wash the paper with a yellow so weak that it became unambiguously yellow only as the water evaporated; he watched him create triangles of shadow with a succession of single strokes.

Then Sidney's hand stopped stirring his brush in the water pot. 'Jesus Christ!' he yelled. 'Bleeding hell! Alex! Look! That's him!'

In front of the columns a long black car was parked, and on the roof of the car lay a grey pinstriped sleeve and a curl of white shirt-cuff. A gold cuff-link flashed.

'Jesus! That's Sir Archibald!' As though his legs were bound by ropes, Sidney writhed to his feet. He raised his arms as high as he could, wincing as he waved. 'That's Sir Archibald!' he cried. The car swung out of the forecourt, away from them. 'That's him,' he told Alexander. 'The great McIndoe,' he said again, his voice falling as the car gained distance.

14. The cave

For almost fifty years the shop had been owned by Mr H. R. Jacklin, whose initials and surname were still on the fanlight, in letters of gilt with thick black borders. The old porcelain door handle and the brass finger panel had not yet been replaced, but the name of Jacklin the Jeweller had been scraped from the window hurriedly, leaving moth-like flakes of white paint on the glass.

A ship's wheel was the centrepiece of Sidney Dixon's display. To one side of it stood a wooden telescope, with a cutlass dangling from its tripod, above a china shepherdess and a matching pair of Toby jugs. In the other half of the window was set a globe that was marked with greasy patches all over Europe, and close to the door, behind a rattan-sided crib, there was a brass diver's helmet on top of a pedestal, which sometimes caught the sunlight in such a way as to give the shop's interior the tone of sunset in the morning.

Inside, a long glazed case that had been made for Mr Jacklin stretched down one side of the shop. In the course of the year it would fill with brooches, medals, pens, watches and rings, but on this day there was nothing in it except the casing of an anti-aircraft shell and a compass that was as big as a cake tin. On the opposite wall, above shelves of miscellaneous books, a trio of photographs showed Metcalf's smithy and Chapel Farm in Eltham, and a line of hansom cabs at the top of Tranquil Vale.

'Take a good look at that one,' said a voice. Sidney Dixon was sitting in a leather armchair behind a roll-top desk at the end of the shop, beyond the rectangle of light that came through the door. 'The blacksmith. See the sign? "Smith & Farrier" it says.'

Alexander put a knee into a space on a bookshelf and leaned forward to scrutinize the faded picture. 'I see it,' he said.

'There's a chap in a cap, working on the horse on the left.'

A crouching, bandy-legged man, wearing a leather cap and a leather jerkin over his white shirt, clamped a massive hoof between his thighs. 'I see him,' said Alexander.

'That's my father, that is.'

'Your father was a blacksmith?'

'My father was a shoe repairer. He was playing the fool.' Sidney turned the switch on the green-shaded desk lamp and beckoned Alexander like a priest summoning a penitent. 'Come and sit down,' he said, and clawed a dining chair towards him with a white-gloved hand. 'Sit down,' he said.

'Are things going well?' asked Alexander.

'Do you see any customers?' Sidney responded, without sharpness, as though the shop were not his.

Alexander looked around the shop, and noticed that the picture propped against the accordion behind the long case was a watercolour of the Freemasons' Hall, which Sidney had painted one Sunday afternoon.

'I have a proposition for you,' said Sidney, straightening his legs gradually then drawing them gradually in again. 'I'm doing all right. Ticking over. I've got good stuff here. People will pay good prices for it. But I'll be straight with you, Alexander.' He paused to await the decision of a man who had stopped to inspect the objects in the window; the man put his face close to the glass, looked towards them, and moved on. The skin around Sidney's mouth bent stiffly into a smile. 'There you have it. I'm not getting any casual trade. People stop but they don't come in. Not many of them, and them that do don't tend to linger. And it's because of me, with a lot of them. I'm a good businessman, don't get me wrong. I've got a head on me, and I know my stuff. But I'm not good for business. Not as the front man.' He regarded his feet, as if finding fault with his choice of footwear for the day. 'Folks come in, Alex, but they don't hang around, not once they get a butchers at me. Not all of them, mind. And I don't blame them that scarper. But a lot of them go squeamish. You can see them struggling with themselves, and off they go.'

'That's bad.'

'It's a shame all right. And it's your father's money.'

'Not really his,' said Alexander. 'He's the man who hands it out.'

'Not how his boss will see it, if I can't make a go of things. He'll be responsible, and I'll be responsible for him being responsible.' He

129

moved the desk lamp an inch farther from him, then put it back where it had been. 'You see what I'm getting at?' he asked.

That morning Alexander had attended an interview at a branch of a building society in Greenwich. He pictured the office in which he might be working, with its desks jammed together like dominoes, under lights that were the same as the lights in his classroom at school. He heard the jangle of the telephones, and saw again the eager, hopeless face of the woman who had taken his name.

'I need a better face to greet the punters,' Sidney went on. 'And I couldn't get a better face than you.'

'I'd have to give it some thought,' said Alexander, looking out into the street.

Sensing that he was winning, Sidney leaned back and placed his hands on the arms of the chair. 'You'd be very good with the public. I know it. You're easy to talk to, apart from anything else. And if I had you here, that'd give me more time to go buying. Auctions, and all that. Auctions are a different proposition. Tend to get the soft hearts there. Folks don't like to bid against me. Reckon I'm a war hero.'

'When would you like me to start, if I said yes?' asked Alexander.

'Whenever you like, Alexander, whenever you like. Tomorrow would be perfect, but I can wait.'

'I'll let you know by the end of the week.'

'That would be good. Now, pick that up for us, will you?' Sidney asked, indicating a covered chamber-pot on the floor by the door to the back room. Alexander lifted the lid, and took out two bottles of stout and two glasses.

He became Sidney Dixon's assistant within the fortnight. On his second day he was entrusted with a key and instructed as to how the mark-up should be calculated and how the books should be kept, and then he was left alone. There was almost nothing to do in the first few months. On a Saturday a dozen people might come through the door, but on a weekday he sometimes saw nobody at all, other than the friends who called to see him after school or after work. Every morning he dusted the shop and cleaned the windows; he might take a message on the telephone once or twice a day; and some days he unloaded from a van the things that Sidney had bought at an auction or from someone's house. And Alexander was quite content, while the pendulums of the long-case clocks maintained their quiet debate, to leaf through Sidney's reference books, learning to recognise the styles of Lalique and Mackintosh and many others whose work he knew he would never see. He was content to sit in the oxblood leather armchair and view the changing picture of the street as the light and the shadows moved and the shoppers dawdled by. An old man with long grey hair, whose name Alexander never learned, walked his dog up the street every morning, and returned with a newspaper under his arm; the postman passed the shop at ten o'clock and three o'clock; at ten-thirty and four o'clock Maureen Doherty stepped out of the shoe shop to smoke a cigarette; once or twice a day Mr Beckwith might drive past, delivering another batch of cards or headed paper from Johnson the Printer's. The days were so alike that time did not seem to pass.

John Halloran was working in a garage in Deptford, and on days when he finished early he would sometimes visit Alexander. They would sit in the back office, where there was a framed photograph of Bert Johnson leading the Charlton team onto the pitch between two lines of kilted girl pipers, and a print of William Innes, standing in his buckled pumps on the turf of the Royal Blackheath Golf Club, shouldering his iron daintily, as if it were a parasol. Alexander would always remember the superior Mr Innes, and the windmill in the background, and the rough-faced caddy in a tricorn hat, with a corked bottle in one pocket, and John Halloran looking at the picture as he rolled a cigarette between his fingers.

'Sid want to sell this?' he asked.

'Don't know. It's not in the book.'

'Pity. The old man might like it.'

'I'll ask, if you like. Sid might take an offer.'

'Yes, do,' said John, and he handed the cigarette to Alexander. 'Big brother's back in town,' he said, sprinkling a line of tobacco into the folded paper on his palm. 'A changed man, I tell you.' His lips made a whistling motion, and he blew out a long breath.

'Six months, isn't it?' asked Alexander, positioning his chair so that he could see the empty shop.

'Long enough, mate. Long enough.' John tapped his cigarette repeatedly on the back of his hand, as if enacting the passage of the months. 'You should see him. Hair you couldn't hide a gnat in. Like having Desperate Dan around the house. Half a bloody pig for breakfast and a bucket of tea. Mister human bloody dynamo. Up on the roof he was this morning, fixing the tiles. Bloody lunatic.' He sent a jet of smoke ceilingwards and shook his head in disbelief. 'I tell you, square-bashing isn't doing that to me. I'm going to be a layabout, mate. Follow your example. You wait till you see him,' said John, passing the ashtray. 'Mister bloody ramrod.'

But he never did see James Halloran again, because James joined the army as soon as he had done his National Service, as did his brother, whom Alexander was to see for the last time in the autumn of 1960. Years later, he would strive to remember their conversation, but succeed in recalling only that John had been serving in Egypt, that his face and bare forearms were tanned, that he was to be posted to Germany later that month, and that he looked over Alexander's head at the clock above the chemist's window before announcing that he must be going, and when Alexander looked back at the clock, after John had strode away, he saw that the clock was not working.

Sometimes Paul Malinowski would come to the shop after school, and begin his homework in the back room, because it was quieter than home, where there was now a baby sister. Some afternoons Roy Pickering would wheel his bicycle into the doorway and stop for a few minutes. Mr Barrington came in several times, and bought an old flyposter for the Lewisham Hippodrome, advertising 'Kit-Kat And His Saxophone Rascals' and 'Mademoiselle Rubina, The World's Most Artistic Dancer'. Occasionally Mrs Beckwith would drop by, with his mother, and leave a slice of cake for him. But John Halloran was the one who visited the shop most frequently, except for Megan, who would come to the shop at least one day each week.

Having peered through the window to check that Alexander was alone, she would deposit her beret on the elephant's-foot umbrella stand by the door and loosen her tie, just as his father did as soon as the front door was shut behind him. Sitting on the Chesterfield that remained unsold for more than a year because one arm had been badly repaired and was no longer upright, they talked about her lessons and the essays she had to write, or about things they could not talk about when Alexander came to her house to work in the garden with Mr Beckwith. 'Dad was talking to himself last night,' she told him once.

'Mum thinks it's you he's talking to,' she said, and she took an exercise book from her briefcase so that he could test her. 'Meanwhile she's getting all worked up about germs. Obsessed. Spent all yesterday scrubbing the kitchen, Dad said. Looks like an operating theatre.' Perusing the incomprehensible diagrams and charts that she had drawn, Alexander imagined her at work in her classroom, and her hand moving across the page, neatly transcribing the numerals from a blackboard. 'And she's not keen on me doing geography. She thinks it's a brawny subject. Not the right thing for a young lady. Not keen on university, come to that. Thinks I'll get led astray,' she sighed, and she moved closer to him, to point out what he should read. The thought of their separation made the ticking of the clocks become louder and a taste of glue rise on his tongue.

In the same month Megan would be leaving to go to university and he would be called up for his National Service, and the closer they came to that month the more often their conversation wandered into reminiscence during their hours together in Sidney Dixon's shop. Asked for the name of the girl who had once brought her cat to school, or the location of a shop in which they had both been accidentally left behind by his mother, or the place where they had seen the woman with the monkey on her arm, Alexander would close his eyes to see the scene that she wanted, and describe its details for her, and Megan would gaze at the ceiling while he talked, as if she were watching a cinema screen. More than forty years later Alexander would remember one afternoon especially. Someone had slashed the awning the week before, and now the rain was falling through the slit, making a noise like a football rattle being turned slowly. It had been raining all day. A man had called to read the electricity meter in the morning, but nobody else had entered the shop before Megan came running across the road, holding her briefcase over her head. Alexander draped her gaberdine over a chair in the doorway and she put her shoes and socks on the radiator in the back room. They sat on the Chesterfield. Mrs Giles, the chemistry teacher, having found an impertinent remark written in chalk on her desk, had lectured the class on the paramount importance of laws in all things. Megan put a cold white foot onto his hand while he tested her knowledge of the periodic table. The rain intensified, tumbling through the hole in the awning as if from a burst pipe. 'Terrific noise,' said Megan, and he propped the door open so they could hear and see the rain better. The pavement shimmered with rebounding water; a car slowed down outside the shop and crept through the pool, raising a wake that lapped the doorstep.

'Remember that time in Cornwall, Eck?' Megan remarked. 'When we took the bus to the other beach, and sheltered in the cave?'

Alexander saw the low arch of black rock and the silver-grey veil of rainwater that hid everything outside. The rain on the beach made a sound like breath drawn in through clenched teeth. Feeling his way along the damp walls, he led Megan into the depths of the cave. The rock became so low he had to crawl, and Megan turned back. Then suddenly the roof was out of reach, and he was in another chamber with a hole high above him and a cord of rainwater gyrating in the shaft of light. Suspended by its roots, a bush swung like a chandelier underneath the hole. He pressed his hand into the chilly sand, leaving imprints as clear as plastercasts. 'You worked out that the tide was coming in,' he said.

'I did?'

'You realized it was coming in, because there was a rock in the entrance with a border of water around it, and you noticed the water was getting wider.'

'I did that?'

'Yes, you did. And you said "We've got to go, Eck," as if there was a bomb that was going to go off.' He imitated her direful whisper, and the way she pulled her fringe from her eyes. 'So we counted to three and ran out together.'

'I remember that bit. And your mother. She was furious.'

'And what did you say?'

'No idea.'

'You said "Sowwy," and that made it worse. "Irresponsible infants," she called us.' Alexander saw his mother's hand on Megan's bare back, and his father and Mr Beckwith in the car park, with their arms crossed as if watching a cricket match on the beach. 'We went and had a cup of tea. My mother kept wiping your head with a towel. There was a labrador under one of the tables that you called Nelson, because it was blind in one eye.'

'You remember all that?'

134

'Of course.'

'You're not making it up?'

'I couldn't make it up.'

Megan rested her head on the arm of the Chesterfield and closed her eyes. One of the clocks commenced its whirring and crunching, as if clearing its throat before the chimes. Then Megan opened one eye, looked intently at him, and said: 'Eck, how can you stand this?'

'Stand what?' he asked.

'Stand this.' She waved one arm over her head. 'This.'

'What do you mean?'

'You know what I mean, Eck.' She sat up and clutched her feet. 'What I mean is, what are you going to do with yourself?'

'I am doing something.'

'You're not. This isn't something. Sitting in a shop all day, staring out of the window. That's not doing anything.'

'I enjoy it.'

'You enjoy staring out of the window?'

'I learn things,' Alexander protested, tapping a foot on a book that lay open on the floor.

'Nothing much. And that's not the point. It's not why you're here.'

'So why am I here?'

'You're here because you feel sorry for your boss.'

'I like him.'

'That as well. But really you're doing this because you feel sorry for him. It's good of you. I'm not criticising you, Eck. But what's the plan? You can't do this for ever.'

'It's not for ever.'

'You're getting settled. I can see it happening. You'll go off and be a soldier, and then you'll come back here. I can see it.'

'You can see better than me, then,' said Alexander.

'Well, that's not right, is it? You've got to have some idea of where you're going.'

'What do you suggest?'

'God's sake, Eck, I don't know. Get an apprenticeship. Learn to make something. Clocks, for instance.'

'Clocks.'

135

'It's not such a dim idea. You need to be patient to make clocks. Careful. Steady. That's you.'

'Right-oh,' he said, glumly.

'A good eye. You've got that. Fine hands.'

Alexander inspected his hands, turning them mechanically at the wrist: palm up, palm down; palm up, palm down.

'Eck, I'm being serious. You can do better than this.' She gathered her books and stood up. 'A bit of willpower. That's all it takes.'

A cloud of ambition drifted over him while Megan spoke, but evaporated as soon as she had gone. He turned the pages of Sidney Dixon's books and tried to imagine himself making cabinets or chairs, or making anything at all. He tried to imagine being somewhere else, but could think only of places he had already been. The sound of the clocks was like a continuation of Megan's argument. He withdrew to the back room and looked at the picture of the three paddle-steamers at Woolwich, and the one of the woman selling crockery from a horse-drawn cart, and William Gladstone at the hustings in Greenwich, addressing a mass of top hats and bowlers and soldiers' caps.

15. 6 July 1958

While he talked to his mother and opened the ledgers for her, Mrs Beckwith would stroll about the shop, giving the pictures and the trinkets a leisurely look, flicking a glove at the things that took her fancy and asking Alexander about their price or origin, and then she would sit down on one of the armchairs, to wait for his mother to finish her assessment of his progress. They never stayed for more than five minutes and it was always Mrs Beckwith who spoke last, calling 'See you soon, Alexander,' or 'Keep busy, Alexander,' as she stood aside and held open the door for his mother, whose style of leaving was that of a shop inspector who had now completed her day's assignment, to her partial satisfaction.

His mother had seemed not to notice when Mrs Beckwith ceased calling him Alex, though the change had been sudden and absolute. From the day Mrs Beckwith kissed him he was Alexander. Nothing in the tone of her voice nor anything in the way she looked at him was different immediately, but he was always Alexander and never Alex after that, and she would use his name more frequently than she had ever used its abbreviation, as though she thought it was a charm that would banish by its repetition his evident embarrassment in her presence. For a time he avoided her whenever he could, sometimes making excuses for not going to the Beckwiths' house on Sunday, as had become his habit. Soon a teasing nuance appeared in Mrs Beckwith's gaze as she pronounced his name. 'Harry's missing his assistant, Alexander,' he would remember her saying to him when they met one afternoon in the street, and it was plain to Alexander that she was rebuking him for his recalcitrance. Eventually he resumed his weekly visits, and the guilt that he felt in the company of Mr Beckwith diminished quickly, though sometimes the afternoon of Mrs Beckwith's kiss would resurrect itself as if through a depth of muddy water, and he would start at the realisation that it had not been a tenacious dream.

It seemed that nobody noticed anything different in his manner with Mrs Beckwith and hers with him, not even Megan, who explained his absences by the moodiness of all boys. And he himself did not notice one particular and significant change, not until the day they all went to Whitstable together and walked to Reculver. Six abreast, hand in hand, they walked into the wind. Alexander, at one end, held Megan's hand. Mr Beckwith, his shirt wrapped as tight as a shroud to his torso, walked between Megan and his wife, whose handkerchief was snatched from her hand and vanished instantly into the fields. Alexander's mother kept laughing as she staggered over the molehills, and his father, folding his glasses away because he could no longer see through the spatter of sea mist, assumed the doughty expression of a polar hero and urged them on. At the Roman fort they huddled in the lee of a wall to eat the picnic that Mr Beckwith had carried in his knapsack, and then Mr Beckwith took a photo. Alexander knelt beside Megan in the hissing grass and the adults stood behind them. 'Chop-chop, Harry,' said Mrs Beckwith. 'We'll be blown back to London in a second.' It was then that Alexander remembered the evening on the beach at Praa. He recalled that he had been happy, and that the windblown sand had rippled on the beach, and that Mrs Beckwith's hands had rested on his shoulders. He glanced back and saw that she was standing close behind him but with her arms linked with his parents', and it occurred to him that he could not remember an occasion when she had touched him affectionately since the afternoon of the kiss. As readily as she put her arms around Megan's shoulders she had used to put her arms around him, but now she did not. When she brought a tray into the garden on a Sunday afternoon she might place it beside Alexander, but her hand would rest on Megan's back or on her husband's, but never on his. Even at Christmas, when the Beckwiths filed into the hall under the arch of holly, she no longer embraced him but instead shook his hand, as if it were his joke to play at being the manager of the establishment.

He had once been a sort of son to Mrs Beckwith but in time he became a sort of ally, who was required to side with her in her disagreements with Megan. When, one autumn Sunday evening, Megan came downstairs wearing coral pink lipstick, Mrs Beckwith called him to the hallway, where she was obstructing Megan's exit.

'I told her she can get that stuff off her face for starters,' she declared. 'She's not leaving this house looking like that. Makes her look like a tart,' she said. 'Doesn't it?'

Megan glared at him. 'It does not,' she said.

'Don't you backchat me, young woman,' said Mrs Beckwith. 'You look like a tart and that's that. Upstairs and get it off.'

'It's your lipstick,' Megan stated.

'Upstairs,' shouted Mrs Beckwith.

'Do I look like a tart to you?' Megan asked him.

'Thank you, Alexander,' said Mrs Beckwith.

'Well?' demanded Megan.

'Better without it,' Alexander replied, and he tried to look at her as he would have done had Mrs Beckwith not been there to observe him.

'Thank you, Alexander,' said Mrs Beckwith.

'Thank you, Alexander,' Megan parroted. 'Stooge MacIndoe.'

She called him the same name during the last argument that Alexander witnessed. He was in the kitchen with Mr Beckwith, filling the watering can, when he heard Megan's voice rising stridently above the blurred sound of Mrs Beckwith's. 'It's important,' she insisted.

'It's ridiculous is what it is,' Mrs Beckwith retorted.

'Mum,' pleaded Megan, making a whine of the single syllable.

'I've said no.'

'Why?'

'It's fifty miles, that's one good reason.'

'I won't go all the way. A few miles.'

'You won't go any of the way.'

'I will.'

'You will not, madam.'

Mr Beckwith tightened the tap and looked at Alexander. 'Trouble,' he said, nodding towards the door. 'Let's retreat.' Alexander followed him out of the kitchen, but was summoned to the bottom of the stairs by Mrs Beckwith.

'How do you bear her, Alexander?' she asked. 'Can you reason with her? I can't.'

'Where's the reason?' demanded Megan. She was standing on the landing, with her hands on her hips, mirroring the stance of Mrs Beckwith.

'Listen to her,' said Mrs Beckwith to Alexander.

'That's the idea,' Megan retorted.

'I am listening to you, Megan, and I'm telling you you're talking rubbish, and you're not going on any damned march.'

'It's not rubbish. You don't understand it, that's all.'

'You're a young girl, Megan. Outside this house nobody cares what a young girl thinks.'

'Not here, either.'

'You chanting slogans isn't going to make a difference to anything.'

'If there's enough of us it will. And they're not slogans. They're called principles. Bertrand Russell doesn't chant slogans. You've heard of Bertrand Russell?'

'Megan,' interrupted Alexander, 'don't sneer.'

'Course I've heard of Bertrand bloody Russell,' said Mrs Beckwith. 'Have you heard of Stalin? Have you?'

'Have you heard of Hiroshima?'

'Will you listen to yourself, you stupid child?'

'I'm going,' said Megan. 'I've made my mind up and you can't stop me.'

'Yes I can. As long as you're living under my roof you'll do as I tell you.'

Megan leaned back against the wall, crossed her arms and regarded Alexander accusingly. 'What does the head warder's stooge have to say?'

'You're not going, and that's all there is to say,' shouted Mrs Beckwith. 'But what do you think, Alexander? Should my daughter be wasting her time with a bunch of dimwit priests and journalists and ne'er-do-wells?' Megan slammed the door of her room before Alexander could answer. 'See what I have to put up with?' said Mrs Beckwith, and she looked out of the hall window to hide her face from him.

There were other arguments that Alexander overheard, but he would be able to recall no later ones, nor anything that happened in the Beckwiths' house between that Easter and the sixth of July, a day that would commence in his memory with the image of Mr Beckwith in the garden and Megan standing beside him, vigilant, but with an expression of suppressed distaste about her lips. Raising a leaf by its

140

tip, Mr Beckwith revealed a ball of tiny flies on the underside, packed like iron filings on a magnet. Alexander doused the flies with soapy water; the froth dripped from the leaves onto Mr Beckwith's legs.

'Another blast,' said Mr Beckwith, lifting the branch higher. 'Let them have it. Never know when they're beaten, these lads.' Every shoot of the plant was infested. Mr Beckwith took the bottle from Alexander, crouched down and waddled under the foliage to get at the back of the bush. The air around them became hazy as he sprayed. 'Need more. More ammunition, Alexander,' he said, handing him the bottle.

Alexander went in through the French windows. He saw that Mrs Beckwith was in the room; the top of her hair could be seen over the back of the settee. The air inside the room was cool and smelled of polish, as it always did, but the atmosphere was unusual, and he could not understand why this was. He looked to his left again: beside the settee was the baize-topped card table, on which were placed Mrs Beckwith's sewing box and a decanter of water. The door, blown alternately by the draught from the hall and the breeze from the garden, knocked the jamb softly four or five times. Straight ahead was the ship's-wheel clock, showing that it was twenty-six minutes past four. And then it occurred to him that he could hear its ticking, and that this was strange.

He crossed the room to the side of the settee. Mrs Beckwith appeared to be dozing; a couple of her upper teeth were exposed, as if a dream were amusing her. A piece of needlepoint work, stressed tightly on its frame, rested on Mrs Beckwith's lap; her right hand held the needle to the petals of a half-formed carnation. Gingerly he stepped around the table; his foot struck something on the floor, lightly, but the contact made him gasp with shock. The fallen tumbler rolled against the castor, and he bent down to retrieve it. Mrs Beckwith's eyes were open, squinting drowsily at him. 'Mrs Beckwith?' he said. 'Mrs Beckwith?' He took a magazine from the rack beside the electric fire and scooped her unresisting, heavy hand onto it.

For perhaps a full minute Alexander looked at Mrs Beckwith. She had been a friend of his mother when they were girls, he told himself; she had been a wife to Mr Beckwith and a mother to Megan; she had been the sister of a man of whom he knew almost nothing; and all that she had been was but a breath that now had gone. And now that this breath was gone, her body was no longer hers. The hands were like replicas of her hands in wax. An artificial tinge of violet had appeared in the skin around her eyes and lips. The feeble smile, which seemed to widen as he looked at her, was no longer like any smile her mouth had ever formed. He thought of her kiss, and the smile began to seem malevolent, as if it were a message from Death.

His limbs were weightless but he could not move. 'Mr Beckwith,' he said, too quietly to be heard. The magazine fell from his quaking hand. 'Mr Beckwith,' he called. 'Mr Beckwith, come here.'

Mr Beckwith rushed past him. He placed his palms and then the backs of his hands to Mrs Beckwith's cheeks. 'Oh God,' he murmured, as if he were looking into the far distance and could see that something terrible was about to happen to some people there. 'Oh God,' he repeated, in exactly the same tone. He touched his brow to the tip of Mrs Beckwith's nose. 'Oh God,' he repeated again. 'Oh God, oh God.' He took hold of her wrist and squeezed it tightly.

Alexander went into the kitchen, where he stayed until he heard Megan scream. He hurried back into the room, where Mr Beckwith was sitting beside his wife and stroking her hand, and Megan was standing on the threshold, her hands flattened over her eyes and her mouth moving.

'Could you phone Dr Simpson for me?' asked Mr Beckwith. 'Tell him that my wife has died, and ask him to come.' He eased Mrs Beckwith's head against his shoulder. And when the call had been made he asked 'Is that done?' and said 'Thank you,' and continued to stroke Mrs Beckwith's hand, as though they were a couple sitting on a bench at the end of a tiring day. 'Go and see to our girl,' he said.

Megan was sitting on the paving stone that formed a step in front of Mr Beckwith's shed, staring at the back wall of the house. Drinking the air into her body in shuddering gulps, she fanned a hand at him to keep him away, then hid her eyes. Tears were dripping from her fingers, but she neither moved nor spoke.

'Shall I leave you alone?' he asked. He fixed his gaze on the grass around her feet, waiting for her to reply.

'Don't go, Eck,' she said at last. 'Not yet.' She uncovered her eyes, and looked at the ground with a resolute vacancy. 'Don't go yet, Eck.'

142

Alexander would remember Dr Simpson glancing at him suspiciously through the French windows, and the undertakers manoeuvring the coffin into the hall, followed by Mr Beckwith, who kept one hand on its lid, and Mr Beckwith coming out into the garden to lead Megan inside, and the blackbird that was singing on the TV aerial as Alexander stood on his own doorstep, rehearsing what he might say to his mother. He opened the door and saw his mother in the kitchen, wiping her eyes, and his father leaning against the wall and looking at her helplessly.

16. Chocolate soldiers

'Let's have a look at you then,' said his mother, leading him to the middle of the living room carpet. She let go of his hands and circled him twice, as if she were checking the condition of a valuable object that had been damaged then perfectly repaired. 'You're taller,' she decided.

'I'm exactly the same height as I was when I left,' he replied.

'No, I don't think so. Taller.'

'So I've miraculously begun to grow again, have I?'

'It's the boots, Mrs MacIndoe,' Sam Saunders interjected. 'Like Frankenstein. It's all in the footwear.' Hoisting a trouser leg at the knee, he wiggled a gleaming black boot for her.

Alexander's mother took a step back and surveyed her son from his feet to his beret. 'Maybe,' she said. 'But you're holding yourself better, Alexander. Not slouching.'

'I never slouched,' he replied.

'It didn't seem so before, but now I'm not so sure.' She came towards him and tugged both his cuffs at once. 'The making of you, this will be,' she said firmly.

'A fine figure of a man,' Sam observed, appraising the knot of his own tie in the mirror and sleeking his hair with his palms.

'Yes, he is,' said Alexander's mother. 'And I'm sure your mother will be just as pleased with you.'

Sam removed his elbow from the mantelpiece and stood at ease for her. 'Nice of you to say so, Mrs MacIndoe. As long as I bring her a few packets of fags she'll be pleased. Otherwise, the odds are against it.'

'That's unkind,' she said.

'Not unkind, Mrs MacIndoe. The truth. The plain truth. Not every mother is like you, Mrs MacIndoe,' Sam told her with a gallant grin. 'I'm the fifth kid in ours, and it's hard enough feeding two, she's always said.'

'Well, we'll be feeding you this evening,' said Alexander's mother, glancing towards the door. She returned her attention to the fit of Alexander's jacket.

His mother's discomfiture with Sam Saunders was what Alexander would remember from the first hour of his homecoming, and that she had set the dinner table in pairs, as if he and Sam were both guests in her house. 'So, Sam, do they treat you properly?' she asked, setting his plate on its mat.

'Alexander's letters don't tell us much about himself,' his father explained. 'Quite good on the weather. Poor on the human dimension.'

'Well enough,' said Sam, prodding his fork on the surface of his chop. 'But you get nothing like this from the NAAFI, I tell you.'

'I should hope not,' said Alexander's father.

'And how are you finding it?' Alexander's mother asked solicitously, laying down her cutlery.

'We'll get through OK, Mrs MacIndoe. Some better than others, but we'll all get through, God willing.'

'That isn't terribly encouraging,' she said, hesitantly lifting her knife.

'Some find it a struggle, but it's OK.'

'Is it a struggle for you?' she asked, frowning as she looked from Alexander to Sam and back to her son.

'Do you want an honest answer?' asked Sam.

'Honesty's always best, I say.'

Sam impaled a potato on his fork and pondered it before speaking. 'As I see it, Mrs MacIndoe, this rigmarole is a waste of time. These should be the best years of our lives and we're hanging around in a stupid camp, keeping the files nice and tidy, doing the paperwork, waiting for life to get going again. Learning all this useless stuff by rota.'

'The breech and the cocking piece and the upper sling swivel and the lower sling swivel,' chanted Alexander drearily.

'By rote,' interjected Alexander's father. 'One learns by rote. One performs tasks in accordance with a rota. Or not, as the case may be.'

'I stand corrected, Mr MacIndoe. But whatever it is, I think it's going to make me a mental case. Patience of a saint, your son. But me, I'm chafing at the bit, morning, noon and night.'

'But you're making friends?' Alexander's mother asked.

'A few, Mrs MacIndoe. But a mite too keen, some of them, if you get my meaning.'

'I'm not sure that I do,' said Alexander's father.

'Bit too enamoured of the old rifle for my liking, Mr MacIndoe. They'd like nothing more than to skewer some lad with a bayonet.'

'A lot of gung-ho,' Alexander agreed. 'Itching for a fight.'

'Useful quality in a soldier,' commented Alexander's father.

'I'm afraid we're not real soldiers, Mr MacIndoe,' Sam responded. 'We're chocolate soldiers, me and him.'

Alexander laughed, and his father's displeased face was turned on him. 'Just a joke, Dad,' he said, as his father shook the salt cellar over his food.

'Graham,' said Alexander's mother. 'Anyone would think you were a general or something.'

Sam watched Alexander's father for a moment, then brightly asked: 'So what did you do in the war, Mr MacIndoe?'

'Civil Defence.'

'A volunteer,' his mother added. 'And there was the desk job too.'

'Keeping the wheels of the economy turning,' his father said.

'The eyesight,' explained his mother, and there was a pause in which the chatter of cutlery on crockery was the only sound. 'But you've made some friends?' she then resumed.

'Not many, Mrs MacIndoe, and Sandy here's the best of them,' Sam said vigorously. 'The thing about your boy is that he has a great capacity for pain, tedium and misery. Whereas I have great difficulties with pain, tedium and misery, and need the companionship of a better specimen.'

'So you're doing well?' Alexander was asked, and his mother's effortful optimism obliged him to say that he was, though it was from a shared sense of futility that his friendship with Sam Saunders had grown.

'He's a good man to have beside you on exercises, is your boy, Mrs MacIndoe. Never gives up. Doesn't make a fuss. Gets his head down and gets on with it.'

'Pleased to hear that,' said Alexander's father, looking steadily at his son.

'And very handy for the social life too. Only one thing impresses

146

the ladies more than a uniform, and that's Sandy's face. Honeypot MacIndoe, I call him.'

'Alexander?' his mother queried.

'Joking again, Mum.'

'It's all right, Mrs MacIndoe. Alexander's a good lad. Keeps me on the straight and narrow, he does. Most of the time.'

'So, son,' said his father. 'Any prospect of an interesting posting?'

'Do you mean dangerous, Mr MacIndoe?' asked Sam. 'Malaya, that kind of thing?'

'Not that I've heard,' Alexander told his father, and he looked to Sam for confirmation.

'No, Mr MacIndoe. No point. They'd give anyone independence sooner than send us to sort them out.'

'What exactly have you been doing these past few months?' his father asked neither of them in particular. 'Tell me. Tell me what you've been up to,' he said, as though rejecting his own annoyance, and Sam, no longer facetious, told him about their drills and their lessons, embellishing his stories with such conviction that Alexander had no difficulty in corroborating them.

At the end of the evening, while his mother and Sam washed the dishes, Alexander went out into the garden with his father. He lit a cigarette and listened as his father talked about Hanif Mohammed's heroic innings. 'Remarkable,' his father pronounced, his chest rising in admiration of Hanif Mohammed. 'Never be beaten, that record, not in my lifetime,' he said, and he groped for his pipe in his cardigan pocket. Fastidiously he packed a pinch of tobacco into the bowl, and as his father's fingertips tamped the tobacco repeatedly, Alexander experienced a burgeoning awareness, like an onrush of nausea, that he was about to speak to his father in a way he had never spoken to him before.

'You can't stand him, can you?' Alexander said.

His father regarded the unlit pipe, then raised it to his lips. 'Matches?' he said, from the side of his mouth.

Alexander struck a match and touched it to his father's pipe. 'You really don't like him, do you?'

'Who?'

'You know.'

147

'Him indoors?' replied his father, and he blew a shot of smoke towards the door. 'I wouldn't put it like that.'

'But you don't, do you?'

'It doesn't matter.'

'Why don't you?'

'Hard to say. Perhaps I've seen a few too many of his sort.'

'And what sort is that?'

'Alexander, it doesn't matter. Leave it be.'

'What sort?'

'Talkers. He's a talker.'

'What's wrong with that?'

'There's nothing wrong with it. Not my type, that's all.' His father craned his neck to look into the kitchen over Alexander's shoulder, and smiled wryly. Sam walked past the doorway, carrying a low stack of plates on a support of splayed fingers, like a waiter. 'Remember a character called Douglas Nesbit? Worked in Stan Porter's shop, until he got sacked?'

'No,' Alexander replied, making no effort to remember.

'He had another line, selling nylons out of a suitcase. You'd see him at the station, flogging his stuff. Any sign of the police he'd jump on the nearest train and put out his stall at the next stop. Remember Iris Evans?'

'Yes.'

'She used to buy her scent and stockings from Dougie. One of his regular customers. Best ladies' outfitter in London, he used to call himself. Kept up his spiel non-stop until he'd emptied his case. Never knew a talker like him.' His father exhaled and smiled, as if the flavour of his recollection resided in the smoke. 'A bit like Douglas, your pal. Similar in some ways. Gift of the gab. Would have made an excellent spiv, your friend.'

'He's a good chap, Dad,' said Alexander, and he told his father about the time that Sam had rescued a boy from the river, and how he punched the boxing champion who was making fun of a boy who stuttered. 'He makes everyone laugh,' he said. 'Even the sergeant-major.'

'I'm sure he does,' said his father, and he knocked his pipe against the concrete post of the garden fence. 'Let's go inside,' he said, though he could not have been unaware that Alexander had more to say.

On the next day Alexander went to the Beckwiths' house. It was not the same as it had been before he went away. New paper covered the walls of the hall, and the pictures of the Cornish harbour and the bullfight had been taken down. The furniture in the living room was different: the cushions of the new settee and armchairs were perfectly flat, as if nobody had yet sat on them; the ship's-wheel clock had gone, as had the glass-fronted cabinet with the two shelves of books; heavy new curtains framed the windows, their folds as hard and regular as plaster mouldings.

Alexander scanned the lifeless room. 'I'll make some tea,' Megan suggested. 'You two go on out. I'll bring it to you.'

Mr Beckwith led Alexander into the garden. They stopped in front of the central flowerbed, by a rectangle of green canvas on which lay the shears and a pair of scissors. A purple and scarlet fuchsia lolled over the step to the shed, and a Spanish broom now masked the water butt.

'Looks nice,' Alexander remarked. Mr Beckwith gave him a look that had nothing in it. 'I miss this as much as anything,' Alexander was about to say, but he prevented himself and said instead: 'My parents send their best wishes.'

'Thank you,' replied Mr Beckwith. He glanced towards the French windows. 'Haven't seen them for a while,' he said.

'You're welcome any time, my mother said to tell you.'

'Good of her,' said Mr Beckwith.

'Give them a call one weekend,' Alexander said.

'Aye,' said Mr Beckwith. Staring at the ground, he stirred a fingertip on the creases of his brow. 'Thank you for coming round,' he said.

'I like coming here,' Alexander replied.

Briefly an exhausted smile appeared on Mr Beckwith's face. 'Must get this done,' he said, picking up the scissors.

'Shall I help you?' Alexander asked.

'Only a one-man job, this one,' said Mr Beckwith.

Megan came out of the house and set the tray on the canvas. 'Staying for a while?' she asked. In her voice there was no clue as to her wishes. Mr Beckwith was walking the lawn's perimeter; he lifted a sawdust-coloured petal from the soil beneath the rose bush.

'Not for much longer,' Alexander replied.

'I've got stuff to do,' said Megan, taking a mug from the tray. 'Sorry,' she said, and she looked at him as she blew across the steaming tea. 'But come up before you leave, won't you? I'm in my room.'

Alexander walked around the garden while Mr Beckwith worked. Neither of them spoke for five minutes. 'I was thinking of our holiday in Cornwall,' Alexander then remarked, though this was not true. 'Remember the drunkards in the churchyard?'

'Aye,' said Mr Beckwith, but in the tone of 'No'.

Alexander surveyed the garden again, and saw Megan at her window, turning back into her room.

'You've better things to do,' said Mr Beckwith. 'Go up now, why don't you? Come back and say goodbye. I'll be here.'

Megan was waiting for him at the bottom of the stairs, holding a book on her knees in such a way that Alexander imagined her as the custodian of a secret society and the book as its list of rules and regulations. 'You OK?' she asked.

'Ready for battle at a moment's notice,' he said.

'That's not what I meant,' she said. 'I meant, are you OK with this?' She took one hand off the book and made a gesture that swooped around the hallway.

'I think so. Should I have stayed away?'

'Like everyone else? No,' she said, and she looked strongly at him. 'I'm glad you didn't.'

Alexander cupped his hand around the newel post, as though it were Megan's face that he was touching. 'What's the book?' he asked. She showed him the title, but it made no sense to him. 'Are you OK, Megan?' he asked.

'We'll cope. Don't worry about us.'

'You sure?'

'Sure. Don't worry.'

'How's university?'

'It's fine,' was all she said, but he could tell that it was better than she would admit to him. 'How's the army?'

'Awful,' he said.

'Really?' she asked, and she seemed concerned for him.

'Not cut out for it,' said Alexander. 'Give me a quiet life any day.'

Megan stood up and put a hand on his shoulder. 'Poor soldier boy,' she said, and she rubbed the cropped hair on the back of his head. 'Let's meet before you go back. Not here, though. I'll try to come over to your house.'

But the last day of his visit came, and he had heard nothing more from her. In the afternoon he saw *Room at the Top* at a cinema up in town, and walked back all the way, from Waterloo to Borough, on through Bermondsey and down Jamaica Road, then up the hill to the Heath. He considered calling at Megan's house, and the thought was still in his mind when he found himself at Sidney Dixon's shop. A stirrup-shaped brass knocker had been attached to the side door that led to Sidney's flat. Alexander rapped on the door and above his head a window rattled. 'Who's that?' Alexander heard, and he stood back from the door and looked up. 'My boy!' Sidney shouted. 'One minute!'

In Sidney's front room they shared two bottles of beer and talked about the shop and Alexander's training until the chorus of chimes under their feet announced seven o'clock. 'I'll have to get home,' said Alexander.

'The hero's send-off, eh?' Sidney jested. Alexander would always remember that he was looking out of the window when Sidney said this, and that the crack in the windowpane was so wide that he was looking through clear air at the wall above the shoe shop opposite. A train was going up to the city. 'Any idea what you'll do after?' Sidney asked.

'Haven't really thought.'

'You know you can have your old job back any time you want,' said Sidney. 'The new boy, he's all right. He'll do for now. But he's not like you. You're like family,' Sidney assured him. 'Remember what I said,' he added as he closed the door to the street. 'If you want it, it's yours.'

Alexander crossed the road, then crossed back to look into the shop. The glass shone like the surface of a dark pool. Inside, the Chesterfield gleamed like a weed-clad rock and the clock faces caught the light like sea-worn pebbles. As though peering into the water in the hope of seeing something move across the sandy bed, he stared into the space where he used to sit.

17. Welcome back, Private MacIndoe

Morosely, as if they were a gang of work-shy assistants, Sidney inspected the rolled-up rugs that leaned against the wall. 'We've got to get this stuff shifted, Alex,' he complained. 'Look at it. Nothing's moved for days. Nothing. Not a single damned thing.' His galoshes squelched on the waterlogged carpet as he crept behind the wall of wardrobes and tallboys.

'Don't worry, Sidney,' said Alexander, dredging a handful of cigarette cards and sweet wrappers and pencil shavings from the back of the desk's upper drawer. 'Things will improve.'

A door clicked open and clicked shut. 'You could grow potatoes in the muck back here.' Sidney reappeared, displaying a smudge of filth on the end of an index finger that was as pink as an earthworm.

'We'll sort things out, don't worry,' Alexander assured him.

'It's meant to be a shop, for Christ's sake, not a bloody museum,' Sidney grumbled, idly dandling the label that hung from a print of the Battle of the Nile. He looked at what his finger was doing. 'What the hell?' he exclaimed. 'Two quid? Two quid? Would have stayed here till the crack of doom at that price. Bloody idiot! And God knows how many times I told him: guineas, not pounds. Always guineas. Not hard to remember, is it?' Once he had checked the price of every picture, Sidney began on the crockery and silverware. 'Oh, for Christ's sake,' he moaned at the label on a teapot that was made in the form of a thatched cottage. He lifted the lid by its chimney and waved it like a porter's bell. 'Here's another one. See the price on this? See that? I paid more than that for it. Running a bloody charity or something.' He lowered himself onto the chaise longue, and gave its tag a disgruntled glance.

'I'll fix them all before the end of the day,' Alexander volunteered, turning the pages of the ledger.

'Good lad,' Sidney smiled, but behind the stiffened skin his eyes were like nail heads.

'This appears to be well kept. Nines look like twos sometimes, but it'll be all right,' Alexander reported.

'Good lad. Job number one, that is,' Sidney intoned. He looked up from the floor, and slowly his eyes became rekindled. 'Job number two: get the desk moved up there, by the window. Get that bloody helmet out the way, and slot the desk in there. I want the punters to see what a nice boy you are. No point hiding your light under a bushel, is there?' he asked, and a smile contorted his anguished skin. 'And job number three. Out the back you'll find a few boxes. Lots of small things: tiepins, cuff-links, cameos, that sort of stuff. Put everything in the big case, Alex. Neatly, in straight lines, labels to the right. Neat as if they was new.'

It took Alexander three days to set the shop in order. Diligently he traced every item in the acquisition book, calculated the mark-up, and attached new labels to every one, writing the prices in a script as careful as that of a registrar of births. He buffed each foggy mirror and clouded pane of glass, restored the gloss to greasy veneers, eradicated the tarnish on the silverware. He glued the peeling corners of the green leather rectangle that was set into the surface of the desk, and moved the desk to its new place near the window. It was there that he was sitting, on the afternoon of the third day, when he noticed a ball of paper crumpled under the door, by the hinge. Alexander peeled it apart and read 'Welcome back, Private MacIndoe', written in pencil, in a squat, loopy handwriting that he did not recognise. The next day, at five to nine, he pushed open the shop door to see on the mat, half covered by the morning's post, a page that had been torn from a magazine. Part of a crossword puzzle was on one side, and on the other a photograph of Cary Grant and Eva Marie Saint, ringed by a circle of dark pencil. A week later, he found amid the morning's letters a sheet of paper folded precisely into quarters, with 'Its too long till Valentines Day' scribbled on the inside. Another note, soon after, had been left protruding onto the tiles of the doorstep, where the sleet had dissolved what seemed to be a piece of verse, so that Alexander could read only 'to be true' at the end of one line and 'you' at the end of the next.

The illegible note was lying on the desk, and Alexander was about to close for lunch, when Liz Gatting came into the shop. She was wearing a white cotton overall and her hair was now blonde, lying in a broad wave against the nape of her neck. The collar of her blouse lay open on a necklace of pink plastic beads that matched the colour of her lipstick. Plucked into steep wiry arches, her eyebrows gave an insolent quality to her expression, which the slight backward tilt of her head was perhaps intended to strengthen.

'Long time no see,' she greeted him, dropping her handbag onto the desk. 'How you finding Civvy Street?' She smiled at him, revealing the gap in her teeth, and her smile amused and excited Alexander, as if a masked actress had accidentally allowed him a glimpse of her face.

'So–so,' Alexander replied, suppressing a laugh. 'You a nurse now?'

Appalled, Liz clutched her hands to her throat. 'A nurse. Me? Mucky bandages? Bed pans? You've got the wrong girl.'

'What then?'

'Receptionist, Alec,' she explained. 'Like you, sort of.'

'Where?'

'The opticians, up there.' She aimed a pink fingernail at the street. 'Five minutes away. You've walked past some mornings. In a world of your own. Can I?' she asked, and she sat down on the chaise longue.

Together they tallied the schoolfriends who had left or were no longer friends. 'I reckon John Halloran's gone,' Alexander told her, and he recounted the conversation that he had sensed would be their last. 'Paul Malinowski's still around, though.'

'Don't know him.'

'And Mick Radford?'

'Tough guy, yes.'

'He's stuck around.'

'Nowhere else would have him,' said Liz. 'But I'll tell you something. A real shocker,' she said eagerly, balancing on the very edge of the seat. 'Jenny Stanthorpe. Little Miss Proper.' Sarcastically she clasped her hands together and regarded Alexander with a demure and saintly gaze. 'Mother opens the door one evening. Big black boy in motorbike gear standing there. Asks is Jennifer in. All polite like. Quick as a flash, Little Miss comes running out the house, jumps on the back of his bike, and they're off into the sunset at ninety miles an hour. Right palaver there was. Her mum screaming blue murder in the road, boys

154

in blue on the scene. Nothing they can do, though, is there? Twenty-one, can do as she likes. Not as if she was kidnapped. Two weeks later the parents get a note. Sorry it had to be like this, I thought you'd never understand. Too right they wouldn't. Run off with a Zulu, far as they were concerned. A boxer, someone said he was.' Liz examined her fingernails and stood up. 'Some people get all the excitement, don't they?' she said, flattening the creases of the overall on her hips. 'None for the likes of us, I tell you. Surgical supports and aspirin all day for me; busted chairs and old junk for you.' She picked up a battered old cricket bat. 'Must be going. See you tomorrow?' she proposed, and as she swung the bat her ankles and stilettos made a shape that brought to Alexander's mind his mother and Mrs Beckwith, walking arm in arm away from him towards the wet pavement outside the Dome of Discovery.

Every day she came to the shop at one o'clock, and he would put the sign on the door and walk up the hill with her, to the café by the concert hall. They sat on tall stools at the yellow Formica table that ran along the window, by the blackboard on which the menu was written every day, though the dishes on offer never changed. She would tell him about her morning's customers, then he would try to make a story out of his, if there had been any. Through the musty net curtains they watched the street as they ate their sandwiches. She had nicknames for the housewives they saw most often: Mrs How Much? haggled with the assistants in the grocer's and the butcher's; Mrs Must Be Going always seemed impatient to get away from the conversations she herself had initiated; Mrs Dog's Best Friend had a Highland terrier that travelled in a wheeled wicker basket with her shopping; Mrs Doomed was never seen to smile. 'Twenty years time, that's me,' said Liz, as Mrs Make An Effort replenished her lipstick at the bus stop, grasping her umbrella and her open compact in the same hand. 'And where are you?' she asked herself, and she stood on the struts of the stool to scan the hill. 'There,' she decided, pointing to the newspaper that hid from view the sole passenger on the upper deck of the bus that was pulling in to collect Mrs Make An Effort.

One day, shortly before Christmas, one o'clock passed and Liz Gatting had not arrived. For a quarter of an hour Alexander kept a lookout from the doorway, but she did not appear. He kept the shop open, and set to work logging some recently bought pieces into the book, transcribing the dates and prices from Sidney's slips of paper. Two o'clock passed. He went to the door again. From a shelf of cheaper items he picked up a battered fob watch that might have been in the shop since his first day there. The watch's case was as dull as mortar. He took it into the back room, put a dab of polish on a cloth, and began to work the sheen back into the brass. Mrs Daniel – Mrs Must Be Going – it was who came into the shop then, leaving the door ajar. 'Just enquiring,' she said. 'I've gone and broken a cup, and I do so want to replace it. Used to be a popular pattern, I believe. So my husband says.' From her handbag she extracted a linen handkerchief, folded into a triangular shape. As though unwrapping a wren's egg, she peeled back the fabric from an eye-sized fragment of china. 'Would it be familiar to you?' she asked, tracing with a fingernail the tendril of orange vine that was painted on the china.

'Hard to say for certain. Not much to go on here, to be perfectly frank with you, Mrs Daniel.' He put down the watch and plucked the shard from the handkerchief. His face assumed an expert's seriousness, but he could think of nothing to say.

'Should I bring a bigger piece? Might that be of assistance?'

'It would be an idea, Mrs Daniel.'

'Yes, it would. That's what I'll do, then. But in the meantime, if you do happen to see anything like it, you will let me know, won't you?'

'Indeed I shall,' said Alexander, and he escorted Mrs Daniel to the door.

He retrieved the watch, put a thumbnail into the notch of the casing and prised the cover open. He turned the winder and raised the watch to his ear; its escapement made a noise like the splintering of a small bone. He was watching the tiny ace of spades at the end of the minute hand move over the pillars of the roman three when his fingertip found, on the reverse of the watch, a smaller indentation by which a second lid was opened. It covered nothing but a back of smooth brass. He was about to close this purposeless lid when he noticed a mark on its inner surface. It was a name, scratched unevenly into the metal rather than engraved, and the name was Simon Ordish. Alexander repeated the words aloud, and then, in the silence of the shop, they repeated themselves to him, over and over again, as if they were imprisoned within his mind, and were seeking the meaning that would give them liberty. He bolted the front door and turned off the lights in the shop; he locked the cash box and stowed it in the safe. And then, as he closed the lid of the pianola, he recalled seeing the name Ordish written on a medicine bottle in the rubble of the Doodle-bug House.

When Liz arrived he was still holding the watch. 'Miss me?' she asked. She unbuttoned her red coat and held it open. 'You like? My mum's, but she got too fat for it. Stylish, no?'

'It's lovely,' he said.

'So why the face?'

'This is very peculiar,' he told her, putting the watch on the desk.

She sat on the edge of the desk and held the watch up, like a nurse taking a reading from a thermometer. 'It's stopped,' she said. 'Nothing strange about that. It's a crappy old broken watch.'

'No, but I know the house it came from. I used to play in it when I was a kid,' he said, and he told her about the Doodlebug House.

'And here it is in a junk shop,' said Liz, shrugging her shoulders.

'But it's strange it's turned up here, don't you think?'

'Got to end up somewhere, Alec. You've got a lump of junk from every house between here and Luton. If there wasn't something from that place, that'd be really amazing.'

'I think it's peculiar it's ended up back with me.'

'If you say so,' said Liz, looking at him as if he were an entertainingly dogged child. 'You shutting up shop now?'

'In a bit,' he replied, having consulted the clocks.

'Waiting for the last-minute rush, eh?' she teased. 'Go on, be a devil. Lock up half an hour early and you can walk me home.'

Alexander opened the cash book and unscrewed the ink bottle to refill his pen. 'Fifteen minutes,' he told her. She eased herself down from the desk.

At that moment the doorbell rang and a man wearing tweeds and a deerstalker hat came in. He had bulging blue eyes and his face was covered in claret capillaries, like minuscule rivulets streaming from his cheeks. 'Interested in something I saw in your window last week,' he said. 'Decanter. Crystal. Silver collar,' he explained. 'Seems to have gone.'

'It has, sir. Sold it last week, I'm afraid. We do have others, however.' He indicated a group of decanters, arrayed on the bottom tier of a cake stand, close to where Liz was standing.

The man looked at Liz, then at the decanters, then mistrustfully at Alexander. 'Sold, you say?'

'Sir. Last week. But do take a look.' Alexander preceded his customer to the stand, and bent down to admire the bottles.

Liz wandered down the aisle of carpets, humming 'He'll Have To Go' as though it were a cheerful song. 'Still got that kettle out the back, Alec?' she called to him.

'I think this one is most similar,' said Alexander, raising the decanter in his palm. Above the sound of the running water, he heard Liz complaining quietly: 'The decenter's gorn, it hes.'

'No, no,' said the customer. 'Not at all similar. No substitute at all.' He looked at the pictures on the wall, at the row of clocks, at Alexander's desk, and seemed to see evidence of poor character in everything he saw. 'Good day to you, young man,' he said. He closed the door with significant firmness.

Liz strode purposefully into the shop and stopped in front of Alexander. In a pompous, matronly voice she said: 'I am interested in something I saw in the window of your establishment, young man.'

'And what might that be, madam?' Alexander enquired.

She reached into her coat and produced a sprig of mistletoe, and pressed her open mouth to his. 'No more dealings with the public today, that's what I say. Go and lock up. Kettle's boiling,' she said, and shoved him towards the door.

When Alexander returned to the back room her blouse was hanging on the chair by the radiator and she was sitting on the threadbare settee with her arms crossed over her chest. 'Locked and bolted?' she asked.

'Locked and bolted.'

'The light?' she said. 'Don't want to make a spectacle of ourselves.' Alexander's fingertips skimmed the wall and pinched the steel bud of the light switch. It snapped like a mousetrap. 'Come on,' she said, and she raised her arms to him. She closed her eyes and kissed him, delicately, as if she had become the one who was being seduced. Her hand touched his chest and he felt the skin of his entire body become tight, and a sound like the shriek of a flock of starlings raced into and out of his hearing. Her lips touched his ear and she said his name, as though each of its four syllables were a new sound to her. 'You are lovely,' she whispered, and she guided his hand to her back. 'A lovely boy,' she sighed.

They fell asleep under his coat, and it was eight o'clock when they awoke. They dressed in the darkness of the back room, and passed through the darkened shop like burglars. While he locked the door Liz waited for him on the other side of the street, rummaging in her handbag.

'I'll walk you home,' he said to her.

'That's kind of you, Mr MacIndoe,' she said. 'Because at the moment I'm not sure where my house is.'

They walked together, not speaking, as far as the street before the one in which she lived.

'See you tomorrow?' he said.

'I should think so,' she said.

'Lunchtime?'

'Who can tell?' she replied enigmatically, shaking a curl down over one eye. She took two steps back from him. 'I meant it, you know,' she said, and then she turned and hurried home.

Alexander's mother called from the living room as he was hanging his coat in the hall. 'In the oven. Burned to a cinder.' Under an upturned plate he found a pork chop and half a dozen wrinkled sprouts and a pair of cracked potatoes. His mother eventually came into the kitchen. She watched him eat for a minute. 'Anything to report?' she asked.

'Sold a chair and a couple of pictures.'

'That all?'

'That's all,' he said. His mother looked at him and left the room.

On her way to the bathroom, in her dressing gown, she came into his room. 'Who is it, Alexander?' she asked, resignedly.

'Who's what?' he replied. He interposed a shirt between his face and hers.

'Please don't try to be clever, Alexander. It doesn't suit you. Who is she?'

'Don't understand, Mum.'

His mother snatched the shirt and threw it onto the floor. 'I can see it in your eyes, you stupid boy. I can smell her on you,' she said, her fury rising. Alexander looked at his mother, trying to divine how much she had guessed. 'Who is she?' she asked again.

No name except the true one would come to him. 'Elizabeth,' he said. 'Liz.'

'Liz who? There're a lot of Lizzes in the world. It's a common name.'

'Liz Gatting.'

'Do I know her?'

'Used to be in Megan's year.'

'I can't picture her. Describe her.' Alexander described Liz Gatting. 'What does she do?' his mother demanded.

'Works in the optician's, near the shop.'

His mother retied the belt of her dressing gown. 'Gangly girl?' she asked.

'She's tall, yes.'

'Peroxide blonde? Brassy?'

'She's fair-haired.'

A flinch of disgust raised a corner of his mother's mouth. 'I know the one. You can do better than that, Alexander.'

'What do you mean by that?'

'You know what I mean.'

'You don't even know her.'

'I know enough.'

'You don't know her,' he stated. 'You didn't even know who I meant when I told you who she was.'

'I know who she is,' said his mother emphatically, opening the door. 'Don't you go doing anything irresponsible. We don't want a girl like that getting her claws into you.'

'Girl like what?' Alexander shouted.

'A girl like that.'

Almost every word of this bickering would be remembered by Alexander for many years, as would his feeling, as he lay on his bed, still dressed, after his parents had turned out their light, that he was no longer the person to whom this room belonged. And he would never forget reaching for the lamp beside his bed and discovering the dust of dried blood under the nails of his right hand, nor the silhouette of Liz's neck and the thin curved shadows of her ribs in the watery grey light from the street.

18. A Name You Can Trust

It was a humid evening around the middle of August, as Alexander would remember, because the Berlin Wall had gone up, and it was still the main story in the papers.

He sat at the bar in the saloon of the George, waiting for Sam Saunders. The landlord's daughter came round the front of the bar, carrying a watering can, and he watched her through the open window as she watered a basket of geraniums that hung from a bracket on the signpost. Every table was occupied, and Mick Radford was in one of the groups.

'How's things, Monty?' Mick asked when he came up to the bar, at the same time beckoning the barmaid with a folded banknote.

'OK,' said Alexander. 'Yourself?'

'Mustn't grumble,' said Mick, and he ordered his round. 'Work all right?' he asked, glancing from the stream of beer to Alexander.

'It's fine,' said Alexander. 'And you? What are you up to?'

'Bit of this, bit of that,' said Mick. He ground his cigarette stub into the chipped glass ashtray. 'Thirsty weather, eh?'

'It is,' Alexander agreed.

'Be good,' said Mick, lifting the tray of drinks. 'See you around.'

'And you,' Alexander replied, and that was the end of the first conversation he had with Mick Radford that year.

Sam punched Alexander lightly between the shoulderblades and planted his elbow on a saturated beer mat. 'What you should know, Al, is that I have already taken a considerable quantity of drink and I intend to take a good deal more.' He slicked his moustache with the ball of a thumb, and smacked his lips like a pantomime glutton. 'Professional obligation, old man. My colleagues cannot bear to see a sober man after seven o'clock. Makes them suspect he might be happier than they are. Cheers, and may the good Lord bless you.' Alexander fitted a pint into the receptive curve of Sam's hand. 'How are things in the mausoleum?'

'Uneventful,' said Alexander, having guessed that Sam's day had not been.

'A laugh and a half I've had,' Sam duly told him. 'Behold,' he grinned. His left hand rose from his pocket and flopped palm upwards on the bar, presenting half a dozen stigmata, ranged in a quarter-circle. 'And a matching set,' Sam boasted, turning his hand to show a rake of scarlet weals. 'First martyr of insurance I am. Saint Samuel Saunders of South London, patron saint of all who struggle for their daily commission.' In a single draught he swallowed half his pint.

'Let's hear it, then.'

'You know what did this?' Sam demanded. 'You want to know? This big it was.' He slanted an arm downwards, swivelled and slipped off the stool. 'This big,' he insisted, levelling a hand beside Alexander's ankle. 'Like a bottle of pop with legs and hair. And teeth. Boggle-eyed little freak. Looked like it had been throttled to within an inch of its life and stuck like it.' Dreamily Sam contemplated his punctured skin. 'Doggie comes skipping down the stairs and stops six steps from the bottom. Rule one: if they've got a pet, be very nice to it, however repulsive the beast is. So I put the hand out. Tickle the little bastard between the ears. Sod took off like a rocket. The fangs go right in. Sharp as a bloody sewing machine, I tell you, and tight as a limpet. The old dear has to prise its jaws off with a spoon. Blood all over the place. "I'm so sorry, Mr Saunders," she says.'

'"He's never done that before,"' Alexander joined in.

'Exactly. "Can't think what came over him." Utterly mystified, she is. But, ever the professional, I seize the initiative. I have her on my side. She feels guilty. I'm magnanimous. "It's nothing," I assure her, all noble like. "Occupational hazard." And then the stroke of inspiration. "But see how easily accidents can happen, Mrs Jarvis. Out of the blue: snap! The jaws of fate." I give her the meaningful stare. The Moment of Truth look. Ten minutes later, she signs.' Triumphantly Sam raised his glass and chinked it on Alexander's. 'You are in the presence of a master. No point making out otherwise. Sam Saunders could sell life insurance to Jesus Christ Almighty. Contents policy to a monk. You should give it a go, Al. Make more than you're getting from Sid's place.' Alexander made a gesture of demurral. 'I mean it. A mint you'd make, with your mug. Charm the chequebooks out of their handbags.'

'Can't do the spiel like you, Sam.'

'No need to do much of that if they like you. Let them natter, that's what you do. That's all a lot of them want. A change from the same old faces, day in day out. You'd make a very nice change, and you're a good listener. All you've got to do is learn a few lines. Recite the script and be pleasant.'

'It's not for me. Really, it's not.'

'Good money, mate. Good money.' Sam smiled regretfully at the floor, as if looking at a heap of cash that Alexander was spurning. He flicked his empty glass to make it ring. 'You could do with it, Al. It's about time you got a place of your own. Nice folks, your mum and dad, but they're still your mum and dad. Know what I'm saying?'

'Time to move on,' Alexander replied. 'I know, Sam. But I can't do what you're doing.'

'Squandering himself,' Sam told the barmaid, and he took a new pint from her. 'Whereas I, on the other hand, am doing some very tasty business.' Having waited until the barmaid was out of earshot, he propped his elbow on the bar and his head on his palm, and slid closer to Alexander. 'Imagine Shirley MacLaine, if you will, but with a bigger frontage in the upper storey. See that, can you? Well, that's the very tasty business I've been doing,' he confided, with a slow, suave smile. 'That's Pauline Alford.' Sam paused, relishing the vision he had invoked for himself; his sleeve slid back along the bar, dragging through a spill of beer. 'Mrs Pauline Alford,' he added, hooding his eyes lasciviously.

Rather than look at Sam, Alexander took out a cigarette and turned to the barmaid for a light.

'Shocked you, haven't I?' asked Sam.

'No,' said Alexander.

'Oh yes I have.'

'No,' said Alexander. 'You haven't. But I wish you'd kept it to yourself.'

'Can't keep it to myself. That's the problem.' A laugh passed quickly across his face, then he looked at Alexander, severe as a magistrate. 'You need to live a bit, Al. Nice girl, your Liz. But there's a lot more to life than holding hands with the girl next door. Know what I mean?'

'She's a nice girl, like you say,' said Alexander plainly.

Sam withdrew his smile and set his glass on the bar, as if replacing something that did not belong to him. 'Meant no offence, Al,' he said, putting a hand on Alexander's shoulder. 'I'm sorry, mate. I'm drunk as a skunk. Let's change the subject.'

'Agreed,' said Alexander, offering a cigarette.

Nothing of the remainder of their conversation would stay for long in Alexander's memory, but he would remember standing in the car park at closing time and Sam taking out a card with the slogan "A Name You Can Trust" below his name, and hugging him as he cried out: 'Save me from myself, Father MacIndoe, for I have sinned.' And he would remember Sam climbing aboard a bus that Alexander realised, as it turned at the traffic lights, was not the one that Sam should have taken. He watched the bus until its roof went under the hill and then he turned to walk home, treading the joints of the paving stones.

Alexander was still within sight of the pub when he heard someone say, behind him, as if making a remark to a companion: 'I'll have whatever you've got.' Listening for the reply, Alexander kept walking. 'Talking to you,' said the same voice, more loudly. Something struck his back and there was the tick of a stone on the pavement. A second stone skittered into the road.

He was a few years younger than Alexander and was wearing a royal blue V-neck jumper under a black leather jacket. A white comb stuck out from behind one ear. His blond quiff bobbed like a little springboard. 'I said, I'll have whatever you've got.' The unfastened buckles of his crocodile shoes made a chinking sound as he shifted his feet.

'Who, me?' Alexander replied.

'No one else here, is there?' said the boy, looking around.

'I suppose not.'

'So what have you got? For a quid I won't kick your head in.'

'Do I know you?' asked Alexander in panic.

'Do I know you?' mimicked the boy, with a prissy squirm of his lips.

'I'm sorry,' said Alexander, thrusting a hand into a pocket and feeling only coppers. 'I don't have much on me.'

'What a pity,' said the boy. He brought a hand forward and hand-cuffed its wrist with his fingers. For half a minute he contemplated

Alexander; a developing thought brought a look of satisfaction to his face. 'You,' he said, 'you're a fucking poof. That's what you are.'

'I'm what?'

'I'm what?' he echoed. He gave Alexander the sort of scrutiny a newly arrived prisoner might receive from a gaoler who already bore him a grudge. Mouthing his words exaggeratedly and without tone, as if addressing a lip-reader, he said: 'You. You're a queer.'

Alexander held a pool of coins on his dithering hand.

'You're a fucking ponce.' Biting his lower lip, the boy looked at the coins. 'What the fuck is that? What the fuck? Money from your ma, is it?' He swiped the hand aside, and the coins were flung into the road.

'That's all I have,' Alexander pleaded.

'Not good enough, pal.'

'Honestly, that's all I have.' Alexander turned his pockets inside out. He pointed at the road. 'That's it. Look,' he said, wringing the empty fabric.

The boy gnawed at his lip and made a moaning noise like a thwarted child. 'You're a fucking poof,' he said, with deliberation. 'You're a fucking nance.'

'Please,' said Alexander. 'This is a mistake.' A car was approaching from behind him. He dashed into the road, but before he could reach the opposite kerb he was tripped. He raised an arm into the light of the headlamps; the car passed.

The boy's eyes widened, flabbergasted at Alexander's attempt to escape. 'No mistake, pal,' he said.

Alexander saw him draw back one arm and, in the style of a fighter in a comic, clench a fist and hold it high in the air, wide of the shoulder. And then two of the distant streetlights disappeared behind the swinging arm and Alexander's cheek was hit by something that felt like a perfectly flat board, not like a hand. The blow seemed not to have hurt him. Benumbed, stupefied, he gazed at the boy as though he had been asked a question that he had not quite understood. There was the moaning noise again, and he was hit twice more. His head bounced on the road and the pain seemed to flow into him through cracks in the bone. A kick to the belly forced the air out of his body with a squeal. He curled on the road, putting his hands to his face. Cold wet

166

fingers wrenched his guard away and a fist swooped down on his temple and rose and fell again on his mouth. He cried out, but it felt as if the noise remained trapped in his head.

He was then at home, bringing his face out of the pink water that was brimming in the kitchen sink. His mother was pressing her hands to her face as if she thought he was in danger of dying. He saw someone he did not recognise and then Mick Radford.

'Smile, please,' said Mick Radford, and Alexander obeyed. 'Teeth all there. Bugger of a headache you're going to have,' Mick Radford diagnosed. 'But no serious damage. Lucky lad.'

'Cavalry arrived in the nick of time,' said the unknown friend.

'Dave, Monty. Monty, Dave,' said Mick Radford.

'Pleased to meet you,' said Dave Gordon, and Mick Radford raised the sopping flannel to Alexander's cheek.

In the morning his cheek came away from the pillow with a soft tearing sound, leaving a sticking plaster behind, in a corona of blood. He looked in the mirror on the back of his wardrobe door and saw a face that was not his face. One eye was like an overripe plum; the lips reminded him of Charles Laughton; his teeth were smeared with a brown paste. He went back to bed and slept. The door opened, and his mother came into the room, advancing reverently with a poultice and a pot of tea. He slept again, then was awoken by a sound on the landing; the sun was low and the walls were the colour of chamois leather; Megan's head appeared at the edge of the door.

'Awake?' she said. He hoisted a bandaged hand. 'Lord above, Eck,' she murmured, and she put a hand to her mouth.

'Not contagious,' he said.

'What happened?' she asked. 'Who was it?' She drew the chair to the side of the bed.

He had not seen her since the beginning of January, when they had sat for an hour in her bedroom, from which every remnant of her childhood had been expunged. The knitted doll with button eyes, which for years had sat on the sill, was no longer there. The red satchel had gone from the hook on the door. The embroidered pillowcase, the annuals with the russet cloth spines, the shoe box filled with plastic farmyard animals, the crayon portrait that a classmate had drawn when she was nine – all had gone. He had sat beside her desk, under a shelf of books, looking at a board to which were pinned photographs of her friends. Broad-striped scarves were looped around their necks, as if yoking them all together. A stone wall, like the wall of a fort, rose behind them. Midstream on a sunny river, there was a boat in which Megan was laughing at the boy who was rowing. Alexander looked at these pictures of people he had never met and would never meet, and it was as though time had become inverted: these faces were gazing at him, seeing nothing, as if he were a ghost who was looking out of a window at Megan and her friends.

Her appearance had changed since then. Her hair was now cut short as a boy's, and she was dressed like nobody else he knew would have dressed, in sky-blue capri pants and a sleeveless white shirt. She put a hand on his bruised fingers while he spoke; she was wearing a silver ring that he had never seen before.

'You've spoken to the police?'

'We had a Sergeant Willoughby here this morning.'

'What are they doing about it?'

'What they can, Meg. There's not much of a chance.'

'But you got a good look at him? If you saw him again you'd recognise him?'

'I can see him again any time I like, broad as daylight.'

'So you gave your Sergeant Willoughby a good description?'

'Of course I did. I'm not a complete idiot.'

'So they know exactly what he looks like.'

'Not really. I described him, but when he read it back to me it sounded like half the people in London,' said Alexander, turning Megan's ring. 'Let's talk about something else.'

She told him about her exams, and her summer job in the bookshop, and the flat that she and Angela and Helen had rented. With phrases that sounded practised, with gesticulations that seemed too artful, she presented to Alexander the person she had become.

'Still seeing that Liz?' she asked him, and he said that he was. 'Happy? she enquired.

'Yes,' he told her. 'Are you?'

'Yes,' she replied immediately, with certitude. 'Must be painful,' she went on, and she lifted her hand towards his swollen eye but did not touch it. She stayed for half an hour more. 'I have to get the train straight back,' she explained, and she picked a hair from the pillowcase. 'I've decided I'm going to do teacher training, Eck,' she said abruptly. 'It's time to sort out a career. I'll be going to Leeds, probably.' She took her hand from his and looked out of the window. 'I'll tell you more next time.' Simulating tiredness, he closed his eyes and smiled. Megan kissed him fleetingly.

Two days later Liz returned from holiday. 'Baby boy,' she called him, pityingly, when she came into the front room. She stood beside his father, and together they assessed his condition. 'Fresh air might do him some good,' she said, turning to his father.

'Indeed it may,' said his father with a sideways glance.

'All right if I take your son for a walk, Mrs MacIndoe?' Liz asked.

'Of course, dear. I don't know why you ask,' his mother replied, taking up her magazine.

'He hasn't got the key of the door yet, Mrs MacIndoe. Go through the proper channels and all that.'

'Permission granted,' his father told her. 'Come back to eat with us, Liz? Rations served at six-thirty.'

'Don't forget Megan said she'll ring after work,' his mother called when they were in the hall.

Liz waited until they were walking along the main avenue in the park. 'Megan will ring after work? Explain, please,' she said, making him halt by hooking his arm.

'She came to see how I was,' said Alexander. 'Dad called her, and she came up for the afternoon. That's all.'

'That's all?' Liz repeated furiously.

'Well, yes.'

'That's all? Florence bloody Nightingale, is it?'

'It was good of her, I thought.'

'Doesn't miss a trick that one, does she? Quick as a rat up a drainpipe. Mop your fevered brow, did she?'

'She's family, practically,' said Alexander.

'Like I'm Princess Margaret, practically.'

'No, Liz, she is. We grew up together.'

'No, you didn't,' said Liz. 'You've never grown up.' She began to walk away. 'She's a bit of skirt, Alec. Not little goody-two-shoes. She's the same as me.'

169

'Liz,' said Alexander, weakly.

'Don't you bloody Liz me.' She shook her hair as though to shake off a bothersome insect.

Alexander followed her to the statue of General Wolfe. Sullenly she picked at the shrapnel holes in the base of the monument, and then she turned to face him. 'But how would you like it?' she demanded.

'I wouldn't,' he admitted.

'It's not fair, Alec.'

'I'm sorry,' he said.

'You're not,' she told him. He took a step towards her. 'Leave me alone,' she said.

He took another step. 'I'm sorry, Liz. I am,' he said.

She put a cool hand on his face and looked at him. 'It's like you've got a mask on. You can tell what people are like when they've got a mask on, because you can only see their eyes.'

'And what am I like?' he asked.

Liz stared into his eyes as if peering through a chink in a curtain. 'You're a dishonest boy,' she said.

'I am?'

'You're not to be trusted.'

'Not so,' he appealed.

'You're unfaithful,' she said, and she kissed him.

'I'm not,' he said.

'Yes, you are.' She kissed him again. 'You are.'

19. Edie the WAAF

The shop became overgrown; its contents rising nearer to the ceiling week by week and narrowing the tracks between the furniture. Alexander's desk became enclosed within a grotto of coat-stands and stacked dining chairs and standard lamps with fringes of dusty braid. Three pianos formed a cul-de-sac near the door to the back room. Cushions and hat boxes rose like enormous toadstools on top of the two Utility wardrobes. Occasional tables, suitcases, model ships, tapestries, typewriters, irons, kettles, roller skates, games sets and books crammed the windows. To make more room, Alexander was told to dismantle the long display case. A family of armchairs soon took its place, and trays of jewellery and trinkets and timepieces were piled onto the seats and under them.

'Look at this place, Alec. Just look at it,' he would remember Liz complaining as she smacked the side of the old gramophone. 'Does anything ever leave this dump?' With distaste she lifted from the shelves a bundle of bone-handled knives, a set of initialled silver napkin rings, a gravy boat, a set of tortoiseshell hair brushes. She took a pinch of needles from the small steel well by the arm of the gramophone, sprinkled them on the platter's brown felt mat, and cranked the machine into motion to spin the needles off. 'Any ideas for tonight?' she asked, as had become her habit.

'Not yet,' he replied.

'I'll have a think,' she said, disdainfully inspecting a china bust of Wellington. She went into the back room, where she would sit for much of each Saturday afternoon, reading the magazines that Alexander's mother had discarded. After an hour or so she would emerge to complain that she was bored, or to put a 78 on the gramophone, or stand in the doorway, with her arms folded, as though it were the fault of the people in the street that time was passing so slowly.

Sometimes he would suggest that she should come back nearer to closing time, but she would always remain with him throughout the afternoon, for a reason that he never suspected until a day on which he went into the back room to find her kneeling on the arm of the settee, her face against the leather-coloured mesh that covered the speaker of the big radio. As if she had not noticed him, she twirled the tuning dial, raising a flutter of voices in different languages. 'What's wrong?' he asked her.

'Nothing's wrong,' she said airily, and turned the dial one degree, then another, then another, like a safe-breaker. Alexander watched the cursor creep under the serried names on the glass panel above the dial. The small recessed window of green glass in the corner of the radio brightened as a French voice came into focus.

'What's he saying?'

'Not a clue,' she replied, and turned up the volume.

'Liz, what's up?' he asked. 'Turn that off, will you? Neither of us can understand it, so what's the point?'

'It's educational. And a bit of company.'

'I have to work, Liz.'

'Oh yes,' she said. 'You have to work. Silly me.'

'I do,' he protested.

'Work, he calls it,' Liz muttered to the radio.

'Liz, what's the matter?'

As if breaking something out of spite, she switched the radio off. 'Alec, do you think I got off the last banana boat or something? Think I'm an idiot? Do you?'

'You'll have to give me a clue, Liz. I don't know what you're on about.'

'Look, I've been stuck back here for, what, two and a half hours?'

'About that. But you don't have to sit around if you don't want to. I'm not forcing you.'

'Not the point I'm making, Alec. I've been in here for more than two hours. Quite a few people have been in and out in that time. Half a dozen at least. What are the two things that all of them have in common? Every single person who's come in through that door, bar none. Go on. Have a go.' Alexander began inwardly to recount the afternoon, but she interrupted the roll-call of faces. 'Jesus, Alec, how slow can a boy be? Number one: they've all got these,' she shouted at him, grasping her breasts. 'Are you following me so far?'

'Yes.'

'Good. Number two: not one of them gets her purse out. I'm right, aren't I? All women, yes?'

'Now you mention it.'

'And every one of them goes away empty-handed, yes?'

'Right.'

'They mooch around for a while and then they bugger off. Having bought not a thing?'

'One way of putting it, I suppose.'

'And what does that tell you? What conclusion do we draw from a procession of women who don't seem interested in buying anything? Come on, Alec. It's not a case for Sherlock Holmes.' The chain of the shop door rattled.

'I'd better go,' said Alexander.

'I'm not budging from back here, Alec, I'll tell you that. Turn my back and one of those cows will be in like I don't know what.'

When he returned to the back room she was sitting on the floor, her ankles crossed and her knees pulled up to her chin, with an open copy of the *Sunday Times* colour section balanced on her head, like a sou'wester. 'Cow gone?' she enquired.

'Was a male cow. An elderly male cow. Didn't buy anything.'

'They're the worst. Can't get enough of you, the old boys.' She made a winsome pout for him, and the magazine slipped down her back. 'I'm sorry, Alec,' she said. 'What can I do to make it up to you?' He crouched beside her and she kissed him vehemently; her fingers freed the buttons of his shirt, quickly, as though shelling peas from a pod.

She always took her bracelet off and placed it on the mat of flattened cardboard boxes under the settee, as he would recall, and for a time there was a burgundy velvet curtain that served as their bedsheet. On the draining board there sat a TV, a set so decrepit that no picture would appear until, after five minutes, figures like reflections in a pool of dirty oil would begin to emerge. For half an hour or more they would watch it, even though the sound was so muffled it seemed to be coming from another room, and sometimes if it had not been for the sound they would not have known if it was a car chase or a variety show they were watching. 'So what'll we do?' Liz would sooner or later ask, and then they would go dancing in Lewisham or up in Soho, or go to the cinema, or to a pub. They saw *Breakfast at Tiffany's* together, and he would remember standing at the bottom of Regent Street, and Liz saying to him: 'Audrey Hepburn, she your type of girl? Fragile and sweet. That your type?'

'I don't have a type,' he told her..

'Rather have Marilyn Monroe or Sophia Loren, would you? Come on, tell me, Alec. I won't mind.'

'They're not real,' he said, and he tried to take her hand as they waited to cross Piccadilly.

'Audrey Hepburn's too soppy, isn't she? Needs a square meal inside her,' she said, and for a second there was an inertness in her eyes, as if a sense of pointlessness had momentarily overcome her.

'I already said, Liz. I don't have a type,' said Alexander.

'Everybody has a type. Be chaos otherwise, wouldn't it? I've got a type.'

'Oh yes?'

'Same type as most girls. Dark and handsome. Cary Grant, Dirk Bogarde, Alexander MacIndoe. That type.' She tucked a hand under his arm and pressed her face to his shoulder. 'What about your other girlfriends?' she asked 'What were they like?'

'What other girlfriends?'

'When you were in the army. Every soldier had a girl. You must have had one. You can tell me now.'

'There's nothing to tell.'

'Come on. Don't be shy. You don't get to kiss like that without practice.'

So they sat on the grass in Green Park and Alexander told her about the regimental dance before Christmas, when the WAAFs were brought in by bus and everyone got drunk. Two signalmen had a fight over a WAAF officer; the next day they were ordered to load a sack of rice using teaspoons. Alexander ended up with a girl called Edie under the stage while the band – Mick Michaels' Mad Men – was playing a set of Bill Haley numbers. 'The drummer knocked his beer over and it was leaking through the boards onto Edie's neck,' he lied, and he continued with the tale of Sam Saunders and the WAAF named Edie, taking Sam's role in the story.

'Bet she still thinks about you,' said Liz. She glanced at him and her mouth alone smiled.

'I doubt it,' said Alexander, gazing up through a plane tree's branches at an aeroplane's condensation trail.

With a thumb she brushed the skin above his collar, and she kissed his neck. 'I love you,' she said, as if she were reminding him of a loan. 'You're never going to say you love me, I know. But you like being with me, I know that too.'

'I do.'

'Always?'

'Always.'

A cyclist rode past them, he would always remember, and the loose chain-guard made a dismal clank with every turn of the pedals. Alexander looked at Liz's hands as they lay loosely meshed on her lap. A gust of damp air passed over them, and he knew that they would soon be finished.

A walk through Greenwich Park, on a Sunday afternoon two months later, was the end. They had walked in silence from the Heath gate to the summit of the steepest path. 'What do you want to do?' she asked him, surveying the river from the top of the hill.

The water shone like crinkled cellophane; over the north of the city, the clouds were thick and white and churned; to the west, the clouds were nothing but scratches on the sky. 'We are doing something,' he replied.

'What's that then?' she asked.

'What everyone's doing,' he explained, gesturing at the whole park.

'Walking and breathing. Bloody hell. The excitement.'

'It's more than that, Liz. It's enjoying the day.'

Liz inspected the park, like a hotel guest dismissing the inferior accommodation she was being asked to accept as a substitute for the room she had booked.

'But it's wonderful,' Alexander urged her. 'All of London laid out. Look there.' A damburst of sunlight sped down distant Hampstead Heath and coursed over the city's streets.

'I'm fed up, Alec. I'm going home.'

'OK. I think I'll stay here for a bit.'

'Suit yourself. I'm going down the George tonight. Jill said she'd be there. You coming?'

'Not this evening.'

She was standing a pace away from him. Her hands fidgeted on her hips and she looked at him as if he were holding up a picture in front of his face and asking her what she thought of it. 'Ah well,' she sighed. Still she looked fixedly at him. 'That's not what you mean, is it? You mean not this evening and not any other evening.' Her expression was one of profound disappointment rather than distress, and when she started crying it was as if for something that had happened a long time ago. 'See you later,' she said, walking away.

'See you later,' Alexander agreed.

Halfway down the path, Liz stopped and turned. 'You look great, Alec, but something's peculiar with you. Sometimes it's like you're the oldest boy in London.' She walked under the canopy of the trees and into the lower part of the park, and Alexander watched her until she was gone.

He made no mention of their separation to his mother nor to his father, until the evening, more than a month later, on which his father commented, as an aside, 'Bachelor again, I take it?' and Alexander took the laden dinner plates from him and merely nodded in reply. He said nothing to Sam Saunders for several weeks, but he told Sidney Dixon within a few days. He was cleaning the piano keys with a rag and a saucer of milk when he noticed, through the spars of a ladder-back chair, that Sidney was standing in the street, looking gloomily at the things in the window. Alexander walked to the door.

'All right, Sid?' he asked.

'Right as rain,' said Sidney, but his gaze did not move from the window. 'Come on up, when you've done the books,' he added. 'Let's have a talk.'

President Kennedy was talking on the television when Alexander went up to Sidney's flat. Sidney patted the arm of the vacant chair; without talking, they listened to the President. 'What do you reckon, Sid?' Alexander asked when the broadcast was over and Sidney had turned the television off.

'Bound to happen sooner or later. If not Cuba, then Berlin. If not Berlin, somewhere else.'

'Yes, but what's going to happen?' asked Alexander, hearing a passing lorry's growl as the noise of a bomber.

'It won't go kaput, don't worry. Your man knows what he's doing, that's what I reckon. Russian lads lost too many last time round. They'll see sense. They'll back down.' For a minute, intent as an astrologer reading the light in a crystal ball, Sidney looked at his own image in the cabbage-coloured glass where John F. Kennedy's face had been. 'Sold anything this week?' he suddenly asked.

'A few things.'

'Sold anything today?'

'One picture. And a vase.'

'And that's the lot?'

'That's it.'

'Bad, isn't it?'

'Not that bad, Sid.'

'No, Alex, it is that bad.' Clutching Alexander's arm, he pushed himself out of his chair. 'You must be bored senseless,' he said.

'No, Sid. I'm never bored.'

'Admirable. But it's time for a change, anyhow. That's what I think.' In the style of an orator, he raised a crooked forefinger. 'It's what I've decided, in fact.' He shuffled to the kitchen and brought back two bottles of brown ale, two glasses and a plastic bag full of magazines. 'Do the honours,' he said, handing Alexander the beer and a bottle-opener. From his bag he withdrew the first magazine. 'Cliff Richard,' he said, as though the picture on the cover were that of a fugitive criminal. He let the exhibit fall to the floor and then produced the next. 'Adam Faith.' He dropped the magazine and extracted the third. 'Cliff Richard again. And his Shadows.' He peered at the fourth cover. 'Chap in a shiny suit. He Billy Fury?'

'He is,' said Alexander, holding out Sidney's glass for him.

'Bloody silly name.' Sidney accepted his drink, laid the bag on an arm of Alexander's chair, and went over to the record-player that stood on tapering sky-blue legs behind the door. 'You know this, I assume?' he said. He lowered the arm onto the record; a muted harmonica's wail seeped from the speaker.

'Course, Sid. "Love Me Do".'

'You like this?'

177

'A lot of people do.'

'Bloody caterwauling if you ask me.' He raised the volume gradually, grimacing as if he were subjecting himself to an electric current. 'Enough,' he declared, and hooked the arm away.

'It'll grow on you.'

'Not any chance of that happening,' said Sidney. 'But,' he pronounced, raising his forefinger again, 'that's neither here nor there. Like it or not, this din is the din of the future. I've done some homework.' He scooped a scrap of newspaper from a trouser pocket and held it up for Alexander to observe. 'It says here that your average kid is spending eight quid a week on clothes, fags, make-up and records. I rest my case. All our yesterdays are going to have to fend for themselves. They've had their chance. In a nutshell, Alex, I want you to flog that junk downstairs for whatever you can get. If anyone so much as stops in front of our window, get an offer out of them. Take anything you can get.' Firmly he prodded the cutting back into his pocket. 'I'll still do a bit of trading, private like. Special pieces for particular people. But the shop, that's going over to music. Are you with me?'

'Well. I don't know,' said Alexander. 'It's a bit sudden.'

'I know, I know. Have a think about it. Tell us next week. But I'd like you to stay, and if you do, you can have this flat. Nominal rent. Virtually free. I'm taking over a friend's place. You and your girl will have somewhere decent to canoodle.'

'We've packed it in, Sid.'

'Is that so?' said Sidney casually. 'Thought I hadn't heard anything for a while.' At Alexander's blush he stepped back, pushing his hands outwards in his pockets, making a shape like clown's trousers. 'Come on, lad. I wasn't born yesterday. Two healthy young people. Nice girl, she is,' he commented, and he looked at Alexander ruefully. 'Packed in good and proper? Not just a tiff?'

'Good and proper,' said Alexander.

'Pity. Nice girl that.'

'She is, Sid, she is.'

'Pity,' said Sidney, and the sadness of it seemed to make his shoulders sag. 'A real pity.' He chinked his glass against Alexander's. 'Don't fret about your girl, though. Plenty more where she came from. Lot more mermaids in the ocean.'

'Aye,' said Alexander, and he stood up to join Sidney at the window.

'To the future,' Sidney toasted.

'The future,' said Alexander, but Sidney's words had made him nostalgic, and he was recalling Liz asleep on the settee in the back room of the shop. With fondness and regret he heard her talking to him on the steep path in the park, as he looked down on the street, where an eddy of dry leaves was jumping in a doorway like a cat in pursuit of its tail.

20. Dixon's Discs

Alexander would remember that he had not been living in the flat for more than a month when Profumo resigned, and it was a warm Saturday morning when he moved out of the house. His father struck his head on the roof of the car as he stooped to push a box of clothes across the back seat. His mother appeared at an upstairs window. He would remember looking up from the car to see her look away and scrub at a mark on the glass with a ball of newspaper. The radio was playing loudly in the kitchen when his father closed the front door; there was a blare of trombones. His mother was at the upstairs window, stepping back.

Alexander's father did not speak during the drive. When they arrived he followed his son up the stairs, carrying the larger suitcase. 'Where do you want this, guv?' he asked, and he played the taciturn porter, following his son's directions, until everything was unloaded. Leaning against the boxes, recovering his breath, he took note of the place in which Alexander would be living, but he made no comment. He lifted a tail of peeling wallpaper, tearing another inch free of the plaster.

'I'll fix it,' Alexander assured him.

'Yes,' his father concurred. 'Easy enough. Doesn't need much.'

'A lick of paint all round.'

'Yes,' said his father. 'Not much more than that.'

'Thanks for the help, Dad.'

'Not at all,' said his father, and he pressed the curl of wallpaper flat. 'One last thing,' he said, as though at an afterthought. He descended to the car.

Through the cracked window, which would never be repaired in all the years that he was to live there, Alexander watched his father reach into the glove compartment and extract a small parcel wrapped in red paper. Already embarrassed, he withdrew to the kitchen to wait for him.

'From your mother,' his father said. 'She thinks you're going to starve without her.' His right hand, having released the gift, moved sideways and rested on the controls of the stove. A plastic dial rattled under his fingers. 'This thing safe?' he asked.

Alexander held the Marguerite Patten cookery book in both hands, high in front of him, as though it rested on an invisible lectern. 'Never harmed Sid, as far as I know,' he said. 'Not that he ever gave it much cause to harm him. Bottle of stout and half a loaf of toast is Sid's idea of a meal.'

'I'd have it checked, if I were you,' replied his father. He plucked the dial from its spindle, replaced it, turned it clockwise a quarter-circle and turned it back.

'I will,' said Alexander.

'I'll give you a name. A reliable chap.'

'Thanks,' said Alexander, and he looked at the book again. 'This'll be useful.'

'Good.' His father found something to look at: Sid's picture of a Varga girl, still taped to the door of the cupboard. 'You'll be redecorating, I imagine,' he observed.

'Sooner or later,' said Alexander. Like strangers in a museum, they looked together at the Varga girl.

'Well, good luck, son,' his father said, and he shook his hand, as he had done on the morning that Alexander left home to begin his Basic Training, and on no other occasion.

Two days later, when the carpenters were on their break, his mother appeared at the shop. 'Anyone there?' he heard her call. 'Alexander, are you there?' He came out of the back room to see her picking a path through the shavings and the stray screws and the turquoise perspex letters that would spell 'Dixon's Discs' on the shopfront. 'Everyone working flat out, I see,' she observed. With the toe of her shoe she pushed aside a sluglike tube of glue.

'They've been at it since six, Mum,' he told her. 'You can't expect them to go all day without food.'

She looked at the walls of the shop, which now were clad with vinyl tiles in a chequered pattern of white and blue. It was a greenish blue, the same colour as the travel-sickness pills she used to make him take.

'Thanks for the book,' he said.

As if affronted by their proximity to her, she regarded the perspex panels that leaned against the new counter. 'My pleasure,' she said. 'What's all this in aid of?'

'For the booth. Where you can listen to the records. It's going there,' he explained, indicating a corner.

She pointed at lengths of timber that lay on the floor in the doorway to the back. 'And that?'

'Racks for the stock room.'

'It looks like a municipal swimming baths, Alexander,' she said. 'With a shower cubicle.'

'It's modern, Mum. Bright.'

'It's that all right.'

'But you didn't like it before.'

'It was like a hovel before.'

'Wait till the records are out. The album sleeves. And I get the pictures up. It'll look good.'

'Look better, certainly.'

'Do you want to see upstairs?' he asked. 'My flat?'

'If what your father says is anything to go by, I'm not sure that I do, Alexander.'

'If what my father says? What did he say?'

'Don't make a fuss, Alexander,' said his mother. 'You know how he likes to exaggerate.' She held out a hand to him, as if stepping across a stream on slippery stones. 'Come on. Let's see for ourselves.'

He put a note on the door, locked it, and led her up the stairs. 'I'll replace the carpet soon,' he volunteered, bending to snap a thread of backing from the rip on the edge of a tread. His cases and boxes still littered the living room, so he took her into the kitchen. She advanced one pace beyond the doorframe; she seemed to make her eyes see only the air within the room rather than the room itself. 'I'm painting it next week,' he told her. 'Plain white, I thought.'

'Not terribly practical, Alexander. In a kitchen.' She raised a foot from the lino and gazed down at its sole, and in looking back she noticed the book on the chair with the yellow PVC seat.

'Thanks for the book,' he said again.

'Tried anything from it?' she asked, and now she smiled at him.

'Not yet.'

'It's all straightforward,' she said, hooking her arm under his and

182

turning to leave. 'You've eaten a lot of her meals and thought they were mine. Your father thinks I'm a genius with the pots and pans, but it's not me, it's Marguerite Patten. Hasn't a clue about some things, your father.' She nudged the living room door ajar and peered in, like a matron checking on her ward at night. 'This place will be nice, Alexander.'

'With some work,' he added.

'With some work,' she agreed. 'If you'd like a hand with the gloss, you know who to ask.'

She visited him a fortnight later, on an afternoon when Mick Radford and a couple of other people were in the shop. Seeing them, she hesitated on the step until he waved her in. Their conversation was brief; she held open her carrier bag for him to look at the cardigan she had bought for his father. On her way out she hesitated again. Standing on the pavement in front of the window, she looked left and then right before walking away. Alexander watched her dawdle up the hill, stopping at the window of almost every shop. At the zebra crossing she waited, though there was no traffic. She looked at the sky and then she crossed the road.

The next day Alexander rang to say that perhaps she might drop by that afternoon, but earlier than before, when the shop would be empty. Some new releases had been delivered by the time she arrived. 'Perhaps you'd like to give them a listen?' he suggested to her, opening one of the boxes. 'Give them marks out of ten,' he said, handing her a pen and the *Melody Maker*, and to his surprise she was instantly persuaded.

Sitting on the booth's blue velvet bench, she raised a thumb to him, like a fighter pilot before take-off. 'Dragonfly' was the first single he played for her. When it was finished he leaned over the counter to face her and raised a questioning eyebrow. A hand lifted from her knee and hovered, palm downwards, ambivalently.

'Another?' he mimed, flourishing a copy of the 'The First Time'.

She nodded quickly and her lips parted, as if she were delighted by the frivolity of the diversion he was giving her. Alexander would always remember this expression, and the fact that when the record ended she held up eight fingers to him, whereas to 'Shindig' she allotted seven. He would know that this had happened because he

183

could recall, as clearly as her delight, looking at the charts in the stock room with her, a month or so later, and remarking that 'The First Time' had gone one place higher than 'Shindig', and then saying to her, as though she were his pupil: 'You're good at this, aren't you?'

'Beginner's luck,' she responded, but it was not. For a long time she would call at the shop regularly, albeit not as regularly as she had used to when it sold old furniture and she was with Mrs Beckwith. She would arrive in the becalmed part of the afternoon, between the lunch hour and the end of the school day, bringing him something from the café by the station. 'So what's new?' she would ask, and then take the release lists and *Melody Maker* from him, like an office colleague taking over the day's only interesting piece of paperwork. Her coat was folded carefully and put under the bench; the lists were placed beside her, like examination papers; from her handbag she took her black lacquered ballpoint, which she would tap against her knee or her lips if she liked the song he was playing her. While Alexander changed the record she marked her verdict: three stars for any she thought would go to number one; a pair for a top ten place; and a single star alongside the top twenties.

Alexander would remember an array of those stars, each one of them drawn as two overlapping open triangles of blue ink and each identical to all the others, in the margin of a month-old list. It was near the end of the year. There were buds of condensation on the tiles when he opened the shop that morning; the shop smelled of damp vinyl and the previous day's cigarette smoke. The picture of Billy J. Kramer had sagged with moisture, bending his legs into waves, like a Hall of Mirrors. His mother was listening to an EP in the booth. Demurely she sat, with her camelhair coat folded behind her feet, her handbag upright beside her, singing to herself. Alexander was comparing her predictions against that day's chart, and yet again she had been right. Dusk was coming. He reached round the doorway of the stockroom for the switch. The fluorescent light shuddered on and seemed to press every object into place around the room. His mother glanced up and smiled at him through the watery ghost of his reflection.

21. Pen

After the death of his wife Mr Beckwith became as neat as a mannequin. He wore his best black brogues in the house, and they were always polished perfectly. His trousers were crisply pressed and his shirt was as smooth as virgin paper. His cheeks had a barbered sheen. A perpetually clean fawn raincoat hung on a hanger from a hook in the hall, like a garment in a gentlemen's outfitters.

Side by side at the French windows they would often stand, as if on the bridge of a ship. 'Things to do out there?' Alexander might remark, although the garden was as trim as the house.

'If you'd like, of course,' Mr Beckwith might reply, and he would go upstairs to change his clothes, while Alexander went to the garden shed where an overall was kept for him, and the smell of the air was the same as it had been since the day he had first talked to Mr Beckwith.

'Do you remember taking me on a tour of the garden?' Alexander once asked him.

'Oh yes,' said Mr Beckwith, after a pause, but it was as though Alexander had asked him if he could recall a fact rather than a day they had shared.

'You had Lavender Cotton there,' Alexander told him. 'And Viburnum over there.'

Courteously Mr Beckwith regarded the places where the plants had once grown. 'Ah yes,' he said. 'Yes, I remember. Yes,' he repeated, in a retreating voice, as his hands kneaded the soil of the flowerbed.

Often Mr Beckwith cooked a meal when the gardening was done, while Alexander watched TV. One evening, which Alexander would always remember, a detective programme had begun and Mr Beckwith came into the room, holding a wide white bowl against his belly. 'Is that any good?' he asked.

'Good so far,' Alexander replied. 'Why not stay and watch it?'

'No, no. It's underway now,' said Mr Beckwith.

'We can wait a bit.'

'No. I must get on,' he said, and Alexander, intending to check when the programme would end, leafed through the newspapers and magazines in the rack as soon as Mr Beckwith had left the room, and found a copy of the *Radio Times* that was six years out of date and a *Woman's World* that was even older.

The moment the programme ended Mr Beckwith called him. The knives and forks were placed in perfect parallel on the laundered tablecloth. Ranks of glasses gleamed on the upper shelf of the dresser, above plates that overlapped like the scales of a cartoon fish. 'How was it?' asked Mr Beckwith.

'So-so,' said Alexander. 'The killer was very helpful with his clues. Didn't need Scotland Yard. I'd have caught him.'

'Always the case when they make it up,' said Mr Beckwith. 'Give me the documentaries any day. Real life.'

'But that Maigret. He's good. You watch that ever?'

'Oh yes, he's good,' Mr Beckwith agreed. 'I like him.'

Alexander sliced the fish on his plate, and bent forward into the fragrant steam that came out of the cut. 'But this is better than Maigret,' he said.

'Pity it's not cod,' said Mr Beckwith.

'Why's that?'

'Because then I could have made a quip.' He raised an unamused face to Alexander, who gave him the requesting look that was invited. 'The piece of cod that passeth all understanding,' said Mr Beckwith. A partial smile made a crimp in a corner of his mouth.

'The piece of cod,' laughed Alexander. 'You make that up?'

'An old one,' said Mr Beckwith, and he applied himself to his meal.

At nine-thirty exactly the telephone rang, and because it was nine-thirty they knew that it was Megan calling. 'That'll be our girl,' stated Mr Beckwith, placing his mug of tea on the hearth. 'You want a word?'

'If she does,' said Alexander.

Mr Beckwith closed the door and Alexander turned up the volume of the TV slightly, to cover the sound that would come into the room. 'Hello, love,' Mr Beckwith said distinctly, and then, as if he knew that these words had been overheard, his voice became quieter. Alexander leaned closer to the screen, but still he could hear the confessional mumble from the hallway. For half an hour the conversation continued, and then at last Mr Beckwith knocked on the door and called to him, as he invariably did: 'Northern bulletin.'

'Eck,' she said. 'How are things?'

'Fine, fine,' he told her.

'Shop OK?'

'You know,' he said, and he told her the things he had already told Mr Beckwith. 'How about you?'

'Exciting, intermittently,' she said. She told him about her work, but she seemed burdened by whatever had passed earlier between herself and Mr Beckwith. 'Family all right?' she asked. Alexander felt his words drag on the silence of the telephone line. While he spoke, he listened for her breathing. 'You look after yourself, Eck,' she said.

'I will. And you,' he said. He returned to the living room; the TV was still loud.

'Doing well for herself,' said Mr Beckwith, looking at the screen.

'She is,' Alexander replied.

'Seems happy.'

'She does. She tell you about the field trip?'

'She did.' Mr Beckwith stared absently at the TV. Tilting his mug towards the screen, he asked: 'What's going on here?'

'Not altogether sure,' said Alexander. They watched to the end of the programme and Alexander went back to his flat.

When Megan was at home for the weekend, Alexander would usually see her, but never at her house. 'There are things Dad has to talk about, Eck. He's different when I'm there. You understand, don't you?' he would remember her saying to him, on Oxford Street, after she had bought a skirt that was the same red as the pinafore his mother had once bought her for her birthday. They jumped onto the platform of a moving bus and rode it to Marble Arch, where they saw *Billy Liar* in a cinema that had a lilac carpet with orange stars in the foyer, and the draught from the street raised a whirl of dust that reminded him of the windblown sand on the beach at Praa. They saw *Lawrence of Arabia* and *This Sporting Life* together as well, he would remember, and occasionally they wandered around the West End in the early evening and stopped for a coffee in Frith Street or Greek Street, but most often she would come to the shop as he was closing and they

187

would walk for an hour or two through the streets of Blackheath and Greenwich. She would tell him about the children in her classes, about their parents and her colleagues. One of the teachers was a mathematics teacher who had been taught by Jesuits but had lost his faith at the shrine of Loreto. He was teaching as a way of doing penance for his lack of belief, Megan thought, because he appeared to find children detestable and once said to her: 'Give me the child and I will give him straight back.' His name was Draper, which was the name of the boy in Alexander's regiment who'd cut off a finger in the breech of a gun and could still feel the presence of it a year after his accident. As they talked about the two Drapers, he would remember, she held his arm as if she were cold, though the evening was warm. She would hold his arm whenever they came to talk about Mr Beckwith, as they always did. 'How does he seem to you?' she would ask, or 'Do you think I should come down more often?' It was the one subject on which she requested his advice, and it seemed that she was reassured by what he told her, or by his presence. 'You're right, Eck. I shouldn't worry so much. He sees you; he speaks to me. He's not alone.' They were sitting against the trunk of a pollarded tree, near the place where Liz Gatting had walked away from him. 'You're right,' she said again, as if to confirm that her anxiety was ebbing. Alexander looked up at a sky that was almost white and saw an arc of pale moon, like a last remnant of melting ice on a pool. 'What's that going up over there?' Megan asked, pointing to a crane in the midst of the East End, but he did not know. For many minutes they watched the river and did not speak. A barge came loose from a wharf downstream and slowly turned. A launch with a steep white cabin cut across the barge's wake. Sensing a change in the quality of the silence, Alexander glanced at Megan and saw her head rise an inch, as though something across the water had caught her attention. Her eyes became fixed on something that he could not see, and her gaze appeared to soften. Gradually the corners of her mouth deepened and furled, but her expression did not become a smile, and as he looked at her face Alexander had the notion that it was not the city but their childhood that she was seeing in the distance. 'Don't stare, Eck,' she said, then kissed his hand.

It was in March, four days after Megan had been in London, that

Pen Hollander came into the shop, late in the morning. Alexander looked up from a picture of Richard Burton and Elizabeth Taylor, and she smiled and turned to the rack of jazz LPs, where she browsed until there was nobody except herself and Alexander in the shop. 'Have you heard this?' she asked, presenting a sleeve that bore the pensive face of John Coltrane. 'It's excellent. Truly excellent. Have you heard it?'

'I don't think so,' said Alexander.

'You don't think so? Then you haven't. Believe me: you hear this, you don't forget it.'

'I'll listen to it later.'

'Do,' she said. 'It's great.' She replaced the sleeve and flicked through another section. 'I'm sorry. You were reading your newspaper. I interrupted you. I'm sorry.'

'Not at all,' said Alexander. Surreptitiously he watched her as she worked along the racks towards the counter. Her face seemed constantly agitated, and her eyes continually startled. Her hair was dyed black and she wore rainbow-hooped socks that reached over her knees. She was so small that her black corduroy smock might have been intended for a young girl. Over one shoulder she carried a bag that was like a school satchel made of patent leather.

'Great-looking guy,' she said, as though in agreement with a proposition someone had just made.

'Pardon?'

'John Coltrane,' she explained, smiling at him. 'Great-looking guy.'

'Yes,' said Alexander. 'I suppose so.'

'You should listen to that album. You really should. You like jazz?'

'Some.'

'Some? What does that mean?' she demanded.

'Louis Armstrong, Duke Ellington, the usual.'

'OK,' she said, relinquishing the subject. She selected an album, looked at it for a second or two, replaced it, and moved on to the next section. Having done the same thing three times, she planted a hand on a hip and made a blowing sound, as if losing patience with herself. She strode to the counter and stood on her toes to offer her hand. 'My name's Pen,' she stated.

'Pen,' he doubtfully repeated.

'Pen Hollander. Penelope Hollander. Penelope Arianna Matilda Hollander. Hence Pen.'

'Alexander. Alexander Gordon MacIndoe. Alex, Alec, Al, Eck, Sandy or Alexander.'

'Alexander, would you object if I took a picture of you?' she asked. 'I mean, would you object if I took some pictures? Would that be presumptuous of me? You can say. I won't take offence.' Her brows buckled as if she were pained by her own persistence.

'What, now?' Alexander asked.

'No, whenever,' she said, and straight away checked herself. 'No, not whenever. Soon. Next weekend? I have a week. I don't live here, you see. I'm visiting. Vacation, kind of.'

'I'd guessed,' said Alexander.

'Ah, no. You haven't guessed right. I know you haven't. Born in New York, but I live in Paris, actually. Didn't guess that, did you? You been to Paris ever?'

'Never been abroad.'

'Really?' she marvelled.

'Nearly got posted to Germany once. Ended up in Wales instead. Halfway to abroad, but not the whole hog.'

Pen crossed her arms on the counter and looked at him. 'Alexander, you would love Paris,' she said, with the conviction of a longstanding friend.

'I would?'

'You would,' Pen affirmed. 'Anyone with a soul would love Paris. Anyone with any life in them. I couldn't like anyone who didn't love Paris,' she told him, patting her arms. 'So, would you mind if I took some pictures?' she asked, and she moved back a step. 'How about it?'

'Can't see why not,' he conceded.

'I take a good shot, Alexander. I'm a professional. Not long at it, but I sell stuff.'

'I'm sure.'

'And you'll take a great shot. No, really. I mean, you don't have any bad angles. Anything that breathes has got a bad angle. It's a rule. Normally. But you don't.'

Two schoolboys came into the shop and stood behind Pen to read the charts on the wall behind the counter. She went back to the jazz albums; the boys went to the opposite side, where they scanned the new EPs and passed a cigarette back and forth. Nervously, rapidly, Pen turned the sleeves she had already checked. When the boys left, she slipped the strap of her bag from her shoulder to her hand, and Alexander knew what she was about to say.

'Alexander,' she said, 'I have a confession.' She swung the bag onto the counter and held it there, as if to prevent its escape. 'I already did take a picture of you.' From the bag she withdrew a paper wallet, from which, wincing in anticipation of his anger, she extracted a stark monochrome photo. He was leaning on a wall, looking up, with one foot flat against the bricks and one hand shading his eyes. 'A few days back,' she explained.

'I know. Sunday,' he said.

'That's right,' she said, as if he had answered an abstruse question correctly. She watched him as he studied the picture; he had been looking at a birds' nest that was dangling under the eaves, tethered by some strands of what seemed to be straw; a couple of minutes earlier, Megan had been standing there as well. 'Are you angry with me?' Pen asked. 'I'm sorry. You should be angry. It's really bad of me. Inexcusable.'

'No, not at all.'

'I was walking by and I saw you. Next moment, it was done. I'm sorry.'

'It's all right. It's interesting.'

'It's like a reflex. Like looking. That's how quick it is. I don't think.' She pushed the envelope towards him. 'The negative is in here. If you want it, take it. You can rip it up. Burn it. Here.' She scrabbled in her bag and produced a lighter.

'It doesn't matter,' he said.

'You sure?' she asked, and before long he had told her about the fairground and the Bovis stove, and later that day, in the living room of his flat, he took the old magazine out of the suitcase and showed her the advertisement in which he stood simpering beside his mother and Geoff Darby. 'That's cute,' she said. 'That's so cute.'

'She's my mother,' he explained. 'But that's not my father.'

'No,' she replied, placing the brittle pages carefully on the seat of the settee. 'That would be too much.'

That Sunday they met underneath the Waterloo station clock and set off for a walk through the city. He took her past the Theatre Royal and into Lincoln's Inn Fields, then back to Leicester Square, where she asked him to stand in the path of a crowd of daytrippers and took a picture of him as they flowed around him. At Trafalgar Square she took a longer lens from her bandolier and made him walk away from her, under Admiralty Arch. From a distance she photographed him by the ivy-covered bunker on the Mall, and then they strolled across St James's Park and he retold the stories that he had heard from Sidney Dixon, about Henry VIII's hunts in the park and the pelicans that the Russian ambassador gave Charles II. He told her about James I's aviary as they went up Birdcage Walk, and she talked about Central Park and her parents' separate apartments and her sister's family in Toronto. 'Like Paris in reverse,' she said, waving him into position by the statue of Achilles. 'You could never like anyone who loved Toronto.' In Kensington Gardens, by the statue of Peter Pan, she unloaded the last film. 'Paris, then,' she said. 'You'll come and see me, yes? I have a nice apartment. There's a room for you. Stay for a week, two weeks. I'm out for half the day, but it's OK. You can treat it like home. Do what you like. Whatever.' She wrote her address on a paper tissue, with handwriting that filled the whole square.

Each week a postcard arrived from Paris, bearing a single message that filled all the space on the back of the card: 'Come on!' she wrote on the Tour Saint-Jacques; 'Bought your ticket?' on the Orangerie; 'Dépêche-toi, Alexandre!' on Place de la Concorde. In an envelope of pink-flecked paper she sent him a photo of his own kitchen, with 'Still think it doesn't look bad?' on the back, and it was when he looked at the tattered Varga girl and the yellow PVC seat and the bubbled paintwork above the cooker, and saw that she had been right, that he decided he would go to Paris.

'Am painting it white from floor to ceiling,' he replied. 'Negotiations with employer have commenced. Date to follow.' The date was a Friday before a morning on which Megan was due home, bringing someone she hoped he would like, but did not name.

Though it was dark by the time the ferry departed, and it was raining, he remained outside throughout the crossing, sitting on a slatted wooden bench underneath the upper deck, watching the rope of the ferry's wake unravel into the black water. A slime of salt covered the steel behind the bench, as he would always remember, and the ropes clanged ceaselessly on the davits like a fire bell. He would remember as well the lights of the quayside, glaring on the crocodile's back of wet cobbles, and an advertisement painted directly onto a wall in dandelion yellow and indigo, and the cocoa-coloured cattle, their hides spangled with raindrops, in the fields he saw through the misted windows as the train carried him to the city. He took the Métro to Denfert-Rochereau, then followed the map she had drawn on the back of a photo of her front door. The door was moss green and heavy, and opened onto the concrete floor of a vaulted hallway, from where a flight of shallow steps with a wrought iron handrail led up to Pen's apartment. Piano music was playing, but there was no sound of any occupant when he pressed the bell.

The music continued; he pressed the bell again. The door opened abruptly and Pen, in a man's white shirt and jeans and leather slippers, smiled at him as though his arrival were a daily pleasure. 'Paris comes to Paris,' she said, and kissed him for the first time. The room behind her was narrow, with huge cushions on the bare wooden floor and windows that rose from the floor to the ceiling and had broad strips of muslin for curtains. She dropped his bag beside a wide brass tray in the centre of the room and led him, through the corridor that was her kitchen, to the darkroom, where several versions of her face were pegged to a cord above the trays of chemicals. 'Know thyself,' she joked, lifting another sheet from its bath with plastic pincers. Her phone rang, with a purring tone. She nipped his lip; under the red bulb of the darkroom, her hair was sea-urchin purple.

He would meet her every afternoon at three-thirty, on the corner of Rue Mabillon and Rue Lobineau, because she could see that corner from the office in which she worked. From there they would wander for a couple of hours, and she would take pictures of him. She photographed him in a café, looking away from the tiny cup he had raised to his lips, as if he were lost in a reverie of Boulevard St-Germain. She photographed his face in profile above the roofline of the Invalides, and she photographed his hands upon a stone lion's head, somewhere in the Luxembourg gardens. He glowered beside the Gates of Hell and lowered his face poetically to the stopper of a perfume bottle in Rue de Rivoli. Wearing a black shirt with outsized cuffs he sat back against a wall of white-glazed tiles in the Châtelet station. He sat cross-legged on a riverbank wearing an unknotted bow tie and a black velvet jacket that she took from her wardrobe. Feigning despair, he stared down the paths of the Parc Montsouris, where she pushed his hand under her denim jacket to touch her breast.

'And what did the morning bring?' she asked him on the first afternoon. He had done nothing but follow the river, walking upstream as far as the Austerlitz station, then downstream on the other side as far as the Palais de Chaillot. 'What have you been up to?' she asked on the second day, but still he had done nothing of which he could make an account, though he would not forget the fern of shadows cast by the carvings on an office building, nor the paving stones that bulged like rising bread, nor lying on a bench in the Tuileries, where the noise of the trodden gravel was as distinctive as any voice and the air beneath the chestnut trees smelled of cement dust and coffee and warmed bark. One morning he walked to the Pont de Neuilly, and then walked all the way back. Next day he walked to Père Lachaise, following no planned route, conducted by the grain of the streets like a bead of water across a board, and then walked all the way back. 'You didn't even go in?' Pen exclaimed. 'Jesus, Allie. Not making the best use of your time, are you? Took half a day to get somewhere you could have been in ten minutes. OK,' she asserted. 'Tomorrow you do some sights. Can't go back to London without seeing the things you've got to see.'

Together they visited Notre-Dame and the Sainte-Chapelle and Sacré-Coeur. They saw the opera house and ascended the Eiffel Tower. On the last day they went to the Louvre, where Pen photographed him at the sleeping hermaphrodite, as he regarded lubriciously its curvaceous rear. She hurried him through the galleries, past walls of battles and disasters and coronations, along avenues of landscapes and saints. She took a picture of him with Ingres' long-backed bathers, and reciprocating the wistful gaze of Watteau's Gilles. 'Come on,' she urged, as he continued to look at Gilles' baggy satin suit. 'There's a lot more to go.'

'What's the rush?' asked Alexander. 'We can see it another time.'

'And you can see him another time,' she replied.

'I like him.'

'Why? It's a bunch of clowns. Big deal,' Pen declared, and Alexander took a last glance at Gilles, and knew that if he ever saw him again it would not be in Pen's company.

That evening, she took him to a party in a house out at Meudon. A man in a tuxedo got out of a Mercedes and preceded them up the path. 'A few familiar faces,' said Pen, as they paused in the doorway of the room in which most of the guests had gathered. Candles burned in iron chandeliers, above terracotta pots and multicoloured banded rugs. At one end of the room a laconic double-bassist and a frantic guitarist accompanied a pianist who sang with a cigarette in his mouth. 'That group's English,' Pen explained, 'and that's American. Be yourself, Allie.'

As soon as he could, Alexander retreated to the garden, from where frequently he would see Pen pass behind a window, always talking, as if her appetite for speech could not be satiated. When he went back inside, a woman wearing a low-necked green dress and a coral necklace touched his arm as he made his way towards Pen. They stood underneath a Moorish arch that creaked when he leaned against it.

'You're Alexander, I assume,' she said, drawing out the third syllable of his name. 'The London boy?'

'Yes.'

'From London myself,' she said. 'Chiswick,' she added, and raised an emerald enamelled lighter to her cigarette.

'Greenwich,' Alexander replied.

'I know,' she said. A stream of smoke flowed over her upper lip. 'I'm Sarah. Pleased to meet you.' By way of a handshake she dragged her long fingers across his palm.

'Do you find these people entertaining?' she asked him.

'Yes,' he said, though it would have been more precise to say that they made him conscious that he was not entertaining.

'Neither do I,' she said, and a pipette of smoke sprang from the tight circle of her lips. 'And what do you do in London, Alexander? Remind me?'

'I work –'

'A record shop,' Sarah interrupted.

195

'That's right,' he said.

'And that's where Penelope found you?'

'That's where we met, yes,' he replied. 'And what do you do?'

Sarah spread a hand over her breastbone, raising a fragrance of rosewater. 'What do I do?' she drawled. 'That is an incisive question, Alexander. I do almost nothing. I am a diplomatic wife. My husband is at the embassy.'

'That sounds like it should be interesting,' commented Alexander.

'Yes. Yes, I should imagine it does,' said Sarah.

'What does he do there?'

'Now that, Alexander, is a real question. What does my husband do? I think what he does is tell lies to people who tell lies to him. And he writes reports on the ghastly creatures with whom he has to mingle. He goes to receptions and asks the Russians if they're going to take over the world, and they tell him it's the last thing on their minds. That's what he does, as I understand it.'

A claret-skinned man with a gold watch chain slung across his white waistcoat pushed between Alexander and the arch. Pen followed, and glanced at Alexander with ambiguous curiosity. 'Dear Pen,' said Sarah, when Pen had gone. 'So good at keeping life fresh. Every week's a new adventure. Never in a rut,' she sighed, extinguishing her cigarette with a sardonic frown.

'A lot of energy,' Alexander agreed.

'Has she taken you to Parc Montsouris yet?' enquired Sarah, turning the biggest of the coral beads.

'She has.'

'Charming, isn't it?' she said.

'I enjoyed it,' said Alexander.

'Pen speaks highly of you,' Sarah observed.

'I'm glad.'

'Most highly,' she told him, still turning the bead.

A remark other than mere agreement was expected of him, but Alexander could think of nothing that might suffice. The superiority faded from Sarah's smile, and then the smile itself withdrew. 'You really don't have any idea what's going on here, do you?' she asked, with a laugh that was not so much an effusion of amusement as a statement that she was amused.

196

In the taxi Pen pushed herself into the angle of the seat and the door. 'Sluiced, was she?' she demanded, jabbing her elbow on the armrest. 'Under the influence?'

'Didn't appear to be.'

'She wouldn't appear to be. She's a professional soak.'

'Forget it, Pen.'

'What a bitch. Class-A bitch.'

'Calm down. It doesn't matter.'

'I don't want to calm down, Mr Serene,' she said with bitterness. 'I like being uncalm. OK?' She glared at the traffic, and her face seemed paralysed by vindictiveness. Her expression had barely changed when she reached for the switch through the chiffon scarf that covered the lampshade beside her bed.

Six weeks after his return from Paris, he received through the post a copy of a French magazine. Page 22 was folded over, and featured a trio of miniskirted girls on Vespa scooters, a Mod in the doorway of a club, and himself beside a Carnaby Street window. The caption to Alexander's picture, translated by Pen in the margin, read: 'A face of young London . . . he lives for today . . . looking good is what life is all about . . . he looks good, and expects other people to recognise it, girls especially.' A photograph of Alexander on a staircase in the Louvre fell out of the magazine. On the back was written: 'Well, I recognised it, and I wasn't alone. It was so good to know you, Alexander – good luck with everything.'

22. The Crown and Anchor

'The ugliest pub in Christendom,' Sam Saunders called it. 'The dullest dump known to humanity.'

A solitary whitewashed and pebble-dashed building, the Crown and Anchor stood next to a boarded-up house and an overgrown plot of land that had once been occupied by prefabs, on the corner of two streets that led to other streets that ended in hillocks of waste ground. There was only one bar inside, and it had the appearance of a room that had been assembled from whatever furniture and materials had been to hand whenever the landlord had decided to make improvements. No two tables were the same, and three-legged cast-iron stools of differing heights were scattered across the peat-brown carpet. Swivelling panels of frosted glass were set into old wooden frames above the bar, but the bar stools were steel and plastic and stood on a track of burgundy lino that was mottled like a ten-pin bowling ball. Half a dozen daffodil-shaped lamps were attached to the walls; the bare neon strip in the centre of the ceiling was used only to signal closing time. To reach the toilets one pushed aside a folding door of plastic panels that were moulded to resemble planks of pine. A three-bar electric fire, with an inset of fibreglass red-hot coals, was installed in the scorched brick fireplace, and along one wall there was a black vinyl banquette that might have been salvaged, as Sam said, from a Soho strip club. Behind the banquette, next to an old advertisement for Guinness, the landlord had wedged a large oblong aquarium; on its gravel floor lay a miniature galleon, a miniature hump-backed bridge and a whisky bottle with its base cut off, through which swam tiny transparent fish with guts the colour and size of apple pips.

At around the time that Sidney Dixon changed his shop, it became Alexander's habit to call at the Crown and Anchor after work, two or three nights a week. He would sit by the larger window, opposite the picture of Sir Gordon Richards, and read his newspaper. Alf Davies, who lived across the road, in the house in which he had been born in the last year of the nineteenth century, was invariably there before him, reading a paperback from which he would look up to acknowledge Alexander's arrival and to which, having said nothing, he would then return. From time to time Alf might glance up at Alexander or at his pint of mild, which he scarcely touched in the hour that Alexander stayed, but the only person to whom he ever talked was John, whose surname Alexander never knew, and whose greeting to Alexander – 'All right?' – never changed and never led to any more substantial exchange. Seated at adjacent tables in the centre of the room, these two would conduct a mumbled conversation for a minute or so, and then Alf would prop his book on his chest and continue his reading, while John studied the door to the street, through which, in the course of the hour, another four or five customers, all known to Alexander solely by their first names, if by any name at all, would pass with a nod on their way to the bar, from where they would cross to a table at the furthest point from the other drinkers, as though repelled by magnetic force. They were all in their fifties or older, except for a couple called Colin and Christine, who would roll up their sheepskins and put them on the banquette beside their padded gloves, as carefully as Alexander used to lay out his army uniform, and would leave after one drink.

'What on earth's the attraction?' Sam asked him the first time they went there together. Sam inspected his surroundings suspiciously, squirming in his jacket as though the room made him itch.

Alexander looked out of the window, at the end walls of the terraced houses, on which the evening light was maturing to the orange of marigolds. 'It's quiet,' he replied.

'It's that all right. Like the mummy's tomb.'

'And the beer's good.'

'Granted,' said Sam. He tilted his glass to salute Alf Davies, who was looking at them as though they were creating a disturbance in a public library. 'Evening,' Sam volunteered, but received no response. 'Life and soul,' he murmured. 'The long-lost brother of Bela bleeding Lugosi.'

Within the hour they had moved on, yet they met again in the Crown and Anchor a few weeks later, and before long it became a routine. For more than two years Sam and Alexander met almost every week in the Crown and Anchor, but when, in his fifty-eighth year, Alexander came to deduce how many evenings they had passed in that pub he was surprised by the answer, because all those hours had left little of any substance in his memory. He remembered John remarking sourly 'Never seen that before' when Sam scored 180 with three darts. He remembered the evening the jukebox was delivered and the evening it was removed, the following month. And he would remember giving Sam the photographs that Pen had sent, and Sam pushing them back across the table and saying: 'I'd like to see her make something out of this hole.' Before these pieces, though, he remembered a scene that commenced with Sam in the street, by the house with the green tarmac drive, smoothing his tie against his chest as he walked.

Sam did not look up as he approached the pub, and when he joined Alexander he kept glancing at his briefcase, as if preoccupied with what was in it. 'Bugger of a day,' he said. 'People. Who needs them?'

'What have they done?' asked Alexander.

'Changing their minds all the bloody time. Their word isn't their bond any more. I'm tired of it, Mac,' he said, rubbing his face with a weariness that did not seem genuine.

They had downed their first pints and Alexander was on the point of going to the bar when the door opened and Liz Gatting was there. She hesitated, pulling her coat close to her, as if she were about to step out of doors into rain. 'Can't believe the awfulness of it,' Sam commented, and he raised a hand. 'Actually, she needs glasses but she's too vain to wear them.'

Liz put her hand on Sam's shoulder and bent down to let him kiss her cheek. Several months had passed since Alexander had seen her, and their last conversation had been easy and trivial, but when she looked up at him now it was as if she had been slighted by him recently and had not decided how she should act towards him.

'You know each other, of course,' said Sam, looking at neither of them.

'We do,' said Alexander. He took the hand that she was holding out to him and guided her to the seat beside him. She gave him a small smile. 'What would you like?' he asked her. 'I was on my way.'

She looked across at the bar and pressed a hand to her hair, which now was straight and a darker blonde. 'I don't know,' she replied. 'What shall I have, Sam?'

Sam swapped two beermats quickly on the tabletop, as if performing a conjuring trick, and Liz watched his hands. 'What say we go somewhere else instead?' he said. 'Down to the river? What say you, Mac?'

'Mac?' Liz interjected. 'Why do you call him that? Makes him sound American.' She put a hand on Alexander's arm protectively and instantly withdrew it.

'We all called him Mac, in the army,' Sam explained to her. 'Don't know who started it.'

'You did,' said Alexander, to make Sam look at him.

'You sure about that?' asked Sam, looking at Alexander from under lowered brows.

'Yes.'

'Really?'

'Yes,' said Alexander, and he chinked the empty glasses against each other.

'What do you say, Liz? Do we move on?' asked Sam.

'All right with me,' said Liz. 'Would you mind, Alec?'

'No, let's go.' It's a two-thirds majority. Democracy must prevail. Take me away from all of this.'

They walked down to Greenwich, three abreast for most of the way, with Liz on the other side of Sam, holding his arm demurely. They went to another pub and sat upstairs, at a table that gave a broad view of the river. Every boat on the water attracted Sam's attention. 'So how long have you two –?' Alexander finally asked him.

'Early days,' Sam replied, patting the back of Liz's hand. 'Early days,' he repeated, and he took his wallet from his jacket. Liz asked Alexander about the shop and about his family, in such a way that nobody overhearing their conversation would have detected any hint of their former intimacy.

Occasionally they returned to that upstairs bar, where Sam was always readily distracted by any traffic on the river. Once the three of them went to the cinema together, to see *Zulu*. Liz sat upright in her seat throughout the film, with a magazine flat on her knees and her hands primly folded on the magazine. They went to the circus on Blackheath, where at last he saw her laugh as she used to laugh, so the gap in her teeth could be seen. And then they all met again in the Crown and Anchor, on an evening that Alexander would remember acutely.

Sam and Liz came in together. He was wearing a brown and white checked shirt with a button-down collar, and a cardigan with leather buttons under his jacket. Liz wore a violet dress that was very short, and a broad white plastic belt and gold earrings. Her eyes were rimmed so thickly with black liner that she looked drowsy. She waited with Sam until he had been served, then followed him to Alexander's table.

'Yours,' said Sam, positioning a pint in the centre of a beermat and sliding it towards Alexander. Daintily he placed Liz's half-pint before her. 'Elizabeth's. And mine.' He raised his glass and gulped a quarter of its contents.

'You look great,' Liz told Alexander.

'He does,' Sam agreed, and he put down his glass. He watched the foam until it had ceased to move. 'Mac,' he began, and as Liz shifted on her stool Alexander knew what was about to be said. 'Thing is, we're going to get married.' He looked at Alexander as if he were looking at a house of cards to which he had just added another piece.

'And we'd like you to be our best man,' Liz added warily.

'Delighted,' said Alexander, but Sam's expression remained watchful. 'Delighted for you,' Alexander insisted, and as proof he took Liz's hand and kissed it.

'Once more?' requested Sam. 'With a touch of joy this time.'

'Sam,' Liz chided. 'Thank you, Alec,' she said graciously.

'Do you have a date?' asked Alexander.

'It will be a short engagement,' said Sam.

'Very short,' said Liz.

'Very short indeed,' said Sam. 'Six weeks from today.'

'From tomorrow,' Liz corrected him.

'From tomorrow,' Sam said.

'Woolwich Town Hall,' said Liz. 'Mum wanted a church, but I insisted. Don't want all that palaver.'

'If a registry office is good enough for David Bailey, it's good enough for us,' Sam stated, easing back and taking out his cigarettes. 'You're OK with being best man, Mac? You'll get the parents to look after. You realise that? Meet the ma, at last.' He pulled a horrorstruck face for Liz, who reached for a cigarette and did not look at him.

Before the ceremony there was no opportunity to meet Sam's

mother, because Sam lost so much time looking for his cuff-links that he and Alexander arrived at the town hall barely a minute before the bride. Neither did he have a chance to talk to her when the wedding ceremony was over, because Liz's parents came up to Alexander immediately, one on each side, smiling thinly, and walked with him across the hall to the cars that were to take the guests to the party, an interval during which they let him know that they had once allowed themselves to think of him as their future son-in-law. 'But not to be,' said her mother, and she drew a glove through the loop of a thumb and forefinger, as if it gave her the consolation that others would derive from rosary beads.

'Nice enough boy, though,' said Liz's father.

'And a friend of yours, Alexander,' said her mother, giving him a winsome, sorrowing smile.

'It's just, you know,' her father insinuated.

'It's just –?'

'Well, you know,' her mother replied. 'Some young men are the steady type. Others aren't the steady type. You always seemed steady.'

'I'm sure he loves her, Mrs Gatting,' said Alexander.

'Yes,' she mused. 'Yes, I'm sure he does.'

'And vice versa,' he added.

Mrs Gatting made no response, but hurried half a dozen steps forward to yoke two children with her arms and steer them down the steps; her husband nodded at Alexander, then followed her.

Inside the restaurant Sam's mother was waiting for him, stocky as a snowman in her pleated gaberdine. As Alexander approached she beckoned her husband, who was still in the street, lifting a lapel to shelter his match.

'Hello, love,' she said. She turned her back to Alexander, offered him a shoulder of her coat, and unwound herself out of it. 'Peculiar we've never spoke, what with you knowing my Sam all these years.'

'It is, Mrs Saunders,' said Alexander, draping her coat on his arm.

Her eyes were dark as mahogany, and she looked at him as if she were determined to discover immediately, and did discover, what it was that had made her son befriend him. She smiled, and in the skin below her eyes appeared scores of lines as fine and clear as the veins of a mint leaf. 'This is Arnold,' she said.

'Son,' said Arnold, holding out his hand in exactly the way Sam did, with the palm almost flat, as if to receive a small object.

'Nicely done, didn't you think?' said Sam's mother. 'Weren't so sure, were we, Arnold? It not being a religious do.'

'We weren't,' her husband responded, surveying the tables nervously.

'But it was very nice. Very tasteful,' said Mrs Saunders. Again she looked at him frankly, as if there were something in his face that she had forgotten to verify. 'Sam said you was a nice-looking boy,' she commented. 'You're a very nice-looking boy,' she told him, conclusively. 'Isn't he, Arnold? A nice-looking boy?'

Her husband was looking in the direction of Mrs Gatting, who was adjusting a slide in her hair while standing underneath a pink wall-lamp which made her hair resemble a hive of candy-floss. At the top table, Sam was kissing Liz for a relative's photograph.

'Giving you trouble, was she?' asked Sam's mother, folding her arms in a gossip's pose. 'Mother of the bride. I saw her giving you an earful.'

'Oh no,' Alexander assured her. 'She was just saying hello.'

'If that was just saying hello, I'm Vivien Leigh,' she laughed.

'Well,' conceded Alexander. 'She's bound to have mixed feelings.'

'Oh, bound to,' Sam's mother agreed sarcastically.

'Giving her daughter away. It must be hard.'

'Oh, very hard.' Mrs Saunders swatted her husband's arm. 'Arnold, stop staring at the poor woman,' she ordered. 'You're making things worse for her.' She presented to Alexander a face suffused with compassion, briefly, and then her smile returned. 'I'm sorry, love. You must think I'm wicked, but I don't like her and she don't like me, and that's the way it is.'

'Doesn't like our Sam,' her husband reminded her.

'She's the same as us, for all her airs and graces. Her dad was a docker.'

'He was,' said Mr Saunders.

'Mind you, if you want to know what I think, Alex, I think it's her reputation she's bothered about most. It's what people will say about her. As a mother.'

'You're right,' said her husband.

'Her girl could have been marrying Lord Muck, and she'd still have

204

that face on her. It's the circumstances that's really put her nose out of joint. The gossiping.'

'The circumstances?' replied Alexander.

The small, dark eyes of Mrs Saunders started, then looked at him quizzically. 'You hadn't noticed?' she asked.

'Noticed what?'

'Look at her, Alex.' Sam's mother stood aside so that Alexander could see Liz clearly, and at that moment Liz looked up at him and waved him towards her table. 'She's in the family way, love. Four months. And a bloody good thing too, if you ask me.'

'Why's that?' asked Alexander emptily.

'Otherwise they'd have never got round to it, would they, Arnold? Three years it's taken them.'

'Three years?' asked Alexander, though there was nothing to be gained from any answer.

'Thereabouts, love. How long they been courting?' Sam's mother asked her husband. 'Three years, isn't it?'

Mr Saunders turned his eyes to the floor, as if to keep from his vision anything that might interfere with the consulting of his memory. 'Something like that,' he said. 'Off and on. Something like that.'

'What was that record he kept playing?'

Her husband searched the floor around his feet. 'That thing about the rocket.'

'"Telstar"?' Alexander suggested.

'Yes, that was it,' Mr Saunders replied.

'That's the one,' said his wife with satisfaction. 'She bought it for him. Whenever that was.'

Alexander looked across the room at Liz's mother, who was straight-ening the zip of her skirt, while her husband held a glass of sherry in each hand, as if weighing one against the other. He heard the warble of 'Telstar' and found a day that matched it. He was walking past Lenehan's the electrical shop, and the tune was coming out of it. And then he saw Liz walking under the trees, towards the gate of Greenwich park, on what he knew was a later day.

'You with anyone then, Alexander?' asked Sam's mother.

'Not at the moment.'

'You've caused a bit of a stir, I can tell you.'

205

'You have,' said Mr Saunders.

Sam's mother pointed to a girl in an aquamarine dress that flared out from her hips like a tutu. 'That's Carol,' she said. 'A lovely girl.' Liz was standing, waving him over eagerly.

When the car arrived to collect the bride and groom, Sam came over to Alexander's table, bowed extravagantly to Carol, and hauled Alexander to his feet. 'Time we were off,' he announced. He seized Alexander by the shoulders and kissed him on his ear. 'Thanks, Mac,' he breathed. 'Took care of the old folks for me. Good job. Good man.'

As Sam was embracing his mother, Liz came up to Alexander. 'You know, then?' she asked.

'About what?' he replied, and Liz glanced at her belly. 'I do,' he said, and he kissed her on the cheek, more coldly than he intended.

Soon after Liz and Sam had left, Alexander returned alone to Greenwich and went to the Crown and Anchor, where a couple he had never seen before had taken the table that normally was his. He sat at the bar until they went, and then he moved to the window. He rehearsed what he would say to Sam if he ever decided to tell him that he knew, and as he watched the steel grey of the sky turn to anthracite his anger weakened into disappointment, which became resignation, which became mere tiredness. Shortly before closing time Alf Davies came back in, and was given a pint, which he flicked with a thumbnail by way of acknowledging Alexander.

23. The Park Rangers

It was a Saturday and Alexander was about to close the shop when he saw them hurrying down the hill, with Mick Radford in the lead. As he reached for the upper bolt Mick saw him and pointed, and they all broke into a run. He went out onto the step, where they gathered in front of him.

'How's it going, Monty?' asked Mick.

'Fine,' replied Alexander.

'You got a minute? We'd like a word. Won't detain you long. Word of honour.' Mick spread his fingers over his heart, showing five oil-rimmed fingernails.

They followed him into the shop, where they lined up, precisely as a firing squad, as Alexander withdrew behind the counter. 'So?' Alexander asked. 'What's up?'

Pondering how to begin, Mick Radford stroked the flattened bridge of his nose. His sleeves were rolled up, revealing 'Mother' tattooed in blue ink on his left arm, on a scroll that wound around a scarlet heart, and 'England' on his right, above a vase-shaped thing that was intended, Alexander assumed, to be the World Cup. 'You know Dave,' said Mick, presenting Dave Gordon, with whom Alexander had exchanged a few words on a few occasions since the incident on the Heath, though more often they exchanged nothing more than nods whenever they happened to meet in the street or in the pub.

'Yep,' said Dave, giving Alexander a look that implied some doubt about their mission. There was always something undernourished and furtive about his appearance, and his outfit seemed to have been chosen to accentuate these qualities, with a close-fitting, high-collared white shirt, now tinged faintly blue, hanging over the waist of a pair of grey drainpipe trousers, which ended well above the tops of his winkle-picker shoes. The block in the pocket of his shirt, pinned tightly to his chest by the fabric, resembled some sort of bony extrusion rather than a pack of cigarettes.

'And of course you know this lad,' Mick continued, dropping a hand onto the shoulder of the shortest and plumpest of his three companions, who wore jeans and a secondhand pinstripe waistcoat, and glasses with red-tinted lenses shaped like letter-box slots.

'Come on, come on,' said the plump young man, scraping his damp and wayward hair. He hooked a finger over the bridge of his glasses and observed Alexander over the lenses, wryly, waiting to be recognised.

'Jesus! Gareth?'

'Jesus Gareth at your service,' Gareth Jones replied. 'Fifteen years wiser, fifteen years wider.'

'Where have you been?' asked Alexander.

'Only went three miles down the road. Where have you been?'

'Here, all the time. I thought –'

'And this is an old friend of mine, Billy. Billy Barton. We go back a very long way,' said Mick, as though there could be no better guarantee of Billy's good character.

'Known each other since the dawn of time,' Billy told Alexander. With his zip-up jacket, freshly pressed trousers, bristly fair hair and large white teeth, his appearance suggested to Alexander the character of an apprentice astronaut. As far as he was aware, Alexander had never seen him before.

Cheryl, from the baker's up the street, came to the door. 'We're closed, love,' Mick called out before she could open it, and Cheryl backed away, craning her neck to see where Alexander might be. Alexander smiled at her and mimed an apology. 'Better lock up,' said Mick. 'You do it, Chuck. Look lively.' Gareth stepped out of the line.

'Chuck? Since when's he been Chuck?'

'A year. In honour of the other Chuck Jones,' explained Billy.

'I see.'

'Creator of Sylvester, the hippest cat around,' added Dave, with a caustic smirk.

'So,' said Alexander, 'what's this all about?'

'Well,' answered Mick, 'what you have here, though you might not believe it, is a band.'

'The premier R&B outfit in the Blackheath, Lee and Mottingham area, we'd like to believe,' said Gareth, straining to push the bolt across.

'I do drums,' Mick went on. 'Dave and Billy are guitars. Chuck's on bass, and writes the songs, with Dave.'

'The Park Rangers,' said Billy. 'We're the Park Rangers. Because of –'

'I think he can work it out,' Dave interrupted.

'But,' said Mick, 'we're in a fix.'

'We need a singer,' stated Dave, seeming to imply that their problem was the fault of one of the other three.

'We had a singer to begin with, but he's out of the picture now. As of four o'clock. Man overboard.'

'Thought he should be getting the biggest cut,' said Billy.

'Of the money that will come flooding in our direction when we finally get out of Mick's garage,' Dave explained.

'No great loss,' said Billy. 'Pissed half the time, he was.'

'Aren't we all?' said Gareth.

'So we have this problem,' Mick resumed. 'I sound like a bus reversing, Dave's got a voice that could stun a mule at fifty paces, and you don't want to know what Billy sounds like. That leaves Chuck.' He bowed and gestured at Gareth as if passing a gift on to him. 'Chuck, if you would? "Wild Thing", perhaps?' Clutching his chest with parodic passion, Gareth howled the first verse, half in tune. 'Now that,' observed Mick, 'is the best we can do. And, as I think you'll agree, it's simply not acceptable to the general public. Not acceptable to anyone, really.'

'Not the best,' Alexander agreed.

'Painful, is what it is,' said Gareth.

'So,' Mick continued, 'you understand the situation. And this is where you come in, we hope. You can hold a tune, can't you?'

'Near enough, I suppose.'

'Better than that, Monty. I've heard you when I've been in here. Singing to yourself in the back room. Quiet, like, but I can tell. When we were kids you could do it. You can do it now. What do you think? Could be a big break.'

All four were looking at him: Mick with his arms spread wide, like a car salesman making a pitch for this week's special offer; Dave sullenly, as if indifferent to Alexander's decision but willing him to make it quickly; Gareth with a vague smile, perhaps elicited by something he was remembering from years ago; and Billy pulled the zip of his jacket right up, as if to make a good impression with a potential employer.

'R&B, you said?' Alexander asked.

'Right,' said Mick. 'Spencer Davis, Yardbirds, that sort of stuff.'

'You do their songs, you mean?'

'And some of ours,' Gareth interrupted. 'Dave and me have written one or two.'

Dave scratched his chin and looked around the shop to avoid Alexander's gaze.

'Give it a go,' Billy urged. 'If you can hum in the right key you'll be better than us. I mean, you look the part.'

'I don't know. I've never done anything like this,' said Alexander.

'We're all beginners, more or less,' Billy countered.

'I should do an audition.'

'If you insist,' said Mick.

'Next weekend?'

'Stuff next weekend. What's wrong with right now? Give us a quick blast, like Chuck did. Only better.'

'You need music, Mick,' Dave protested. 'You can't tell anything without music.'

'You can tell if someone's crap,' Gareth pointed out.

'Anyway,' said Mick, sweeping an arm out, 'we've got music. Tons of it, haven't we?'

'So we're going to have a sing-along right here?' Dave mocked. 'For the benefit of the good folks of Blackheath, Monty's going to stand here and make a screaming great tit of himself?'

'No, Dave, not here,' said Mick. Putting a hand on Alexander's back, he looked significantly at the ceiling, and then at Alexander.

Five minutes later they were filing into the living room of his flat. 'Like a monastery,' observed Gareth. 'I expected a bachelor pad, Alex. Cushions and posters and all that.'

'A year from now and you'll be in a penthouse in Mayfair,' Billy laughed, but nobody followed the joke. Billy took a seat on the settee beside Gareth. They looked like reluctant jurors, Alexander thought.

In an upper corner of the long white wall there was a lozenge of goldfish-orange light, reflected from a window across the street. As

Alexander looked at it he heard, in a lull of the traffic, the descending note of a plane flying away from the city, and the combination of the piece of radiant colour and the distant, falling sound made him acutely conscious of the absurdity of what he was about to do.

Dave Gordon was rifling through his records, urgently as a burglar who hears footsteps on the landing. 'The Supremes,' he called out. 'The Temptations, The Supremes, The Temptations. Lot of Tamla here,' he complained. 'John Coltrane? The Beach bloody Boys? You sure you're on for this?'

'Well –'

'Hang on. Here we go. Small Faces. That's more like it.' Like a marksman parading the target he has hit in the bull's eye, Dave displayed Alexander's copy of 'Sha La La La Lee'.

'We have blast-off,' Mick confirmed, settling on the windowsill. 'To the controls. Ready, Monty?'

Before Alexander could reply the music was playing. He joined in behind the beat, and skipped a word to catch up. Dave altered the tone to dampen the vocals, but before a minute had passed Mick raised a hand. 'No, no, no,' he moaned, and Dave lifted the arm off the record. 'We're not going to be singing for our mums and dads. You're being too – what's the word?'

'Wet,' said Dave.

'Yeah. A bit. Let yourself go, mate. Another try? Once more, Dave.'

Billy cleared his throat as if he were the one being asked to perform. Gareth pressed his glasses back into place, crossed his legs and uncrossed them immediately.

Again Alexander stepped into the music, and again Mick stopped him. Rubbing a forearm as though his tattoo were a rash, Mick grimaced at him. 'Better. It's louder, but you're still too posh. This isn't choir practice. Needs to be rougher.'

'Too Rex Harrison,' Gareth admitted. 'Loosen up, Monty. Relax.'

'Can't be done,' Alexander told him. 'Not with you lot watching me. Makes me feel stupid.'

'Imagine we're not here,' said Mick. 'Look the other way. Go on. Let's try again.'

Alexander stood at the end of the room, facing the door to the kitchen, but the third attempt was no improvement. 'Not right,' Mick pronounced, and he gazed out of the window. 'You're all strangulated, Monty.'

'Adjourn to the pub?' suggested Billy, but he received no response.

A bus arrived at the stop on the opposite side of the street. Alexander looked at the skin of its roof, which quivered with the vibration of the engine. He glanced at Mick, who was staring resentfully at the bus, as though its clattering had impaired his consideration of their problem. The bus pulled away and still nobody spoke. Gradually, however, the tension in Mick's face slackened, as if he had seen, in the vacated space across the street, the solution to their predicament. 'Remember that bastard Owen?' he asked. 'The psycho?' He scrutinised Alexander as Alexander had scrutinised the transformed Gareth Jones. 'You had him off perfect, didn't you? You could do him so good his own mother couldn't hear the difference. You know what I'm thinking? I'm thinking this isn't working because you're singing like you. What we want is for you to be singing like him on that record. I reckon you could do that. What do you think?'

'You want me to copy him?'

'That's it. Don't sing along with him. Be him. Try it, Monty.'

'You want me to do impressions?' Alexander laughed.

'To get it going. Once you break the ice, we're away. This'll work. I know it'll work. Believe me.'

'White boys with the blues,' added Gareth. 'It's all impressions, sort of.'

'Yeah,' said Dave. 'Go on, Monty. Fake from the heart.'

'Go through there, if we're putting you off,' said Mick, pointing to the kitchen door.

'Don't be bloody daft,' Dave protested. 'We can't stick him in another room when we play, can we? The Park Rangers, with backstage vocals from Monty MacIndoe.'

'Short-term answer, Dave, that's all,' said Mick. 'We all agreed we'd ask Monty. Can't let a bit of nerves beat us. Let's see if this gets us going.'

'Got a better idea?' Billy asked Dave. 'If you have, let's hear it.'

Dave put his hands on his hips and looked askance at Alexander. 'No,' he replied heavily. 'I don't have a better idea.'

So Alexander retreated to the kitchen, where he drew the curtains

212

because someone was standing at a window in the flat above the estate agent's. This will come to nothing, he told himself as the record started again, and he closed his eyes to release a voice that was not his and yet was no one else's, as if he were an instrument played by another's breath.

24. Mitchell

Most of their bookings were for Friday evenings, and it was on a Friday that they played in a pub that was close to Charlton House, as Alexander would remember, and had all its windowframes painted black. At the rear of the pub, between the fire escape and the lines of empty barrels, there was a black door on which 'The Playroom' was written within the bands of a rainbow. Inside, the flock-patterned wallpaper on the walls of the corridor had been covered in black paint, which had made the plumes and bouquets of flock as rough as brick.

Halfway down the corridor a second black door opened into the narrow back room, where the publican was stacking crates behind the bar. He had the girth of a wrestler and wore a black T-shirt that rode up over his belly when he straightened.

'Afternoon,' said Dave Gordon.

'A Stones fan, I presume?' Gareth called out from behind him.

The publican regarded Dave with morose irritation. 'You what?' he muttered.

'We're the band,' explained Mick Radford.

'Oh,' said the publican dully, wiping his hands on his T-shirt.

'The Park Rangers,' said Dave.

'Yeah,' said the publican. 'I didn't think you was Jehovah's Witnesses.'

'That's the Sunday job,' said Gareth.

The publican screwed a towel into a ball and lobbed it through a hatch below the inverted whisky bottles. 'He your John Lennon?' he asked Mick.

'Sort of,' said Dave. 'He's the smart-arse, but he plays bass.'

'I'm Ringo,' said Mick, holding out a hand. 'Otherwise known as Mick Radford.'

'Steve, the boss,' the publican responded, reaching over the bar. 'You're on at half seven. Break at half eight. Then nine till ten. Cash as agreed, when you're done. And two pints on the house, each of you. That's where you play.' He pointed to the end of the room, where two spotlights were bolted to an iron pole, above a rectangle of bare floorboards. Around the row of electrical sockets on the far wall someone had drawn a ring of chalk, indicated with a chalk arrow and the words 'The Juice'. A sour smell of old dishcloths rose from the lino.

'All right if we get unloaded now? Do a quick sound check?' Mick asked Steve.

'Sure. Go ahead.'

'Welcome to the Shea Stadium,' grumbled Dave Gordon, as he led them back out to the car park.

At seven-thirty the only other person in the room was the publican's son, who had been put in charge of the bar and stood stroking his knuckles as he surveyed the place, as if stoking a grievance against the people who should have been there. Two girls in identical pink minidresses, with identical belts made of huge silver loops, were the first to turn up. Arm in arm they came through the door, took two steps into the room, conferred, and walked across to the bar, their heads down as though huddling against a freezing wind. The girls went to a table against the side wall, where they hunched over their cigarettes and whispered to each other, mouth to ear, until half a dozen boys, each with a drink in his hand, came in to see what was happening, and the girls stopped talking. The boys turned, but were pushed back into the room by a group of couples whose arrival Mick heralded with the 'Bits and Pieces' drum roll. Dave grabbed the microphone from Alexander. 'Hang around,' he shouted, through a shriek of feedback. 'We're South London's finest, I'm telling you. We're bloody hot. Hotter than Old Nick's arse.' The publican's son chewed the nail of a thumb. One of the two girls clapped and whistled as Alexander sang the first line of 'Sweet Marie', the song Dave had written for a French girl he said he'd met one night in Dover, who was known to the others as Sweet Mirage.

After four or five songs all the chairs were taken and the door to the corridor seemed to be opening every few seconds. Through the hatch Alexander could see people leaving the front bar to come and listen. As they were about to start the last song of the first set, a boy in a mauve shirt sat down at the front table and folded his arms as if considering a verdict that would make or break the band, though he

215

looked no older than twenty. 'Yeah, that was a day,' sang Alexander. 'C'mon, I'll take you away,' he cried, roughening his voice in a way he had learned from Eric Burden. 'Babe, let's do it again,' he yelled, and then the door opened again and he glimpsed hair the colour of Megan's at the opposite end of the room. He shielded his eyes from the spotlight's glare, but all he could see clearly were the plates of cigarette smoke that floated in the shaft of white light. In the shadows, faces looked at him like dolls. Everything he saw was the colour of smoke. Staring at the boards in front of his feet, Alexander missed his cue for the last verse.

When he went to the bar to collect their drinks, Megan was standing there. Behind her, propped on his arms, with one leg extended and the other crossed over it at the ankle, was a man with a Buddy Holly hairstyle and long sideburns that tapered. His jacket was burgundy velvet, and he wore, askew, a thick velvet tie of the same colour. He was perhaps ten years older than Megan. 'This is Mitchell,' said Megan, stepping aside to present him. 'Mitchell, this is Alexander.'

Having taken a drag on his cigarette, Mitchell gave a low wave with the hand that held it. He nodded as he looked at Alexander, as though recalling something that Megan had said about him and judging it to be true.

'Pleased to meet you,' said Alexander.

'Likewise,' replied Mitchell, and then there was a pause.

'You're good,' said Megan. 'They're good, aren't they, Mitch?'

'Sure,' Mitchell conceded. 'You write your own stuff?'

'The guitarists do,' said Alexander. 'How did you know we were here?' he asked Megan.

She explained that they had driven past his shop the previous night and seen the flyer in the window. As she spoke, Mitchell put a hand on her waist, and watched the caressing motion of his fingers, as if nobody else were there.

'I didn't realise you were back,' Alexander remarked.

'Spur of the moment,' she said. 'Dad seemed low.'

'Seemed OK last week,' said Alexander.

'Yes, he's OK, I suppose. Up and down, you know.' She took hold of Mitchell's hand and stopped it.

'You know the old man, then?' Mitchell enquired.

'I told you he did,' said Megan.

'Must have slipped my mind,' Mitchell replied airily.

'I know him,' Alexander confirmed.

'Rare privilege,' said Mitchell. 'I've yet to have the honour,' he said. 'Deemed inappropriate at the present moment. I don't know whether to be flattered or not. Rival for the daughter's affections, perhaps.'

'Nothing to do with that,' said Megan tersely, looking at Alexander.

'No?' replied Mitchell.

'No.'

'So one day I'll get my admission ticket, eh?' said Mitchell, quickly tickling her ribs.

From a flickering of Megan's eyes, Alexander knew that Mitchell would never meet Mr Beckwith. 'I'd better get back to the lads,' he said to Mitchell. 'Talk later?'

'Later,' said Mitchell, making a gunslinger's draw with his hand.

The second set began badly and did not improve. Under Megan's gaze he heard himself singing about things he had never done and would never do, in a voice that was faked. Removed from himself, he forgot whole lines, came in on the wrong beat, was too quiet or too loud. The guitars sounded clangorous as scraped steel lids. The drums were like a hammering on hollow doors. He almost talked his way through the final song. The two girls in pink applauded with their hands above their heads.

Afterwards they went through to the front bar, where Megan and Mitchell were waiting. 'I thought it worked. What did you think, love?' Mick asked Megan before Alexander could introduce her. 'Speaking the words like they was poetry. Makes you sound sincere I think.'

'It was interesting,' said Megan. 'I'm Megan, by the way. And this is Mitchell.'

'How do,' said Mick, and Mitchell greeted them all with a wave identical to the one he had given Alexander.

'Shambles, if you ask me,' said Dave. 'Utter bloody shambles after half-time.'

'It was fine,' said Megan.

'Wasn't how it was meant to be,' said Gareth.

'You wouldn't have known,' Megan assured them.

'Making it up as we went along, some of us,' Dave complained.

217

Billy fetched the drinks, and then Mitchell laid his arms along the back of his and Megan's seat, in the manner of a host relaxing with his guests, and asked: 'So, how are you guys doing? Making a few bob?'

'We do all right,' Gareth told him.

'Lots of gigs like this,' Mitchell speculated.

'Wouldn't say lots,' Mick replied.

'But all in places like this,' said Mitchell. 'Nothing more ambitious.'

'Not yet,' said Dave, cleaning a fingernail with his plectrum.

'Building our following,' said Gareth.

'No sign of anything bigger?' asked Mitchell.

'Some bloke said he'd have a word with another bloke who knew a bloke who worked for some label or other,' said Dave.

'Never turned up, though,' added Billy.

Mitchell singled out Dave for his attention. He leaned forward, drawing smoke noisily through his teeth. 'Could be doing better, I'd have said. You've got talent. You can play.'

'Why thank you, kind sir,' said Dave.

'But you're not going anywhere without some changes, I can tell you that. For one thing, the shirts are a mistake. Round necks, white cotton, makes you look like dentists. Get rid of the shirts. Burn the shirts.'

'And then?' prompted Gareth.

'Some of your songs are good, OK? But this earthy old R&B stuff is getting stale. Pink Floyd, Hendrix, drugs – that's the way things are going.'

'Thanks, Mitchell,' said Mick. 'We'd noticed.'

Mitchell shifted nearer to Dave; he rested his elbows on the table and his chin on his thumbs. 'Guys, can I be absolutely straight here?' he asked earnestly. He gave Alexander a glance that might have been taken as a request for Alexander's permission to disclose a secret shared only by the two of them.

'Down the line, Mitch,' said Mick.

'What I'm about to say may seem strange,' Mitchell warned.

'Can't be stranger than Mick after six pints,' said Gareth.

Mitchell turned his cigarette and regarded it as though it were a fine figurine. 'I think – and I know it's only one view, but hear me out – that you need to think about the impression your front man makes. No offence, Alexander,' he added, raising his hands in appeasement.

'What, Alec?' Billy exclaimed. 'Fuck off.'

'He had an off night. We all do,' said Mick.

'That's not what I mean,' said Mitchell.

'He's the best thing they've got going for them,' Megan interrupted. 'No offence, boys.'

'None taken,' said Gareth.

'So what's the problem?' asked Mick.

'Yeah. What's the problem?' Billy demanded. 'I've heard plenty worse. Plenty worse than him sell millions.'

'Not arguing with that,' said Mitchell calmly.

'He can sing better than Jagger,' Billy insisted.

'I'm not arguing with you. It's a decent voice. More than decent. But that isn't the point. Singing isn't what it's about. Jagger's big because of the way he looks, not the way he sings.'

'You what?' said Mick indignantly. 'Al's miles better looking.'

'Exactly.'

'Exactly what?'

'Well, perhaps he's too much.' He smiled at Alexander as if to offer him the gift of his honesty.

'How d'you mean, too much? The girls really go for him.'

'Too bloody right,' said Gareth.

'Look,' said Mitchell, 'this is how it works, as I see it. It's about how you look, OK, but it's not about being good-looking. Jagger's no looker, but he really appeals to both camps, and that's the essence of it. The girls want to have Jagger, and the boys want to be Jagger – those that don't want to have him too. But your boy, he's too much for the guys. The girl vote, he's got that. But the girls don't buy the records. The girls don't do the deals. It's the boys you've got to impress. The boys want to be Mick Jagger. He can kid himself he's the same as Mick Jagger. But no bloke's going to be like Alexander here without major surgery. And he's too nice. He's obviously a nice boy. A really nice boy. But Jagger isn't nice. Lennon isn't nice, not really. Roger Daltry isn't nice. Cliff's nice, but that's not the same thing.'

219

'It's not, and neither's Mick Jagger,' objected Megan. 'They don't want a five-year plan for stardom.'

'No, but –' began Mitchell.

'They don't need a Brian Epstein.'

'She's right. We're a pub band, Mitch,' said Mick. 'Thanks for the advice, but that's all we are. We're not out to be anything big. More money we could handle, but we're not the next Stones.'

'We're going down in a blaze of obscurity,' Dave declared.

'OK,' said Mitchell, with a disavowing shrug. 'No more to be said. It struck me, that's all, when you were playing. Just a thought.'

'It's all right,' said Mick. 'Give us something to think about.'

'OK,' said Mitchell. 'I liked your stuff. But, you know –'

'Yes. It's OK.'

'I was impressed,' said Mitchell.

'Glad to hear it,' said Mick.

There was a silence, then a few minutes of broken chat, which lasted until Mitchell, having drained his glass, looked at his watch and said that it was time to leave. 'Right, guys. It was good. But got to hit the road.'

As if he were observing some peculiar social ritual, Gareth watched Mitchell helping Megan with her jacket. 'What do you do, Mitchell?' he asked.

'I'm at art college,' Mitchell replied.

'Doing what?'

'Teaching. Painting. Why?'

'Just wondering. No reason. Idle curiosity.'

'Drive carefully,' said Mick, drilling his cigarette butt into the ashtray.

'Got to make a call,' said Mitchell to Megan, and he kissed her and hooked her arm. 'Catch you again some time,' he told Dave.

'Look forward to it,' Dave replied.

'Bye, Megan,' Mick called out.

'Sorry,' she mimed to them behind Mitchell's back. With a jerk of her head she beckoned Alexander.

'Bye, Megan,' repeated Dave and Gareth and Billy in chorus.

Alexander followed Mitchell and Megan along the corridor. Under the lamp by the back door Mitchell turned to him. 'Don't take any of that stuff the wrong way, will you?' Mitchell urged, seemingly oblivious to Alexander's indifference. 'You're a good band. All of you. I mean that. I was being a bit controversial. Force of habit,' he admitted, winking at Alexander and patting his shoulder. 'See you again, I hope,' he said. He flipped his collar up and hunched his shoulders, though the night was mild, and he crossed the gravel car park to the phone box. He struck a match on the concrete bollard beside the box and cupped the flame for a few seconds before lowering his cigarette to it. He looked, Alexander thought, like a B-movie spy.

'Not pleased, is he?' Alexander remarked to Megan.

'About what?' she asked. They walked towards the car.

'About being banned from the house.'

'Banned is a bit strong,' she said. Ambling towards the car, Megan scuffed the gravel with each stride, as she used to do when she was a child, when she was bored.

'But he's not at all pleased.'

'He's not. But it's not what he thinks, Eck,' said Megan. She glanced towards the phone box. In the dowdy light of the cubicle, Mitchell was gesticulating as he talked, as if demonstrating a repertoire of argumentative poses.

'Isn't it?' Alexander replied.

'No. Dad's got his ways. It's not easy.'

'I know. But Mitchell's not going to pass the screen test, is he?'

Megan bumped her elbow against his side. 'Don't be smug, Eck,' she told him.

'I'm not being smug,' he protested. 'But he's not, is he?' he asked, and he heard the tone of his voice change, as if of its own volition.

'He's an intelligent person. Whatever he may say,' she laughed. 'But,' she continued, then stopped, and Alexander waited. 'He likes the sound of his own voice too much sometimes.'

'I can imagine.'

'And he wants me to marry him,' added Megan, casually, but with an incredulous widening of her eyes. She slipped her bag from her shoulder and fumbled for the key. 'Can't see a damned thing,' she said, and she looked up at the sky, where the upper half of a half-moon, as Alexander would always remember, stood up like a sail in a flow of starling-coloured cloud. Holding it wide open, Megan tilted the mouth

221

of her bag towards the light of the phone box. 'But I am not getting married, Eck,' she said, squinting into the bag.

'On principle?' he would have asked, but Mitchell had finished his call. 'See you, Mitchell,' he called. 'See you,' he said to Megan, and he returned to the back door, from where he watched the tail lights of their car shrink and then vanish at the junction. Dejection was rising within him, but he seemed to feel no jealousy. It was as though Mitchell had been nothing more than the means by which Megan had been brought into the evening and then removed. He stared at the place where the scarlet lights had disappeared, and then he went inside.

The girls in pink had now joined his friends. Full glasses filled the tabletop. 'What bollocks, eh?' said Billy to Alexander.

'Must be dynamite in the sack,' remarked Mick. 'Only reason a girl like that is going to be with a berk like him.'

'A big noise in his own trousers,' Gareth commented.

'What's that supposed to mean?' asked one of the girls.

'Don't know,' said Gareth contentedly. 'Catchy line, though, isn't it?'

'Nice girl,' said Mick.

'Very,' said Billy, with what was meant to be a lustful grin.

'I remember her, I think,' said Mick.

'I do,' said Gareth. 'Definitely. She did your reputation a lot of harm, Al.'

'How do you mean?'

'Hanging around with a girl when you could have been playing football. Not natural when you're eight, mate. Sissy MacIndoe, that's what you were.'

'On our block, all of the guys call him sissy MacIndoe,' Dave sang, to the tune of 'Pretty Flamingo'.

'Leave him alone,' objected the blonde girl, flicking ash at Dave.

'Yeah, leave him alone,' said Gareth, in a schoolboy's whine.

'My name's Lily,' the blonde girl told Alexander.

25. Gone but forgotten

The pleasure of being in the group was like the pleasure of appearing in a play on an irregular tour, in a succession of darkened and unfamiliar rooms. They had created roles for themselves, it seemed to Alexander, with ways of behaving that were so secure it was as if they had been written. He said as much once, to Gareth, as they walked back to Greenwich along the Woolwich Road, having played in a club that was run by a friend of Billy Barton. 'And we shouldn't be called The Park Rangers,' Gareth agreed. 'Should be The Misfit Labourers. That's what we look like.' Mick was Brickie Berserk, smacking the drums like he was throwing lumps of mortar all about the place. Dave Gordon was The Frustrated Craftsman, obliged to demean himself with a bunch of horny-handed artisans. Billy was The Genial Hodcarrier, happy enough to make a few quid on the side, while Gareth himself was The Clumsy Carpenter, fussing over his guitar as if trying to get his angles to come right. 'And that leaves you. You're not one of the labourers, of course. You're the front man, the focus of all our efforts. You're The Statue.'

'The Statue?'

'Yes. It's like you're a statue and we're building this room around you, to show you off.'

A couple of weeks later, Gareth gave him a T-shirt with the head of Michelangelo's *David* printed on the chest, which Alexander wore whenever they played. At the first bar of the opening number he would close one hand on the stand and the other on the microphone, then plant his feet wide apart and lock his legs and tilt his shoulders, adopting the posture of a hero of Soviet industry, from which he would barely move, no matter how loud the band or how boisterous the audience. He would train his gaze for as long as he could at a point to the side of the spotlight, so that when he looked away everything in front of him was blurred, like sandy seawater. Often he would close his eyes to inhale the air of the room, which changed from place to

223

place as little as the parts they played. It was an air compounded of smoke and beer and perfumed skin and the smell of hot dust and glass and metal that came off the lights, and Alexander inhaled it like a diver's oxygen. When he sang he thought of nothing; his voice seemed to be impelled not by his will but by the music that rushed into him. His head would ring in the noise they made, as if he were immersed in a breaking wave, and when the last song was over, and the lights in the room went up, a feeling of being stranded would overwhelm him for a moment, as if he had been washed ashore and unfamiliar faces were looking at him.

With the other four he would sit around a table and drink for a while, and talk about how the set had gone. There was rarely anything else for Alexander to talk about, not even with Gareth, whose boyhood friendship with Alexander was like an invisible and tedious companion who would not leave. Once or twice a month for almost two years, the band played in the pubs and clubs of south London. Almost forty times they played together, but those plentiful evenings would decay into meagre memories of half a dozen rooms, and a brawl one night in November, when a firework was thrown behind the bar, and parts of the evening on which Megan and Mitchell turned up, and Billy Barton arriving drunk because his girlfriend had left him and then tripping on a cable in the middle of a song and gashing his arm. Some faces and names he remembered, and a kiss by a grass-green door in the light of a bare fluorescent bulb, and sitting alone in a cold kitchen, with his hands on a clammy red oilcloth, looking out at a street he would never see again. And of all the nights on which he and Gareth walked or drove back together after playing, he would be able to recall substantially only the last one.

Gareth had written the words for a song, which he'd given to Dave a couple of months before. 'It's complicated, very intricate,' he assured Alexander, as they approached the town hall. 'A lot of wordplay. Like Dylan Thomas, that sort of thing.' He recited some lines. If you hadn't read *The Magus* you wouldn't understand it properly, he explained. 'Dave doesn't understand it, I reckon. That's why he's dragging his feet. Just doesn't get it.' It was not raining but there was water in the air, and a silvery coating had formed on the sleeves of Gareth's velvet jacket. They passed under a streetlamp and Gareth swiped the water

224

from his arms, as if someone had clumsily stained his clothing. 'He's not too subtle, if you ask me,' he went on. 'Can play the guitar, but he's too straight down the line.' He recited the last verse of his song. 'Now that's OK, isn't it?' he asked, and Alexander replied that it was. They walked in silence for a while, and then, for some reason, they stopped across the road from the pub where Eric Mullins had lived. Its name was the same as it had been, but the mane of the plaster unicorn had crumbled and its crown, once scarlet, was now white-washed. 'The good old days, eh?' said Gareth, with no clear meaning.

'Whatever happened to Eric?' asked Alexander.

'Christ knows,' said Gareth. 'Left years ago,' he added, and then he looked at Alexander pityingly. 'You don't get it either, do you?'

'Get what?'

'The song.'

'No,' said Alexander, in a tone not so much of admission as of refusal.

'Thought not,' said Gareth, and he walked off.

One morning the following week, Mick Radford phoned Alexander at the shop and told him that Dave Gordon had quit. An hour later he phoned again, to say that he had a replacement in mind, and that they should get together that evening. In the afternoon Mick called to postpone their meeting and by the Saturday the Park Rangers had been disbanded. Alexander removed the photo from the noticeboard behind the counter. 'The end of an era,' he announced to the half-dozen people in the shop, dropping the picture in the bin. One of the school-boys looked into the bin as if to see if Alexander had disposed of something valuable. The stolid young woman at the classical music section, whom he would not remember as having been there on that day, glanced over her shoulder, smiled sympathetically, and resumed her browsing. She was the only person under the age of thirty who regularly went to those racks, and since the beginning of that year she had called at the shop every month, always on a Saturday. Other than 'Hello' and 'Goodbye' and 'Thank you' she had never yet said anything to him. Methodically she would work her way through the month's new albums, seeming to take note of every word on the front of every sleeve; some she would take out and turn over to read the essay on the back, unselfconsciously and without haste, as though she were standing in her living room and reading a magazine. There was an air of deliberation and self-sufficiency and imperturbability about her, though she appeared to be no more than a year or two over twenty. Sometimes he would see her coming down the hill, or watch her walking away. She always walked slowly, as if enjoying an amble along a country lane, even when everyone else in the street was hurrying out of the rain. With her wide hips and long plain skirts, her deep-set blue eyes, her pale and mole-dotted skin, and her oak-blonde hair drawn back in two stout plaits, she put Alexander in mind of an alpine villager.

It was in October – Bob Beamon's picture was on the back page, he would remember – that they first had a conversation of any extent. Only she and Alexander were in the shop, and he was playing the Jeff Beck album. Leaving one hand in a gap between the album covers, she looked out of the window as if considering an idea that had suddenly occurred to her. Her hand lifted a cover free of the rack. She looked at it, and then at Alexander. 'Would you mind?' she asked, with a fatigued smile. 'That music. As there's no one else here, would you mind if we did without it? For a minute or two.' He took the album off the turntable. 'Thank you,' she said, and for five minutes or so the shop was like a library, as she reviewed that month's releases while Alexander turned the pages of his newspaper. And then he read something that made him laugh aloud. 'What's funny?' she asked, in a tone so plain it took Alexander aback. It was as though they were colleagues who were used to spending every day in the same room.

'A misprint,' he explained. 'I'm sorry.'

'What does it say?'

'No,' he said. 'Really. It's not funny. I'm sorry.'

She came over to the counter, carrying a sleeve. 'Come on. What is it?'

He placed a finger on the notice of the second anniversary of the death of a Mr Reginald Irvine of Charlton. The heading read: 'Gone but forgotten'.

She bit her lip guiltily. 'That's terrible,' she said.

'I shouldn't have laughed. It's not funny.'

'It's terrible,' she said, hiding her laugh behind the portrait of Beethoven.

'We shouldn't,' said Alexander. 'The poor family.'

'You're right,' she replied, and she composed her face into an expression of earnestness.

'Would you like to listen to that?' he asked.

'No thanks. It's not necessary. I've already heard it.' She placed the sleeve on the counter precisely, like a picture-framer aligning a watercolour on its backing card. 'I'll take it,' she said. Alexander went into the back room to find the record. 'My brother saw you, in your group,' she told him when he returned. 'He thought you were pretty good,' she said, intending, it seemed, simply to relay her brother's opinion rather than to please him.

'But you weren't tempted to check for yourself?'

'I'm happy to take his word for it, when it comes to things like that,' she said. 'And I'm not much of a one for pubs, to tell you the truth.' She put the money into Alexander's palm.

Two weeks later she appeared again, but she stayed for no more than ten minutes in the crowded shop, turning over the records she had seen a fortnight before, and left without talking to him. The following Saturday she returned, and after that she did not miss a week. Once, he would remember, she asked if she could listen to something, and she sat on the chair at the end of the counter, put the headphones on, and began to smile with such delight that one of the other customers – the jazz fan from the sorting office – glanced at her uneasily, as though he had found himself trapped with someone who was shouting nonsense. 'What are you reading?' she asked Alexander on another afternoon, after Mick Radford had called to pay the two pounds that he owed him from the last gig, and Alexander showed her the copy of Gilbert White that Mr Beckwith had given him for his birthday. She nodded, as if uncertain what conclusion should be drawn from his choice of book, but then somebody came in and the conversation ceased. That afternoon she bought an LP and wrote a cheque for it; Alexander watched her hand moving sinuously, writing the name Jane Nesbit. And then, on the last working day of the year, she arrived in the last half-hour, wearing a navy blue duffel coat and a vast navy blue pullover with a roll-neck collar and a partly unravelled cuff that protruded from a sleeve of the coat. 'Did you have a good Christmas?' she asked him casually.

'Quiet,' he said. 'And you?'

'The same,' she said. She pulled the hood of her coat down and went to her habitual section, like a machinist clocking on for her shift. 'Some cash from the aunts and uncles,' she explained, slapping her coat to make the coins chink in her purse. 'No point in delaying. Seize the day.' She picked up an album, scanned it, and dismissively replaced it.

'There's a few newer ones at the back,' he informed her.

'Yes,' she said, but she continued with the batch she had begun. For five minutes or so she persevered, and then Alexander looked up from his book and saw her glance at her reflection in the window and notice that he had seen her glance. She took up the record on which her hand was resting and brought it to the counter. It was a recording of Bach concertos, as he would always remember.

'You don't want to listen first?' he asked.

'Time for you to close. I wouldn't want to delay you.'

'I'm in no hurry.'

'No, really,' she said. 'I'll chance it. I have a good feeling.'

'OK,' he replied, and he stooped to take a paper bag from the lower shelf. When he stood up again his gaze was met briefly by hers, which seemed to have remained fixed on the place where he had been standing.

She looked down at her purse and prised it open. 'Do you have any family, Alexander?' she asked.

'A full quota of parents,' he replied.

'Oh,' she said, and seemed embarrassed. 'I'm glad. I'd assumed you didn't.'

'Why's that?'

'From your eyes,' she said. 'I thought I could tell. But obviously not.' She took from her purse a banknote that was folded into quarters and put it in Alexander's hand. Her gaze moved from his hand to his face, and she frowned as if trying to complete some connection of her thoughts. 'You do have the most fabulous eyes,' she stated, but like someone a generation older than she was. Still looking at him, she asked him directly: 'Are you happy?'

'Happier than most people, I think,' he said.

She looked at the wall, considering his answer. And then she raised

228

herself onto her toes, leaned across the counter and kissed him on the lips. 'Was that a mistake as well?' she asked. 'You look perplexed.'

'I am perplexed.'

Again she leaned forward, but this time she brought her face to within an inch of his and stared smilingly into his eyes for a moment, and then she kissed him as his hand touched her hair. Her lips, he would remember, seemed to be whispering as she kissed him, and the faintest perfume of lemons was on her skin.

'Still perplexed,' he said. 'Perplexed and not at all unhappy.'

'Well, you have a think, and I'll come back,' she said. 'You're with your parents for New Year?'

'I am.'

'And I'm with mine. But never mind,' she replied, and she held her hands out flat to receive the record she had bought.

'See you next year,' said Alexander, to which she said nothing. She sauntered up the road and did not look back, or betray an awareness that he might be watching her. When she had gone he locked up the shop and went upstairs to his flat, where he sat for an hour before phoning his parents.

26. Shipping Supplied

On the first Saturday of January she phoned him at the shop, and at six o'clock she came to the flat. She waited downstairs, in the hallway, while he fetched his jacket. They went up to town to see a film. On the train she sat facing him, and asked him how the New Year had been with his parents. It had been the usual routine, he told her: they watched TV, had a glass of the Christmas scotch, sang 'Auld Lang Syne' at midnight. 'My father goes all vague when he hears a bagpipe,' he said. 'I think it makes him pine for the glens.'

'And your mother?'

'Bagpipes make her ill. She prefers to be within a ten-mile radius of Oxford Street.'

'A city girl.'

'Through and through. She's OK for a week or two in the country, but she needs her magazines with her. To stay in touch with real life.'

'But they get on?' she asked. 'Your parents?'

'Oh yes. They get on. I've never heard them argue. Not really argue.'

'How unusual,' she commented, smiling. 'And what is it your father does?'

'Works in a bank,' he said.

'A banker with a soul?' she queried, and she kept him talking about his parents all the way into Charing Cross, where she took his hand and they walked to Haymarket to see a film of which, when he endeavoured to reconstruct this day many years later, he would remember nothing.

Of their Sunday morning walks he would remember reciting the description of the ancient yew tree in Selborne's churchyard, and Jane repeating, as if the sentence were the end of a fairy tale: 'This is a male tree, which in spring sheds clouds of dust, and fills the atmosphere around with its farina.' There was a bench on which the name of her schoolfriend Maria could still be seen, carved on the underside of the seat. One Sunday they drove to Rochester, but a downpour started before they reached the town, and the water was dripping into their hair through a rip in the canvas roof, so they took a turn down the high street and then drove back. Somewhere in the West End, waiting for traffic lights to change, she told him that she loved her mother, with an emphasis that made it plain she did not care for her father, but then, for some reason, nothing more was said. He recalled how she would decline to come up to his flat, with a kiss that was like an affectionate reproof. 'Not yet,' she would sometimes say to him, and raise a forefinger to his lips. He would remember going into her flat for the first time and seeing the records she had bought from him, arranged behind the armchair; she lit a stick of incense that evening, as she always did, and when she left the room he looked at the objects on the shelf above the record-player – the tiny cross-legged brass elephant, the postcard from Iona, the bottle of minuscule glass beads, the photograph of Jane by a canal in Amsterdam, the little tree made out of cork – and anticipated the time when he would understand how these things were connected. On that first evening they sat on cushions on the floor to listen to the Bach concertos, with her back against his chest, and occasionally she would press his hands tightly, as if to transmit her contentment to him. When he left he stood under the tree on the other side of the street, to see her shadow moving in the room as she cleared away the plates. He did this many times, and often he stayed until her light went out. Once, he would remember, he saw her take the glass he had used and touch it to her lips.

Then, one evening in April, they were walking up to the Heath from her flat when a wolf-whistle, not loud but protracted, made them turn. On the other side of the street, walking in the same direction, was a boy of fifteen or so, in jeans and a denim jacket that was studded across the chest with small enamel badges, and with straggly dark hair, parted down the centre. He kicked a flattened can off the pavement, then looked at them and gaped. 'Stay here,' Jane sighed. 'I'll be back in a minute.' The boy had turned and was walking away with a rapid, cringing gait, but Jane caught up with him quickly, and pulled him back by the shoulder. He raised a hand to knock hers away. Alexander called her name and stepped off the pavement, but she stopped him with a flat hand, like a policewoman on traffic duty. She pushed her face towards the boy, who was smiling now. Jane poked a finger at the boy's chest. Laughing, he ducked and weaved, leading with a loose left fist. Alexander ran towards her. 'Stay back!' Jane shouted at him, and contemptuously walked away from the boy, who stayed on the spot for a few seconds, shadow-boxing. 'What a creep,' she cursed quietly.

'What was he –'

'My brother Martin,' Jane told him.

'Not how I imagined him,' said Alexander. Over his shoulder he saw Martin watching them, rubbing at his chin to erase his smirk.

'A brat and a nuisance,' she complained, looking back. Martin, walking their way again, waved heartily at her, like a hiker hailing a pair of fellow enthusiasts on an upland footpath. 'Now we've been found out,' Jane said. 'You'll have to meet the family.'

He met the family the following week, on the Saturday evening. He wore the blue suit he had bought when the band had tried a change of image, and the blue silk tie his father had passed on to him the year before, to smarten up his wardrobe. Standing on the pavement outside her flat, Jane appraised his outfit. 'You look lovely,' she said. 'Mum will adore you.' She buttoned her duffel coat over the outsized blue jumper and inspected him again. She adjusted the knot of his tie and stroked it as though it were a talisman. 'An hour,' she said. 'That'll do for the introduction.'

It was her mother who came to the door. Blue-eyed and pale and broad at the hips, with fair hair that was pulled back into a bun, she was so similar to Jane that it was like looking at Jane's face under a disguise of creases and little pouches of flesh. 'Mrs Nesbit, you'll have guessed,' she said, wiping her hands on her apron. 'Very nice,' she said to her daughter as she shook Alexander's hand. 'I do like a man in a blue suit. Come on in.' Behind her mother's back, Jane raised her hands as if asking for heaven's aid. 'You see what you're letting yourself in for?' said her mother to Alexander, having halted halfway down the hall. With a thumb she pressed at the creases that crossed her brow and curved towards her eyes. 'All the women in this family go wrinkly before their time. Wonderful when you're a youngster.' Cherishingly she put her hand to her daughter's cheek. 'Beautiful milky skin. Never had a spot in her life. But soon enough she'll get the wrinkles.' She took them through to the living room, where Martin was watching a flock of flamingos on TV. 'Say hello, Martin,' she instructed him.

'Yeah,' said Martin, lifting a hand from the bowl of crisps in his lap. 'We've met.'

'No you haven't,' said Jane.

Rustling his crisps, Martin simulated fascination with the antics of the feeding birds.

'Martin. Where are your manners?' demanded his mother.

'Missing, presumed dead,' Jane interrupted.

'Evening, boyfriend,' said Martin.

'Good evening, Martin,' Alexander responded.

'A cup of tea?' asked Mrs Nesbit. She went into the kitchen, leaving Alexander and Jane to sit at the table, while Martin heckled the wildlife. A cheetah was running a small antelope to ground when Mrs Nesbit came back, bearing a tray on which were set three cups and a teapot enclosed in a brown and beige tea-cosy.

'Left, left, you stupid bastard!' Martin shouted.

'Martin!' snapped Jane.

'Taken a left he'd have been home,' explained her brother, gesturing at the screen in his defence. 'Now look at him. Cat food. Should have looked both ways before crossing.'

Mrs Nesbit shrugged hopelessly at Alexander and gave him a rapid smile that the others were not intended to see. 'Knitted by Jane,' she told him, tweaking the bobble of the cosy. 'When she was eight.'

'Finished when she was sixteen,' said Martin.

'Ignore the oaf,' said Jane to Alexander, and her mother nodded in agreement. For a while they chatted at the table, and then the front door slammed.

'The boss is back,' said Martin, raising both hands in awe.

Mr Nesbit presented himself in the doorway, but did not come into the room. Scratching his dusty hair, he looked from his wife to Jane to Alexander, and when his gaze fell on Alexander a twitch seemed to occur in the muscles of his hairline and eyelids.

'This is Alexander. Jane's young man,' said Mrs Nesbit.

Mr Nesbit took the rolled newspaper from his back pocket and lifted it in greeting. 'Evening, Jane,' he said.

'Hail,' called Martin, without turning round.

'I'll get cleaned up,' said Mr Nesbit, indicating his overall. 'Excuse me – Alexander, was it?'

'It was.'

'Yes,' said Mr Nesbit. 'Excuse me.'

Ten minutes later he returned, with his hair combed and oiled, wearing a waistcoat over a fresh white shirt. Passing behind Jane's chair he stroked her hair lightly, and Alexander thought he saw a slight cowering of her shoulders. 'So, Alexander,' said Mr Nesbit loudly as he sat down on an armchair, but instead of completing his sentence he took a pack of papers and a pouch of tobacco from his waistcoat and began to roll a cigarette in his palm.

'Alexander works in the record shop,' his wife explained. 'In the village.'

'Oh yes,' said Mr Nesbit.

'You know it?' asked Alexander.

'Oh yes,' he replied. 'I know it.'

'And he's a singer. In the Forest Rangers. That's right, isn't it?'

'Park,' Martin snorted. 'The Park Rangers.'

'Martin went to see them,' Mrs Nesbit continued. 'Didn't you, Martin?'

'I went somewhere and they were there.'

'He said you were very good,' Mrs Nesbit told Alexander.

'I said they were OK.'

'We had worse reviews,' Alexander said to Martin. He took the replenished cup that Mrs Nesbit was offering him. 'Actually, Mrs Nesbit,' he said, 'I'm not a singer any more. The band broke up.'

'Oh dear,' she said. 'That's a shame.'

'We'll recover,' said Martin.

'Turn that off,' Mr Nesbit ordered his son.

'It's educational,' Martin replied.

'You're not going to get leopards in your exams.'

'They're not leopards.'

'I don't care what they are. Turn it off.'

Martin jabbed a thumb on the switch and kept it pressed there, rocking it as if squashing a fly.

'So anyway, tell us about yourself, Alexander,' resumed Mr Nesbit, with a half-smile that seemed almost resentful, and which was directed at Alexander several times in the ensuing conversation. Martin watched with evident pleasure at his discomfort, while Jane seemed to conduct a dialogue of glances with her mother, to whom Mr Nesbit addressed not a word in all the time that Alexander and Jane were there.

'You'll stay for a bite?' Mrs Nesbit asked Alexander, after a story about Sam Saunders and Sam's mother's cigarette supply had made nobody laugh except Jane.

'We'd better get going,' said Jane. 'We've got friends coming round,' she lied.

'Well,' said Mr Nesbit, rising from his chair with alacrity to give Alexander a forceful handshake.

Alexander shook hands with Mrs Nesbit, and said goodbye to Martin, who was already moving towards the TV. 'See you,' said Martin. 'Bye, your ladyship,' he called to Jane. Only Mrs Nesbit came out into the hall.

Outside the house a van was now parked. 'D. S. Nesbit: Builder & Decorator' was painted on its sides. Jane leaned against a lamppost, scowling at the lettering on the van as though it were an abusive message directed at her. 'That was awful,' she said.

'It wasn't the social event of the decade,' said Alexander.

'I'm sorry.' She glared at the house then threaded a hand under his arm. 'He's ruined the evening for us. I'm sorry. You had the third degree.'

'Did I say something wrong?'

'No, you were lovely. He takes against people sometimes. I knew he'd take against you.'

'Why?'

'Because you're with me, for one thing. He's jealous,' she said, taking a kick at a tyre. 'I have to go home, Alexander. He's put me in a mood. Are you OK?'

'Unscathed.'

'Shall we go out tomorrow?' she asked him. 'Let's have a day away. I'll call for you?'

At precisely nine o'clock his doorbell rang, and he looked out of the kitchen window to see her Morris Minor parked below. She had fastened the canvas roof back and the steel spokes of the steering wheel glinted as if they had been polished that morning. Hearing the window rattle, she stepped backwards out of the doorway. She was wearing a sleeveless white shirt and a long blue skirt, and her hair was arranged in a ponytail that was tied high on her head and swung at the slightest movement. 'Very Grace Kelly,' he called down. She crossed her ankles and curtsied, ballerina-fashion, holding her hem between her fingertips.

When Alexander came out of the flat she was in the car, with a map draped over the dashboard. 'How about a trip to Canterbury?' she suggested, and with a finger she demonstrated the route to the city. He kissed her on the cheek, and from the way she accepted the kiss he understood that the visit to her family's house was not to be mentioned. Canterbury was fine, he said. 'Open top?' she asked, gesturing at the sky. He smacked his hand on the outside of the door and pointed up the road.

For the first few miles they hardly spoke, but then Jane seemed to relax, as if the last trace of the previous day had now evaporated from her mind. She told him about the day she first went driving after passing her test, when she ended up on the coast, not far from Brighton, and had so little petrol in the tank that she was turning the engine off at every set of lights on the way back and coasting down every hill. 'Befuddled by the thrill of independence,' she commented. 'So I did it again the next weekend, but with enough money this time. A one-woman victory parade, down to Brighton and back.' She looked from the rear-view mirror to Alexander and back again quickly. 'Silly, is what you're thinking.'

'No, I wasn't,' he said, and he told her how, when he moved into his flat, he would sit in the living room at night, with the lights off, enjoying the silence of the place. Sometimes he would lose all sense of time and find, when he awoke from his trance, that hours had passed while he sat at the window. 'Mad, is what you're thinking,' he said. She smiled and put her hand to his face.

They were about ten miles from their destination when Alexander sensed a vapour of salt water. Resting his head against the window, he closed his eyes to sniff at the air, in pursuit of the saline taste.

'Alexander, what on earth are you doing?' Jane asked.

'The sea,' he replied. 'You can smell the sea.' She breathed deeply, but was unconvinced. 'You can,' he insisted, smiling with his eyes closed, like a sunbather.

'You can smell the engine, and that's about it,' she said.

'The sea, the sea,' he yearned, like a feverish young poet repeating to his pillow the name of his lost beloved.

Jane raised herself in her seat to put her face into the air that streamed over the windscreen. 'I'm getting nothing,' she said.

'We're there, practically,' said Alexander, and he showed her the map, spanning the distance from the city to the coast with a thumbnail.

'You're advising a change of plan?'

'A small diversion. We could go to Canterbury afterwards. A stroll by the water. What could be more pleasant on a day like this?' he asked, with a florid, poetical wave of a hand.

A minute later she turned onto the road to Whitstable, where they parked in a side street and followed the signs to the harbour. They stopped to look at the tiny frontage of the Foresters' Hall and the gulls that stood like trophies on the stepped gable behind it, and again at St Alphege's church, where the tone of another visit to the town, a visit made in his childhood, made itself present clearly, like the note of a tuning fork. He remembered seeing that the church had a name that was almost the same as the name of the church in Greenwich, and being confused by it, and deciding that this misspelled building was in some way a faulty version of the London church. At the two white clapboard cottages in Harbour Street he smiled, as if encountering a friend who had thought to surprise him. 'What?' Jane asked him, and he told her what he was remembering: his father in his Harris tweed jacket, despite the heat of the day, and his mother in her polka-dot dress, holding his father's hand and waving her other hand rapidly at Alexander, because he had his thumb over the lens of the Brownie camera.

'Down here,' he said, 'there used to be a shop with advertisements painted around the upstairs windows. Royal Daylight Lamp Oil was one,' he recalled, and they continued down Harbour Street, where 'Royal Daylight Lamp Oil' was still legible on the brick, above 'Shipping Supplied', which had excited him with the notion that the seafront would be thronged with adventurers, making their last preparations before departing from England.

They walked along the wharf, past the fish market and the row of tall sheds. On the harbour side of the sheds, nets were draped to dry

237

on the balustrades of the upper storey; at the back, windows oozed a steam that reeked of shellfish. 'Now I can smell the sea,' Jane said, and she strode ahead, down the shingle-strewn path that led to the beach. Everything he saw was delicious to Alexander, and he would remember avidly the details of the hour: the thick grey planks of the slipway, frosted with mustard-yellow lichen; the slate-grey wooden walls of the huts behind them; the calm grey sea, which darkened with distance and became, in front of the low promontory across the bay, a colour identical to that of the sky above the headland; the farther strip of land, dark as an eel; the newly sawn lengths of timber stacked on the concrete pier, which were brighter than anything else on the waterfront. He watched the syrupy ripples of the water, while Jane read the book she had brought.

Jane dozed for a while, and when she awoke a breeze was gathering. Now there were dashes of iridescent olive-green in the open water, between dashes of black. Under the pier, between the rusting iron columns, the light on the agitated water made shapes like new springs of thin steel, coiling and uncoiling. Her hand rose to take his. 'Alexander,' she said softly, as if his name were an exotic word that made a pleasing sound. She released his hand and looked at him for a long time. 'Alexander,' she said again, putting his fingers over her eyelids.

They had something to eat in a café at the end of a street of low cottages, and drove back to London. The street lights were not yet on, Alexander would remember, when Jane drew the curtains. In a corner of the room she undressed without hurry, laying her clothes on the seat of a chair, carefully, as if she were laying them out for somebody else to wear. Unabashed, she crossed the room slowly, moving exactly as she did when clothed. She stood beside the bed and bent over to kiss him. She had not said anything since they had come into her flat. All this he would remember, and the coolness and the elusive salty perfume of her skin.

27. All My Appointed Time

Late in the evening Alexander's mother brought the biggest of the photograph albums downstairs and placed it in Jane's hands. Jane lowered it into her lap as if she were holding a box of blown glass, raised the front cover on her fingernails, and peeled back the leaf of tissue paper that covered the first page.

'Alexander's grandparents,' said his mother, with a fond, respectful cadence.

'Paternal?' asked Jane, and she gave Alexander a glance for corroboration.

'Hamish and Helen,' said his father.

'On the occasion of their engagement,' his mother added, wiping a crease from the tissue.

As Jane raised the album closer to her face, Alexander leaned over the back of the settee to regard the portrait of his father's father. Hamish Alexander MacIndoe always looked to Alexander not like a man who was alive but like an effigy of himself, with his waxen white skin and wig-like hair, and his mouth as straight as a spirit level, and his wide glassy eyes. The shining eyes and the rigid mouth gave his grandfather's image the expression of a man stupefied by his own probity.

'A handsome man,' Jane remarked, angling the page in the light of the standard lamp, and Alexander could tell by the tightening of the skin at her temple that she, like he, could see no resemblance at all between Hamish MacIndoe and Hamish's son.

'By all accounts,' said Alexander's mother. 'A good-looking and flinty kind of man.'

'I don't recall him,' his father told Jane. 'I was five when he died.'

Jane half-closed the album, as though by way of expressing condolence. 'In the war?' she asked.

'He survived the fighting. It was the flu that killed him,' explained Alexander's mother.

'Killed more than the war,' said his father. 'Far more. Twenty-five million in all. Thereabouts. He died in the second wave, in 1920. Worst epidemic since the Black Death.'

'I'd no idea,' Jane apologised.

'That's all right. Few people have. Flu's not dramatic enough, I suppose,' said his father, peering with one eye into the bowl of his pipe. 'No sense of the heroic, the Biblical. Not nasty enough. Outdone by the Somme,' he reflected. 'I don't know. Died of the flu. Scarcely better than "slipped on the soap".'

'He was an engineer,' said Alexander. 'A steam engine man.'

'Went up to York on a Friday, right as rain,' his father told her. 'Came back with an ache and a cough. Dead the following Thursday.' With a fluting breath he expelled the debris from his pipe.

'I'm sorry,' said Jane.

'No need, dear. C'est la mort,' his father responded, with a loose-wristed wave of his hand, like a gallant salute. 'But thank you.'

'Yes,' said Alexander's mother wistfully. 'They didn't have long together, did they? They married late, for those days. This would be 1910, wouldn't it, Graham?'

'It would.'

'They moved down to London, for his work, soon after they married. Then they had a five-year wait for their son,' she said to Jane.

'Remission,' muttered his father from the side of his mouth, and he winked at Alexander as he struck a match.

Alexander looked down at his grandparents again. Like busts on a tomb they stared out from behind the sandstone-coloured frames, Hamish to his left and Helen to her right, in perfect symmetry, so that their gazes met at a point midway between them, a short distance above the plane of the page, as if to seal their union in death and exclude whoever in the living world regarded them.

'She had a twinkle to her,' said his mother, brushing a fingertip across the lace of Helen's blouse, which looked as hard as porcelain, like the substance of Hamish's collar. She touched the brooch at Helen's throat, which was as big and as dark as a bar of coal tar soap, and the lips, which were the only part of her face in which Alexander could recognise anything of his father. 'I think the photographer had told her to stop smiling a second before he pressed the shutter, don't

240

you?' she asked Jane, and Jane agreed. 'I met her only once before we were married. We took the train up to Edinburgh, then a taxi out to her house. She moved back, as soon as Graham left home. To the same street, just a few doors down. I was frogmarched up the garden path, and Graham's mother opened the door. Before she could say a word, Graham said to her: "Hello Mother, this is Irene. We're getting married." And she inspected me for a minute, then she grabbed my hands and laughed, didn't she?'

'Screamed.'

'Laughed,' she assured Jane. 'We had shortbread and sherry in the garden, and she kept her hand on my knee all the time. And when we had to go she said "You'll do," and she sort of patted me, didn't she?'

'On the bottom,' explained his father, striking a second match.

'She came to our wedding, of course. Played the piano at the reception for us. What was it, Graham?'

'"The Dance of the Blessed Spirits".'

'That was it. She had a funny way of playing.'

'As if there was a nasty smell emanating from the keyboard,' said his father, pressing his head into the back of the chair and flaring his nostrils. 'One of her wee ways.'

'Like open windows.'

'Always had the windows open. Ice Station Zebra, our house in winter. And she didn't like handling coins and notes with her bare hands. You never know what diseased flesh has fingered them. Thought I was risking my life when I went to work in the bank. All that unwashed currency.'

'She was a character,' his mother sighed, and her eyes, directed at her husband, became momentarily vacant with the recollection of her.

'What was her name?' asked Jane. 'Before she was married?'

'Cruft,' said his father, batting aside the curls of smoke. 'Helen Clementine Cruft.'

'What a wonderful name,' Jane commented, and she blushed.

Alexander heard the refrigerator shudder and its bottles clink. Unobserved by his parents, he touched the upper arch of Jane's right ear. 'Moving on,' he said, reaching over to turn the page.

'Alexander never met her,' said his mother, settling a cushion in the small of her back. She craned her neck to see the picture that Jane was now studying, in which Helen and Hamish, out of focus some twenty yards from the camera, grasped the top bar of a fence to balance on a tandem in front of a crag and a stretch of blurry water. 'Where's this, Graham?' she asked. 'The tandem.'

'Dunsapie Loch. Holyrood Park. Same year, I think.'

'She loved Holyrood. When she was a girl she used to go there every day. Before school in winter, after school in summer. Her favourite story was King Arthur, the once and future king, asleep under his hill. She used to imagine that Arthur's Seat was the hill he was under, she told me. And she used to imagine herself asleep under the hill.'

'The view from Arthur's Seat was the most beautiful in the world, she thought,' said his father. 'Very romantic city.'

'Cold,' his mother retaliated, encasing Jane's arm in her hands.

'Not necessarily a contradiction.'

'Cold and wet.'

'A city of all weathers and for all temperaments. The Old Town for the heart, the New Town for the head.' With the stem of his pipe his father made crosswise incisions on his chest. 'When I am dead and opened, you shall find Calton lying in my heart,' he proclaimed.

'I've never been,' Alexander whispered to Jane, turning the page. 'They never saw fit to take me.'

'We took you to Scotland once,' said his mother.

'But not to Edinburgh.'

'No, to –'

'Pitlochry,' his father interrupted.

'He can't bear the way I pronounce it,' his mother confided to Jane.

'When I was twelve,' said Alexander. 'For a week.'

'A week of rain and midges. Bitten raw, my arms were.'

'Bitten raw,' his father mocked.

'They were. Clouds of the things, every evening. Thousands and thousands of them. Horrible little specks. In your hair, in your eyes, in your ears. Everywhere.'

'Tried spraying them with Chanel, to no avail.'

'Never again,' said his mother, fiddling with the chain that fastened her bracelet and then with the strap of her wristwatch. 'Anyway,

Alexander preferred Cornwall. And we've been to Edinburgh a few times, Graham, you and I.'

'We have,' his father conceded, and received from his wife a tender glance, from which Alexander looked away.

Alexander turned the page, revealing the photograph of his mother's father that used to hang in a frame in Nan Burnett's front room. He started to turn the page again, but Jane stopped him. 'Wait a second,' she said, raising a forefinger, almost peremptorily.

'My father,' said his mother. 'Stanley. Stanley Burnett. He died before I was born. In the war.'

'Let's pass on,' his father said. 'The poor girl's had enough death and gloom for one evening.'

'We're not gloomy, are we, Jane?' his mother responded, taking a corner of the page. Alexander saw her gaze slide from Jane's pale hand to her own, and stay for an instant on a varnished nail, as if noticing a flaw in its colour. 'Alexander, why don't you make us all some coffee?'

He went into the kitchen, and when he returned they were still looking at the photographs. 'The years of short trousers,' Jane smiled, holding up a page on which Alexander, wearing shorts and a V-neck jumper and a narrow tie, sat beside Jimmy Murrell on the kerb of a street he did not recognise, and his father stood under a tree in Greenwich Park, frowning at an entangled kite, and his mother slept in a deckchair in the garden, with the fingers of her left hand curled so elegantly on the armrest it looked as if a cocktail glass had been erased from her grasp. Jane studied the page again, as if wanting to make sure that she had memorized each image before proceeding. When she came to the photograph of his parents and the Beckwiths on a boat by Tower Bridge she commented: 'Now I know what he looks like.' She pointed to Mr Beckwith, and his father looked at her over the rim of his cup.

Once or twice a month his mother would invite them for a meal, and sometimes the album would be brought down again, at Jane's request. Lingering on the portraits of Hamish and Helen, resting her fingertips on the page as she listened, like a medium at a seance, she would ask his father about his mother and their holidays in Edinburgh. His father would lower his newspaper far enough to allow Jane to see his eyes, and recount what he could recall, or what he thought might suffice, in a way that made it seem as if the anecdote were a story rather than a recollection. He told her one evening about visiting the High Kirk of St Giles, with his grandfather, Duncan Manus, on a day so windy that his grandfather's beard was blown into a shape like a swallow's tail. Underneath a stained glass window his grandfather put his hands on his shoulders and talked to him about the prophets, whom he described with such familiarity and esteem that thenceforth his grandson had imagined the City of God as a town that was somewhere on the other side of the world, with streets like the streets of Edinburgh, but wider and cleaner and with no horses or automobiles, and with buildings made of stained glass, one of which was a building like a parliament in which the prophets made their speeches. When his grandfather left him to contemplate the Israelites crossing the River Jordan, he passed the time by counting the pieces of glass in the window, which seemed to tremble like a sheet of greaseproof paper in the wind, and when they stepped outside a flock of crows went over Lawnmarket sideways, like black paper bags blown off the rooftops. His hand skittered out from the arm of his chair, the fingers rippling like wind-beaten wings, and it was then, Alexander would remember, that Jane closed the album softly and said: 'We should go, one day. To Edinburgh.'

A couple of months later, a week before Jane's birthday, they travelled to Edinburgh on the sleeper, on a night that was very humid, as he would remember. They lowered the window and lay together in the upper bunk to see the lightning splash the hills and houses to the west. After Jane fell asleep he stayed awake for another hour or more, watching the light of the train as it raced over fields of black grass, through sidings in which the wrecks of old carriages were herded, across empty streets and stations. He slept for no more than an hour, and his tiredness enhanced the evanescent pleasure of emerging from the station into a city that was perfectly strange. Breathing an air that was like the air of no other place, he saw in the hills and buildings varieties of colour he had never seen before. The sound of the morning's traffic seemed as rich as the sound of an orchestra tuning up. He kissed her, and then she took out the map his father had marked and pointed the way to the guest house. She reversed her signet ring

244

to make a wedding ring of it while he signed the register, a sleight of hand that the receptionist noticed. They were given a room that was barely larger than the train compartment and provided a view not of the castle, as he had been assured it would, but of the glow of the floodlights on the castle, which radiated above the roofs like the nimbus of another moon.

As soon as they had unpacked they went to the Royal Mile. He bought her a pair of earrings from a shop on Lawnmarket, where they were served by an obsequious and breathless young man who had shaved so hurriedly that he had left sooty tufts of whisker under each nostril. In the High Kirk of St Giles they gazed up at the prophets and the River Jordan. 'Is it what you expected?' Jane asked him, and Alexander could not recall what he had expected, because he was thinking not about the building but about his father, whose own father had died so early. It wasn't quite, he replied; nothing ever was what you imagined it would be. She gave him a sceptical look, which she cancelled as she took his hand. They had lunch on Canongate and in the afternoon they visited the castle, where, as they surveyed the city from the Argyle Battery, an American man asked them if they were on their honeymoon. He looked at them through lenses so thick his eyes were like olive stones in the bottom of flesh-coloured cups. That was right, Jane said, reaching for Alexander's hand behind his back. They were spending the weekend in Edinburgh, and then they were going on to Pitlochry, she said, and her fingers caressed Alexander's as she spoke.

The next morning, having been roused at ten o'clock by Mrs Donaghy, who told them loudly, from the other side of the bedroom door, that they were now too late for breakfast, they took a bus to Mayfield, to find the houses in which his grandmother had lived. Following the map, Jane eagerly led Alexander up the street, as if she were hurrying to see a place that she was thinking of buying. 'This is the one,' she said, at a drab little house behind a privet hedge. 'This is where she lived until she married.' Alexander looked at the slug-shaped scars that had been left on the bricks by a web of ivy; he looked at the lank green nylon curtains in the upstairs windows, and all he felt was a redundant compassion for his father, like an echo of the emotion he had felt in the church. Jane gazed at the building, as if it were a screen and she was waiting for something to appear on it. 'Her room must have been at the back,' she observed, pointing at the hill that rose over the roof. Alexander agreed, and continued down the street. The house in which his grandmother had died was fifty yards away. It was now a guest house. Where there had once been a garden there was now an area of concrete paving, on which three cars were parked. 'This is disappointing,' she said. 'But I want to go on. You don't mind, do you? It's your roots, after all.'

They walked to the cemetery in which Helen was buried, and Alexander would always remember Jane striding between the rows of gravestones, as if the grave of his grandmother were something immensely precious that she had mislaid. 'Over here,' she called at last, beckoning him. On a low white stone was inscribed: 'To the memory of Helen Clementine MacIndoe, née Cruft, b. 1880, d. 1941', and underneath, carved in a fluid and uneven script, like letters scraped quickly into soft clay, 'All My Appointed Time Will I Wait, Till My Change Come.' Jane crouched by the stone, with one hand resting on its upper face; Alexander read the words again, and wandered away, towards the perimeter wall.

He sat on the ground with his back against the wall, by an overspill of buddleia. The name of Eliza, the beloved wife of George McFarlane, was spelled in grey lead letters on one of the four bars of marble that enclosed her burial plot, a rectangle of coarse grass on which plantains and mint and daisies sprouted. Next to her, a slab of stone that had become as dull as cardboard recorded the deaths of Lieut. Gordon Petrie, R.N., who crossed the bar 3rd Feb 1914, and Charles, youngest son of the above, died in action in France, 14th August 1917, aged 22 years. Behind them lay Richard Guise Davidson, who ceased not to preach Jesus Christ and was called suddenly to rest in a year that was lost under moss. Alexander breathed the honeyed air beneath the buddleia and recited the words that his father must have ordered to be carved for Helen Clementine, who was alive in the memory of his father, as she was alive in the memory of the unknown people in this city who had known her and could remember her, just as, perhaps, Eliza McFarlane and Gordon Petrie and his son were still alive, and Hamish MacIndoe was still alive, though he was dead to his son.

246

Jane contemplated the stone for a minute more and came over to Alexander. She put an arm around his shoulder. 'Does this upset you?' she asked.

'No,' he said. 'Not at all.'

'I would have liked her,' she said, stroking his neck. 'I know I would.'

'I'm sure,' said Alexander.

'Shall we go up the hill?' she suggested, and they walked from the cemetery to Dunsapie Loch, where Jane asked a hiker to take a picture of them, near to the spot where Helen and Hamish had been photographed with their tandem. They went on to the summit of Arthur's Seat. Sitting cross-legged on the grass, Jane watched the sunlight bloom and shrink on the roofs of the city. She closed her eyes for a second, and her face was as beautiful as it was when she listened to music and it was as though he was not in the room. 'Your father was right,' Jane said, opening her eyes narrowly, as if wavering on the edge of sleep. 'And Helen Clementine was right.' She put her arms around his waist. The sea flashed in the distance, under a flotilla of speeding clouds, and Alexander looked down the hill and recalled the ride to Kinloch Rannoch from Pitlochry, along the shore of Loch Tummel, in the cold bus that smelled of mud inside and had no padding on the seats. The rain had made the lake look like a field sprouting short black shoots, and the dripping leaves beside the road were as vibrant as wet green ink, and when he had pulled the narrow window back he could hear a sound like thousands of tiny cogs within the trees. Something broke through the surface of the water, like a portion of the tread of a spinning tyre. It was an otter, the driver had said, without looking. They had passed a boat that was gliding very close to the shore, with a man in a sou'wester standing in it, immobile, watching the bus go by. And he remembered from that week two fragments that he would still remember in the last years of his life: a bright red hosepipe, leaking water from its new brass nozzle onto the sunlit gritty tarmac of a railway platform; and striding with his father up to the Pass of Killiecrankie, where the wind battered the heather and the parting clouds spread a blush over the hills, and his father lowered his head, as if he were thinking about a difficult question, and Alexander kept quiet and stayed a couple of paces back, like the cabin boy standing behind Nelson in the picture in one of his books at home, until his father said his name and they walked down the springy path towards the tiny figure in the white hat, who was his mother.

'What are you thinking?' Jane murmured, and he told her that he had been reminded of the holiday in Pitlochry. 'Tell me,' she said, so he described the bus, and the sound of the rain in the trees, and the otter spinning in the water. 'Was it better than this?' she asked him.

'Of course not,' he told her.

'So you'll remember this, when we're old and decrepit?'

'Yes.'

She sat up and gazed over the city, at the sea and at the hills on the horizon, and her face again looked as it did when she listened to music.

28. Edwin

Alexander would recall that they were standing at the sink, facing their rain-pocked reflections, when his father mentioned Douglas Nesbit. Jane was very pleasant, very pretty, his father remarked, and then he was silent for a minute. They talked about the department in which she worked, and another pause followed. 'Her dad's name,' he resumed, 'wouldn't be Douglas, would it?' Alexander confirmed that it was. 'What's he like?' his father asked negligently, and Alexander described Mr Nesbit. 'Could be the same one,' his father remarked, as if to himself. 'I thought I'd told you about him,' he said, when Alexander requested an explanation, and when told that he had not, not as far as Alexander could recall, he merely said 'Oh well.' Alexander persisted, and his father, arranging the cups and the coffee pot and the jug of milk on the tray, answered that Douglas was something of an operator, a long time ago, during rationing. 'He had a way of lifting his finger,' he said, copying Jane's almost peremptory gesture, the gesture that Alexander had noticed that his father had observed and seemed to find interesting. 'Apart from that, you'd never know she was his daughter. If she is his daughter,' he added, nodding at the door. 'Nothing like the Douglas Nesbit I remember,' he said, but later Alexander saw him steal a look at her, as though intrigued by other similarities he had noticed between Jane and her supposed father.

But Jane would never talk about her father, and so rarely did Alexander visit her parents' house that he learned little more about him until the Sunday evening they went to see Edwin, her mother's brother, who was in London for the day.

Edwin was waiting for them, alone, in the living room, but he affected not to hear them enter. With his fingers intertwined behind his back and his back gracefully bent, he continued to peruse the face of the barometer until Jane was at his side, and then he turned and gave her a smile that showed that this was always his way. He was tall and narrow-shouldered, and his slenderness was accentuated by the close cut of his black suit, which he wore with a lemon shirt and a loosely knotted silk tie that was a slightly darker shade of yellow. His hair was as thick and the same colour as Jane's and her mother's, and was swept back in tight rigid waves that reminded Alexander of patterns drawn with icing sugar. 'Hello, my dear,' said Edwin, in a voice that was gentle and actorly. He cupped a hand around Jane's waist and touched her cheek with his moustache, which was trimmed so that its fringe followed perfectly the rim of his lip. Edwin's fingernails, Alexander noticed, were cut as neatly as a woman's, and on his middle finger he wore a large signet ring, into which was set a flat oval bloodstone. 'And this must be your beau,' said Edwin to Alexander, uncovering bloodstone cuff-links and a watch with a gold-coloured face as he held out his hand. He had a strong and affable handshake, which left a perfume like sandalwood on Alexander's skin. 'How do you do, Alexander. As my niece's young man, you are by definition a fine chap,' he informed him. 'If you'd be so kind,' he requested, pointing to a paper bag on the seat of one of the chairs. 'A belated Christmas present,' he said to Jane, as she took the bag from Alexander and the record from the bag.

'You gave me a Christmas present, Edwin,' Jane said, as though talking to a friend rather than to an uncle.

'Did I?' Edwin replied, smiling at his absentmindedness and at Alexander. 'Well, think of it as an advance against next Christmas.'

'I caught my taste in music from Edwin,' Jane explained. 'He took me to a concert once, for my birthday. My twelfth. I was never the same again.'

Edwin gave a modest bow from the neck. 'Do you like music, Alexander?' he asked.

'I run a record shop.'

'How nice for you,' said Edwin. 'What kind of record shop?'

'A standard record shop,' said Alexander. 'We sell all sorts.'

'And what sort do you prefer?'

'Nothing in particular. Some –'

'I'm working on him,' Jane declared, clutching Alexander's arm. 'He used to be in a pop group.'

'Oh, really?' Edwin smiled genially. 'How frightful,' he commiserated, unbuttoning his jacket before sitting down on the settee. He crossed his legs, raising high an uncreased shoe, and smoothed the adjacent cushion to make Jane sit down beside him. 'And tell me, Alexander, how are you finding your in-laws?' he asked.

'Jane's mother's lovely,' Alexander replied.

'Nicely put,' said Edwin, raising a hand languidly to point at him, and letting it slowly fall. 'Jane is her mother's daughter, isn't she? The face, the complexion, the sweetness of temperament. Very determined genes on the female side.'

'They are,' said Alexander.

Edwin looked at the shelves to the side of the settee, as if reacquainting himself quickly with the ornaments displayed on them. 'So tell me, my dear, how have you been?' he enquired, squeezing Jane's hand. 'What tales of corruption and deviousness from the corridors of local government?'

No sooner had Jane begun to speak than Martin appeared in the doorway. 'Food,' he announced drearily, as though enervated by the duties that had been imposed upon him. He walked off, letting the door swing back before Alexander could reach it.

'That boy,' Edwin remarked plaintively to Jane. 'No music has charms to soothe that savage breast.' Before they left the front room he removed his jacket, fitted it carefully onto the back of a chair and, with the demeanour of a man who was about to undergo a medical examination, removed his tie and posted it, rolled, into a pocket.

Alexander was seated between Edwin and Martin, who remained silent throughout the meal, except when Edwin asked him about the supermarket where he worked, questions which Martin answered in sentences of a single clause. 'Good, good,' Edwin concluded, when it had become clear that Martin had nothing more to say, and he glanced at Jane, who was staring at her plate as if she were reading something of scarcely bearable inanity, an expression that Martin noticed and copied when Edwin was telling them all about his argument with his manager at the Pump Room, which had almost led to his resignation a week before. There was a conversation about Edwin's holiday in Ireland, as Alexander would remember, and almost every time Jane's father addressed Edwin he used his name like a full stop. Describing the evening he had come across a poacher brandishing a hunting knife,

Edwin rested his hand on his sister's wrist to accentuate the drama of the encounter, and he left his hand there while Jane was speaking. Mr Nesbit glanced at Edwin's hand, as if at some broken object that he had long intended to mend. And when they all rose from the table, he would remember, Jane was the last to get up; carrying a plate past her, Edwin touched her on the shoulder with his fingertips, at which she smiled; her father, following, touched her arm, and Jane did not respond in any way.

When the dishes had been cleared, Martin went out to meet some friends at a pub, and they went back to the table, where they opened the bottle of port that Edwin had bought. After a while Edwin returned to the subject of Alexander's shop. Alexander told him how he had met Sidney Dixon, how he had come to work for him, how the shop had changed over the years. While he was talking, Jane's father leaned over to open a drawer in the sideboard and took from it a box of cigars; having offered one to Edwin, who declined like a reformed sinner banishing temptation from his sight, he unpeeled the cellophane wrapper with his teeth and clamped the cigar in his mouth as he fished for his lighter.

'Not in here, please,' said Jane's mother. 'You'll make the house smell for a week. Outside, if you don't mind.' Closing his lips on the cigar, Mr Nesbit glowered at his wife, at his daughter and at his brother-in-law in turn. His mouth made a chewing motion, and he bowed to his wife like an usher to a magistrate. He left the table, bowed once more at the door, and closed it behind him silently. 'I don't know why he's being like that,' said Jane's mother to Alexander. 'He knows it's the one thing I can't abide.' Edwin recounted another episode from his holiday, which in turn prompted from Jane's mother the reminiscence of a girl from Ballymena who had been in Edwin's class at school. Deirdre, her name was; she used to bring an apple to school every day, wrapped in a white handkerchief; she had a crush on Edwin and wrote his name on the wall of their house once, with a lump of coal. Edwin laughed, but could not recall her. 'Wait till you see this,' said Jane's mother; she went back to the kitchen and returned with a newspaper. Pointing to a small photograph above a story about a mother who had reported her own daughter to the police for shoplifting, she asked: 'Ring any bells? That's her.' Edwin held the page as far from his face as he could and said that he would need his glasses, which were in his jacket. Alexander offered to fetch them.

Alexander opened the door of the front room and saw Edwin's jacket by the light from the hall. As the door swung shut, he crossed the carpet to the chair on which the jacket hung. He brushed a sleeve with the back of his fingers to feel the sleekness of the fabric, then hooked the collar with a finger. The door met the jamb and bounced back, so that a blade of light traversed the room to Alexander's left. From Alexander's right came Mr Nesbit's voice. 'I hope you've washed your hands,' he said. Mr Nesbit was sitting where Edwin had sat, a tumbler in one hand and the unlit cigar held in front of his face, as if he had been about to light it when Alexander had intruded. 'Cost a lot of money, an outfit like that,' he said, and he raised the tumbler to take a judicious sip. 'How much do you reckon?' he asked, squinting through the gloom.

'I've no idea,' said Alexander, suspending the jacket at arm's length as though to test its weight.

'Nor me,' said Mr Nesbit, showing his teeth as the bite of the whisky made him grimace. He rested the tumbler on one knee and the other hand on the arm of the settee, in the attitude of a man enthroned. 'Stay a minute, why don't you? Let's have a chat. You and me.' Again he showed his teeth, perhaps in a smile.

Alexander sat on the chair and draped the jacket across his lap two or three times before leaving it.

'Enjoyed your evening, son?' asked Mr Nesbit.

'I have.'

'Good,' said Mr Nesbit, and he took another sip. 'Ridiculous, isn't it?' he said, exhibiting the cigar. 'A man can't even have a smoke in his own home. What's the world coming to, eh? An Englishman's home is his castle? Prison, more like.' He put the cigar between his teeth and picked up the lighter from the cushion. 'Well, bugger them, I say,' he said staunchly. The flame illuminated his face; his eyes and brow were clenched, as if at a harsh noise. He drew on the cigar three times, quickly, smacking his lips on it, and then he asked: 'So what do you make of our Uncle Edwin, son?'

'Very pleasant, he seems to me.'

Mr Nesbit directed a long breath of smoke towards the ceiling. 'Nice man, isn't he?'

'He is.'

'He knows how to tell a story.'

'He does.'

'A cultured kind of man,' Mr Nesbit proposed. 'Very – sensitive,' he said, as he knocked the ash into the fireplace. He brought the glass to his mouth, smiled at it, and drank.

'I should take this through,' said Alexander, cradling the jacket

Mr Nesbit ground the back of his head against the settee, as though to relieve a tension in the muscles of his neck. 'She's told you, of course,' he stated, with a weakly interrogative accent.

'Who, Jane?'

'Who else?'

'Told me what?'

'About our Edwin. Taking care of things.'

Alexander looked blankly at him, but Mr Nesbit was looking away. 'No,' he replied.

'The year of Uncle Eddy,' said Mr Nesbit, stirring an arm to the side of the settee. His hand came up, holding the bottle of whisky. He poured a deep measure, with one eye wincing in the thick stream of smoke. 'Uncle Eddy's year at the helm,' he snarled, as though repeating the words of an unpalatable toast

'I don't understand.'

'Yes you do. She told you,' said Mr Nesbit. 'Course she told you. I can tell,' he cajoled, with a hostile leer.

'I hadn't even heard of Edwin till last week,' insisted Alexander.

'Get away with you.'

'It's true,' Alexander protested.

Mr Nesbit lowered the glass and swung the cigar far from his face, as if throwing open a window. 'That can't be true. How long you two been going out now?'

'It is true.'

Staring at Alexander, Mr Nesbit gulped his drink. 'So it must just be because your old man's a banker,' he surmised. His heels bounced on the carpet, like a boxer's as he waits for the bell to begin the round.

'What must be? I still don't –'

'Why you're like you are.'

'I beg your –'

'Why you reckon you're better.'

'Why I what?'

'Why you reckon you're better than me.'

'I don't think any such thing, Mr Nesbit.'

'You reckon you're better.'

'I don't think I'm better than anyone.'

'Yes, you do. You and her both –'

'I don't think I'm the one who –' Alexander interrupted, but Mr Nesbit then interrupted him.

'How's Sid then?' he demanded, as if by this interjection he had clinched an argument.

'How's Sid?'

'Fuck me. You're like a bloody parrot sometimes, son. You know that?'

'You know Sid? Sid Dixon?'

'I know Sid. Sid knows me. We know each other. We had the same sideline, for a while. During the war. After his –'. He waved the cigar, sketching over his face in the air. 'Scavenging Sid Dixon. A smart man, Sidney. Knew some things would be worth a bit, one day. Knew what he was doing. Wily as an Arab. Always been doing deals. Behind the scenes, if you know what I mean.'

'You mean –'

'Bent as a nine-bob note, in other words.'

'Are you sure?'

'Lord love a duck,' Mr Nesbit laughed sourly. 'A right ten-watt bulb you are. Of course I'm sure. I know. I've put a lot of business his way over the years. I could have shopped him. I could have shopped a lot of people over the years. Sid and a lot of others.' Pinching the cigar between two fingers, he pointed it at Alexander. 'That's your boss, son. That's who you work for. So don't you go looking down your nose at me.'

'Mr Nesbit,' Alexander responded, 'I've told you, I don't –' and then Jane came in and turned the light on.

Her father held up a hand to shade his eyes, and Jane looked at him, at the cigar, at the glass of whisky. Standing with her feet almost touching his, she looked again at her father's face, on which Alexander saw a childish shame and defiance, and a pitiable awareness of his daughter's distaste. She glanced at Alexander. 'Edwin will give us a lift,' she said.

'Good old Eddy,' said her father. Ostentatiously he set the empty glass down on the edge of the arm of the settee, in demonstration of his sobriety.

'I'll be there in a minute,' Jane said to Alexander, and he left her with her father.

Ten minutes later he was waiting with Edwin by Edwin's car, an old crimson Jaguar with handles and chrome trim that shone like dental mirrors. They leaned against the doors, gazing up at the Plough, the only whole constellation they could see in a sky that had no visible clouds but seemed to have congealed into opacity. 'When I was a boy,' Edwin observed, 'the London sky was clearer, I'm certain. It was like looking at a chart. You have to go up Ben Nevis now, to get a view like that.' With his arms crossed to signify his dissatisfaction, he surveyed the desultory stars.

'Edwin,' Alexander began, seeing shadows move on the front room's curtains. 'Can I ask you something?'

'By all means,' Edwin replied, still scanning the mediocre sky.

'I was talking to Jane's father.'

'So I gathered.'

'I think he's had a bit too much.'

'Wouldn't surprise me, dear boy. Wouldn't surprise me at all.'

Jane appeared in the hallway, and her mother came out of the dining room. 'He was going on about the year of Uncle Edwin, but I don't know what he was talking about. What did he mean?'

'Ah,' Edwin protractedly exhaled.

'If you'd rather not –'

'No, no. If Douglas brought it up –'

'He assumed I knew.'

'Yes,' Edwin drawled. Jane took her coat from her mother and put her arms around her. 'Well, once upon a time brother Douglas was away from home for a year. And I lived here while he was away, to help Patricia with the children. Hence the warmth between Jane and

256

myself. And the extraordinary warmth of my relationship with her brother.' Still he was looking up at the sky, as though this were a trivial chat to pass the time. 'A guest of Her Majesty, you understand.' Now, noticing that Jane was approaching, he at last looked at Alexander and whispered, as if conveying an item of ribald gossip: 'Receiving stolen goods.' Making a chauffeur's salute, he held the door open for Jane.

Alexander saw a spasm of displeasure in the corner of Jane's mouth, but she said nothing about his conversation with Edwin as they drove away from the Nesbits' house, which Alexander was never to visit again. But as soon as they were in the flat she turned to him and said, with a tone of accusation: 'He told you, didn't he? He told you.'

'Oh God,' laughed Alexander. 'Here we go again.'

'It's not funny, Alexander,' said Jane, with her hands on her hips, as she had stood when she argued with her brother on the hill.

'You mean Edwin?'

'Of course.'

'He told me a bit. Yes.'

'How much is a bit?'

'That he lived in your house for a while.'

'And why?'

'Yes, and why?'

'Anything else?'

'He only had a couple of minutes, Jane.'

'He shouldn't have,' she said, but her anger had gone.

'I asked him. He didn't have any choice.'

'But he shouldn't have. He should have left it to me.'

Alexander put a hand on her shoulder and she stepped back from him. 'I don't see it's such a terrible thing,' he pleaded, but she stared morosely at the floor. 'It was a long time ago.'

'He's a bad man, Alexander,' said Jane quietly, as if making a confession. 'There's more. You don't understand.'

'Then tell me.'

'He's a bully. I don't like him. Let's leave it at that.'

In bed they read for a while, then she turned out the light on her side. Alexander read his book for half an hour more. He was almost asleep, he would remember, when she put the light on and leaned over him. 'Was he horrible to you?' she asked. She held his face between her hands as she looked at him searchingly, as if his face were a mirror, before she kissed him.

29. Esmé

Megan left Mitchell not long after they came to see the Park Rangers play, and by the beginning of the next school year she had left Leeds to take up a job in Berwick, where eventually she met Shaun Clarke, a teacher at a different school, with whom she was living by the start of 1971. Of this date Alexander would be certain, because he could recall that the card on which she had written her new address and phone number, and no other message, arrived in the week the currency changed.

After she had moved to Berwick, Megan did not come down to London as often as she used to, but she continued to visit at least once during every school holiday, and at some half-terms, and Alexander still spoke to her every two or three weeks, until she went to live with Shaun. They talked about little else but Mr Beckwith, whose fondness for him was all that sustained the friendship with Megan now, Alexander would sometimes think as he put the phone down, feeling an undertow of regret that weakened once he was with Jane, and in time vanished entirely. Jane was sometimes with him when Megan rang, but she met her only once, in the half-term break after the trip to Edinburgh. Megan had called in at the shop, and when she was about to leave he said that if she could wait for another half-hour she would get to meet Jane, and Megan, as he would remember, opened the bag that she was carrying to take out a textbook, which she carried into the stockroom, where she sat making notes until Jane arrived. She came out of the room as if she were the owner emerging to greet a customer, and spoke to Jane with a familiarity that Jane seemed to take as condescension. When Megan asked Jane what they had done in Edinburgh, she replied in a single sentence. Megan asked if they had visited a certain shop, which she located in the wrong street. Alexander corrected her. 'It's maddening, isn't it?' Megan remarked to Jane. 'He's been there once and he knows it better than I do, and I'm there every other week.' Jane smiled sympathetically, but as if

Megan were talking about something that had nothing to do with her. When Megan asked Alexander a question about Mr Beckwith, a question she had already asked him, Jane sidled to the nearest rack and took a record out. She was nicer than she looked in the photos was all Jane said when Megan had left, but in the weeks after Megan's visit she began to seem resentful of the time he spent with Mr Beckwith. Putting down her book as Alexander set the phone down after talking to Megan, she asked why it was impossible for her to meet him. She became almost petulant. 'You know everything about me,' she would protest. Why should she be excluded from this part of his life, she wanted to know. And after Edwin's visit it seemed at times as though she had determined that they should spend the minimum amount of time apart. She rarely spent an evening with her friends unless he agreed to come along. For several weeks she would appear outside the shop every night as he closed, as if she suspected that he might sneak away. Often, when she kissed him, she would hesitate as her lips were about to touch his, and look into his eyes, as if to ensure that he comprehended the significance of her kiss. 'You're mine,' she would say, locking her hands over the buckle of his belt as she nuzzled at his neck. 'And I'm yours,' she would tell him, and he would not turn round, because he would not be able to look at her honestly.

One Wednesday lunchtime, having closed the shop for the afternoon, he went into Greenwich, and as he was about to cross the road in front of St Alfege a noise from the riverfront made him look to his left and he saw Jane. Sauntering past the shops on the other side, with one hand on the strap of her shoulder bag and the other in the pocket of her dress, she resembled herself as she used to look, when he would see her walking slowly down the hill, as if nothing could hurry her or disturb her self-possession.

Alexander stepped into the churchyard to watch her as she passed. At the newsagent's window she stopped to read something that produced a smile like the smile he had used to see sometimes when she browsed through the records in his shop. When she turned into Nelson Road he followed her, at a distance. She stooped to look at a picture in the window of the framer's shop, where she stayed for some time. Curious to see what had absorbed her attention, Alexander ran over as soon as Jane had reached the next corner. The picture was an engraving of the Rotunda in Ranelagh Gardens, and Alexander studied it with such concentration that years later he would still be able to see the colossal circular hall with something at its centre that looked at first like an altar but was in fact a brazier, and the orchestra playing on a structure shaped something like a typewriter, and the groups of gentlemen in tricorne hats and ladies in wide-hipped skirts dotted here and there on the vast disc of the floor. He followed her as she rounded the block and crossed the road to walk back towards the town hall. One would have thought that she was taking a long afternoon's stroll in the springtime sun rather than returning to a job that bored her. He watched her until she had gone, and what he felt, he thought, was perhaps a last upsurging of love.

Soon after Easter they spent an evening with Sam and Liz. She barely spoke during the drive back from Croydon, as if she were brooding over some remark that he had not heard. It had been raining lightly, and she kept the windscreen wipers going after she had turned the engine off, until the blades screeched on the glass. She left her hand on the switch, but took it away when he touched her. Raindrops as fine as pollen were filling the tracks of the wipers. She opened the door and then closed it again. 'Alexander,' she said, in the tone of someone who has listened long enough and now must speak, 'I want to be married, and I want to leave London. I am not going to wait for ever.' She turned in her seat and challenged him with a gaze in which humiliated anger was stronger than affection. 'I don't want to mess around any more.'

'We're not messing around,' he said.

'Time's passing. A few more years and I'll be thirty. I'm not going to be a sad old spinster.'

'Come on, Jane. Nobody's a spinster nowadays. Spinsters became extinct after the war.'

'I want to get married, Alexander.'

'Why?' he asked, and the word had the taste of a farewell.

'The same reason as anyone. Why don't you want to? That's the real question. You won't marry me, will you?'

'It's not that I don't want to.'

'Don't lie to me, Alexander. Clearly you don't want to. So what is it? Is it my family?' she demanded.

'Of course it's not your family.'

'It's not my father? Because he doesn't like you?'

'Your father? Of course it's not.'

'So what is it? Explain. I want to know.'

Thinking of the day he had followed her, he did not answer immediately, and then he replied: 'I don't know why you need to be married.'

'I don't need to. I want to,' she told him.

Fifty yards down the street a fox squeezed itself under an advertising hoarding and trotted along the pavement, away from them, he would remember. For a second or two he was distracted, then he looked at Jane, who was staring at the animal, with her hands gripping the steering wheel tightly, as if she intended to run it down. 'Oh, go away, Alexander,' she said, staring at where the fox had been. 'Go away, go away, go away,' she said, her voice dwindling hopelessly. She stayed in the car until he reached the corner of the street; as soon as he turned the corner he heard her drive off.

She would phone him at the shop every second or third day, to berate him for his weakness, for his fecklessness, for his cowardice, his laziness, his selfishness, his charm. She implored him to come back, she reminded him of days they had spent together, she swore at him for deceiving her. One afternoon she came to the shop and berated him in front of one of his regular customers, and after that the calls became less frequent. 'You'll be back,' she told him, the last time she rang.

By the end of August the calls had ceased. It was at the end of August that Megan came down from Berwick for the weekend. Fischer was playing Spassky in Reykjavik, he would remember; in a shop window on Oxford Street a chess board had been set up with a Stars and Stripes next to the white pieces and a Russian flag by the black. They had not seen each other for almost half a year, since she had begun living with Shaun.

Alexander took the afternoon off to meet her up in town. As he crossed the last road before Bond Street station he saw her waiting for him at the top of the steps, watching him as he approached, as though she had instantly detected that some aspect of his appearance had changed but was trying to define what the change might be. It was not until he was a couple of yards from her, and she put out her hand to take the hand of a small dark-haired girl who was wearing, like Megan, a white shirt and a denim skirt, that he realised she had brought Shaun's daughter. 'This is Alexander,' said Megan to the girl, putting a hand on the front of Alexander's shoulder. 'And this is Esmé.'

'Hello, Esmé,' said Alexander, smiling at the girl.

'Say hello, Esmé,' said Megan.

Esmé screwed up her eyes at him, as if she were looking up into the clouds. 'We've been to the zoo,' she told him, and her fist unfurled from a pair of crumpled tickets.

'And now we're going to the big shops,' said Megan. Over Esmé's head she winced at Alexander, miming 'Nothing I could do.'

'We're going to ride the stairs.'

'She means the escalators. Madame Tussaud's, the zoo, the big shops. Our mission for the weekend.' There was an infinitesimal delay, then she leaned over and kissed him gently on the cheek.

Alexander touched her arm and smiled at Esmé, who was scowling at him as if he had told her to be quiet. She tugged at Megan's hand and they crossed the road to Selfridge's, where they took the escalator to the first floor. At the second flight Esmé stamped up the steps to get ahead of them, and stood with a hand on each handrail, her head pushed forward, leaning into an imagined gale. Following Esmé, they travelled up to the top floor, turned, and went back down to the basement. 'You look well,' said Megan as they returned to the ground floor, giving him a wry look.

'As do you.'

'Are things all right?'

'Things are all right. Everything all right with you?'

'Oh yes.' Megan held Esmé back to allow a family to overtake them, then let her go. She looked at Alexander earnestly and pressed her lips together as if she were dissatisfied with him. 'Are things really all right?' she asked.

'I'm not with Jane any more,' he told her. He had told no one else.

'Bloody hell, Eck,' Megan muttered. 'I thought something was up.'

'Bloody hell indeed,' he said, with a smile of resignation.

'You were together for ages. How long?'

His last conversations with Jane seemed to obstruct his mind, preventing him from seeing the months that lay beyond them. 'A long time,' he admitted.

'I thought you two were in love.'

'I think we were. Most of the time.'

'What happened?'

'Nothing happened, Meg. We split up,' he said, now wishing he had said nothing.

'But why? I thought –'

'I don't know,' he interrupted. 'It was good and then it wasn't. It became too –' he said, making a circle of his arms as though to clutch a figure on the step beside him. Hearing the tone of complaint in his voice, he stopped.

'Too what?' she asked, but Esmé took hold of her skirt and pulled her towards the door. They left the shop and walked along the street to John Lewis, where Esmé clung to Megan on every flight of the escalator until they arrived at the floor with the toy department. Megan and Alexander stood by a pillar while Esmé explored the shelves of toys. 'And how's Jane?' she resumed.

'We haven't spoken for a while. I've hurt her.'

'So you were the one who ended it?' asked Megan, apparently intrigued.

'You could say that. She wanted to get married. And I said no.'

'You said no?'

'In effect. I couldn't say yes.'

'Why not?'

'I told you,' he said, looping his arms again.

'Not much of an explanation, Eck.'

'Well, it's the best I can do,' said Alexander, looking for Esmé. 'She thinks it's because I'm weak and chronically indecisive. Says I'm just drifting through life.'

'She might have something there,' smiled Megan, stroking his arm glancingly. 'But you're not chronically indecisive. You have made a decision, after all. Or might you get back together?'

'I very much doubt it,' said Alexander. 'It was marriage or nothing. She won't change her mind.'

'And neither will you?'

264

'Highly unlikely.'

She hooked his arm and they walked down the aisle in which Esmé stood, gazing at a menagerie of soft toys. 'It's sad, Eck,' said Megan, as if agreeing with him. 'Perhaps we're the same. I could never get married to someone who wanted to marry me.' Alexander laughed briefly, dutifully, almost silently. 'Remember Mitchell?' she asked, as if something she saw had reminded her of him.

'I do,' he said, having waited for Megan to continue. 'Try as I might to forget him.'

'Married a German girl. A teenager. Who then ran off with someone even older.'

'How terrible for him,' said Alexander, feeling a nip of jealousy.

'He was a fool,' she sighed, as if only now arriving at that conclusion.

'He was.'

Megan smiled at Esmé, who still had not noticed they were near. 'Anyone else on the horizon?' she asked.

He was watching Esmé, and did not answer. Pushing a hand into the depths of a shelf, she angled her shoulder to reach farther, and extracted something as if easing it from a trap. Unable to see what she had taken, Alexander crept up behind her and peered over her head. She was holding a small velour elephant. She held the toy firmly in both hands and turned it in front of her face, enraptured, it seemed, by the dark plum colour of its body, by the buttercup yellow of its eyes and mouth and the tuft of its tail. Suddenly aware that Alexander was behind her, she turned and held out the elephant. 'Will you buy me this?' she asked, with a jubilant grin.

'Good Lord, child,' said Megan, clamping Esmé's head between her hands. 'Curb your avarice.'

'What?'

'Alexander is a friend, Esmé. He's not Father Christmas.'

'I want it,' Esmé sulked, crushing the toy to her chest.

'I can see that. But you can't have everything you want all the time,' Megan reasoned.

'It's lovely. I want it.'

'It'll be your birthday soon, Esmé. If you still want it then, we'll see what we can do,' Megan countered, but Esmé crumpled her face, as if she were hearing gibberish. 'Elephants are today's great passion,'

Megan explained to Alexander. 'Aren't they, my love? We wanted to free all the elephants from the zoo, didn't we?'

'When is your birthday?' asked Alexander, but Esmé would not look at him.

'November,' said Megan, shaking her head at the recalcitrant girl.

Crouching in front of the girl, Alexander made a bowl of his hands and Esmé relinquished the toy. 'Come on,' he ordered her, ignoring Megan's disapproving frown. Esmé followed him to the till, drumming her hands on her legs.

Somewhere near Manchester Square they had a cup of coffee and tried to keep Esmé entertained when she had finished her ice cream, and then Megan and Esmé went off to Shaun's brother's house, where Shaun was waiting for them. They stood in the mouth of Bond Street station, waving goodbye to him together. Megan seemed happier now than she had been since the day Mrs Beckwith died, Alexander thought.

A cool, damp breeze blew along Oxford Street, and the sunlight gave a concrete wall the lustre of oak. The temper of the street was changing, as the shoppers climbed onto buses and descended into the station, crossing the people who were up in the West End for the night. For a minute Alexander continued to stare at the station steps, from where Megan had disappeared into her life, and then he went back into his. He walked to Oxford Circus and down Regent Street, feeling as if an atmosphere of thicker air enveloped him and muffled the sounds of the crowds. Later that evening, he would remember, he walked across Greenwich Park to the street in which Jane lived. Her flat was in darkness, and at the sight of the black windows his sense of guilt abated temporarily. He went to the Crown and Anchor for an hour, and then he went home, where he played the recording of the Bach cello suites that she had given him for his thirtieth birthday, which brought to mind, intermittently, the drowsy pleasure of a Sunday morning, with the curtains of her bedroom window rising and falling slightly, and casting a sapphire light on the wall beside the bed, and the music rising and falling in the other room.

266

30. The riot in Buenos Aires

In the same way as he would know that this was the year of his thirty-third birthday, there were things Alexander would know had occurred in 1973 but had left no mark in his memory. There were some things that were attached securely to that year but were recalled as mere information, as if recorded as incidents or facts in a disembodied memory that existed alongside the memory of his experience. And there were many others – coming home late and seeing Sid Dixon smoking a cigarette behind the counter of the unlit shop, or standing by Mr Beckwith in the garden while he listened to the ringing of the phone until it stopped, or recognising the overweight man outside the bank as the boy who had attacked him outside the George a dozen years before, or rowing on the Serpentine with Nicola Cowell and her identical twin, who kissed him as Nicola stepped out of the boat – that had become detached from the time of their occurrence, to rise and fall with fragments of other years, like debris in a river. But twenty-five years later, the year 1973 would evoke spontaneously only one replete memory that was rooted in that year of his life, and it consisted of this: it was the morning of Midsummer's Day, and Alexander stood in the doorway of the shop, in the shade of the awning, and opened a newspaper at a page on which, alongside a photograph of a riot in Buenos Aires airport, the name Penelope Hollander was printed, and when he glanced into the shop he saw her there, with her black corduroy smock and patent leather satchel, and the pleasure of seeing her was such that it seemed a perfect recapitulation of that day in March, nine years ago, as if the intervening time, and his present self, had been annihilated.

31. The light on the stairs

After Edwin's visit, several months passed before Alexander mentioned Douglas Nesbit to Sid Dixon. Some days he foresaw the consequences of speaking and told himself to say nothing. Some days he decided that this was the occasion to speak, but the words would break apart and change in a moment, as if unwilling to be composed into an utterance. And then one afternoon, as he was writing an order by the light of the lamp on the counter, he found himself seeing the watch from the Doodlebug House, on the day that Liz came into the shop in her mother's red coat, and he said: 'I've met an old acquaintance of yours, Sid.'

'Oh aye?' Sid replied, from the back office.

'Does the name Douglas Nesbit ring a bell?'

'Doug Nesbit? Of course.'

'My girlfriend Jane. He's her father.'

'Is that so? Your girl's Jane Nesbit?' Sid was standing in the office doorway, and his expression was one of benign curiosity.

'She is,' said Alexander. 'You know him?'

'I knew him,' Sid replied, as though it were a subject of no consequence.

'During the war?'

'Aye.'

'And after?'

'Aye.'

'He says he used to do business with you.'

'Hardly anyone round here he didn't do business with. A finger in a thousand pies.'

'Used to sell stockings, didn't he? From a suitcase?'

'He did that. Nylons, fags, sweets. Anything that people wanted, Doug could get.'

'A dodgy sort of character?'

'Some would say.'

'Would you say?'

'I'd say tricky. Resourceful.'

'He said he used to sell you things.'

'He used to sell to everyone, like I say. Everyone bought from him.'

'Sell to the shop, he meant.'

Sid paused and scrutinised Alexander before replying. 'He sold me things. Once in a while.' Now there was impatience in his tone, and his impatience was stoked by the look that Alexander gave him. 'What point are you trying to make, Alex?' he asked.

'I wanted you to know what he told me.'

'No, you don't. You're accusing me.'

'I'm not accusing you, Sid. I suppose it just bothers me –'

'Bothers you!'

'He said –'

'Bothers you! Bothers you! Who do you think you are? The Archbishop of bleeding Canterbury?'

'No, Sid –'

'So what's this bloody holier-than-thou stuff!' Sid shouted, and he flung away the receipts he had been holding.

'I don't think I'm being holier-than-thou, Sid.'

'That's exactly what you're being. You don't know what it was like. Remember that, will you? What are you saying? That Doug did some things that were a bit shady? He did. He did all sorts of stuff, and he got caught, and he took what was dished out to him. When he was your age he had a wife and kid to support, and things were a bloody sight tougher then than they are now, I can tell you.'

'I know, Sid.'

'You saying that I wasn't spotless? Possibly I wasn't. Sorry I don't have your scruples. It would have been nice to live by the book, but I didn't much fancy eating out of bins. There didn't seem much choice at the time. Didn't seem to be many avenues open to me,' he said bitterly, jabbing a ruined finger at his own face. 'And I'll tell you another thing. Douglas Nesbit was bloody decent to me. He was a bloody good friend. Like your father was.'

'I wasn't –'

'Yes you were. There's nothing I can do about it now, is there?

Can't take the past back, can I? What do you want me to do? Sack you to save your soul?'

'I know,' Alexander started, but Sid had already left.

Each offered an apology to the other the next time they met, but for a while afterwards the affront was perceptible in the evasiveness of Sidney's gaze and the crispness of his manner. And when that episode was over there was a new civility to their dealings with each other, as though they had agreed to conduct themselves more conventionally, as employer and employee. It took almost two years for the wash from their disagreement to dissipate. It was early in 1974 that they were wholly reconciled, through what happened with Mr Beckwith.

For years the quality of the friendship between Alexander and Mr Beckwith had not changed. Spending their time in the same few rooms and in the garden of Mr Beckwith's house, they acted as though in observance of a rule they had established tacitly. Like scribes they worked together assiduously, slowly, similarly contented by their shared and unfinishable task. Yet there came a point at which, it seemed to Alexander, their friendship began to lose its efficacy for Mr Beckwith. Their talk had always been sparse, but their silences became longer, and Mr Beckwith's silence became a thing that clothed him like a heavy coat. When Mr Beckwith knelt to tend a plant, his shoulders seemed to curve under a weight. Sometimes Alexander would ask him if he had spoken to Megan recently, knowing from Megan that they had spoken. 'She's doing well,' Mr Beckwith would invariably reply, and he would talk about her in such a way that it was as if he had forgotten how long and how well Alexander had known her. He seemed to be forgetting the significance of the things that were around him. Sometimes Alexander would observe an expression of dismayed concentration on Mr Beckwith's face, as if he were trying to make himself remember that this was his house, that this was his garden, that this was a person with whom he had spent innumerable hours. Or he would stop what he was doing and get to his feet and go into the house, where Alexander might find him later, sitting in an armchair as if waiting for something to be brought to him, or standing at the sink in the kitchen, staring at his hand on the cold water tap as if the hand and tap together formed a single apparatus, the function of which he could not understand. Crossing the garden, Mr Beckwith would often come to a halt and look down at his feet, as he had done when Megan, as a girl, had led him through the park, and Alexander would ask, quietly, without moving from where he was: 'Mr Beckwith? Are you all right?' Promptly Mr Beckwith would reply 'Oh yes,' in a voice that was tranquil. 'Thank you, yes,' he would say, and then he would resume his work, tamping the moist soil around the stems with light movements of his fingers.

The frequency of Alexander's visits had begun to diminish at around the time that he joined Mick Radford's band. One Sunday evening, when Alexander had locked the shed, Mr Beckwith said to him: 'Don't feel obliged to come here, Alexander. You have your friends to see.' There were other evenings for them, Alexander replied. Mr Beckwith surveyed the garden. 'There's not so much to do at the moment,' he said. 'Let's leave it for a couple of weeks.' Gradually it became common for two weeks to pass between their afternoons together, and then it became customary for Mr Beckwith to suggest a longer interval, which he would do in a manner that made it seem not a rejection but rather an affirmation of the value of Alexander's understanding, as if the absence of company were a positive thing that Alexander could give him. By the time that Alexander was with Jane Nesbit, his visits had dwindled further, and some months he would see Mr Beckwith no more than once. He was rarely in the house when Megan phoned, because Mr Beckwith preferred to spend the evenings alone now. 'I get so tired,' Alexander would remember him saying, as he gazed at the keys in his hand as if looking at the cause of his weariness. They no longer ate together. In the cupboard in the kitchen, he would remember, tins of beans and tomatoes and corned beef were packed onto the shelves in perfect, complete rows. In the drawer to the side of the sink there was a single fork, a single spoon, a single knife.

Other than his workmates, the only acquaintances Mr Beckwith ever mentioned were George and Cynthia Carmichael. When Mr Beckwith returned to England after the war, it was Cynthia Howett who had nursed him in the first few months, Alexander eventually learned. She was known to all her patients as Georgie, on account of the Orwell books she was always reading, and she had met George Carmichael in a bookshop on Charing Cross Road. When they married they moved to Southwold, the town George's family came from, and there George and Cynthia ran a small hotel, overlooking the harbour. They had two sons, the elder named George, the younger Eric, and that was almost all Alexander knew about the Carmichaels, even though Mr Beckwith had been to stay in their hotel once or twice a year every year, from some time in 1960, when Alexander was completing his National Service.

Towards the end of 1973 Mr Beckwith went to Southwold for a few days. Early in January, more than a week after the date on which Mr Beckwith should have come back, Alexander went to the house, as they had arranged. The front lawn had recently been trimmed and there were rake marks on the grass. The empty dustbin was set perfectly in the centre of its plinth of paving stones. Every curtain on the upper floor was closed. Alexander knocked at the door and waited, and knocked again, more forcefully. He opened the letterbox to look in. The doors were all shut, and no light could be seen under them. There were no scuffs on the hall carpet. Alexander put an ear to the open letterbox and listened, and heard nothing but the ticking of the radiator at the foot of the stairs. Pressing his brow to the glass of the living room window, Alexander peered through the net curtains. The room was as lifeless as a showhouse. The gate at the side of the house was locked. Alexander went back to the door and rapped the knocker a dozen times. From the call box at the end of the road he rang Mr Beckwith's number, but there was no answer. He phoned Megan, but there was nobody at home. He ran back to the house and called Mr Beckwith's name through the letterbox. For five minutes he watched the house, and then he returned to his flat. At nine o'clock that night he went to the house again. The curtains had not been touched, it appeared, and the rooms at the front were dark. He knocked at the door, but there was no response. He looked through the letterbox: a pale light was on the higher stairs. He clattered the flap of the letterbox; he called Mr Beckwith's name. Still there was no response.

When he phoned his parents his mother answered, but she handed the phone to his father as soon as Alexander had explained why he was worried.

'Perhaps he's decided to stay away longer,' his father suggested.

'Another week?'

'Could be.'

'It's not like him. He likes everything to go to plan. If he says he's coming back on such-and-such a day he's coming back.'

'It's not impossible. There's no reason to panic.'

'I'm not panicking. I'm worried. He's in the house. There's no post on the mat. He must have picked it up.'

'Do you think he gets much post?'

'Dad, he's there. The heating's on. I can hear it clicking.'

'He could have left it on. Some people do. Stops the pipes freezing.'

'He wouldn't, Dad. I know he wouldn't. He's there.'

His father paused. 'Let me give him a call,' he said, which he did, but still there was no answer. 'I'll go over there,' his father volunteered when he called Alexander back, and now there was some concern in his voice.

An hour later Alexander's mother rang to tell him that a light was on upstairs at Mr Beckwith's.

'At the front of the house?' Alexander asked, and he heard his mother repeat the question to his father.

'Yes, at the front,' she said. 'Was there a light at the front before?'

'No.'

'There you are, then. Obviously he's not fallen or anything. He's moving around the house. There's no need to call the police out.'

The following morning, before opening the shop, Alexander rang the printer's. Mr Beckwith was not well, Alexander was told; he had sent a note from his doctor and would not be back for a week. On the hour at nine, ten, eleven and noon Alexander rang the house, and there was no answer. In the afternoon Mr Beckwith's line was engaged every time. Again he rang Megan, and only then did he remember that she had told him she would be away that week. In the next moment he had the idea of asking Sid Dixon for his help.

'But I've never met the man,' Sid objected, as Alexander had known he would.

'I think that'll be in your favour,' he replied.

'How do you reckon that? You're his pal. Doesn't want to see you, he isn't going to want to see a total stranger.'

'You're not a total stranger, Sid. He knows about you.'

'Like saying Ted Heath's not a stranger. He doesn't know me from Adam.'

273

'And if he doesn't, that might work. You're the same age. The same generation.'

'What's that got to do with it?' Sid laughed. '"Come on in, mate. I see you're as old as me." How's that work?'

'I don't know. But it might.'

'And I might find a thousand quid lying in the gutter,' said Sid, but from his voice it was evident he would do the favour that Alexander had asked of him.

At nine o'clock Alexander turned into Mr Beckwith's street and saw Sid waiting by the telephone box. 'Bloody barmy plan,' Sid mumbled, stamping his feet on the pavement to hammer sensation back into them. His brusqueness seemed a performance, as if he were offering to resume the style of his former self with Alexander.

'Not a plan, Sid,' Alexander smiled. 'A hunch.'

'Bloody barmy hunch then,' said Sid. He turned up the collar of his overcoat and with a sweep of an arm invited Alexander to lead the way to Mr Beckwith's house. As before, all the rooms overlooking the street were in darkness, and a pallid light lay on the segment of staircase that could be seen through the letterbox. Over the edge of his collar Sid Dixon observed the house while Alexander rapped the steel bar of the knocker and called Mr Beckwith's name repeatedly.

'I get the picture,' said Sid. 'I'll see what I can do.'

'I think I should go away and leave you to it.'

'I do too,' Sid replied. 'I'll report back.' Thrusting his hands deep into the pockets of his coat, he sat down on the doorstep. Furtively he looked to right and left, like a sentry making sure that there is no one to see him taking an illicit rest. 'Away with you,' he ordered.

Two hours later Sid came to Alexander's flat. 'Siege over,' he announced. Behind him his car was parked with its nearside wheels on the pavement and its engine running.

'You spoke to him?'

'Contact made.'

'How did you do it?'

'Introduced myself by the letterbox method and said I wasn't leaving. Sat down on the path for a bit. Repeated message. A curtain twitched eventually. I showed my face.' He flapped the wings of his coat and made a bow. 'Waited a bit longer, then open sesame.'

'He let you in?'

'Course not. Reckon you'd need a search warrant to get in that house.'

'But is he all right?'

'Not what you'd call a jolly bloke,' Sid pronounced, after a hesitation. 'Doesn't look like he needs looking after, though.'

'So he's not ill?'

'Healthy as you or me, I'd say. Skinny bugger, but so are whippets.'

'Did you talk to him for long?' asked Alexander.

'Long enough, Alex. Long enough,' said Sid, glancing at the lorry that was passing close to his car. 'He says not to worry yourself. Leave him be for a while. That'll do the job.'

'That's what he said?'

'That's the gist of it,' said Sid tersely. Waiting for further instruction, he stamped his feet and huffed a mouthful of steam into the air.

'What do you think, Sid?'

'What do I think,' Sid pondered ruefully. He sniffed loudly and wrapped his coat more tightly about him. 'I think he knows his own mind. I think there's no point in pestering him.' He presented his face frankly to Alexander, inviting him to read it, and it was clear that he had not liked Mr Beckwith, and that there was nothing more to be said.

'Thanks, Sid,' said Alexander. 'Come in for a nightcap?'

'Better be off,' said Sid, looking at the multicoloured sequinned shirt and trousers that Alexander had pinned in the window. He smiled and shook his head. 'Some other time,' he said, and he patted Alexander on the elbow.

Once or twice each week in the ensuing months Alexander would take a walk that would pass Mr Beckwith's house. Most weeks he would talk to Megan, who seemed to gain reassurance from reassuring him. 'He's no different with me,' she told him. 'I'm sorry he's gone like this. All you can do is wait. He'll come out of it.' One night, having seen the four square windows of the door light up, Alexander opened the front gate and approached the house. He raised his hand, but as he was about to knock he heard a chair scrape on the kitchen floor and the sound of a plate being set on the table, and in that moment he saw himself as the violator of Mr Beckwith's cloistered life, and he lowered his hand and walked away. Still he continued to walk past Mr Beckwith's house, but he never again went up to the door.

And then, one Sunday afternoon in June, he saw Mr Beckwith on the path beside the house, exactly where he had first seen him, more than twenty years before. His arms were thin and tanned, and hung from his shoulders as straight as chains from a yoke. He was holding a carrier bag in each hand. Like a surrendering fugitive he put the bags down and came to the gate. His cheeks were concave and looked as if the flesh had been scoured by a pestle.

'Alexander,' he said, making his name sound like a remark made reluctantly. 'How are you?'

'Same as ever, Mr Beckwith. How are you?'

Mr Beckwith looked at him, but he might have been gazing into air. 'Sorry to have caused trouble,' he said. 'People have to be alone from time to time. You understand.'

'Yes,' said Alexander, meaning to go on, but already Mr Beckwith had taken a step away from him.

'I'll give you a call,' said Mr Beckwith. He went back down the path, and that was the last time that Alexander saw him.

32. Mr Harvey

'That must be him,' said Megan, pointing to the man who was stepping into the porch. He was wearing a black blazer and a broad black tie, the knot of which was obscured by a beard that was bardic in its length and taper. His hair, which like his beard was white and streaked with strands of nicotine yellow, stuck closely to his scalp and turned up on his collar in a greasy curl. He seemed somewhat older than Mr Beckwith, perhaps in his seventies, and he carried a slender walking stick for which he appeared to have no need, for he mounted the steps as nimbly as Alexander's father.

Alexander gave Megan the letter that Sidney Dixon had written to her, and went into the church. Mr Harvey had taken a seat in the second pew from the front and was perusing the order of service. As soon as Alexander sat down behind him, he put the card aside, then linked his hands on the greyhound's-head handle of his walking stick, which he clamped upright between his knees. His fingernails, Alexander would remember, were long and hooked and ridged like almonds, and he stared at the altar as if rigorously keeping guard over it. A ragged high note, like a pig's squeal, was emitted by the organ. The old man did not flinch.

'Pardon the intrusion,' said Alexander, 'but would you happen to be Mr Harvey?'

The old man turned his head a few degrees, sufficiently to ascertain who had spoken to him. Heavily the lashless eyelids closed over his eyes and rose, uncovering half the iris. 'I am,' he replied, and resumed his vigil. His lips were bracketed by hinge-like indentations of muscle. It seemed like a face that could never express any spontaneous feeling.

'I hope you don't mind my talking to you, but I'm a friend of Mr Beckwith's daughter.'

Mr Harvey leaned towards Alexander, like a passenger in a cornering car. 'And you would be?' he asked.

'Alexander MacIndoe. I –'

'Yes. You were mentioned. The gardener,' he stated, and he sat upright again, knotting his fingers more tightly on the head of his walking stick.

Alexander eased forward to ask: 'You had known Mr Beckwith for a considerable time, I believe?'

Now Mr Harvey did not move at all, nor react in any way to indicate that he had heard the question. Alexander was about to repeat it when Mr Harvey said: 'Yes. A considerable time.'

'How long, would you mind my asking?'

'Since 1943.'

'And you last saw him, before –'

'1946,' Mr Harvey interrupted crisply.

'Never since?'

'1946 was the last time I saw him.'

Obdurately immovable, Mr Harvey obliged Alexander to address him in the manner of a courtier petitioning his master. 'Did it strike you as strange that he reappeared, after so long?' Alexander enquired, lowering his voice.

'It did not,' replied Mr Harvey. 'He did not reappear. We were not strangers to each other. Letters were exchanged. Infrequently, but sufficiently. He did not arrive out of the blue.'

'Did he give a reason for wanting to see you? A particular reason?'

'Time was passing. We had intended to meet for many years.'

'Nothing more particular than that?'

'Young man,' said Mr Harvey, dropping his gaze to the back of the pew in front of him, 'I should be grateful if you would modify your tone. You are not addressing a suspect in a murder case.'

'I apologise.'

'I accept your apology.'

Alexander waited for Mr Harvey to resume, but was obliged to ask again: 'But nothing –?'

'No, nothing. He informed me that he would be coming to Evesham. He thought he might take the opportunity to visit me.'

'Did he say why he would be in Evesham?'

'He did not.'

'Do you think there was in fact any other reason for him to be there?'

'I would regard it as inappropriate to speculate.'

'Did he seem distressed?'

'No, he did not.'

'Did he strike you as being unhappy?'

'I could not say he seemed happy, but then Harold had not been a happy man when I knew him. None of us had been. We were not in a place where one could be happy. And thirty years of life tends to put a weight on one's mind, wouldn't you say?' Alexander gave a mild smile, which Mr Harvey, by a flickering glance, appeared to accept as assent. 'We passed a pleasant afternoon,' he continued. 'We took tea in my garden. We exchanged reminiscences. Such, I think, is what customarily passes for conversation.'

'So there was nothing out of the ordinary?'

'Nothing was said, I assure you, that you would regard as being of any significance.'

'Nothing that you –'

A spasm of vexation tightened Mr Harvey's grip. 'Nothing,' he reiterated.

'I'm sorry. It's just that his daughter –'

'I understand,' replied Mr Harvey, with a taut nod. Father Medlicott appeared at a door in the transept; sorrowfully he regarded the congregation and touched the silver crucifix that hung from his belt; he turned back into the sacristy. 'He drowned, Mr MacIndoe,' Mr Harvey resumed. 'That is fact, and the only fact.'

'His daughter finds it –'

'Of course, of course. But the choice is simple: an act of will, or an accident. An accident I would regard as improbable, and a strong will was always a characteristic of Harold Beckwith,' asserted Mr Harvey dispassionately. 'But then,' he added, with no apparent feeling, 'he used to be a courageous man as well.'

Father Medlicott came out through the doorway and walked down the aisle with his head bowed, as though in a procession that nobody else could see. 'I'm not sure I understand you,' responded Alexander.

'I should have thought my meaning was abundantly clear,' said Mr Harvey. Then, as if further provoked by a comment he had imagined Alexander to have made, he twisted to face him directly. 'Mr MacIndoe,' he said, 'I am here to pay my respects to a man I once held

279

in the highest regard. I should appreciate it if I may be allowed to do so without disturbance. As for Harold Beckwith's state of mind in recent years, I think you know as much as I – more than I do, in fact. There let us leave the matter.'

Of Father Medlicott's speech Alexander would remember not the text but rather its inane cadences, which sounded as if they had been composed for words that were not the words he was speaking, and he would remember looking from the lectern at people he did not recognise, then at Mr Harvey, whose impassive eyes were trained constantly on the altar, then at Megan, who was staring at the floor. He would remember beginning to read, and finding that his voice became the voice with which he used to speak to Mr Beckwith, and did not falter as he had feared it would. He would remember that Mr Harvey raised his eyes briefly as Alexander descended the steps, but that neither spoke to the other until the interment was done, whereupon Mr Harvey offered his hand and said: 'It is unfortunate that we should have met in such circumstances, Mr MacIndoe. Harold held you in some affection, I believe.'

'Thank you,' said Alexander.

'Thank him,' replied Mr Harvey, flourishing his stick at the open grave.

'I meant, thank you for talking to me,' said Alexander.

'I see,' said Mr Harvey, and his small, upturned nose made a snuff-taker's sniff, as though this were his habitual means of closing a conversation. He presented himself to Megan, and left her as soon as he had shaken her hand. Rapidly he read the messages that were written on the wreaths, then for a minute he lingered at Mrs Beckwith's headstone, holding aside the flower stems with his stick to read the bottom line of the inscription. Shunning the other mourners, he strode off down the path, swinging the stick to waist height and jabbing it into the gravel in unison with his heel.

Megan, enclosed within a circle of black coats, watched Mr Harvey leave, and once he had disappeared behind the screen of poplars she peered over a shoulder to find Alexander. She gave him a beseeching look; he pointed out of the churchyard and mimed a word he hoped she would understand.

Sitting on the hill, below the statue of General Wolfe, Alexander looked around him. Behind him a man held out his arms to catch a small girl on clattering rollerskates. To his left a French woman and her two daughters posed for a photo, straddling the Meridian line. The leaves of the oak trees shimmered in a gust too weak to stir the parched cigarette packet near his feet. The walls of the Queen's House were sugar-white, and there was a constellation of platinum spangles on the river. On the boating pond, a red canoe met a blue canoe with a knock that was barely audible. The dome of St Paul's seemed so small, like a cork on a pool of brown water. A dog, a golden retriever, ran down the hill, its head raised for the tennis ball that came out of the sky and bounced across the path. Everything Alexander saw and heard was delightful, and his delight seemed to have a quality of commemoration. When he told himself to think of Mr Beckwith he saw him beside the house, with the trowel in one hand and the clod of earth in the other, like a gift. He saw Mr Beckwith walking the Cornish lanes, with his white shirt cracking in the wind. He saw him fit his hand around the head of a rose and lift it slightly towards Alexander's lowered face, as if inviting him to sip from a glass of wine, and he saw him walking behind Megan in the park, holding out his hand, limply, for Megan to take, and making a cap of his hand to rest on Megan's head as she read to him.

Megan sat down beside him and hooped her arms around her knees. 'That was really horrible, wasn't it?' she asked, squinting straight ahead as if trying to read a distant notice.

'Didn't like the vicar much,' Alexander agreed.

'Dum-de-dum, de-dum, de-dum, de-da,' Megan recited, mimicking the emollient dolefulness of Father Medlicott.

'How were the relations?'

'Can't say I paid much attention, Eck. "A blessed relief," someone said. Can you believe it? "A blessed relief." Accidentally said what she meant. Great-aunt Enid. What would she know? Hasn't picked up the phone in thirty years.' She dabbed her cheeks on her skirt and looked at him. 'What of Mr Harvey?' she asked.

'Waste of time, pretty much. He didn't want to talk.'

'No opinion?'

'Not an approachable man, Meg. Perhaps today wasn't the day. Did he say anything to you?'

281

'"My thoughts are with you," and that was it. And a manly handshake.'

'It was certainly that.'

'Never heard of Iain Harvey until a week ago.'

'And we'll never hear from him again.'

They sat in silence for a while, and then suddenly she seized his arm and her mouth made a sipping motion. 'Eck, he's slipping away,' she whispered. 'I want to hold on to him, but he's fading already.'

'He won't go,' he told her, putting a hand on her shoulder to pull her closer to him. He closed his eyes and saw his father's arm moving like a compass needle as he listed the names of buildings his son could not make out amid the crumpled roofs of the city, and his mother, to the side of them and apart, peering towards the docks, and Mr Beckwith under the chestnut tree, gathering the chestnuts that they then cupped their hands to receive, and Mr Beckwith, as their hands overflowed with the dark brown nuts, putting the palm of his left hand on Megan's cheek and the palm of his right on his.

They sat in silence for many minutes, and then Megan said: 'I think I'll be coming back to London, Eck.'

He felt the air change, as if a tunnel had formed around him. 'Why's that?' he asked.

'Shaun will be going back to his wife,' she said flatly, plucking a blade of grass. 'Sooner or later. I may have to go first. And if I go, I'll try to get a job in London.'

'I'm sorry,' said Alexander.

'No need, Eck. It's been bad for a while. A long time. She wants him back, and he wants to go back. She called a year ago, and he's wanted to go back ever since, but he was too weak to admit it. Instead, it's my fault he's unhappy. Everything I do is wrong now. He drinks because I've trapped him. He hates his job because he's trapped. So I think I'm leaving. I should have made my mind up sooner.' She pressed his hand to her face, and she began to cry. 'I should have done it before. If I'd been here, then Dad –'

'No,' said Alexander.

'It might have helped.'

'Might not. Probably not.'

'But it would have been different.'

'Might have been worse, if he'd known you weren't happy.'

'But I wouldn't have been unhappy. It would have been better.'

'We don't know.'

'It would have been,' Megan insisted.

'We don't know,' Alexander repeated. 'We can't know.'

'God only knows, eh?'

'Nobody knows. Not even 'im. He's not even there.'

'You think that?'

'Of course,' he said. 'Don't you?'

'Yes,' she said.

'I'm sure he's not there,' said Alexander. 'Sure as I am of anything.'

And then Megan looked at him in a way that was unfamiliar, and the trembling of her lips ceased for a moment.

33. All Saints

Sam came to the shop that morning, as Alexander would remember. It was a few minutes before midday, and Alexander was pulling the awning out when Sam appeared on the other side of the road, whistling the theme from *High Noon*.

'Heard anything?' Sam called, crossing over.

Alexander shook his head. 'Sam, what on earth are you wearing?' he said, tweaking the lapel of his friend's jacket. The jacket was the colour of fudge, and its buttons were fat as chequers. 'That's the most horrible garment in all of London.'

'Fashion. You wouldn't understand, you scruffy Herbert,' Sam replied, giving Alexander a consoling pat on the shoulder. 'Time for a fag?' He took a steel cigarette case from his jacket and released its catch with a flip of a little finger.

'This a social call?' Alexander enquired.

'Pleasure and business combined,' said Sam, burrowing for his lighter. 'A bit of freelance spying,' he explained. He drew avariciously on his cigarette, making his cheeks bow inwards. 'Let's step inside.'

'Who's the victim?'

'The suspected miscreant, Mac, is what you mean. Who's the suspected miscreant?' Sam sniffed the air of the shop. 'Nice,' he remarked, batting the mobile of albums in the window. 'Diesel and joss sticks. Summertime, and the smell is disgusting.'

'The miscreant?'

'A not very smart fraudster,' said Sam, exhaling thoughtfully, regretfully. He pointed up the hill, to a building encased in scaffolding. 'See that bloke up there? In the jeans? The fat bugger? Well, his brother-in-law has been seen by my informant drinking with a bloke whose name must of course remain *sub judice*, but who, I can tell you, has had his van nicked three times in four years. Which is at least once too often, in my book. He lost the last one a couple of months back. Expensive vehicle, with a lot of expensive tools in it, allegedly.

284

And unless I am very much mistaken, that's it, over there,' he said, pointing to the green van that was parked beside the scaffolding. 'New plates, a respray, new set of documents, and Bob's your uncle. Always up to something, that one up there. Used to work with a very dodgy crew in New Cross. They got caught doing a real daisy of a job.' He picked a thread of tobacco from his gold tooth. 'Fitting a roof they were, over in Peckham. Their boss, who reckons they're on the fiddle, sits in the back of a car and watches what's going on. Nothing amiss, it seems for a while. Two blokes winching timber and slates up into the roof. Half a dozen industrious lads up top, sawing and hammering. Right beehive. But then he fixes on one bloke and keeps an eye on him. Half an hour he watches this bloke hammering away. At the same bloody length of joist. For half an hour. Making a noise, that's all he's doing, while his mates are carting the stuff across the roof and winching it down into the garden at the back. Then it's over the wall and onto the lorry, and off we go to flog the stuff we're supposed to be using on Mrs Reilly's roof. Who's going to notice? Not going to get old Mrs Reilly shinning up the drainpipe to check if she's being conned, are you?' Watching the fat man on the scaffolding, Sam stroked the ends of his drooping moustache with a thumb and forefinger. 'The dishonesty of some folks, eh?'

For fifteen minutes or so they chatted about Sam's work and his children and Liz's new job, and then Sam said he should get back to the grindstone. 'Good to see you, Mac. Must have a pint one night. I'll see if I can get an evening pass from the wife.' He stepped out into the sunlight and gave Alexander a sideways look, as though deciding between admiration and amusement. 'Give my regards,' Sam said, turning away.

It was nearly five o'clock when the phone rang. A clerk from the post office was in the shop, wearing sunflower-yellow flares and a tomato-red blouse, he would remember. For a moment Alexander rested his hand on the phone. He lifted the handset and listened.

'Hello, Eck?' she said, and he heard the reverberation of the hallway around her voice.

'You're home?' he asked.

'I am. Arrived this minute.'

'You OK?'

'I'm OK,' she said. He heard the chink of the chain on her front door. 'I'm back,' she added, as if to be more precise.

'How was the journey?'

She told him, and then she interrupted herself. 'Are you free tonight, Eck?' she asked, and she said it as though she were in the habit of speaking to him every day.

'Yes, nothing planned,' Alexander told her.

'I don't want to stay in. Not tonight.'

'Of course.'

'Let's go out to eat. Do you mind?'

'I'll come over straight after work,' he said.

'You OK, Eck?' Megan asked.

'I'm fine.' He looked at the back of the clerk's blouse as Megan was speaking, and found its match in the colour of a skirt that Megan had worn when she was twelve or thirteen. He saw her sitting on a wall beside a friend he could no longer name, with the red skirt spread over the glossy black bricks, and her hands wedged under her legs as she listened to her friend and watched Alexander pass.

She had let her hair grow long again, and her face was bare and tight, as if she had plunged it in icy water. 'Calamity Jane returns,' she sang, spreading her arms. An old blue trunk with wooden battens on its lid lay open in the hall, which now was pink. A greasy stripe marked the wall at elbow height. 'This is nothing,' she said, looking at what he was looking at. 'Wait till you see what they've done to the rooms.' She took his hand and towed him to the living room. A track of flattened grey pile ran between the French windows and the door. Scabs of melted fabric scarred the arms of the chairs, and a pattern of overlapping white circles covered the surface of the table. The room smelled of cigarette butts and damp newsprint and old beer. 'Little left alive out here,' she said, walking to the windows. The lawn was like an oval of hardboard, the flowerbeds were nothing but arrangements of naked black stems, and the door of the shed was ajar, hanging on a single hinge. 'The best is yet to come,' muttered Megan, and she led him upstairs. Her room was now lilac, with a zigzag of white aerosol paint across two walls. The walls of the room in which Mr and Mrs Beckwith had slept had been painted lime green, but there were bars and triangles of pale paper where the shelving had been, and grooves of white plaster where something had gouged the walls repeatedly. 'But the *pièce de résistance . . .*' said Megan enticingly, and she flung open the bathroom door. The bath was ringed by a dozen horizons of dirt and there was no lid on the cistern. Water dripping from the cold tap had cut a course as clean as boiled bone through the basin's pumice-coloured grime.

'Depressing, isn't it?' she laughed. 'Owed two months' rent as well.'

'You going to do anything about it?' asked Alexander. 'I know the man to track them down.'

'No, Eck. I want shot of them. Good riddance. I start again from today. Let's get out.'

They went for a drink in a pub that he had never been to before, and then they took a train up to town and ate in a Charlotte Street restaurant, where the pauses in their conversation grew longer as her tiredness increased and her unhappiness seemed to leak into her face. She looked at herself in the darkened window as if at a companion to whom she no longer had anything to say, and later, tipping the last of the bottle into her glass, she pointed a toe towards the neighbouring table to show him the scar on her calf. 'He did that,' she said. 'Went bananas one night. Half a bottle of whisky and half a gallon of self-pity. And everyone thinks he's Mr Nice Guy. Poor Shaun. Poor, poor, unlucky Shaun. His women done him wrong. Wife left him with the baby. Bitch from London ran away.' They raised their glasses to the bitch from London.

A week later they began to restore the house. She bought an estate car, in which they collected chairs and tables and a new bed. Almost every Sunday and one or two evenings in the week he would bring a new album from the shop and they would put the record-player in the centre of the room, under a canopy of polythene. Often, without her noticing, he would watch her while she painted. Reaching into a corner of the ceiling, she would bite the tip of her tongue and frown as she worked, and he would be reminded of the way she used to play in the park with him and his friends, as if something more than merely the winning of the game depended on her tenacity. Afterwards they might cross the Heath for a drink, or he might cook a meal for her while she prepared her lessons for the following day, and sometimes, after the meal, she would phone Berwick and he would overhear her talking in a voice that was tinged with an accent: 'Hello, Esmé. Hello, darling,' she murmured. 'Same here, pet, same here, same here,' she repeated wistfully. And once, Alexander would remember, he heard her shouting: 'Put her back on. Put her back on now!' and he went out into the hall and took the dead telephone from her, and she rested her head against his shoulder.

Alexander relaid the turf in the garden and planted bulbs from the nursery that Mr Beckwith had used. He scoured the moss from the path at the side of the house. He replaced Mr Beckwith's rusted tools and repaired the shed door and the roof of the shed. One afternoon, standing at the workbench where Mr Beckwith had stood and explained about Tollund Man, Alexander looked across the garden, across the barren flowerbeds and the rectangles of new grass, and he saw Mr Beckwith at the kitchen window. The white shirt flashed like the sun off an opening metal door and then was gone, but Alexander saw clearly, in that portion of a second, Mr Beckwith gazing out at the garden as he did after his wife had died, and smiling as if she were there. Many times, when he was working in the garden, Alexander glimpsed Mr Beckwith at that window, and he would find himself smiling as well, and then, as if cause and effect were reversed, he would sense the hush of the breeze in the Cornish lanes, or the egg-yolk yellow of bird's-foot trefoil, or the touch of Mr Beckwith's hand on his. And more than once, coming into the living room from the garden, he sensed a shadow passing across the wall, as if Mrs Beckwith had risen from her chair and left the room, and he seemed to pass through an atmosphere that bore the scent of her clothes.

It was a Sunday, and the clouds were so low that they walked into mist as they came up onto the Heath. They crossed the road at exactly the place, he reminded her, at which a gust had whisked off Mrs Beckwith's hat when they were on their way to the Christmas service, and she had released Megan's hand at the same moment as Alexander's mother had released his, and the two women had gone racing up the hill like a pair of children. At All Saints church he remembered seeing a display by the Royal Horse Artillery, around the time that Megan arrived in London. Men in white vests had vaulted one-handed over an enormous vaulting horse, while a brass band played and the gun carriages were taken off the lorries. He told her about the time Mr

Beckwith had turned off a programme about the Boer War because he never wanted to see another army as long as he lived.

Megan looked at the ground while she listened, as though to picture what he was describing, and then she remarked: 'You know, Eck, your mother really doesn't like me at all.'

'I don't think that's true,' Alexander replied.

'It is true, and you know it,' she said, patting his forearm. 'She thinks I was a bad daughter and now I've got what's been coming to me.'

'No, that's not right,' said Alexander. He returned to the subject of Mr Beckwith, and how he used to swear at any politicians who appeared on TV.

Megan talked about her colleagues in Berwick. 'They knew what'd happened. They knew Dad had died. And no one said a thing.'

'Doesn't altogether astonish me,' he remarked.

'Not one single word. Nobody. It's as if I went out to the toilet and was gone a long time. I think some of them thought I was bad luck. Not yet forty and a double orphan. But most of them simply didn't care, I'm sure of it. Didn't care about anything unless it was about them.'

'Or they didn't know what to say,' said Alexander. 'A lot of people have no idea what to say. I had no idea what to say.'

'But you're different, Eck. You don't need to say anything. You understand.'

He looked at her to ascertain what she had meant, he would remember, and he noticed the pearls of water on the fibres of her scarlet mittens. Her breathing changed, though they were walking slowly.

'Eck. There's something I must ask you,' said Megan gravely.

'OK.'

'Something personal.'

'By all means.'

'Very well. The question is this: do you find me attractive?' With her hands on her hips she stood in his way.

'Of course you're attractive.'

'Not in the abstract, Eck. I'm not asking you if you can conceive how someone might possibly find me attractive. What I'm asking is whether you yourself have an interest in me.'

Alexander said nothing. The grass appeared to become darker; the cars seemed louder than they had been a moment before.

'At this point I had imagined you might say: "Yes, Megan, I do. I have found you attractive for a considerable period of time. I have been battling against myself to suppress certain emotions that your presence provokes, but now that you have raised the subject I must confess that I have feelings for you that are not without an element of sexual desire." Something along those lines.'

'You know what I think.'

'I do not know what you think. If I knew what you thought I wouldn't be asking you.' She glanced upwards, as though a bird had caught her attention, and then she was glaring at him. 'In the interests of absolute candour, allow me to say that I have feelings for you that are not without an element of sexual desire, and that these feelings are not of very recent origin, although they have, I admit, become somewhat stronger of late.'

'You do know what I think,' he told her.

'Damn it, Eck!' she yelled. 'Are you ever in your entire fucking life going to act? What are you? A fucking Buddhist or something?'

He placed a hand on her cheek, and her eyes closed and her lips opened in a smile, and he kissed her.

Her arms closed on his back. 'Well, well,' she marvelled. 'Aren't we the master?' she said, but her eyes were searching his, for assurance that he understood what they might be about to do. He kissed her again.

34. Nafplio

His mother was pleased for them, she said, but occasionally there was now a suspiciousness to her manner, as though it had been revealed that he and Megan had been conspiring against her for years. When she at last came round to the house she stood in the hall and looked about her as if to enumerate all the alterations that had been made. They all followed Megan into the living room, where none of Mr Beckwith's furniture remained. 'Very bold,' his mother observed, having scrutinised systematically each wall, the ceiling and the carpet she stood on. 'Isn't it, Graham? Very striking.'

Holding his glasses behind his back, Alexander's father was looking at Mitchell's painting of Megan, which hung where the ship's-wheel clock had been. 'Yes. Very,' he replied, closely reading the stencilled name and date on the pavement underneath Megan's feet. 'Interesting,' he remarked to Alexander, seemingly engrossed by the way Megan's hair had been painted around her face like the rays of a child's sun.

'Who's that?' asked Alexander's mother, coming over to the picture.

His father stepped aside, and Megan took his arm to lead him away to see the rest of the house, while Alexander made tea for his mother, who stood by the French windows, looking out at the garden. 'You haven't changed everything, then,' she remarked, taking her cup. When she sat in one of the armchairs she sat forward, balancing the saucer on her palm, as if preparing to rise and leave.

'How's the hip?' he asked her, ending a silence.

'Good days, bad days,' she replied.

'And today?'

'It's been worse,' she said, and she gave the room another look. She asked him how the shop was faring. He told her that Sid Dixon had mentioned that he was considering selling it some time in the next few years, and had once asked him if he might be interested in taking it over. At the first lull, when they were eating, his mother repeated to his father what Alexander had said about the shop, and his father took up the subject with such energy that his mother began a separate conversation with Megan, as she used to do with the wives of his father's clients and colleagues, whenever the discussion at the table turned to finance. Alexander heard her asking Megan how her work was going. She nodded politely as she listened, and politely asked more questions, but she barely glanced at Megan while they talked.

After his parents had gone they cleared up and drank the last of the second bottle of wine. He went to bed before Megan, leaving her to read downstairs. A couple of hours later he woke up. Her bedside light was on, and she was lying close to him, her back curled into his belly. A sprig of hair was bent over her neck and bobbed with the pulse of her throat. Alexander slid a hand over her waist. 'It's all right, Eck,' she said. She kissed his hand, and he felt the tears on her skin.

'Meg?' he said, touching her hair.

She kissed his hand again. 'It's all right, Eck. I'm a bit agitated. Made me think of Dad, your parents being here. But it's all right. Go to sleep.'

This was one of many nights on which he would wake to find that she had not yet slept. 'I keep thinking of him,' she would reply, gazing at the door in the darkness. He would put an arm around her, and she would take his hand and clutch it to her face, as though she had the proof of something in her grasp. Once he woke up to see Megan bent double on the end of the bed. 'It's getting worse,' she said, shaking her head to rid it of its thoughts. Once she was sitting upright and staring with such alarm that for an instant it seemed possible that she had glimpsed Mr Beckwith, as Alexander had often glimpsed him, in the corner of his eye, as he came into a room that was empty. And then there was the night he was awoken by a click and saw her standing in the doorway. 'Eck,' she gasped, as if horrified, and he went over to her, thinking that she might be sleepwalking. She let herself be led back to the bed, and she told him how she used to listen to her father walking around the house at night, padding for hours from room to room ceaselessly. 'He's gone,' she grieved, holding his arm tightly. 'I keep expecting to see him, but he's gone,' she said, as if repeating something she could not comprehend. They lay in the dark for an hour or more, and then Megan reached back and touched his face and tentatively asked him: 'Eck, do you really like this place?'

'Yes. I've always liked it,' he said. 'Why?'

'Because I don't, now. Not much.'

'I thought you did.'

'I did. But I'm going to miss him too much as long as we're here.'

'You think it'll be better if we move?'

'I don't know. But it doesn't feel right, not for us. It doesn't feel like it's ours,' she said, and she turned the light on. They talked until it was time to get up, and by then the decision had been made. She would sell the house and they would rent somewhere for a while. They would do something with the money, have a holiday or two. 'What do you think, Eck?' she urged, kneeling to face him. 'I'll take you away for a fortnight in the sun. I'll pay. Let me pay. Your reward for putting up with a madwoman. Let's go, Eck,' she said, jumping off the bed as though she meant to leave that day.

Two months later the house was sold and Alexander left the Beckwiths' house as easily as he had left the flat above the shop. They rented a two-storey flat, which they intended to leave within the year, but never did leave. A week after moving, as soon as everything had been unpacked, they flew to Athens on their first holiday together.

While waiting for their luggage to appear on the airport carousel they decided that they would go to Nafplio the following day. There, after trying every hotel in the town, they found a room to rent above a clothes shop, on a slope above the main square. The owner led them up a brick staircase at the back of the building, to a whitewashed room that was a couple of feet longer than the bed it contained, and was a perfect cube. 'Please,' the man said to Alexander, gesturing eagerly at the single square window. Alexander pushed open the window and put his head out. In the yard a lemon tree cast its shade on a dismantled motorbike; over the roofs he could see a portion of a ship in the harbour. Unlatching the inner door, the owner presented another whitewashed room of identical dimensions, with a rusted shower head protruding from the centre of the ceiling. Megan gave him payment for a week, and when he had gone she tucked their bags under the bed and lay down.

Alexander was still by the window, looking at a broad tin disc that was nailed to the wall above the door of the grocer's shop across the street. A bicycle with lumpy tyres and a frame like a triangle of logs was painted on the disc, as he would remember, and its profusely moustachioed rider wore a scarlet and white hooped bathing costume that covered his arms and legs, which tapered evenly to dainty hands and feet that resembled tiny squid. Enjoying the sight of the capering Edwardian gentleman, and the whine of the mopeds on the harbourside road, and the street's smell of warm tarmac and engine smoke and the sea, Alexander stayed at the window until Megan said his name. She raised one hand to him, and she closed her eyes as though to relish the breeze. The mattress curved like the hull of a canoe when he lay down beside her. They lay together, her head resting on his chest, until it was dark.

They went down to the waterfront, where every restaurant was busy, and returned to the square along a narrow street that was choked with tables, all of them occupied. They walked past the church and the bus station, and reached the train station before turning back and following the road that flanked the cathedral. 'I'm ravenous,' laughed Megan, as though something had been troubling her for some time and she had only now realised what it was. The lights of the ship appeared at the end of a side street. They walked towards the quay, and at the first junction they looked to one side and saw two tables on the pavement outside what seemed to be an ordinary house. A middle-aged man, stocky as a wrestler, stepped through the beaded curtain that hung in the doorway and, seeing Megan and Alexander peering into the twilight of his alley, hoisted a pair of wooden chairs above his head. He pushed an arm through the curtain and extracted it almost instantly, holding a water carafe and a bottle of ouzo. 'That's the one,' said Megan, and before they reached the table it had been set with dishes of aubergine and olives and tomatoes, and two young tourists were approaching from the opposite end of the alley, lured by another brandished pair of chairs.

Standing behind Megan and Alexander, the couple scanned the front of the house. 'It is a restaurant?' the woman asked.

'It would seem so,' Alexander told her.

'Thank you,' said the woman to Megan, and hesitantly she took a seat at the other table, on which four or five dishes, carried into the street on a forearm, were spread as quickly as a hand of cards. Her companion had taken a phrasebook from his pocket and was flicking its pages anxiously. She raked his hair with her fingernails and huddled against him to read the page.

In the course of the next hour or more a dozen dishes were placed on each table with scarcely a word. The young Germans smiled at each course, and at the man who had brought it, and occasionally at Alexander and Megan, but they spoke only to each other until the meal was finished. They could not stop touching each other. While the young man read aloud a passage from their guidebook, his girlfriend ran a finger up and down his arm. When she edged closer to him to look at the page he stroked her hair, her face, her legs. Whenever they took a sip from their glasses they kissed straight afterwards, savouring the taste on the other's lips.

Noticing that Megan was watching them over his shoulder, Alexander tapped her plate with his knife. 'HQ to Agent Beckwith. Do you read me? Over.'

'Sorry,' said Megan, returning her attention to her plate.

'You envious?' he enquired.

'Of what?' she asked. 'Their tans?'

'The first careless rapture.'

She glanced over his shoulder, pressing her lips together in disapproval. 'You're kidding,' she said.

'Not entirely.'

'Why should I be envious?' she replied.

'You know,' he shrugged. 'We've never been like that. We skipped a stage.'

Megan looked at him for a moment, as if considering an idea that had never occurred to her before. 'And perhaps they'll never be like this, Eck,' she said. She leaned across the table to kiss him, and the other couple smiled at each other, thinking, it seemed, that Megan was following their example. 'But I do envy the tans,' she told him, pressing his hand to her sun-reddened brow.

When recalling their first holiday, Alexander would remember this conversation before anything else, except for the day that was as hot at eight o'clock in the morning as the previous days had been at noon, and they hired a scooter because even the beach at the end of the rough track was crowded. They went to Epidavros, where the heat

was so intense that when he sat on the uppermost tier of the amphitheatre and looked across the ruins at the dark green mountain, it was
as though he was looking through a slow flow of clear liquid that was
continuously warping the line of the horizon and making the trees rise
and fall in low waves. His sweat, dripping onto stone, became a dry
stain within seconds. Birds circled high above the hills, never
descending, like particles of iron stirred in thick transparent oil. Megan
advanced across the hot earth, treading the ground as if there were
only one path that would take her across it safely. In front of her, a
man in chequered shorts and a singlet the colour of lemon sorbet
wiggled his forefingers at his temples and kicked up the dust with long
scrapes of his sandals; his wife giggled, waving him away. Two boys
tussled over the circle of white stone in the centre; their teacher called
them back to their group, and Megan stepped onto the circle. A party
of students walked in single file around the tier two rows below the
one on which Alexander sat, their sketchbooks held above their heads
as parasols. In the gaps between them, Alexander saw Megan far below,
hitching his white cotton shirt onto her shoulders. She looked at the
ground; her hair glistened as if it were wet; he saw her mouth moving.
'Hello, Eck,' she whispered. 'Hello, Eck,' she repeated softly, and her
voice was so close it seemed that her lips were almost touching his
ear. Passing behind her, a woman paused to look at Megan, and then
scrutinised the stone terraces, but her gaze did not find Alexander.
Megan whispered at the ground, and her voice floated through the
rasping of the feet of the people around her. 'Hello, Eck. Hello, love,'
she said. Again the woman gazed up at the terraces.

   That night, as on every other night of that week in Nafplio, they
went back to the taverna in the alley by the harbour. After the meal,
as was their habit, they strolled around the main square for a while then
followed the path around the headland from the waterfront. Halfway
between the town and the beach Megan looked back and, assured that
they were alone, climbed down from the path onto the platform of
rock where they sunbathed. At the edge of the outcrop she began to
undress. 'Come on,' she said, holding her dress with her fingertips
and letting it fall. He sat on the path and he watched her as she lowered
herself from the rock. With strokes that barely moved the surface she
swam towards the boat that was tethered some twenty yards from the

shore, and when she reached it she put a hand on its bow to rest there. 'Come on, Eck,' she called. Directly across the bay, a charcoal cloud was running aground on the hills and crumpling upwards, and underneath the cloud the headlights of a car flashed at the curves of an invisible road. Against the dark purple water her skin was as pale as a snowberry. In the bushes the cicadas creaked in a regular rhythm, as if singing the seconds away.

35. MacIndoe's

As soon as they had decorated the flat and Alexander had uprooted the weeds and dug out the debris and put the garden in order, they invited his parents for a meal, and this was to be the one evening on which his parents were their guests, because all subsequent invitations to his parents were discreetly turned by Alexander's mother into an invitation from her to them. From time to time Alexander and Megan had an evening with Sam and Liz, but never at the flat, because it was difficult to get someone to look after the children for long, and whenever they spent some time with any of the five or six of Megan's colleagues whom she regarded as friends it was nearly always at a pub or a restaurant in Greenwich or up in town. The only person who came to the flat more than once in the first year was Sid Dixon.

It was around the time of the bank robbery in Nice, as Alexander would recall, that Megan first met Sid. She and Alexander were redecorating the Beckwiths' house, and she came into the shop one Thursday afternoon before term started, bringing a swatch of paint samples that she had borrowed. Ten minutes later Sid arrived, to pick up a Jack Teagarden record he had promised to deliver to one of their regular customers, who had broken an ankle.

Alexander and Megan were standing by the window, holding the fan of colours into the light, when Sid came in. He looked at Alexander, then at Megan, and then at the swatch they were holding, but before he could form a conclusion Megan smiled at him and said his name. 'I still owe you my thanks,' she said before he could respond.

'For what?' asked Sid, directing his bemused reply to Alexander.

'For never having thanked you,' said Megan.

'For what?' asked Sid again.

'For talking to my father that time. It was very good of you.'

'You're Megan?' said Sid, now closing the door.

'I'm Megan,' she verified. 'Alexander told me all about it. I should have called you, instead of leaving it to him. It was remiss of me,' she said, and she looked at Sid steadily, seeming not to see the disfigurement of his face.

'I wasn't much help,' Sid demurred.

'No, Sid, you were,' said Alexander.

'You were,' Megan agreed.

'Some light refreshment?' Alexander suggested, sidling towards the counter.

Sid nodded, but did not follow him. 'All those years, and we never met,' he said.

'I was away a lot of the time,' Megan explained.

'I always wondered what you looked like,' Sid told her. 'And vice versa, I suppose.'

'I knew,' said Megan. 'I saw you a few times, through the window. When I called to see Eck after school. I didn't come in.'

'A common reaction.'

'No,' said Megan firmly. 'I didn't want to get Eck into trouble.'

'I see,' Sid replied, with a sceptical half-smile that shrank away under Megan's candid gaze. 'A lot of people used to run away,' Sid jested. 'That's why I employed your man here.'

Alexander, waiting in the doorway of the stockroom, took a bow. 'A decision never rued,' he declared, waving the kettle enticingly.

'Anyway, I'm pleased to meet you, after all this time,' said Megan, and Sid, who never shook hands with anyone, let Megan take his maimed right hand in her palm, and he smiled as if entranced by the boldness of her.

They invited Sid Dixon to the house on Boxing Day of that year, and a couple of weeks after Alexander's parents had visited them he came to the flat, bringing as a housewarming present a blue and white china plate on which was painted a rustic schoolhouse with a procession of children filing through its door. On the next visit he brought a little onyx box, in which Megan was to keep her rings and earrings, and after that he gave her an old cut-glass perfume bottle, which she never filled because a trace of jasmine still lingered in the empty bottle. And one evening, soon after the end of the spring term, as Alexander would remember, Sid arrived with a large object wrapped in newspaper under his arm and a briefcase in his other hand. It was raining, and the saturated paper came off in strips as he unwrapped the gift hastily on the kitchen table. 'A bit risky,' he warned Megan, 'but I hope you'll like her. Found her in a jumble sale,' he explained to Alexander. A globe of fluted glass emerged, supported on the forearms of a pewter figure with a helmet-like bob, who was naked but for a tiara, a sash knotted slackly around her waist and a bow slung over a shoulder. At her feet, a borzoi lay asleep, its muzzle nestled between its paws. With a rag of dampened paper Sid erased a mark from the base of the lamp. 'We had a similar one in the shop once, didn't we, Alex? Got snapped up straight away. Less than a year, anyway,' he laughed, glancing at Alexander in such a way that Alexander then knew what Sid would be telling them later.

They kept the lamp in the centre of the table while they ate. Megan was turning it, admiring the nymph's sleek little thighs and small-breasted torso, when Sid, looking up at the drawing of Malham Beck that Megan had made on a recent field trip, at last said: 'I've made up my mind, kids.' They stopped eating, but he could not look at them. 'This is the year I pack it in,' he went on, with a determined tensing of his jaw, and then he turned to Alexander. 'Time to pass it on to a younger man. I'm getting too long in the tooth. Walk down the street now and it's like I'm in a foreign country. All this effing and blinding and wearing stupid clothes, I can't be doing with it,' he told Megan.

'We had quite enough of that kind of thing in the army,' Alexander said, fetching more beer from the fridge.

'Country's going to the dogs, I reckon. I don't know what their problem is, these kids. Life of Riley, they've got.'

'No future, Sid,' said Megan. 'Not as far as they can see.'

'No sense, more like. How you going to have a future if you go round sticking two fingers up at everyone? Shoving pins through your face. It's stupid.'

'They'll grow out of it,' Megan assured him.

'Maybe,' said Sid, fiddling with the switch of the lamp. 'But I'm off. I'm retiring to Jersey. Half-retiring.'

'Jersey?' Alexander exclaimed. 'What happened to the man who needed noise?'

'Who needed noise?'

'You did. First time I met you, that's what you said.'

'I did?' Sid queried. 'Well, that's what getting old does for you. You'll find out, in the end.'

'So why Jersey?' asked Alexander.

'There's a cousin out there. Runs a garage. I'll help him out a bit.' He clicked the switch rapidly, four or five times, then said to Megan: 'I'd like Alex to take over the shop. I'd hate it to become a branch of an off-licence or something. I want it to continue as it is, and I know it'll be in safe hands if he's still running the show.'

'It will.'

'We can trust Alex.'

'We can,' she said.

'When do you think you'll be going?' Alexander asked.

'As soon as I can,' said Sid. 'In the bag I've got the accounts for the last ten years. Get your old man to give them a once-over. Check you're not taking a pig in a poke.' He turned to Megan again. 'You'll make sure he takes over, won't you, love?' he urged.

'I'll see what I can do,' said Megan.

'Good. It's right that he should have it,' Sid told her. 'It's what should happen. Just like you two are together. Some things are meant to happen,' he said, with a sentimental cadence that prompted Megan to reach across the table and put an arm around his shoulders. He glanced at Alexander and winked, but Alexander glimpsed in his eyes an inflection that raised the memory of the desolate smile with which their friendship had perhaps begun, as Alexander's father held Sid's coat open for him in the hallway of their house. Alexander would always remember this, and the frail jocularity of Sid's voice when, standing at the door and glancing over Megan's shoulder, he said that they would have to come out and see him. And he would remember that at two o'clock that night, having leafed through the accounts and found nothing unexpected, he drove to the shop and sat for an hour or more in the half-light. Hearing in the silence of the shop some of the records that he had played there, he sensed something of the portions of time that had become attached to the music. He heard Roy Orbison howling 'It's Over' while two schoolboys counted their money on the doorstep, and Led Zeppelin blaring at the end of a quiet afternoon when for several seconds there was not a single person and

301

not a single car in the street. Summoning the sound of Leonard Cohen's voice, of Dusty Springfield, of 'Somebody to Love', he saw bars of shadow under a striped awning, and a girl's white PVC coat, and a bag made from a piece of dark tapestry, from which had arisen the perfume of patchouli. He recalled the shop as it had been when Megan used to call after school, and heard again the ticking of the clocks. Gazing up the hill, he pictured the faces of the people who worked in every shop, and of the people who had worked there before them, back to the year when he became Sid Dixon's assistant, when the girl who looked like Connie Francis was the clerk at the train station. He could not imagine himself anywhere else.

One afternoon, three months after Dixon's Discs had become Mac-Indoe's, Alexander was in the stockroom, filing the week's mail orders, when he heard, through the music that was playing in the shop, the catch of the door. It was one of the Bach cello suites that was playing, and Pope John Paul II had recently been elected, which he would remember because he could recall the picture of the new pope address-ing the crowd in St Peter's Square on the cover of the magazine that showed through the plastic bag that Jane was holding.

At around the time of Mr Beckwith's funeral he had spotted her Morris Minor parked outside a bank in Greenwich, and had then seen that she was getting out of it and turned back before she could notice him. Many months later, shortly after Alexander's parents had been to the flat, he was walking past the cinema in Lewisham as the audience was leaving, and Jane, with her brother, had looked up to see him on the other side of the street, and seemed irritated by the sight of him, rather than upset, and walked on quickly, without acknowledging his wave. These were the only two occasions on which Alexander had encountered her since their last conversation on the phone, some six years ago, and now she stood in the centre of the shop, holding a bag of magazines in front of her like a breastplate, with her hands crossed over it.

She glanced at him and observed his surprise. 'Hello,' he said, but she did not speak.

Unhurriedly she surveyed the newly painted walls and the racks of records. Without shifting her feet she turned to look into the corner of the shop where she used to browse, as if to make certain that there was no one there. 'You've smartened it up a bit,' she remarked, examining the green glass panels that now covered the ceiling.

'Under new management,' he told her.

'Yes,' she said. 'I saw the sign.'

'What do you think?'

'Not an inspired choice of name,' she replied, with an anaemic smile.

'Well, you'd deter the older customers if you went for something trendier.'

She looked around the shop once more, gradually, until her eyes had used up all the things there were to see. 'How are you keeping?' she asked, neutrally.

'Well,' he replied. Jane nodded, but as if she was not listening to him and she did not reply when he asked: 'And you?'

Squinting at the speakers above the counter, she laughed silently to herself. 'So I made some sort of lasting impression,' she observed. 'The music.'

'I play this all the time,' said Alexander. 'It's pretty well all I listen to nowadays.'

'Can't beat the old tunes,' Jane agreed, with a sardonic twist of her lips that lasted no more than a second or two. The last movement of the suite was playing, and they listened to the end. As he removed the record from the turntable she noticed the book that lay on the counter, its open pages downward.

'What are you reading?' Jane asked, and he handed over *The Great War and Modern Memory*. She perused the book like a border guard with a suspect passport, then put it down in its former place. 'Interesting?' she asked, uninterestedly.

'Very,' said Alexander.

Gazing at the Blondie poster behind him, she enquired: 'I assume you don't live upstairs any more?'

'No, I don't.'

'No,' she said. 'I didn't think the curtains were quite your style.'

'He's from Delhi. The tenant.'

'Ah. Delhi.'

'A medical student.'

'Hence all the books on the windowsill.'

'Exactly.'

'I'm leaving, Alexander,' she said, in the same expressionless voice. 'I'm finally leaving London, and I thought I should say goodbye.' She lifted and dropped her shoulders, releasing a sharp, conclusive sigh, then looked at him in a way that at once demanded a response and denoted an indifference to whatever that response might be.

'You've packed in that job?'

'That would tend to follow, yes.'

'I'm glad,' he said, and she looked away. 'Where are you going?'

'Brighton.'

'To do –?'

'I've enrolled on a course. Acupuncture. Inflicting pain to a good end,' she smiled, at which point the receptionist from the estate agent's came in to collect a record she had ordered. Jane remained precisely where she was while Alexander served his customer, as if he were a painting that had been briefly blocked from her view. As the door closed she raised the bag again and clamped it to her chest. Resting her chin on the edge of the magazine, she looked at him inquisitively, and casually asked: 'Alexander, do you ever think of me?'

Alexander accepted her gaze. 'Of course,' he said. 'Of course I do.'

'I think of you sometimes,' she said. 'But the funny thing is, when I think of you I can hardly ever see your face clearly. Which is odd, isn't it? It's as if you're so beautiful you're almost invisible. Does that seem possible?' she asked. 'When you think of me, do you see me?'

'Yes, I do,' he replied, as another customer, a man from the sorting office, came in. The man went to the country albums; Jane put her bag on the counter and turned to the racks on the opposite side of the shop.

Her hair was loose, and she kept stroking a thick lock of it as she turned the albums over. When she lifted an album sleeve and read it, the calmness of her eyes and the angle of her head and neck reminded Alexander of her appearance on the day she had first spoken to him. Her lips made the tiny pulsing movements they would sometimes make when she was considering something, or was about to kiss him. Watching her, he saw that she was as desirable now as she had been when they met, but he felt no desire for her. He felt no desire, and yet he had not, after all, ceased to love her, he told himself, because he intensely desired her to be happy; more intensely, it seemed, than he had when he had wanted her.

'I must be going,' she said, as soon as the man had left. She came over to the counter and held out her hand. He felt a tremor that was barely perceptible, but he could not tell whether it was in her hand or his. He opened his mouth to speak. 'Don't you dare,' she ordered him. 'Goodbye, Alexander,' she said, detaching her hand from his after one last strong grip.

'Good luck,' he said.

'Fine words.'

'Sorry,' he said. 'I mean, I'm sorry –'

'It doesn't matter, Alexander,' she said, shaking her head. She went, leaving the door open. Closing it, Alexander looked for her. She was almost running up the hill, to reach the bus stop before the bus that was approaching, he thought, but she did not get on it.

It was not until four days later that he told Megan about Jane's visit. Coming into the kitchen, he saw that she had a pair of greeting cards on the table. One was for a colleague who was having a baby and the other was a birthday card for Esmé. He took the food out of the cupboard to prepare the evening meal, and then he told her that Jane had called and that she was going to Brighton. 'Interesting career move. I hope it works out for her,' said Megan as she wrote on an envelope, and that was all she said about Jane. She examined the photograph on the front of Esmé's card. 'Do you think this is appropriate, or is it one for the boys?' she asked him, sliding across the table a picture of a slender blonde girl in hot pants, who was riding a bicycle through a field of high corn. 'A teenager already,' she murmured. She shook her head, and Alexander kissed the back of her neck.

36. Pont des Arts

They were sitting on a bench beside the river, where they had been for perhaps an hour, having spent most of the day on the islands. The late-afternoon sunlight on the pale stone piers of the Pont des Arts had a sweet and deliquescent quality, Alexander would remember. Underneath the footbridge, the arches of the Pont Neuf glowed with the same easeful tone as the piers, as did the flank of the bridge that was framed by the spans of the Pont Neuf, and the spire of the Sainte-Chapelle, which rose above the foliage of a dark tree on the opposite bank. The river shone between the bridges, but where they sat the water was ruffled and its surface held all the colours of a magpie's wing. Shadow covered the front of the buildings that overlooked the river on the Ile de la Cité. The sun put an apricot blush on the faces and hands of the people who were leaning on the railing of the bridge. Megan was drawing on the pad she had bought the day before, soon after they had checked into their hotel, from an old shop in which powdered pigments and flakes of glue were stored in jars like the jars that confectioners and chemists once used. She hunched over the pad, glancing from the paper to the bridge to the paper, moving the pencil slowly across the page, as if she were carving the bridge's profile into wood.

Since she had begun the drawing she had not spoken a word, and neither had Alexander, who was reading the booklet they had bought that morning at the Sainte-Chapelle. An amplified shout made him look up; a boat that resembled a river-going greenhouse was approaching. Having passed under the Pont des Arts, the boat swivelled cumbrously in midstream, churning a dilute pink froth; an incomprehensible sentence boomed from its windows, and a dozen faces turned to regard the Louvre. 'What language do you think that is?' Alexander was about to ask, but when he glanced at Megan he saw that her hand had frozen at the apex of an arc and she had lifted her head to look at something on the bridge, something she found curious and disconcerting. Tracking the line of her gaze brought him to the figure of an elderly woman, who was standing next to one of the lamps, holding a full shopping bag in one hand and an empty bag in the other. The woman put the bags on the ground and looked back, as though seeing where she had come from might remind her of where she was going. They watched her burrow in the full bag and retrieve from it an object that resembled a shrivelled orange, which she dropped into the other bag. She shot a look over her shoulder, then walked off towards the Louvre, holding both bags with crooked arms, as if about to hand them to someone who was offering to take the load from her.

Megan watched the old woman until the trees obscured her. She directed her face again at the place where the woman had been standing, but she was no longer looking. Her expression did not change and her hand did not move.

'What are you thinking?' Alexander asked.

'Daydreaming,' she replied quietly, without turning her head. She looked down at her hand and extended the line that had been interrupted.

'Tell me.'

'It's silly, Eck,' she said. She made a mark and gave him a smile that did not erase the tension from her eyes.

'Tell.'

For a few more seconds she examined the bridge. 'I was only imagining,' she began, and then she hesitated, staring at the spot where the woman had stood, and suddenly he knew what she had been thinking. 'For some reason,' she went on, 'it struck me that my mother might be here. That old lady might have been my mother. I mean, any old lady in Paris might be my mother. I suppose she would have come here, sooner or later. Perhaps she stayed. If she's alive she's as likely to be here as anywhere else, I suppose.' She gazed up at the featureless sky and Alexander touched her hair. 'It's OK, Eck. Really. A passing thought. It's a peculiar idea, though, isn't it? I haven't a clue what she'd look like, and she wouldn't have a much clearer idea of me. We could have walked past each other and neither of us would have known it,' she said, casually, as if this were a diverting situation for a play. 'Perhaps she's in London. Perhaps she's dead. Who knows?' Holding up the pad, she compared her drawing to its subject, and seemed quite pleased with what she had done.

Alexander tried to recall the last time she had made any mention of her mother, and he could find nothing except a day when she was a girl of ten or eleven, when Mrs Beckwith told her that her mother had taken all of her photographs with her when she went away, and Megan had cried in his room and called Mrs Beckwith a liar. 'I often wonder what happened to her,' he said.

'Do you?'

'You must do, Meg. Now and then.'

'Not often. I know I'm supposed to feel I'm not complete, but I don't, not any more. If I ever did. I don't have a biological craving,' she said plainly, as if stating her blood group. 'She's a shadow behind my parents, that's all. I can remember a stripy kitchen apron, and I think I remember her opening the outhouse door, but that might be someone else. And that's about it. I don't resent her going off the way she did. I might have done the same thing. But I don't miss her. I hope she found someone, but I can't say I feel anything. She's nothing to do with me any more.' She continued with her drawing, but a few seconds later she stopped again. 'I wouldn't want to meet her, not now,' she told him. 'Say she got in touch, out of the blue. I'm pretty sure I wouldn't want to see her. That's what I was thinking. Does that sound bad?' she asked him, and he shook his head. 'Things would become unravelled. Do you know what I mean? This is what I want,' she said, and her eyes surveyed the river as she kissed the back of his hand. 'Come on, we should make the most of this weather.'

They went up the steps, crossed Place du Carrousel and walked along Rue Saint-Honoré. On Place Vendôme he took her photograph in front of a window in which a small silver lizard with emerald scales clung to a small blanched twig. Peering through the viewfinder he saw a familiar look, vivified yet clouded by anxiety, such as often came into her eyes when they had talked about Mr Beckwith, and he saw her fingers spread and contract on the stone of the wall, as if to embed the memory of its texture into her skin. In Galeries Lafayette he detected within the stew of perfumes a scent that Megan had once said she liked, and quickly bought a bottle of it for her, which he dropped into her bag as they stood on the kerb of Boulevard Haussmann. They walked the length of Avenue de l'Opéra, crossed the river by the Pont des Arts, and had a drink in a bar near Saint-

Séverin, before eating at Le Procope. While he paid the bill she left the table to splash water on her face. 'Let's stay out a bit longer,' she said, widening her eyes as if to stare the tiredness out of them. They called into a bar near Saint-Sulpice, where the barman poured the unlabelled wine into squat little tumblers, which they took to a small round table near the head of the stairs. In the cellar a man was singing to the accompaniment of a strummed guitar, and above their table hung a row of wrinkled photographs of young men in roll-neck jumpers, each with a guitar across his lap and an expression of irresistible sincerity on his face. Megan smiled at the pictures, at the bare wooden floor, at the haphazard array of bottles and glasses behind the bar, at the backs of the two men by the doorway, whose perfunctory and easy manner of conversing suggested that they had been meeting in this place, at this hour, for a very long time. The older of the pair, who wore a hand-knitted cardigan that was holed at the elbows, directed the tip of his beard at someone passing in the street; his companion thoughtfully drained his glass, as if to signify his understanding of the point that had been made. 'This is bizarre,' said Megan, cupping her hands around the tumbler. 'You wouldn't have thought something like this still existed. It can't have changed in twenty years.' They drank their wine, but when Alexander brought two more glasses back from the bar she looked at him from under her narrowed brows, to prevent him from being evasive, and said to him: 'It wasn't good luck finding this bar, was it? I mean, you didn't just happen upon it.'

'It was not,' he replied.

'You've been here before.'

'I have.'

'I knew it.'

Levelling a finger at Megan's nose, he cried: '*J'accuse.*'

'You were here with that bloody American.'

'Harsh, Meg. But yes, I was not alone,' he said, as if giving a witness statement. 'I was here with Pen.'

'At this table, I'll bet. Listening to one of those lads,' she said, scowling at the gallery of singers.

'I thought you'd like it. And I was right, wasn't I?' he replied, clinking his glass on hers.

'Some of its charm has faded, for some reason.' She looked at the chair on which she was sitting, as if pretending there was something on it that might stain her clothes, then gave him an uneven smile.

They had a third glass, but as soon as they left the bar she again brought up the subject of Pen. 'Don't think about her any more,' he said, stopping by the portico of Saint-Sulpice.

'I can't help it. I don't want to think about her. I wish I'd never heard of her. She's the one you should never have told me about.'

'You can't be jealous of her, Meg. It's fifteen years ago.'

'I'm not jealous of her. I don't like the sound of her. There's a difference.'

'Neither do I.'

'What's that supposed to mean?'

'That she doesn't sound very nice now.'

'What were you playing at, traipsing after that one?' she asked.

'I wasn't playing at anything, and I didn't traipse,' Alexander replied, walking away. 'In retrospect, it would have been better if I'd never set eyes on her, but I did, and I liked her. Now let's drop it.'

At the road that ran past the Luxembourg gardens they turned left and walked past the front of the palace. By the Odéon theatre she moved closer to him. 'I'll tell you what it is about your American friend,' she went on. 'It's that she doesn't fit. I can't account for her, and she makes me worry that I don't really know you.'

'That's ridiculous.'

'I'm all right with Jane, because she was serious. But I wish that one had never existed.'

'Meg, you know me better than anyone on the face of the planet. And it was fifteen years ago, for God's sake.'

'No, it's not fifteen years ago. She's here now. In your head.'

'Like that goon Mitchell's in yours.'

'Hardly. And I don't drag you to bars I went to with him.'

'I didn't drag you anywhere,' said Alexander sharply. For a minute or so they did not speak, and then, as they were waiting for a gap in the traffic, Alexander asked, as if merely requesting clarification: 'You mean you were here with Mitchell?'

'I was,' said Megan, allowing her attention to be taken by a passing police car.

'I thought you went to Paris with what's-his-name.'

310

'Mitchell too.'

'That must have been a lot of fun. Was it?'

'I can't remember,' she told him pertly, as if by this remark she was exculpated.

'Bet he sorted the locals out,' Alexander smiled.

'Eck, don't make out you're not bothered about Mitchell. You're as bothered by him as I am by that American tart.'

'Tart? Tart?' he repeated, scandalised.

'Yes. So don't try to act blasé.'

Resting against the door of a van, Alexander imitated Mitchell's leer. 'Baby, I am blasé,' he bragged, ticking the air with a finger. Megan was deciding whether to make use of the dregs of her annoyance, but she was standing in front of a shop that had in its window a poster of a fireman who had his back to a blazing house and was wearing nothing but a set of thermal underwear. 'Moi? Froid? Jamais?' Alexander read aloud, and he took her hand.

They carried on up the hill to the Panthéon, where midnight struck as they were circling the church. They descended towards Boulevard Saint-Germain, and an hour later they were a couple of blocks from the hotel, looking in the window of a clothes shop, in which were hung, on two crosses of thick bamboo cane, two shirts which seemed to be black until the light of the revolving spotlight struck the fabric and changed its colour to the blue-black of new iron. It was past two o'clock when they returned to their room, and when Alexander woke up Megan was not there. In the bathroom a ribbon of toilet paper was draped over the rail of the shower, and on it was written: 'Gone for an early draw. See you for breakfast.' He went back to bed and was later awakened by something falling onto his face. His hand closed on a piece of thick, soft cotton, which instantly was plucked away. Smiling at him, Megan swept the shirt backwards and forwards, caressingly, across his chest. 'Arise and greet the day, you lazy git,' she said. She touched a tiny cold mother-of-pearl button to his lips.

He put on the new shirt, and after breakfast they crossed the Pont des Arts and went to the Louvre, where they had decided to spend the day. Together they strolled through a sequence of galleries but soon, amid a thicket of Roman emperors, they halted to check their map of the museum, and agreed to meet for lunch. Megan went off to look at the paintings, leaving Alexander to wander, with only an approximate notion of where he was going, through the antiquities and beyond, through corridors and rooms he was certain he had never seen with Pen, until he found himself in a room full of swords and enamelled vessels and ivory boxes, and realised that he was far from where he had to be within the half-hour. He arrived at the café moments before Megan, who had seen only a fraction of what she wanted to see, because she had stayed so long with a single picture. 'It's wonderful, Eck. I've no idea why I didn't find it before,' she told him. 'It's so beautiful, and so simple and sad, for some reason. I tried to draw it, but I couldn't get it right at all. It's like trying to draw the air,' she said, and she showed him her abandoned sketch and drew an X on the plan of the museum.

In the afternoon they again explored the museum apart. After an hour or so he sought out Gilles, but he was not touched by him, because, it seemed, he was remembering that he had been touched by him before and could not see him without the interference of that thought and of his memory of Pen, who had stood a step to his right, with an expression of impatience that encompassed both himself and Gilles. Following the plan, Alexander came to the room that Megan had marked, and Megan was in it, sitting on a low bench in front of *The Astronomer*. He sat beside her and she put a hand on his, but she did not break her contemplation of the painting, in which the light seemed to be fading as it was fading in the silent room in which they sat, and the astronomer regarded the globe on which the tips of his fingers rested, as if it were a thing that might destroy him. With the alert and solemn demeanour of the astronomer she regarded the picture, and then she lifted Alexander's hand and kissed it. 'Love you, Eck,' she whispered. 'See you later,' she said, and he left her.

Alexander would remember her in the room, with the painting of the scholar and the sunlit globe, and he would remember waiting for her in the Tuileries, sitting on a green steel chair by one of the pools, facing the high buildings on Rue de Rivoli, with a bed of cerise tulips and euphorbia to his right, and a chestnut tree and a bedraggled willow to his left. A boy in an old-fashioned child's sailor suit pushed across the pond a toy yacht with a single linen sail. Megan arrived and pulled a chair next to his. They rested their feet on the rim of the pond and sat for a while, to feel the evening come in. She put her hand on his neck to soothe his skin where the new collar had chafed. Back in the hotel room, before it had become dark, she sat in the half-length bath and he washed her hair. A tongue of cool shampoo slid from his palm across his wrist and onto her head. As she leaned back a slurry of bubbles ran over her throat. She closed her eyes and drawled, in the voice of the fop in *Barry Lyndon*: 'Et maintenant, je suis fa-ti-guée.' This he would never forget, and one evening, many years later, when Sam Saunders put down the magazine in which he was reading an interview with an actor, to ask Alexander what he would say to someone who wanted him to name the time when he was happiest, Alexander replied immediately that he couldn't answer, and then, when Liz insisted, chose this day, this hour, in Paris in 1979.

37. A Night at the Opera

A photograph of all the school's teachers and children was always pinned over Megan's desk. Because the headmaster liked to surround himself with the more attractive members of his staff, Megan was to be found near the centre, not far from Dominique Seaton, the French teacher, and Valerie Clough, who taught PE, and, in one year's picture, Claire Mowbray, who lasted four terms and then took a post at a private school in Birmingham. Above the photograph there was a shelf of box files in which she kept the question papers and drawings and notes she had prepared for her classes, and above that there was a second shelf, holding the folders of notes on her pupils, and examples of their work. Many of the names on those folders would remain in Alexander's memory for a long time, and the faces of some of them, but one boy he would remember more fully than all the others, even though he saw him just twice, and that was Courtney Wilson, who was twelve years old when Alexander first met him.

Megan was at work when Alexander came home from the shop on this Friday evening. The door of her room was open, and he saw her at the desk, with one elbow propped on a pile of exercise books, wearily circling in red ink a sentence on the page she was marking. Massaging her shoulder, Alexander read the words within the red circles: Altantic Ocean, Gulf Streem, Dartmore. 'He's a bright boy, Eck,' she told him, in response to Alexander's exhalation. 'Has problems with the written word, but he's a very bright kid. Very imaginative. Look at this,' she said, reaching for one of the folders. She took out a photocopy of a crudely drawn map, which was labelled, in uneven capital letters, as a map of Jamaica. 'He's done lots of these, a whole series of them. Courtney's islands of the Caribbean.'

'That's not the shape of Jamaica, is it?'

'Not really, no. He's made it up. He makes all of them up. But Courtney's islands make perfect sense. They're not like most kids' imaginary maps. He hasn't slammed things together willy-nilly. His

314

rivers make the right shapes, his trees grow where trees would grow, the beaches are right, the shoreline is realistic. He understands the principles.' With the cap of her pen she followed the course of a river from its source to the ocean. 'See? The loops get wider as the terrain flattens out. He might not be able to write words very well, but he sure can draw a map.' Megan swivelled in her chair to kiss him.

'Shall I get you something? Modest glass of wine?' he asked.

She nodded, and put a finger on the photograph. 'That's him,' she said, and Alexander looked at a broadly smiling face in a company of smiling and slightly blurred faces, two rows behind Megan. And then she said, with a small cringe, as if confessing to a mishap: 'He's coming over, tomorrow morning.' Ultimately, it was down to Claire Mowbray, she explained. Observing that *Fawlty Towers* had awoken the nation to the qualities of well-written farce, Claire had decided that the school was ready for something a bit more ambitious than a musical. She was mounting a production of *The Comedy of Errors*, with her favourite pupils, the Fielding twins, cast as Antipholus of Ephesus and Antipholus of Syracuse. The Cartwright brothers, who could pass for twins as long as they remained sitting down and one of them dyed his hair and both wore dark glasses, had been persuaded to take the roles of Dromio and Dromio, and an audition had been held for the other parts, at which Courtney, who was nurturing a blatant crush on Claire, had presented himself. Declining to read from the script, he had delivered instead a scene from *Jaws* that he had learned by heart. He had performed both parts of the dialogue, convincingly enough to put Claire in something of a quandary. 'She thinks he's dim, and can't possibly learn the lines. But I know he's not, and I'm pretty sure he can, and so I agreed to coach him. She's given him the part of Luciana,' Megan laughed, 'because he's prettier and speaks more clearly than any of the girls.'

They were still eating breakfast when Courtney turned up. He was wearing black nylon shorts and football trainers and a T-shirt with the Ferrari logo across the chest, and he regarded Alexander with eyes that were huge and marvelling and melancholic. Cupping a hand to the back of his head, he asked if Miss Beckwith was in, then followed Alexander as far as the inside doormat, where he remained, staring at his feet so as not to see anything he was not supposed to see, until Alexander beckoned him from the doorway of the living room. Courtney ran into the room and halted abruptly at the sight of Megan in her jeans and old sweatshirt.

'Good morning, Courtney,' Megan greeted him, folding the newspaper.

'Morning Miss Beckwith,' Courtney replied, and he dipped a shoulder in a paroxysm of bashfulness, as if dodging something that had been thrown at him. He glanced at Alexander through his eyelashes.

'This is Alexander, my boyfriend,' said Megan, at which Courtney gave him a dubious smile. 'Would you like a bowl of cereal, Courtney? Or some juice?'

'No thank you,' said Courtney, as his hands searched for pockets that were not there. 'Is that what we doing?' he asked, jerking his head at the book on the table.

'It is. Shall we start? No point hanging about, is there?' said Megan. She indicated the chair in which Alexander had been sitting.

'No point, Miss Beckwith,' Courtney agreed, and with sideways steps he advanced to the table.

Alexander went out of the room. Taking his coat, he indistinctly heard Megan explaining something to Courtney, and then she went on, in an assuaging voice: '*Good sister, let us dine, and never fret.*' There was a pause; through the gap between the hinges of the door Alexander saw Megan wave the book over the table, like a conductor's baton. '*Good sister, let us dine, and never fret,*' she coaxed.

Courtney rubbed the heels of his thumbs on his eyes and grinned at the newspaper. '*Good sister, let us dine, and never fret,*' he recited, in a light, bouncing treble.

'*A man is master of his liberty,*' Megan reasoned.

'*A man is master of his liberty,*' repeated Courtney, to the same melody as he had given to the first line.

'*Good sister, let us dine, and never fret;*
A man is master of his liberty,' Megan reprised, with emphatic expressiveness.

'*Good sister, let us dine, and never fret;*
A man is master of his liberty,' Courtney recited, exactly as before, but when Alexander returned, nearly five hours later, Courtney's deliv-

316

ery of his words was so different it was as though he had been pretending not to understand what he had been saying.

Packets of biscuits and crisps, various mugs and glasses, a bottle of lemonade and a carton of juice were strewn about the table. Megan was sitting where she had been before, but Courtney was strolling around the room, gesturing at an imagined companion, whom he comforted with arguments that were self-evidently sound. She got up when Alexander came into the room, took up a position in front of the window, and waved Alexander to the settee. 'Your attention, please,' she announced, and looked to Courtney.

The boy approached her, raising a graceful hand, and while walking he began to speak:

> *'Good sister, let us dine, and never fret;*
> *A man is master of his liberty;*
> *Time is their master, and when they see time,*
> *They'll go or come; if so, be patient, sister.'*

Sweetly condescending, he touched a finger to the back of her hand.

Furrowing her brow, Megan responded: '*Why should their liberty than ours be more?*'

'*Because their business still lies out o'door,*' explained Courtney.

'*Look, when I serve him so, he takes it ill,*' Megan complained, assuming a petulant expression that melted only when Courtney, with a demeanour of great wisdom and patience, pressed Megan's hand and told her:

> *'Why, headstrong liberty is lash'd with woe.*
> *There's nothing situate under heaven's eye*
> *But hath his bound in earth, in sea, in sky.'*

And so Courtney expounded the natural law of the beasts, the fishes, the winged fowls and man, rolling his hands in a way that, as Megan later explained, was a parody of the headmaster's most conspicuous mannerism. Alexander would remember Courtney's hands with particular clarity, and the courteous bow with which he took the glass of lemonade from Alexander, as Megan applauded, and he would

317

remember Courtney's ease on the stage of the school hall, from which the portly, fair-haired Fielding twins kept scanning the half-filled rows to locate their parents or Claire, whereas Courtney occupied it as if it were his room at home and spoke his lines as though they were occurring to him while he strolled across it, and at the end of the scene, stepped back to allow the jealous Adriana to precede him and took her arm supportively, with a grace and genuineness that Alexander found moving, though Courtney was swathed and hooded in a length of turquoise curtain material and Adriana was some three or four years older than him, and perhaps eight inches taller.

In the foyer they encountered Mr Wilson and his wife. Their son had been the star of the show, Megan told them. Scraping a hand across his silvery stubble, Mr Wilson replied that it was bad enough that the boy had been made to dress up like a girl, but if they'd known he wasn't going to be in action for more than five minutes they wouldn't have bothered coming. He stooped to look through the doors of the hall. At the foot of the stage, still in their togas, the Fielding twins were receiving the praise of their family. But Courtney was so good, Megan persisted, smiling at Mrs Wilson, who looked at her husband, as if to deflect a compromising question. 'Didn't understand half of it,' said Mr Wilson. 'Did we?' he demanded to his wife, and his wife glanced self-deprecatingly at Alexander, then allowed her gaze to drift to a place between himself and Megan. 'Whose idea was it, doing a thing like that?' asked Mr Wilson, peering through the doors again. The children had enjoyed it, Megan suggested. 'Those as were in it, I suppose,' Mr Wilson conceded. 'Didn't see many of them in there, did you?' With a shrug Mrs Wilson conveyed to Alexander her sympathy with his disappointment at the poor attendance. Alexander and Megan left, having asked Courtney's parents to pass on their congratulations to him.

The hostility of Mr Wilson was not unexpected. As a boy Lloyd Wilson had built boats with his uncle, but on his uncle's death in 1958 he came to England, where he worked as a joiner on building sites, mostly in the Midlands and the north-west. Within two years he had married the daughter of the boss of a roofing firm in Coventry and established his own joinery and carpentry business, which by the time of Courtney's birth was employing Mr Wilson's brother, a cousin, and the cousin's brother-in-law. Determined that his son should join the family firm as soon as he was old enough, Mr Wilson could be relied upon to set himself against anything that might divert Courtney from his destiny, a destiny that Megan, whose affection for the boy was in part due to his manifest respect for his parents and most of his teachers, tended to regard gloomily, often envisaging his future as a life on rails. 'I can see it,' Alexander would remember her saying, after she had spoken to Mr Wilson about Courtney's progress, and he would picture her slamming her forearms onto the table, locked in parallel. Over the years there were disagreements between Mr Wilson and Megan and several other teachers at every parent-teacher meeting, until a week in the summer of 1980, from which Alexander would remember two evenings.

On the evening of the meeting he went to his parents' house as soon as he had shut the shop, bringing the video recorder that he had bought on his father's behalf. Before they ate he connected and tuned it, and set it to record *A Night at the Opera*, which, while Alexander was unpacking the machine, his father had noticed was being broadcast at the time they would be eating. They left the doors of the front room and dining room ajar, Alexander would remember, and his father raised a finger expectantly as seven o'clock approached, and offered a handshake when they heard the whirr of the cassette in the other room. Some people thought that Betamax was better than VHS, his father admitted, and perhaps they were right. But he didn't think quality was what would decide the issue. It was the length of the recording, that was what would settle it. And there would have to be a winner, he said. Had Alexander seen the piece in *The Times*? he asked, though Alexander never read *The Times*. Someone had written a long letter to the paper, arguing that the music industry had managed to sustain two different record speeds, so it followed that two different video formats could survive. Which was missing the point somewhat, wasn't it? It seemed to be, Alexander replied, and the conversation continued between Alexander and his father, with his mother saying little, except, as Alexander would remember, to complain that watching films on TV was not the same thing at all, a proposition with which his father could only agree, patting her hand in commiseration.

Alexander helped his mother clear up, while his father, instruction manual in hand, stopped the tape and tried to set the machine to record a programme the following day. 'Shall we see how the film's come out?' his father called. 'Or shall we wait for Megan?' There was no telling when Megan would be finished, Alexander replied; it could be another hour yet, if some of the parents misbehaved. 'Let's give it a look, then,' said his father. 'All right with you, Irene?'

His mother said nothing as she loaded the dishwasher and wiped the draining board. She gave the taps a twist to make sure they would not drip. Finding a jug that was not where it should have been, she carried it to the cupboard, and opening the door she said to herself, in a sigh that Alexander was meant to overhear: 'I don't understand it.'

Suppressing his annoyance, Alexander asked: 'Don't understand what, Mother?'

'It doesn't matter.'

'Yes, it does. You couldn't keep it in, therefore it matters.' He took the jug from her and placed it precisely in its gap on the upper shelf. 'Out with it.'

'All that time for those children,' she reluctantly told him. 'But none of her own. I don't understand it.'

'Yes, you do, Mother. It's not a mighty conundrum. We've had this before.'

'I know, Alexander,' she said sadly, moving towards the light switch.

'Not again, please. We've done marriage, mortgages and kids, God knows how often.'

'Megan's not the maternal type, I suppose.'

'Nothing to do with being a type. It's a choice, and not an easy one. I've told you before.'

'The career is more important, I know. Girls today put themselves first. I know that, but still –'

'It's a choice we both made.'

'Was it?'

'Yes, it was.'

'Like not getting married?'

'Exactly. Neither of us is sure it'd be a good idea, so we decided no.'

'Why? Because she's so up and down?' said his mother, using the very words Megan herself had once used.

'No, Mother. A lot of reasons. Our age –'

'Nonsense.'

'Mother, we've had this conversation,' said Alexander, stepping out of the room.

From the living room his father called: 'All systems go.'

'Perhaps she'll change her mind,' said his mother.

'Perhaps we will, Mother. If we do, you'll be the first to know. But we're not getting any younger, so don't set your heart on it.'

'A pity, Alexander,' she mourned, turning off the light, and she nudged him to go ahead of her. 'There should be more MacIndoes.'

After half an hour of the film Megan arrived; she kissed Alexander's mother and simply made a balancing gesture when Alexander asked how the meeting had gone. 'Only just begun,' said his father, sitting beside Megan on the settee. 'Can't have Megan missing the opening. Nobody minds if we go back to the beginning, do they?' he asked, having already started the rewind. He laughed at each scene as if he had never seen it before, and Megan found hilarious everything that he found hilarious. Together they rocked backwards and forwards in their seats, while Alexander's mother watched the antics of the Marx brothers with little more amusement than Margaret Dumont. There was a moment when his father laughed so much that he had to take off his glasses and hand them to Megan so he could dab his eyes. 'I'm so sorry,' he said to Alexander, who had stopped the tape so that he could recover. He laughed again, and his laughter tripped Megan's laughter. 'How childish of me,' he apologised to his wife, who shook her head, resigned to her incomprehension. 'Let us resume,' he said, controlling himself, and he put out a hand, palm upwards, over Megan's lap, and Megan, straight-faced, slapped his glasses into it, like a nurse giving an instrument to a surgeon.

And that Friday, when Alexander returned home, Megan came out of her room when she heard the door and led him into the kitchen, where tubs of food from the Italian delicatessen were piled on top of a box containing a VHS recorder. 'We're always moaning that there's nothing decent on at the cinema,' she explained. 'And I felt like splashing out on something.' From the fridge she took a bottle of prosecco.

'He's staying. Courtney. He's staying on. His mother has prevailed, God knows how.' She took the bottle and the food out into the garden, where they put the bottle in the little pool that Alexander had created, and spread the dishes on the circle of short grass in the middle of his enclave of wild flowers. They drank to the career of Courtney Wilson, who would leave the school before the end of the year to work for his father, then resume his studies at a sixth-form college, and eventually become a draughtsman for a firm of civil engineers in a town ten miles or so from the city in which his father had met his mother.

It was a pleasant evening, and they stayed in the garden until they could feel the dampness in the grass. Megan brought a book out, but put it aside after only a few minutes; Alexander uprooted some weeds here and there, then sat down next to her. He plucked a poppy bud, he would remember, and put a thumbnail into the red crack in its side, to break it open. As Megan watched, he unfolded the flower meticulously, then held it up to the sunlight, above her face. She took it from him and turned it against the light. When she lay down, Alexander dropped a poppy over each eye. Poppies were the most beautiful flowers, she said. The petals were like a skin of supple scarlet glass. 'Looking at the world through poppy-tinted glasses,' he would remember her saying, as she lay with her hand touching the water and the poppies on her eyes, and then she whispered, still smiling: 'She's a dragon sometimes, isn't she, your mother?' He held her hand as he gazed through the flowers, and soon afterwards they went inside, and listened to a record, and went to bed early.

38. The Greta

'It's your friend. He's gone mad,' said Megan, dangling the phone over the back of the chair, and Alexander heard a tiny voice singing in the earpiece as it turned. 'I've no idea,' she replied to his look as he took the phone.

Alexander listened for a moment, as 'Diamonds are a Girl's Best Friend' became, mid-phrase, a strenuous and tuneless hum. 'Desist,' he instructed.

'And a very good evening to you, Mr MacIndoe,' said Sam, in a compère's croon. 'How are you this evening?'

'I am well, thank you,' Alexander bantered. 'And how are you?'

'I am exceedingly well.'

'It gives me great pleasure to hear that.'

'Did you, by any chance, happen to catch the end of *Grandstand*?'

'Now why would I be watching *Grandstand*?'

'You never know.'

'No, I did not catch the end of *Grandstand*.'

'So you would be unaware that the entire civilised world is, as we speak, engulfed in controversy? That a travesty of justice occurred in the last minute of one of the season's crucial games? That the result of said game was decided by a goal scored by a player standing in excess of the regulation mile offside, as was clear to everyone in the ground except the ref and his linesman?'

'Passed me by, I'm afraid.'

'Well, I recommend you watch it on the box tonight, and while you're watching it you can think of me and the wife, because that goal made it a one-all draw, and that one-all draw means that my boat's come in, after twenty-odd years. What it means is that those columns of little crosses you and me filled in, after a lot of pints, as I recall, in the Crown and Anchor – those columns of pretty little crosses, that I've stuck to through thick and thin, have brought me a nice little packet. I've struck lucky at last.'

'Congratulations.'

'Not the jackpot, I shouldn't think. We're not looking at a Rolls, or anything like that. We won't be retiring to the Costa del Sol. But a nice little packet, all the same. A proper holiday, a few things for the house.'

Alexander heard Liz in the background, muttering, before she called out: 'Ask him how much he's spent over the years.'

'I'm ahead of the game, Mac.'

'About two quid ahead,' Liz heckled.

'Well ahead,' Sam stressed. 'So what are you two doing next weekend? I thought we'd have a little party over here, on Saturday. We'll pack the kids off to the grandparents, get in a crate of fizz. You on?'

'All right for a drink with himself and Liz, a week from today?' Alexander asked Megan. 'Champagne on the house. A windfall.'

Megan sat on the floor, reading the cinema listings. 'Sure,' she replied, turning the page.

When Alexander and Megan arrived at the house Sam and Liz were standing on the drive, beside a black BMW. Walking down one side of the car, Richard Ellis was peering through the windows the way a child might look into a tank in a reptile house, uncertain whether anything lived there. A younger man, whom Alexander had never seen before, braced his hands on the nearside wing and stooped under the raised bonnet. Watching the two men, with her arms crossed, Maureen was talking to a tiny young woman whose stature and tense demeanour and tousled dark hair reminded Alexander instantly of Edith Piaf.

'What do you think, Mac?' Sam called out, wiping a fingertip along the edge of the roof, as if testing the sharpness of a blade. 'One previous owner. Under twenty thousand on the clock. Full service history. Could eat your dinner off the engine.' He patted the shoulder of the younger man. 'My protégé, Matthew Stimpson,' said Sam, 'and Anne, his charming wife.' Anne glanced at them, fingering the zip of her black denim jacket, and gave a nervous nod. Before shaking hands, Matthew threw his cigarette into the road, with the deliberate action of a man aiming a dart; his new white shirt still had a square of creases on the chest. Richard, now in the driver's seat, wound down the window to say hello. 'Shall we crack open the bubbly?' suggested Sam after they had chatted for a couple of minutes. Holding the front door open, Matthew brushed a piece of ash from his new blue jeans. Richard aimed a playful blow at his midriff as he passed; Matthew flinched, and gave Megan a wearied look.

There was a stack of holiday brochures on the table at the foot of the stairs, and in the living room the standard lamp had been moved from its place by the window, which now was taken by a tall black loudspeaker, perched on a pedestal of black steel. The other speaker had displaced the small table on which had stood the florid majolica vase that Alexander had bought for Liz from Sid Dixon's shop after she had said that she liked it. A record was spinning under the smoked plastic lid, which was raised an inch or two, revealing the gleaming bevel of the turntable.

Sam brought two bottles of champagne from the kitchen. 'Here's to the most outrageous decision of the season,' he said, lifting his glass.

'To the blind man with the flag,' Richard responded. 'And to Mr Saunders, our generous host.'

'To Mr Saunders,' they all repeated.

'You've got to hear this,' Sam told them, going over to the stereo.

'Sam,' said Liz.

'A second, I promise. It's special,' said Sam, lowering the arm onto the record. From the speakers came a splintering noise, like a piece of heavy furniture being dragged on ice, and then an explosion like a bursting balloon. 'Listen,' Sam urged them, as fingers squealed on the strings of an acoustic guitar. Between two notes they heard the sound of a ring-pull coming off a can. 'Hear that? Isn't that what hi-fi's all about? The drummer having a beer. Listen carefully and you'll hear him light a fag in a minute.'

'We can have that treat later, love,' said Liz. 'Come and sit down.'

While Sam searched his record collection, Anne and Maureen were looking at the pictures on the mantelpiece. 'Your children?' asked Anne, touching the portrait of Robert and Clare. 'And is that you?' she asked Alexander, holding the photograph of Sam and Liz and their guests on the steps of Woolwich Town Hall.

'The Swinging Sixties,' Sam scoffed. 'Never guess it, would you? Looks like we've all been freshly stuffed half an hour before. Check out the mother of the bride. Got a small dead animal stuck down her front, by the look on her face.'

'Amazing,' said Anne, giving the photograph a sentimental smile.

'We've known each other a long time,' Liz explained. 'Megan and me were at school together. I went out with Alexander for a while, before I married Sam. And Sam was in the army with Alexander before I was going out with Alexander.'

'But Megan was there first,' Sam added. 'She's known himself since she was so high,' he said, smacking the top of the television. 'Isn't that right?'

'Since I was five,' Alexander confirmed.

'That's amazing,' said Anne, with a quick, timorous smile for Megan.

'A good story,' Matthew agreed, but he regarded Megan, when she looked away, as if there were something about her appearance that he could not reconcile with what Liz had told them.

'But it took a long while,' Liz continued. 'For them to get together, I mean.'

'Years and years and years,' Sam groaned. 'Thank Christ, we said, when we found out, didn't we? We couldn't have stood the suspense any longer.'

'Thank you, Sam,' Megan interrupted.

'Thought they were never going to get round to it.'

'Thank you.'

Sam held up a Simon and Garfunkel album for their approval. 'OK if it's quiet,' said Richard, making a queasy face.

'Very quiet. So we can't hear it,' said Alexander, and Sam defeatedly put the record back into its place on the shelf and sat on the floor beside the television.

'So,' Matthew resumed, turning again to Megan, 'do you live near here as well?' Sam cackled at the question, and hid behind his glass. 'What did I say?' asked Matthew.

'They live in Blackheath,' said Liz, in the tone of someone defending a friend out of loyalty rather than from conviction.

'Blackheath's nice,' Anne commented.

'Visit us once a year. With a string of garlic and a crucifix,' Sam told Matthew plainly. 'They think Croydon's the city of the unburied dead.'

'Well, I think it's nice,' declared Maureen, nodding at Anne as if to secure her support. 'Very convenient for the city, but not in the thick of it. And good shops too.'

'And a tip-top cemetery,' said Sam.

'We live on the edge of Blackheath,' Megan told Matthew. 'We're from there. Alexander works there. We like it.'

'And hate Croydon.'

'No, Sam. But prefer where we are. You prefer here, we prefer there.'

'It's where you belong,' said Anne, making Megan's meaning explicit for everyone.

'It's where we want to be,' said Megan.

'How nice,' said Matthew. 'We live in Forest Hill.'

'A friend found us a flat there. We thought it sounded attractive,' Anne explained.

'Sort of foresty,' Matthew laughed. 'Trees. Open spaces. That kind of thing.'

'We'll move out one day, before too long,' Anne insisted, taking Matthew's hand as if making him join in her promise.

'We came down from Durham,' Matthew told Megan.

'And given half a chance he'd go back,' said Sam, aghast at the perversity of the notion.

'To live by the Greta is all I desire,' Matthew declaimed, as if ironically quoting a poet.

'The Greta? What Greta? Greta Garbo?' asked Richard.

'It's a river,' said Megan.

'My family's from Bishop Auckland,' Matthew told her.

'Lot of history there,' Richard commented.

'There is.'

'Once a fine team. Very snazzy strip as well.'

'Dark blue and light blue halves?' Sam proposed.

'I do believe you're right,' said Richard, impressed by Sam's knowledge.

'Before my time,' Matthew regretted.

'I went to Bishop Auckland once,' Megan said to Anne. 'The castle,' she recalled, 'and the chapel, and the park with the deer house.'

'Lovely,' Anne concurred.

'How come you were there?' asked Richard.

'I lived in Leeds, and one day I saw a picture in the gallery. Of Brignall Banks, by John Sell Cotman? You know him?'

'Never heard of the lad,' said Richard.

'Afraid not,' said Matthew.

'A gorgeous picture. A wonderful atmosphere to it. I couldn't take my eyes off it, and it made me want to go there, so I did. It rained every day I was there, three or four hours at a stretch, every day for half a week of walking. But it was wonderful. So beautiful.'

'I swam in the Greta, when I was a kid,' said Matthew, stroking his handsome narrow nose as he looked at Megan. 'And in the really hot summer, seventy-six, I went skinny-dipping with a girlfriend.'

'I never knew that,' Anne protested.

'Best thing there is,' said Sam, giving Liz a salacious smirk.

'Did you go to Hell Cauldron?' asked Matthew, moving his glass a couple of inches aside on the coffee table, as if he were moving a chess piece, and for ten minutes or more he and Megan talked about the Scotchman's Stone and the Greta Bridge and Hell Cauldron. As they talked a sadness bled into Alexander's mind, not because Megan was reciprocating Matthew's flirtation, nor because it was a visit with Mitchell that she was recalling with such pleasure, but because, as he watched her talking and gesticulating to invoke the landscape of the Greta, it struck Alexander, more forcefully than before, and memorably, that episodes such as this, in which Megan was seized by an enthusiasm that was almost as intense as those of her childhood, were now infrequent and remarkable. And he would remember that the conversation turned to the subject of what else Sam would be doing with the money he had won, and Sam said that he had thought of taking Liz to Paris, at which Anne said that she had always wanted to go there but Matthew didn't think that a holiday in a city was a holiday at all, and Megan edged forward in her seat and confided: 'Make him go, Anne. You'll have a fantastic time. We had a great week, didn't we, Eck? I tell you, a walk around Notre Dame at night. The shadows on the old stone, and the perfume the stone gives off, after a hot day. It's magical. And all the lights on the water.' Alexander joined her in describing the things they had seen together, and she smiled at him as he spoke, but when they had finished with Paris, and Maureen and Liz were taking it in turns to recommend the Algarve, Alexander glanced at Megan as she reached for her glass, and he knew by the way she looked at her own hand as it closed slowly on the stem that for her that week in Paris belonged to a receding past, whereas for him the memory of it was a quality of the present, of himself and of Megan as she was. She sipped her champagne quickly and lightly, as if she were trying not to be observed, and he became suddenly aware of the emptiness that was in the room, of how little space was occupied by their bodies and by the things the room contained. Having taken out another album, Sam insisted that they had to hear Alexander doing Lou Reed's voice. Megan looked at Alexander pleadingly and shook her head, he would remember, and then the doorbell rang as more of Sam's colleagues arrived.

When Alexander and Megan left, Sam came with them to the door. 'Come and have a spin some time,' he said on the doorstep, pointing a half-full glass in the direction of his car. He looked up at the sky and scowled at the encroaching clouds. 'Better get it in the garage,' he decided, scraping the keys from a pocket.

'You're pissed, Sam,' said Megan from the end of the drive. 'Leave it.'

'Good advice. The voice of reason. I'll leave it. What do you think? It's only ten feet. Can't make a bollocks of that.'

'Yes you can. Leave it,' said Alexander.

'I'll leave it.'

'Bye, Sam,' Megan sang.

Sam winked at Alexander; inside the house a saxophone blared, and Liz shrieked. 'Be gone,' Sam ordered, losing some of his drink as he raised his hand.

The air was cooling quickly as they walked back to the station, and when the rain began to fall they went into a shop to buy some food for that evening. When they came out the water was spilling from the drainpipes in gouts, as if pumped, and some car headlights were on. Holding the bag above their heads, they ran across the road, jumping the gutters. Their train emerged through a veil of water that was the colour of gelatine, with ribbons of rain flying from its roof.

329

Sitting opposite each other, neither Megan nor Alexander spoke. They wiped the condensation from the window to look out. The houses on the far side of the car park were all grey; a car edged towards the barrier, enveloped in a haze of shattered rain. A young man drowsed in the corner of the carriage, his head back and his mouth open; from his girlfriend's headphones leaked a synthesizer's thin monotone.

The train pulled away, but before it reached the next station it slowed to a halt at a signal, and while the train was stationary the rain stopped as abruptly as it had begun. Angled under the clouds, a cold sunlight, like a halogen beam, made everything in Alexander's vision appear distinct and urgent, and stamped it all into his memory. Curds of translucent beige grease were lit up around a junction, with particles of sand embedded in them. A long crust of dirt under the lip of the live rail reminded him of the soot that used to fatten on the chimney-breast in his parents' house. Ragwort was sprouting in a cone of ballast by a corrugated iron shed, and in a nearby garden the wet outer leaves of a young maple glowed like a mesh of small electric lights. He looked at the oil-spattered stones and steel plates between the sleepers, at the slick black cables that turned under a rail like the sinews of a wrist, at the fox-coloured stains on the lengths of concrete conduit discarded beside the track. He looked at Megan. Her face was freckled with the shadows of the raindrops, and her eyes were directed towards the houses as if she were seeing a place in which she had once lived. He leaned forward to touch her hand. 'What is it?' he asked her.

'The wine's made me a bit glum,' she said. 'I shouldn't drink without eating.'

'Just the wine?'

'Oh yes. I think so,' she said. 'But I'm never going to see the world the way Liz sees it. She thinks I'm a snob.'

'But you are,' he said, and she smiled. He noticed, in another garden, a boy prancing as if under a swarm of wasps, slashing the air with a thin long stick. 'Strange lad,' Alexander remarked. Megan nodded, but did not speak. A train sped past, going away from the city, and she watched the faces recede. Their train heaved into motion. The clouds were becoming violet and opaque, and the gaps between them made Alexander think of gaps in hedgerows, with the sea beyond.

Megan went into the living room and turned on the television. A few minutes later she turned it off. Alexander passed her a few pages of the newspaper he was reading. She read them quickly, then went upstairs to mark some homework.

39. La Plaza de Toros de la Real Maestranza de Caballeria de Ronda

The river could not be looked at, and the walls and roofs of the buildings across the river were all scorched white. The shadow of the tower was like a trench cut into the stone of the pavement. A dog with hempen fur stood in the road, one paw raised, as if stunned in mid-stride.

'This is purgatory,' said Megan. 'I don't know how people function in it.'

'That's Triana,' Alexander told her, gesturing with the guidebook. 'Used to be the gypsy quarter, it says. Nothing much to see there now, according to this.'

'God be praised. I'd fry before we got over the bridge.' She removed her sunglasses as they stepped into the shadow. 'Stop for a second, Eck. Show me how much farther.' She touched her forearm against his. 'Look at you, mahogany man. And look at me: half woman, half radish.'

A drop of sweat fattened on a peak of darkened hair at her temple, and fell onto the paper. 'We could go back to the room,' Alexander suggested. 'Or there's the cathedral. That'll be cool.'

'And full of people like us. We wouldn't want that.' She replaced her sunglasses decisively. 'The park it must be,' she said, shoving him into the light. 'Onward.'

He bought a bottle of water from a cabin at the Plaza de España, where Megan stood beside the miniature canal, grimacing into the sun as if testing her resolve against it. They found a lawn of stiff broad-leaved grass and there they sat, under the leaves of a dusty myrtle. Megan rested her head on his lap, and he dripped water onto her lips. 'That's nice,' she murmured, but she did not open her eyes. 'So what's left to see?' she asked, tapping the guidebook.

Alexander skimmed the pages. 'The art gallery.'

'Featuring?'

'Carthusian monks by Zurbarán. An El Greco.'

'OK. Anything else?'

'Modern art gallery.'

'With?'

'Doesn't say. And Don Juan's hospital. Founded by the real Don Juan, apparently. Don Miguel de Manara. A lot of pictures by Murillo. And a painting of a rotting bishop.'

'A whatting?'

'A worm-riddled bishop in his coffin.'

'Great. And when you say hospital –?'

'A real hospital. Still in service, it would appear.'

'Give it a miss, shall we?' she said.

'We haven't seen the famous weeping Madonna either,' Alexander continued.

'Enough already,' said Megan.

She curled an arm for a pillow, and within a few minutes she had fallen asleep. For almost an hour she slept, while the fiacres trundled up and down the incandescent avenue beyond the trees, and car horns bickered in the city's streets. A young couple spread a blanket underneath another myrtle and placed a radio on it; lying down beside her lover, the woman reached languorously for the switch; an impassioned male howl came out of the speaker. A policeman rode his horse at a walk along the narrow path behind the couple and back again; the saddle flashed like brass through the foliage.

'That been going on for long?' asked Megan when she awoke, nodding in the direction of the couple.

'A while.'

'Should have given me a kick. We could have moved.'

'You get used to it. Like the sun.'

'The sun I'm never getting used to. Not if it stays like this. I mean, are you enjoying yourself?'

'Of course.'

'You're so adaptable,' she said, and she kissed him on the neck.

'You're really not enjoying it?'

'It's too much for a paleskin. Like having a headache all day.'

'We needn't stay, you know.'

'You have a plan?' she asked. 'Been plotting while I dozed?'

'There are two options, as I see it. Number one: we dash to the coast and get in the sea. Number two: we flee to the hills.'

'Let's go for a drink,' she said, and by the time they reached the bar they had agreed to leave the following morning.

At the counter a man with dyed black eyebrows and hair and an azure satin shirt was drumming his heels on the tiles to amuse two students, who squatted on their backpacks beside the door to the toilets rather than take a stool at one of the casks that served as tables. The man ceased his footwork when Alexander stood beside him. He regarded Alexander askance, and then said something that Alexander could not understand. 'English?' the man enquired.

'Si,' said Alexander.

'English,' the man approved. 'I like English. I like English very much. Bobby Charlton. Winston Churchill. Florence Nightingale.' He gestured to the barman, who put two cold glasses of fino on the counter. 'Enjoy,' said the man, and he smiled at Alexander and at the students and at Megan and at the students again.

'Mistaken for a native?' asked Megan.

'Not for one second,' Alexander replied, raising his glass to the man in the azure shirt, who raised his to Alexander, and to Megan, and every other person in the room. 'I think he assumed I might speak a few words of his language, as I'm in his country. Shameful that I don't, really.'

'Well, we can go and be ashamed somewhere else tomorrow,' said Megan, and she pinned the guidebook open on the cask. 'I've narrowed it down to two: Ronda or Cádiz.'

No sooner had Megan reached the end of the account of Cádiz than the students came over to ask if they could look at the book for a moment. Their names were Linda and Amy and they were from Wisconsin. It was past ten o'clock when they left.

'Do you think they found our book instructive?' Megan asked Alexander.

'I hope so.'

'Saucy little minx, that Linda,' she said. 'How many times were you given an eyeful of that cleavage?'

'Eighteen.'

'Dirty flirt,' Megan reproved. The man in the azure shirt bowed to her. 'Your friend's a bit miffed. You'd better buy him a drink,' she said.

'Could you go?'

'He's your friend.'

'Go on. For the price of a drink he'll be yours too.'

'A singular drink? We're going to be here all night, my dear,' she said, and she went up to the bar, where the man in the azure shirt made her laugh by taking their empty glasses from her and making them dance a flamenco on the bar top. This, as Alexander was to recall many years later, was the last occasion on which he heard Megan laugh wholeheartedly.

The fifth hotel they called in Ronda had a vacant room. 'Corrida,' the receptionist explained, and then he took them up a concrete staircase to a room at the back of the building, looking onto a light well from which a smell of hot cooking oil infiltrated the room through the cream plastic shutters. On the plywood bookcase beside the bed stood a lamp in the form of a melting candle and an ashtray that bore the name of a different hotel. The frame of the low steel bed screeched when Alexander lay on it. 'You OK with this?' he called, over the sound of running water.

'It's fine, Eck,' she replied. 'Cold water is all we need. And I'm the one that brought us here. I can't complain. You OK with it?'

'A case of this or nothing, I think,' he said.

'You're right,' she said, too brightly. 'But the room's bearable any-way, isn't it?'

'It's fine,' said Alexander, and he closed his eyes to exclude the room, which seemed the image of his mood, not its cause.

It was in the restaurant that Megan first put forward the idea that they might go to the bullfight. The waiter took them to a table beside a dresser that had a half-consumed leg of ham on it, and as he pushed Megan's chair closer he looked at Alexander and said to him: 'Orson Welles sit here. Where you are. Orson Welles.' He pointed above Alexander's head, where, in the midst of a mosaic of small framed photos, Orson Welles sat in the front row of a bullring, his mouth puckered and eyes tight with concentration, beside a handsome, pensive, black-eyed man whose braceleted wrist rested loosely on the barrier.

'And that?' asked Megan.

'Antonio Ordóñez.' The waiter came round the table and rapped a finger on the glass of several pictures in quick succession. 'Ordóñez, Ordóñez, Ordóñez,' he repeated. 'Of Ronda,' he added, as though to authenticate the man, and then smoothly withdrew.

'We're eating in an abattoir,' Alexander remarked.

'Offputting,' agreed Megan, but throughout the meal her gaze would slide onto the wall and linger there, as though on a long inscription that was indistinctly legible. 'Look at that one,' she would say, and Alexander would turn to look at Antonio Ordóñez sweeping the ground with his cape to usher a bull into the earth, or fluttering the cape behind him like the skirt of a dancing aristocrat, or glaring at a defeated animal in proof of the potency of his will. 'There's something about that one,' she said, pointing to a picture in which Ordóñez, accompanied by an older and bald-headed man, stood in his full regalia on the edge of the ring, staring at the camera as if at an unwelcome intruder to whom he was affecting indifference. 'Looks like he's up before a firing squad in five minutes,' she commented.

'Too glamorous,' Alexander replied. 'More like a film star than a prisoner.'

'And they're so feminine, in a way. Look at all those curves,' said Megan, and Alexander followed her finger to the picture of a plump-buttocked matador, arcing his arms in the shape of an urn. 'Would you want to go?' she asked.

'Not especially.' To his left a smiling fighter, carried shoulder-high by a jubilant gang, clutched an amputated hoof and a pair of severed ears. 'Would you?'

'I don't know.' She twisted in her seat to inspect a picture to the side of the dresser. An elegant rider, with immaculate white collar and cuffs, and hair sprucely parted and oiled, leaned out of his saddle to place a sword between the shoulders of a charging bull, as fastidiously as a butler setting a bottle of fine wine in the centre of a table. A blanched strip of typescript, like the label on a reliquary in a church museum, identified the rider as Angel Peralta. 'I feel I should go,' said Megan.

'Why?'

'To understand.'

336

'But you won't understand. We can't understand. We're tourists.'

'Then to misunderstand less badly,' she retorted.

Alexander regarded the gaunt Manolete, whose sorrowful eyes seemed to ask forgiveness of the beast that had collapsed in front of him. 'It's so bloody morbid,' he complained.

'I know,' she replied, and then the waiter returned and placed the coffees on the table. 'Qué es?' Megan asked him, standing up to indicate a bull's head on a wooden shield.

Like a gallery owner with a prospective purchaser, the waiter stood alongside Megan and insinuatingly adopted a stance that was a copy of hers. 'Bailador,' he explained. 'He killed Joselito. Joselito was great. Very great. The very greatest,' he said, and he directed her to the reposeful face of the martyred Joselito and to the bronze pallbearers of his tomb.

'In Seville?' Megan enquired.

'Sevilla. Yes.'

'We should have seen this, Eck,' she said, and she brought her face closer to the dead Joselito's.

Megan bought a couple of visors from a boy outside the ring and fastened one around Alexander's brow. He held her hand and together they beat time as the band played a raucous paso doble, and the trio of matadors crossed the sand in their pink and sky-blue costumes, attended by their harlequin teams. The picadors made you think of Don Quixote, said Megan. Below them the matadors took their capes from the barrier and began to rehearse their passes. The capes fluttered like gigantic yellow and magenta wings. Megan lifted Alexander's hand to her cheek and kissed it and smiled at him, but there was something like panic in her eyes.

The first bull was grey, and its hide caught the sun like zinc. The ground boomed under its hooves when it charged the banderillero's cape; its horn gouged the wall, and Alexander heard the rending of the wood and the furious sound of the bull's breathing. Distracted by a second banderillero, it crossed the ring at a trot then swerved to run at a third, who scampered behind a barrier. Back and forth the bull was passed, until the matador, having studied its course to his satisfaction, looked up as if consulting the sky and came out of the crescent of shade to take his stand. Swinging his cape behind him, he turned contemptuously from the horns. The crowd applauded and Megan leaned forward, as if straining to follow an engrossing debate. Alexander opened the guidebook. 'Says here that the pope once excommunicated all bullfighters,' he told her.

'Reasonable move,' she said.

He tried to read rather than watch, but a change in the noise soon made him look up. People around him were whistling, and it appeared that their derision was intended for the picadors, who were now manoeuvring their horses in the outer circle of the ring. 'Are you understanding this?' Alexander asked. 'What've they done?'

At that moment Megan clapped a hand to her mouth. The bull was pushing at one of the horses, buffeting the quilted blanket that hung from its flank. The picador stood in the stirrups and turned the head of his blindfolded horse to the barrier, then thrust his spear into the crest of the bull's neck. Leaning on the spear, he stirred its point in the wound it had made. Rearing, the bull scraped the horse against the wooden wall; it shuddered and sprang upwards, dislodging the picador from his saddle. The horse fell twistedly, its forelegs remaining straight as its hind legs buckled, and then it was on its back. Its hoofs clattered the planks of the barrier as the bull dug its horns through the blanket, which now was stained maroon. The banderilleros flurried about, flapping their capes at the bull's head.

'This is horrible,' said Alexander.

'It is,' replied Megan.

'Shall we leave?'

'Not yet.'

'But this is truly, profoundly, inexcusably nasty,' he said.

'It is. It's meant to be,' said Megan firmly.

Fascination and pain were in her face as she watched the bull canter below them. The skin of its flank shone like a throw of threadbare crimson satin. Jigging as if on a springboard, a banderillero incited an attack and sprinted on tiptoe to the side of the onrushing bull. Stiff-backed, bridling like a man who has been insulted, he planted a dart in a manner that elicited applause and a waving of handkerchiefs. 'Megan, this is horrible and ridiculous,' Alexander commented, and she nodded as though his remark were irrelevant.

In unison with the crowd, Megan applauded when the matador

turned a circle in the centre of the ring and saluted them with an upraised arm. When he spun the animal around his body, so closely that a smear of its blood was left across his chest, she edged forward on her seat. When he snatched the muleta straight up, and the bull leapt under it, grazing his sleeve with the tip of its horn, she made a sound that was in part a cheer and in part a gasp.

When Alexander next looked up the bull was banging its brow against the matador's legs. The matador skipped back, transferred the muleta to his right hand, and shook it goadingly. The bull walked up to the cloth and scooped its horns at it exhaustedly; it walked away, coming to a halt facing away from the man. The matador strutted into its line of sight and knelt, flinging his arms back in defiance. 'I'm not sure I can stand any more of this,' said Alexander.

'It's nearly over,' Megan replied.

'No, it's not. Five more victims to come.'

A sword was passed to the matador. He pointed it at the bull as though in accusation. The bull touched its bloodied muzzle to the sand; the matador rushed forward and impaled its neck. Escorted by the matador, the bull plodded around the perimeter of the ring, its head lolling, its tongue protruding and drooling blood. The matador swung the muleta, guiding the bull along the path to its death. The bull's head rocked; its front legs gave way; the matador turned his back, his chin jutting like a boy who thinks he has crushingly won an argument.

Alexander looked at Megan, but she would not look away from the dying animal. 'Well?' he demanded.

'Yes, I know,' she said. 'It's appalling.'

'It's that all right.'

'But it has to be.'

'It doesn't have to be at all, Meg.'

'It's a sacrifice,' she stated.

'A sacrifice? It's the end of the twentieth century, for God's sake. We're not Aztecs.'

'A tragedy, then.'

'I don't think the bull's acting, Meg.'

'That's the point. It's really happening. It's real death.'

'Butchery is what it is. Butchery in fancy dress.'

Then at last she looked at him and she said: 'You don't have to stay, Eck. I agree, it's horrible. It's repulsive and barbaric and horrible. I'm not enjoying it. But I'm going to see it through, right to the end. I'm staying. But you don't have to.' A plough-like harness for the carcass was being dragged into the ring. The crowd applauded something, and Megan joined in.

The streets were as empty as at siesta time. Alexander went to the bridge and looked down at the old mill for a while. He took the path along the lip of the gorge to the little park with the bandstand. On the terrace of the park a drunk man in a dirty white singlet and brown corduroy trousers was stamping his feet and serenading an imaginary companion. A bugle in the bullring fizzed like a kazoo, and the drunk man flourished an imaginary cap. Alexander returned to the hotel, where a chambermaid was rinsing the steps with a liquid that reeked of ammonia. He did not go in, but continued across the square and down an alley of restaurants and into streets he did not know. Near the bus station he was overtaken by a white Mercedes taxi, with a woman passenger whose hair was the colour of Megan's and caused his chest to tighten instantly.

He came to a path that followed the brink of the cliff beyond the park, and where the path widened there was a bench set into the wall. Here Alexander sat, to look over the valley. A dog was barking in one of the farmhouses below. Amber clouds were massing on the farthest hills, where a mist of indigo was rising in the folds of the slopes. Four boys, all perhaps nine or ten years of age, all in hooped T-shirts, all with hair like moleskin, came running up the path and stopped at the parapet in front of Alexander. One of them rested his hands on the wall, bent backwards slowly from the waist, then threw his torso forward and yelled. The cry echoed once, weakly, from the valley, and was answered, after a few seconds' silence, by a child's strident voice, replying with what sounded like a single slur of vowels. The four boys slapped hands, then the one who had yelled did the same again, but the noise of cheering in the bullring flooded over his voice. He shrugged and shouted again, and the same protracted syllable was screamed in response. Alexander went over to the parapet. He scanned the valley in the direction the boys were facing, but saw nobody, nor anything that was moving except a drift of smoke that had risen from no source that he could see. 'Donde?' he asked the boys. One of them laughed and made a megaphone of his hands and shouted. As soon as its echo had ceased a joyous scream came up from the plain. The four boys pointed triumphantly to the valley floor. Alexander's gaze investigated the house to which they seemed to be directing him, but could see nobody in the doorway or in the paddock around the house. Together the boys shouted and leaned out over the wall, each cupping a hand to an ear to receive the cry from the abyss. Laughing, they looked at Alexander. He smiled, and looked down on fields in which nobody stood and nothing grazed.

Alexander would always remember the boys and the empty fields, and the fallen horse and the last minutes of the bullfight, and Megan's clenched face as the harness was scraped across the sand. And he would remember waking in the early hours of the morning in Ronda and seeing Megan sitting on the end of the bed, facing the moonlit wall of the light well. He touched her back. 'It's OK, Eck,' she said softly, but she did not turn round. 'Don't worry,' she said. 'Go back to sleep.'

40. 27 April 1983

On the table in the hall there were three letters for him. He opened them in the kitchen and read them there while the kettle boiled. It was shortly after five o'clock; he turned the radio on and listened to the news bulletin as he drank his tea. On the back of one of the envelopes he jotted a couple of questions about his accounts, to ask his father.

Passing the open door of their bedroom, he saw that Megan had left the curtains drawn that morning. There was a furrow on the sheet where she had been sleeping when he left for work. The impression of her head was on the pillow.

He went into the bathroom. He sat on the edge of the bath, removed his shirt and deposited it in the laundry basket, on top of Megan's red silk dress. The catch on the louvred window was not fastened. A lawnmower whined in a neighbour's garden, and someone was talking loudly. On the tiles above the bath there was a zone of barley-sugar light. The door was speckled with the shadows of leaves. In a row on the shelf above the basin stood his shaving brush, the wooden dish of shaving soap, his razor. His things seemed estranged from him as he looked at them, and then he realised that there was nothing on the shelf that was not his. Megan's perfume was not there. Her nail file was not there. He looked at the sill at the back of the bath. All her bottles were missing.

In the bedroom his clothes lay exactly where he had left them. His blue jacket was draped on the back of the chair, but Megan's jeans were no longer under it. His shoes were under the chair, but her sandals were not. He slid back the wardrobe door: every one of Megan's shirts, every skirt, her coats, her jackets – all had gone. Automatically, like a watchman testing doors he has already checked a dozen times in the course of the night, Alexander pulled open the empty drawers of the chest by the window. A rectangle of dust on the windowsill marked where her jewellery box had been.

He crossed the landing and pushed at the door of Megan's study, but could not bring himself to cross the threshold. It was as though Megan's absence now occupied the house, and he was an intruder in it. He descended the stairs without making a sound, grasping the banister tightly. He stood in the centre of the living room. The books and records leaned where Megan's possessions had been subtracted. He sat on the stairs, immobile as a fisherman watching a river's surface. After a while he went out into the street. There was a seam of pain under his ribs, as though he had been running too fast.

It was dark now; the faulty streetlight outside the house flashed and hummed. At the garage a man in a three-piece suit watched the traffic, smiling, as he refuelled his car. Alexander walked past the garage, past the church, past the row of shops. Soon the coolness of the air became apparent to him; he considered returning to the house; he carried on walking, taking a route of which he would have no memory. Fragments of conversation irrupted into his hearing. 'No, Eck, that's not it,' she wailed, slapping the wall in her frustration. 'I'm the one making us like this,' she told him, jabbing a finger on her forehead. He saw her crying at the kitchen table, fists against her temples, sorrowfully regarding her half-empty plate, speaking sombrely and quietly, as though she were the only one there: 'I don't know, Eck. It's as if I've got lost again.' She stood on the stairs, wrapped in the green towel, her hair wet, and explained to him: 'I want it to be different. But I can't make it different. For me it's gone. What can I say, Eck? It's gone.' He tried to summon a scene from their holiday in Paris, but his thoughts were steeped in white noise. He found himself at the bottom of the rise to Oxleas Wood, and there he turned back.

He sat on the stairs in the artificial twilight that the streetlamps made. A triangular cobweb quivered above the door; the neighbours' TV sent out sporadic applause; footfalls drummed on the stairs next door. Eventually he noticed a pulse of pale red light on the wall at the foot of the stairs. In the living room, the ruby bulb of the answering machine was blinking. There was a message from the garage. 'Hello, Mr MacIndoe?' was all he listened to. The second voice was Megan's.

'Eck? Are you there? It's me,' she said. Her breath came out of the machine. 'Are you there? Pick up the phone, please, Eck.' Something knocked the mouthpiece, as if she had dropped it; she sobbed, and there was a long silence. 'Pick up the phone. Please, Eck.' A door closed in the room in which she was speaking. 'I'm sorry,' she said, and paused again. 'I'm sorry, but – I'm sorry. I don't –' She was crying now. 'I'll call you.'

Twice more he played her message, holding the speaker to his ear. It was the sound of the door, closing in a room he could not imagine, that he could not bear. He removed the cassette from the machine and placed it on the floor. He lay on the floor, with a hand clenched on the cassette, hearing her breathing in the room that was not the room he was in. Later he went out into the street again and walked until the lights began to come on in the houses, as the day commenced.

41. Bank

They arranged it so that she would have taken the rest of her things by the time Alexander finished work, but when he looked down the street he saw a van behind his car, with its back doors open, and Mary Garthside, one of Megan's colleagues, standing on the pavement, holding a crate. She turned sharply towards the house and said something, and then she carried the crate to the open doors and shoved it across the floor of the van. Part of the pewter lamp was visible between two plastic sacks, as he would remember. Alexander turned back and went on to the park, where he walked a circuit of the outer path. He sat on a bench in front of the Ranger's House. Everything he saw was tedious to him, and yet he could feel the pulse, quick and irregular, punching at his chest.

Alexander left the flat a month later, in June. Sam helped him, and together they emptied the rooms briskly, as though they were moving the belongings of a third person. As they were about to drive off, Sam stooped forward in the driver's seat and looked sideways through the windscreen. 'Forgot the curtains,' he said, pointing up at the bedroom window. Alexander regarded the curtains. Beyond them, a bare lightbulb hung on a kinked flex. 'Forget it?' Sam suggested and Alexander gave the dashboard a smack, and they drove to the agent's office to give up the key, and then to Alexander's new flat. By the middle of the afternoon they had unloaded everything. When Sam had gone, Alexander moved the armchair to the window and there he sat until seven, watching indifferently the street in which he now lived, and then he went out to meet Sam again. Though they stayed in the pub until closing time, Megan's name was never mentioned.

Not until August did he see her again. He would remember waiting by the exit from Leicester Square station and seeing her at the turn of the steps, and he would remember that the tiredness vanished from her face, momentarily, when she noticed him.

With her hands jammed in her pockets, she stood an arm's length from him and hunched her shoulders as she looked at him. 'Hello, Eck,' she said uncertainly. The skin beneath her eyes was clammy and in the inner corners was as dark as the underside of a mushroom. 'Where shall we go?' she asked, looking up and down the road. He led her down the alley beside the theatre, and they went into the first pub they came across, where the only place to stand was beside the cigarette machine. 'So how's the flat?' she asked. Listening to him, she glanced from his face to the carpet to the mirror opposite, from which she turned away, as if her reflection were an eavesdropper.

After one drink they left, and wandered along St Martin's Lane and down to the Strand, and ended up at the boat at the Victoria Embankment. It was not yet dark, so they sat outside, on the upper deck. Sitting beside him on the slatted bench, she cradled her glass as if it were a fragile object that someone had asked her to hold for a few minutes. She told him she'd spent a weekend in Yorkshire, with Mary Garthside. Her flat was OK, but the neighbours weren't exactly welcoming. She was thinking about moving to another school, she said. Their conversation sagged, and was silenced by the rising noise of the groups around them. For a while they regarded the river, and then she put her half-full glass on the seat beside him. 'Eck, I have to go,' she said, though it was not late. When she had pushed her way through the drinkers, Alexander poured her drink into his glass. He spent some time watching the figures that moved in the windows of the Festival Hall across the water. It was almost midnight when he arrived home. He looked at his bedroom by the light from the hall and felt as if he were coming back to a hotel room.

They met in the afternoon next time, and on every subsequent occasion. For an hour or two they would stroll together and talk, but their talk was circumspect and trivial, and they stayed constantly a hand's span or more apart, as though it were imperative for Megan that they should not touch. They might stop for a drink, and when they did it was always at a place to which they had never been as a couple. Only once, during this time, did their past intrude openly into the present. In a café in Old Compton Street she called for the bill and opened her wallet, and he saw, alongside the photo of Mr and Mrs Beckwith, a picture of himself and Megan, peeping around the flap of the tent that his father had pitched in the garden. 'Let's have a look,' he cajoled. Reluctantly she held the wallet open on the table. In the background of the picture, above the tent, there was the window of Mrs Caton's bathroom, with the sill that had crumbled over the years and had come to look like a slab of cod's roe. The shrub above the wall was forsythia, and as Alexander perused its blurry flowers the picture imparted to him something of the pleasure that the jubilant yellow blooms used to give him, and he seemed to taste the March breeze. In his fingertips he could sense the texture of the stiff green canvas; he heard the muted crunch the tent's fabric made when his father folded it into the grey cardboard box with the fat brass staples at its corners. Staring at the wooden barrier around the building site on the other side of the street, he saw the rectangle of sapless grass that was revealed when the groundsheet was lifted. He looked at Megan, who was looking at him wonderingly, ruefully, and slipping the wallet back into her bag. She went to visit a friend in Camden and he went to the cinema, as he often did after seeing her. Sometimes the sense of her presence was so strong that he would feel the touch of her head as she rested against his shoulder.

Months went by, and every month they met for a few hours, and nothing changed until an afternoon in February. They met in Bow Street, outside the opera house. 'Three hours shopping, and this is all I get,' she said, showing him the new gloves on an outstretched hand.

'Want to do three hours more?' he asked.

She smiled and shook her head. 'You don't want to slog around the girls' shops,' she replied.

'Not the worst job in the world,' said Alexander.

'No more shopping,' said Megan. 'Let's just walk. Away from here,' she said, and she swung her bag to get them moving.

They walked down to Aldwych. On Fleet Street they decided to go up the dome of St Paul's, but halfway up Ludgate Hill she pointed to the gallery at the top of the dome. 'Bit busy for my liking,' she said, and Alexander knew from her eyes that this was an excuse, and that Megan felt there was no longer any reason to do such things together. 'How about you?' she asked.

'Walking's fine with me,' he said, and so they continued up Ludgate Hill and around St Paul's, talking about what each had bought, or thought about buying, or failed to find in the winter sales. They walked into the wide, empty streets of the City, along Watling Street and Bread Street and Cheapside, past rows of dark and shuttered shops.

They were near the Guildhall when Megan made a sound as if something had startled her. 'Eck,' she began.

'I know what you're going to say,' he interrupted. 'You're going to say it would be best if we didn't do this.'

She stopped and looked at him. 'I was,' she admitted.

'Those bloody gloves,' he said, and he tried to smile. 'I could tell by the way you showed them to me.'

'And you agree that it's best?'

'I can't, Meg. It's not what I want.'

Forlornly she gazed along the street. Traffic lights changed for traffic that was not there. 'Look at us, Eck,' she said, gesturing at the abject man and woman who faced them from the window of the bank. 'We used to be such friends. Now we're a miserable couple, same as the other miserable couples. I went and wrecked it.'

'It's not wrecked, Meg. And it wasn't you.'

'It was me,' she insisted. 'You wouldn't have done anything.'

'Sooner or later I would have.'

'I doubt it, Eck,' she said tenderly, and she started walking again.

'Anyway, it was what we both wanted.'

'We should have known, Eck.'

'Known what? That we'd be happy for years?'

'And then we'd be utterly miserable.'

'We're not utterly miserable. We're not happy, and that'll change.'

'But we can't go back,' she protested. 'Not to what we were like before.'

'No, we can't. But it's not going to remain like this. Be patient.'

'It's not a question of being patient,' she lamented. 'We're not friends who've fallen out with each other. We're ex-lovers. We failed, Eck. All we can do now is talk about things that are beside the point, and there's nothing else to talk about.'

'For now.'

'No, Eck, not for now. All those years, when we were kids, and after. They've gone. I can't feel them any more,' she said. She looked at him imploringly and then stared at the pavement in front of her, and she did not seem to notice when his hand touched her back.

'It's not like that for me,' said Alexander.

'I know it's not. I regret it and you don't.'

'No, I don't,' he confirmed. 'I knew you'd leave, in the end, but I never regretted it and I won't ever regret it.'

Megan came to a halt and confronted him. Her eyes were smarting. 'You knew I'd leave?' she demanded.

'I thought you would.'

'When did you think this?' asked Megan, jamming her hands on her hips.

'From the beginning,' Alexander stated.

'What?' she exclaimed, and she stamped a foot on the ground. 'Why, for God's sake?'

'I thought it wouldn't be enough for you. Eventually.'

'You always thought that?'

'Not always. Sometimes.'

'From the beginning?' she asked, as if she wanted him to admit that he was embellishing his story.

'Yes,' he replied.

'So you came to live with me, knowing it wouldn't last?' she said, her brow creasing quickly with sadness and perplexity.

'Well, for one thing I'd say it did last. For another I hoped I was wrong. And it was what we both wanted.'

'And all that time you were waiting for it to end.'

'Of course I wasn't. You make it sound like a prison sentence.'

'But if that's what you were thinking –'

'It wasn't what I was thinking. I thought you'd be the one who would end it. That doesn't mean I was moping around waiting for my eviction order,' he explained, but Megan continued to look at him doubtfully. 'It's not hard to understand, Meg. I love you.'

'Please, Eck,' she said, ducking her head.

'No, I do. I'm not pleading my cause. I'm not asking you to come back. I accept that we've parted. I want to see you still, but I'm not going to argue. It's pointless. I know that. I'm only telling you that I love you.'

'Eck, please. Don't be a saint. I feel guilty enough.'

'There's no reason to feel guilty.'

'There's every reason.'

'There isn't, Meg. Everything ends,' he said, but she appeared not to hear him.

Neither of them spoke for a minute. The street lights were coming on as they came to the corner of Princes Street. Standing on the kerb, Megan surveyed the façade of the Mansion House, her gaze moving up storey by storey to the roofline, as though the building were inexplicable. The road was clear, but she did not move. She regarded her shoes. 'Eck,' she said, very quietly, and her body seemed to become rigid, as though she were in a situation of such peril that she could not raise her voice or move a limb. 'I can't bear it,' she whispered. 'I'm sorry.' She turned towards him and raised her hands to cradle his face. She looked at him desperately, as if fixing every aspect of his face in her memory. Her lips parted slightly. With a thumb she smeared the tears from her eyes, and then she walked away.

Alexander watched her until the steps of Bank station hid her completely. A car with a rusted roof drove past, he would remember, and the pattern of the clouds was like the imprint of the skin of a palm on glass. When she had gone he turned and walked back west, down Queen Victoria Street and Cannon Street, past St Paul's, along Fleet Street and the Strand, noticing nothing.

42. The Bellevue

He was drunk with boredom and he would remember as little of these months as a man would remember of months of drunkenness. He could be certain, though, that when he drove out of London, late one Friday afternoon in February, he had no plan but to spend a few days somewhere other than London.

He drove west and stopped at a village near Salisbury, where he took a room above a pub. The next morning he continued westward, intending to stop wherever he happened to be when the daylight expired. Soon he found himself on roads that were familiar from the shape they made across the land, passing farms and petrol stations that were as conspicuous as waymarks, and in the late afternoon he saw the first sign for Penzance. At the fourth or fifth sign he followed that direction, and as dusk fell he was driving through the outskirts of the town.

Without thinking he turned into the street in which he and his parents had stayed the year after the holiday with the Beckwiths. He parked the car close by, took out his suitcase, and walked back to the hotel that had been the Tivoli and was now the Hepworth. He looked at the façade of the closed hotel. The breakfast room had smelled of turpentine, he remembered. Someone's woollen swimming costume was left hanging in the bathroom every evening and would drip all night, like a clock that was running down.

From a street corner he took a look at the seafront. The pavement he had run along looked meagre and drab in the misty yellow light of the streetlamps. A scrap of black bin-liner, caught by a gust off the sea, flew into the window of a supermarket that had not been there when he was a boy. He circled back, and after wandering for half an hour he came across a street where the loudest sound was the screech of signboards swinging in the wind. Attracted by the tub of snowdrops beside the steps, he stopped outside the Bellevue Hotel. As he stood beside the tub, brushing the waxen flowers with his fingertips, considering whether to return to the car and drive on, a hand appeared

351

in the window of the Bellevue's front door and straightened the sign on which the word 'Vacancies' was written, and then a woman's face appeared.

A dozen hooks in the shape of anchors were ranged above the table in the hall, and a key hung from every hook. The landlady took the key from hook number twelve and surrendered it to Alexander. 'Top floor, Mr MacIndoe,' she said, with the air of someone bestowing a special favour. Room twelve was at the end of a windowless corridor and its door had been wallpapered to match the walls, with such care that it was only when he noticed the keyhole that Alexander saw where he should go. This he would remember, and what he saw when he opened the door. The bed was immense and its quilt was covered with a sunburst in tones of mauve and pink, a motif repeated on the curtains. A blazing sun was embossed on the headboard, which was made of a brass-coloured metal that the pressure of a thumb could dent. A shroud of thick plastic still encased the plinth of the basin; the taps were cubes of perspex tinted the colour of ginger ale, and the mirror was set inside a plastic scallop shell. A chair with a red plastic seat and a back of curved black wooden slats was pushed under a flat-pack table from which the veneer-effect surface was peeling at the edges. On the table stood a portable TV with a broken dial. Next to the wardrobe hung a painted view of Penzance in a tropical sunset, printed onto card that was slubbed like canvas. A fringe of grime extended a third of the way down the lower windowpane, shining like petrol in the light of the room. Rain dribbled on the glass. Through the droplets and the reflection of his face he could see a portion of the beach, and surf rushing up.

In the morning he sat in the bay window of the dining room, where Mrs Deveral served him a breakfast of thickly sliced ham and toast and eggs, and laid a sheaf of Sunday newspapers on the edge of his table. 'Anything else you need, Mr MacIndoe?' she asked him, knitting her fingers underneath her bosom. Everything was perfect, he thanked her. 'I'll be popping out. Back in a mo,' she said, and she withdrew, closing the door behind her. A minute later she appeared on the steps outside; knotting her pink chequered headscarf, she surveyed the sky as if to decide what she should do, and then she strode off in the direction of the sea, purposeful as a policewoman who has seen a fight brewing. Left alone in the building, it appeared, Alexander read the newspapers as the day brightened; when Mrs Deveral returned, soon after ten, he went out.

He knew the street on which the Bellevue stood, he realised. On a hot afternoon he had walked down this street with his father, and they had seen a man brewing tea on a stove in the back of a van. His father was holding a pouch of tobacco, which he had bought from a shop that was very near. Within a few minutes Alexander found the shop. It was now an estate agent's office, but its windows were the same, with decorations like rosehips on the foot of each mullion. He had been there on another day, with his mother, he remembered; she had bought a postcard to send to the Beckwiths, and behind the counter there was a picture of the Queen and Prince Philip, next to a bigger one of Tenzing on the summit of Everest. The floor used to be bare pine, which was worn to the colour and softness of balsa by the sand carried inside by the customers' shoes. He leaned against the glass and closed his eyes, and saw the sea and his father's arm outstretched. He had been somewhere by the harbour, sitting on a bench between his parents. He walked down to the water and stopped where the bench had been. His father had spotted a seal between two boats. 'There, there,' he cried, standing up to point to the place, and his excitement made Alexander's throat constrict with affection for him, as he stood beside his father's quivering arm and stared out at the sea, seeing nothing but the seal-coloured humps of the swells.

All morning Alexander walked through the town. He found the place where the huge black Mercedes with headlights as big as colanders had been parked, the corner of the market where toy gliders had been strung on a line like fish, the street where, he suddenly remembered, a girl with eyes that slanted upwards had stroked his hand quickly, while she stood on the kerb with her mother, waiting for a bus with cherry-red paintwork to pass. On the outskirts of the town he found the field in which people from Birmingham had pitched their small green tents in a single straight line, like an army encampment. On the beach a clump of fleshy yellow seaweed brought back the weeds he and his father had seen in a stream, which had looked like creatures jostling for a view of the world above the water.

Enlivened by the vividness of these memories, in the afternoon he drove to Praa, and climbed the clifftop path to the hummock where

353

he and Mr Beckwith had sniffed the ground for the apple aroma of chamomile. Making a cup of his hand, he saw the pellet of desiccated earth that Mr Beckwith had put in his palm and crumbled with a thumb to expose a backbone curled inside the fragile ball, like a tiny white zip. He went down to the beach and walked over the rocks where he had sat with Megan, but as he picked a path towards the cliff he became aware of the ridiculousness of what he was doing. He stood near the place where Megan had danced in a skirt of seaweed. Mrs Beckwith had stood behind her, with a towel knotted on her hip. He closed his eyes and saw them, but they faded instantly, like shapes breathed onto glass. The sun had almost gone. It was cold. Tedium returned, as forceful as the hissing of the sea.

He went back to his room in the Bellevue, where he watched TV and read the catalogues he had brought, and wrote some orders. The next morning he drove back to London.

43. The Rotunda in Ranelagh Gardens

It was not long after the last conversation with Megan that Charlie Williamson came into the shop. He was with three friends, who stood outside while Charlie went in. For a couple of minutes he browsed through the new CDs, then his friends rapped on the glass and pointed at their watches. One of the boys pointed a stabbing finger at Alexander. Charlie examined the back of a CD, and again his friends knocked the glass. 'Fuck off,' he shouted, swatting the air. Rubbing his face as if he were waking up, he brought the CD to the counter. 'What I was going to say,' he said, 'was I don't suppose there's any chance of a job, is there, because I know my music and films and I'd like to work here, but I suppose if there was a chance there isn't now, is there, not after that?' His friends were shouting something that might have been a nickname, and one of them was bowing and cringing by the doorstep, kneading his hands unctuously. Charlie watched his friend's performance until it was over. 'Excuse me,' he said to Alexander, smoothing a five-pound note onto the counter. He took a deep breath, went to the door, pulled it open and said, in a tone of reasonableness: 'Will you three bennies do me a big favour and just go and fuck right off out of it? Like fuck right off away over the hill?' Clutching at his mouth, the cringing boy gave an effeminate shriek of alarm, as the other two hugged each other in terror. Charlie closed the door on them and returned to Alexander. 'Sorry about that. They are good lads, really they are, but there is no meaning to their sorry little lives,' he said, and he smiled in a way that reminded Alexander of John Halloran, which was the explanation Alexander would later tend to give himself for his promise to Charlie Williamson, a few minutes later, that he could have a part-time job whenever his current assistant decided to move on.

On the mornings and afternoons that he had free, Alexander would often take a train up into the city, where he would walk for a couple of hours, as he used to do with Sidney Dixon. At first he would do nothing more than roam, pausing at whatever street or building gained his attention, sometimes returning to the shop having seen nothing he had not seen before. Soon, however, it became his habit to choose a small zone of a borough and sedulously explore every street and square in it, every notable building and monument. Sitting in a pew or on a bench, he would feel the air change while he read the guidebook or journal or history book he had brought, as if the words were a rarefied incense, and he would briefly be somewhere that was not perfectly in the present. Intensely he imagined buildings that were no longer there. In Leicester Square he looked up from a picture and saw the minarets of the Royal Panopticon rising in place of the Odeon cinema. In Soho Square he imagined the Soho Bazaar, with its gloves and laces spread on mahogany counters. He envisaged the magnificent rooms of Carlisle House, the home of the Viennese singer Mrs Cornelys, who was once the lover of Casanova. On a foggy morning in February he imagined the rag-clad villains who lurked in the lawless warren of Alsatia, where the Carmelite monastery had stood. He crossed the Strand to Lincoln's Inn Fields and there, standing on the spot where he had sat with Sidney Dixon and seen Sir Archibald McIndoe, he closed his eyes to see the Sardinian Chapel, where Fanny Burney, once a guest at Mrs Cornelys' house, was married to General d'Arblay.

It was during one of these walks that Alexander made up his mind that his shop would no longer sell music. Soon he would forget the nights he spent pondering the future of his business, though he would remember Charlie holding the sleeve of a Madonna record as he clutched his head, moaning that music had died with Sid Vicious, and he would remember his father at the dining room table, rapidly filling sheets of square-ruled paper with figures, and taking a cup of tea from his wife with a 'Thank you', as though he were restored to his office at the bank and she was his secretary, and putting his thin old hands over his eyes when he had satisfied himself that Alexander's plan stood a chance of succeeding. And although he would be able to recall little of the process by which the shop was converted, he would know that it was refitted in the middle of the year, because he would remember a hot morning in July, on which the smell of new plastic boxes filled the shop, and the phone rang as he was standing on a chair to adjust the monitor above the counter.

Hooking the phone from the counter, he answered: 'The Video-centre.'

'What?' said a woman's voice, not aggressively, but rather as if their conversation had commenced some time ago and she had not properly heard his last remark.

'The Videocentre,' Alexander repeated.

'Since when?'

'I beg your pardon?'

There was a silence, and a soft laugh, and then she said: 'My God, that is you, isn't it? Alexander?'

Now he recognised the voice. 'It is,' he said.

'You're still there,' Jane marvelled, and she laughed again.

'Evidently. How are you? Where are you?'

'I don't know why I thought you might have gone,' she said. 'Of course you're still there.'

'Are you in London?'

'Yes, I'm in London. Can't you hear? Listen.' A door squealed, and an unintelligible announcement echoed under a high roof.

He heard the word 'Eastbourne' amid the echo, before the door squealed shut. 'So how are you?' he asked.

'You sound nervous, Alexander,' she observed, with a tinge of mockery to her tone. 'You sound a bit tense.'

'That's because I'm balancing on a chair with a drill in my hand.'

'Get down then, Alexander,' she said, as if addressing a child. 'There's a couple of minutes left on the meter.'

Climbing down from the chair, he heard a sharp rhythmic tapping on the glass of the phone booth. 'How are you?' he asked again.

The tapping stopped. 'I'm very well. But I think what you want to know is why I'm calling, isn't it?'

'Well, not quite in those words, but –'

'A whim. Nothing more than a whim,' she sighed. 'I got off the train and the first thing I saw was an aftershave advert, and the boy in the picture made me think of you.'

'Do you want to meet up?'

'I think so,' she said casually, after a pause.

At six o'clock he walked into the café. He scanned the crowded room but could not find her. About to leave, he looked around the room one last time, and then he saw that it was Jane sitting at the corner table, by the open window, fanning herself with a magazine. Though she was facing the door she had made no attempt to catch his attention, and now she watched him approach without any alteration in her expression, as if she were disinterestedly analysing his response to her appearance. She was slimmer than she had been, her hair was cut short and razored very closely at the sides, and her clothes – a loose-fitting sleeveless black cotton top, loose black cotton trousers and a pair of thin-soled black pumps – were of a style quite unlike the clothes she used to wear. Laying the magazine down beside her sunglasses, she leaned forward to request a kiss. Lines as fine as cobwebs were visible in the strokes of suntan below her eyes. Through the perfume she had dabbed on her neck he could detect the familiar saline scent of her skin. Settling back, she handed the menu to Alexander.

'You're looking good,' she said.

'As are you,' he replied.

'You approve of the oriental theme?' she asked, folding the sunglasses into their case.

'I do,' he told her. He read the menu, conscious that she was watching him, with her hand against her cheek and her elbow on the sill of the window, in an attitude of lukewarm curiosity.

'I'm getting a salad,' she said, as if she thought he might need assistance in making his choice. 'They're always good here.'

'You're a regular?' he asked, not looking up.

'I've been here a few times,' she admitted. She looked out into the street, where a man in a gold-buttoned blazer was manoeuvring a wicker hamper into the back seat of an open-topped car, while in the driver's seat sat a woman in a cerise headscarf, staring down the road as fixedly as a bust, as if unaware of the presence of the man and of everything around her. 'I've been raiding the sales,' Jane informed him, patting the carrier bags that hung on the back of her chair.

'What did you get?'

From a bag the size of a small suitcase she extracted a black silk raincoat, which she ran over her outstretched arm, as though to furnish proof of the taste she had developed in recent years. The coat slithered into the bag with a noise like a fall of dry sand.

'Things are booming in the alternative health sector, I take it?'

'Don't be facetious, Alexander. It doesn't become you.'

'It wasn't meant to be facetious,' he said, and it was then that he noticed the ring.

'I do well enough. And I'm careful with my money. I save.' She turned the ring towards her face and made a frowning smile, as though she were grudgingly impressed. 'Didn't make it before thirty, did I? Closer to forty.' In the look she gave him there was a hint of fondness and sadness, but quickly she was watchful again. 'His name's Philip. Perhaps you'll meet him one day,' she said wryly.

'When did you –?'

'Six months,' she said, as the waiter came to their table.

'Congratulations.'

'Thank you.' When they had placed their orders she asked about the shop, and he told her how he had come to take it over from Sid Dixon, and how it had changed. Jane listened, in a manner that was both attentive and uninvolved, until the food arrived, and then, glancing at the street, she asked: 'And how's your Megan?'

'Megan's fine,' he replied, and though he heard nothing in his voice that might betray him, Jane looked at him keenly now.

'What's she up to? Teaching still?'

'I should think so, yes,' said Alexander, and he began to eat.

Jane replenished her glass of water and topped up Alexander's, which he had not yet touched. For a minute she did not speak. She looked at him, but he did not return her gaze. Taking a sip of water, she looked up at the rotating wooden blades of the ceiling fan. Alexander saw her lips begin to form a word that was instantly rescinded, and then she said, in a low voice, as if the subject made her tired: 'I can't say I'm surprised.' She held her fork above her food, and her eyebrows shrugged. 'Sorry if that seems unsympathetic. But I'm not surprised, not really.'

'No,' he replied. 'I shouldn't imagine you are.'

She met his glance with a small frown of pique. 'What do you mean by that?'

'I mean, given my record –'

'That's not what you mean.'

'Yes it is.'

359

'It isn't, Alexander. You think I'm pleased.'

'Aren't you? A little?'

'I am not. And that's not what I meant.'

'I apologise.'

'I didn't mean you.'

'OK,' he replied.

'I'm not at all pleased. I might have reason to be, but I'm not. I want you to be happy, believe it or not.'

'Thank you.'

'But I'm not surprised it didn't work out.'

'You seemed surprised.'

'No. That's not the right word. It's like hearing that someone old has died. You're not surprised they've died, but it's still a bit of a blow when you hear it.'

'A nice analogy,' Alexander commented, and he could not prevent himself from smiling.

'There's no need to be nasty, Alexander. I am sorry it didn't work out with Megan, but if you don't want to believe me, so be it.'

'I wouldn't say it didn't work out, but let's leave it, shall we? Tell me about your Philip.'

'In a minute. Let's settle this first. I do not want you to be unhappy, Alexander. Look at me. Do you believe me?' she demanded, holding her head up as if challenging him to find evidence of insincerity in her face.

'I believe you,' he said. He lifted the bottle to pour her some water, but she put her hand over the empty glass.

'I want you to be happy. I always wanted you to be happy and I never thought you were going to be happy with her. It was obvious she wasn't right for you.'

'I was happy with her. I was happy with you and I was happy with her.'

'For a while, but not for long, I'll bet. Am I right?'

'You met her once, for ten minutes,' Alexander reminded her.

'It was enough,' Jane said, accepting the water now. 'She was too hard for you. Too cold.'

'Jane, you wouldn't know,' he stated.

'It takes seconds to see things like that. How long did it take you to decide you liked me? Did you have to go away and think about it? Of course you didn't.'

'So you didn't like her. I did,' Alexander replied, taking his cigarettes from his pocket. 'There I think we might leave it.' Jane pointed to the No Smoking sign on the wall behind her. 'Let's hear about your Philip,' he suggested.

'To tell you the truth,' Jane went on, 'I was disappointed in you, when I found out. I may as well tell you this, while we're on the subject. I thought it was a bit lazy of you, like getting together with your pretty cousin. A bit like using a safety net, if you see what I mean?'

'I'm not going to argue, Jane. There's no point,' said Alexander, but Jane persisted and the conversation continued, on the brink of becoming an argument, until at last he asked her simply why she had wanted to see him.

'I could ask the same question,' she replied.

'To see how you are.'

'Well, there's your answer,' said Jane, flipping a nonchalant hand. 'And how am I?'

'You seem well.'

'I am well,' she said, raising a hand to summon the waiter.

She was going to Victoria station, and Alexander walked with her as far as Pimlico Road. They never did talk about Philip, nor did they mention her family or his. They hardly spoke as they walked, but at the junction of Pimlico Road and Chelsea Bridge Road, as Alexander would remember, he pointed across the street, at the Chelsea Hospital. 'That's where the Rotunda used to be. The Rotunda in Ranelagh Gardens.' Jane smiled at him, wondering why he was telling her this. 'A huge building, with orchestra stalls at one side and tables around the edge. Mozart played there.'

'That's interesting,' she said, looking in the direction of the station.

'You saw a picture of it once.'

'Did I? Once?' Jane replied, shaking her head. 'Dear Alexander,' she said, and she patted his cheek as if to humour him. 'Plus ça change.' She took a step back, raised a hand in a wave. 'Perhaps I'll phone you again,' she called from the far side of the road, and she walked away rapidly, though her train would not leave for more than half an hour.

Alexander walked down Chelsea Bridge Road to the river. In the grounds of the hospital a jammed sprinkler had waterlogged a slender oval of grass, in which the sky was reflected so sharply he mistook it for a sheet of blue tarpaulin. The Rotunda was built by a syndicate headed by the man who owned the Drury Lane Theatre, which became the Theatre Royal, he recited to himself. It was demolished in 1805, he went on, seeing the colour of that year in his mind, a tarnished silvery blue that was the colour of the smoke that rises from a match at the moment it ignites, a tone of blue he imagined as the colour of the walls of the Chinese pavilion that once had stood by the canal in Ranelagh Gardens.

44. The desk

Alexander's mother sat at the table in the living room, with the solicitor's letters and papers arrayed before her in a broad arc that encompassed a smaller arc of cards and letters. 'Iris Evans,' she said, showing a signature to him. 'How did she hear?' she asked herself, and replaced the card in its position.

From a box by her elbow she took a sheet of paper and wrote her message to Iris. She passed it to Alexander, who signed his name and folded the page into an envelope, which he sealed and placed on a tray beside the fireplace, underneath the flowers that Jane had sent. He picked up his newspaper and turned the page quietly, as his mother slid the next card across the tabletop. Somewhere in the street a car was started and driven away, and the mid-morning silence filled the room again.

At the chime of one o'clock she rose from her chair and went out into the kitchen, from where she returned, twenty minutes later, with two bowls of soup and a basket of bread. She set his bowl on the round table and carried hers to the armchair by the window. Slowly she raised and lowered her spoon, gazing at the aerials on the roofs across the road. The visible part of the sky was a blemishless blue. 'I might take a holiday,' she remarked at last. 'Do you think that would be a good idea?' she asked him, still facing the window.

'On your own?' Alexander asked.

She glanced at him without expression. 'I should think so,' she replied.

'Where will you go?'

'Somewhere we never went,' she said. 'I don't know. I haven't thought.' She looked up at the sky again, while her hands turned the empty bowl on her lap, an inch at a time. Alexander crossed the room and took the bowl from her. 'I should write to Jane,' she commented absently, to the window. He detached the note from Jane's flowers and put it on the arm of the chair. 'I'll do it now,' she said, but when

363

Alexander came back into the living room she was asleep, with the note held against her chest. He knelt at the side of her chair. A veil of shadow was cast across her face by the lacework pattern of the curtains. Her eyes were motionless under their lids, but her lips moved, as though she were striving to deny something that she was hearing in her dream.

Leaving her to sleep he went upstairs and stood outside the room that had become his father's study. As if preparing to shift a great weight, he gripped the porcelain handle. The door had stuck to the jamb, and cracked as he pushed at it. He saw his father's desk, ponderous as a sarcophagus, in the centre of the darkened room. Behind the desk, the gold and scarlet seals glowed weakly on his father's certificates. The air bore a smell of ink and old paper and cold tobacco pipes. Suspended on a strand of spider's web in the angle of the doorway, a tiny piece of wood swivelled in the draught of his breath.

Alexander opened the blinds. His father's journals and books were yellowed and inert. The castors of the leather-padded chair, he noticed, had been displaced from the little wells they had worn in the carpet. He sat in his father's chair. Striking the long steel lever of the Underwood typewriter, he watched the turning of the wide black rubber drum, on which was softly embossed a pattern of words, the residue of all the letters his father had written on it. To the side of the green glass lamp there was the rack of pipes, and next to that the puck-shaped glass paperweight with the Saltire in its base, and next to that the shallow wooden trough in which were laid two pencils and his father's antique pen, the pen with the gilded clip and the scratches on the barrel that he knew as well as he knew the lines around his father's mouth. He rolled the pen between his fingers, examining the quarter-inch of pitted enamel that he used to see as an elephant's eye.

Sitting in his father's chair, Alexander surveyed the room. For more than twenty years, before it had become his father's study, this room had been his bedroom. He stated this to himself, as if his estrangement might be dispelled by the utterance of the fact. His bed had once been set where he was now sitting. His wardrobe had occupied the place where the shelves of books and journals now were. There had been a chair where the files were stacked, and pictures where the certificates were fixed. He tried to see the colour of the walls in his room, but he could not overcome the presence of his father's things. He lay on the floor, below the window, as often he used to lie and read a landscape of rivers and deserts in the imperfections of the ceiling, which long ago had been erased, as had the pawprint of blotches on the cornice above the door. Not a trace of himself was to be seen in the room, it seemed, but then he found, on the underside of the windowsill, the initials of his name, which he had scored into the wood with a fingernail one afternoon, during a winter when the snow had piled up against the glass and turned into prisms of ice in which the walls and roofs of the houses were broken up and inverted. At night the light of the moon was spread by the ice in such a way that it radiated over the whole windowpane, and Alexander would lie, with his lamp turned off, watching the colour of the frosted window alter as the lights went on and off in the kitchens and bedrooms of the neighbours' houses. Sometimes, as he recalled, the changing whiteness of the ice so entranced him that he did not at first hear his mother's voice calling him down to eat, and he would have to splash water on his face to awaken himself before going downstairs. And one Saturday evening that winter, he remembered, he sat on the carpet beside his father's desk in the corner of the smallest bedroom, while his father worked through a sheaf of accounts. Snowflakes alighted on the black window and quickly lost their form, blossoming into extinction, and a skid of smoke rose from his father's pipe. Alexander watched his father as he wrote, made calculations, considered. The light of the desk lamp was reflected as a misshapen disc in each of the lenses of his father's glasses, and such was his father's concentration that these reflections barely moved for as long as Alexander looked at them. The shining, unmoving lenses were the emblem of his father's knowledge and his seriousness, just as the eye-mask was the image of the shiftiness of the thief in Alexander's comics. The desk at which his father worked had the weight of a factory machine, it seemed to Alexander. He put a palm to its flank to feel its solidity. His father noticed, and smiled, and continued with his work.

Alexander put a hand on the upper drawer of his father's desk and opened it, expecting to see files and folders arranged as precisely as the publications on his father's shelves. Instead he discovered a Silvikrin jar that contained a farthing and three single cufflinks, and a ring of keys that he did not recognise, and two science fiction novels he had never seen before, and a rusted penknife in a buttoned leather pouch, and some advertisements, cut from newspapers, for '*Elsie Carlisle (Radio's Most Popular Songstress)*' and one for '*Eddie Gray (You Can't Help Laughing)*', and another for '*Jack D'Ormonde (Scientific Nonsense)*', and, at the back of the drawer, under an old book of interest tables with a battered primrose cover, Alexander's school reports, bound together with rubber bands. He placed the reports on the top of the desk, squarely against the typewriter, as if in observance of a ritual that demanded his precision. The perished bands had the texture of pigskin, and snapped when he pulled at them. Starting with the earliest, Alexander read the teachers' judgements of the mediocrity whose name was Alexander MacIndoe, a character who was only intermittently himself. He came to Mr Barrington's name, and he repeated aloud Mr Barrington's sentences. He shut the report book and rested his fingers on the pale blue cover, as his father's fingers had rested on it, and he closed his eyes and heard his father's voice say: 'But this is good, son. This is good.' As if to give his memory a note from which to take its pitch, he repeated his father's words, again and again until they made another scene appear. 'Listen,' said his father, putting an arm around his shoulder and holding him. There was a wall, a wall of the fort at Reculver, and Alexander was sitting between his father and Mr Beckwith, who was crouching on one knee and looking around them as though scouting the terrain. Megan sat on a stone fifty yards away, near Mrs Beckwith and Alexander's mother, who held each other's arms like dancers. On a fence post a seagull turned and turned, like a weathervane. The long evening was beginning, and they would soon be going back to the car. His father put an arm around Alexander's shoulder and said: 'Listen. Listen to that. Isn't that a glorious noise?' The breeze moved through the long dry grass with a swishing that could have been the sound of a legion marching across the meadows. He told his father what he had imagined. 'Yes, it could be,' his father agreed, and he raised a hand theatrically to invoke the name of Julius Caesar, and said something about a phalanx, a word that made a brassy tang come to Alexander's tongue, as the thought of the word did now.

The door opened, and his mother stood on the threshold of the room. She looked at the desk, then at him. 'What are you doing?' she asked drowsily.

'I came across these,' he told her, lifting a report.

She looked at him, not at what he was holding. There was no reproof in her gaze, nor any interest.

'Leave them, Alexander,' she said, and she stepped out of the doorway.

When all the cards and letters had been answered they cooked a meal together and ate at the table in the living room. They watched a film on TV, and his mother fell asleep before it was over. Alexander kept the TV on until there was nothing more to watch, then turned it off, and all the lights except the lamp beside his mother's chair, and then he went back to his chair, where he slept. He awoke a few minutes before three o'clock. Coming out of sleep, he averted his eyes from the glare of the lamp. Then, distinctly, he glimpsed his father's face. His father looked tired; it was the face he often had when he worked late in his study and Alexander went in to say goodbye. His father's eyes would sometimes look aside, quickly, when Alexander was leaving, as though he had heard a quiet sound outside, a sound he did not recognise. Anxiously Alexander glanced at his mother. She was asleep still, and her lips were moving silently.

45. Titus Egnatius Tyrannus

Soon after their meeting in the café near Sloane Square, Jane rang the shop to propose that they should try to forget what had been said that afternoon. Alexander promptly agreed, and she said that she would call again before long, as she did, a month later, when they had a conversation that led to other calls, which in turn brought about another meeting, when she came up to London for a weekend course and they went out for a meal in Covent Garden. And when Alexander phoned to thank her for the flowers she had sent his mother, she invited him to stay with herself and Philip in Brighton, an invitation she repeated each time they spoke, and which Alexander finally accepted not long after the October storm, as he would recall, because he would remember the team of tractors pulling trees across a field that was strewn with branches, somewhere near Hayward's Heath.

She opened the door and said nothing for a few seconds, as if to denote by this pause, and by the way she stood aside to allow him into the house, that a new episode of their lives was now commencing. Flooring of polished pale wood extended into every downstairs room, through doorways in which there were no doors. Jane took him into the kitchen, where a bottle of wine and three tall glasses were laid out in a triangle on a bare steel surface that was the size of a single bed. Music was playing in the front room, a piece of piano music he had heard once or twice but could not name. Philip was finishing off some work upstairs, Jane told him, and she took the bottle and glasses through, and set them on a dining table that was a rectangle of thick oak, supported by six square legs as broad as a hand-span. She lowered the volume of the music, turning one of the pair of dials on the amplifier's bald steel fascia, and sat down at one end of the enormous white settee. Alexander sat at the other end, facing the steel-framed fireplace, in which was placed a tall square vase that held a bouquet of stripped pale twigs on a bed of grey pebbles. Above the fireplace hung a monochrome photograph of a single plump tulip. 'Luscious, isn't it?' said Jane, rubbing a wetted finger on the cuff of her raw linen shirt as she admired the tulip. Alexander stood up to examine the flower in the picture, which glistened like an olive dipped in oil. 'What do you think?' she asked, smiling at the whole room, and Alexander looked around, recalling the cushions and trinkets and perfumed fabrics of her flat. It was very nice, very luxurious, very tasteful, he told her, and Philip, who had soundlessly descended the stairs, thanked him for his kind comments.

'Please excuse the lack of civility,' said Philip, offering his hand and looking at Alexander as if he had heard his guest described as an invalid and was mildly puzzled to find him robust. Perhaps a year or two younger than Jane, he had frayed-looking sandy hair that appeared to be carefully unkempt, and the gait and posture of a man who had once been a proficient sportsman and was still quite fit, though his shirt was tight above the waist and his eyes were slightly bloodshot. 'You have no drink in your hand. Why is this?' he asked Jane, who explained that she was letting the wine breathe, a notion he dismissed as nonsense, and he kissed her on the forehead on his way to the table. Passing a glass to Alexander, he asked him about his journey. Philip turned the stem of his glass between his fingers while he listened, apparently still thinking of his work. 'I'd better get the meal under way,' he said, as soon as there was a pause, and he went off to the kitchen, taking a drink with him.

Over dinner the talk was mostly of Jane's clinic and then of the language school where Philip worked, until he mentioned a Belgian boy who, he had discovered that week, had been earning good money as a DJ in Ostend since he was fifteen, and Jane told him that Alexander had been the singer in a group that her brother had seen. 'What year was that?' Philip asked. 'I might have come across you,' he said, after Alexander had worked out when The Park Rangers had formed and when they had disbanded. 'I was at King's then. Used to go to gigs all the time.'

'It's not very likely you saw us,' said Alexander. 'We were as obscure as they come.'

'You don't know. I saw some fantastically obscure acts. Some of them so obscure they hadn't even heard of themselves. I could easily have seen you,' he said, as if he believed Alexander would be flattered if it turned out that he had seen him sing.

'Honestly, there's not a chance. We never played north of the river. The quest for fame failed at the Blackwall Tunnel.'

'The Park Rangers,' Philip murmured. 'I'm sure I saw an outfit called The Park Rangers,' he persisted emptily.

'We were really bad.'

'No, you weren't,' said Jane.

'Every band was really bad in the places I went to,' said Philip.

'If you saw us you wouldn't have forgotten.'

'Depends how much drink was taken on board,' Philip retorted, pouring some wine for Alexander. 'There's one night at the back of my mind. I've got a vague idea, but –' he fretted, scratching his scalp. He filled his own glass, squinting at the bottle as if to bring a memory into focus. 'Did you ever play around Blackfriars Bridge? The south side of Blackfriars Bridge?' he asked.

'Not as I recall.'

'I definitely saw a band with a name like that, somewhere near there. Where the hell was it?' he asked himself, with an impatience that seemed rhetorical. 'Somewhere in that area, I'm sure. Near the bridge. We went to see a couple of groups. The night before a spoken exam, it was. I couldn't hear a bloody thing the next day. Failed miserably. We came out of the pub, but straight away I had to stop for a leak.'

'Philip,' Jane interjected. 'We don't need the intimate details. I think we've established that you didn't see Alexander's group.'

'Perhaps, but let me work this one out. It'll come to me,' Philip assured her, directing at Alexander a gaze that seemed to stop at the surface of Alexander's eyes. 'I stopped around the corner from the pub. I remember peeing through some railings, and there was a patch of grass that stank of cats, and an old window, a stone window, in a brick wall. High up.' He raised a hand, as if reaching for a mirage of the window.

'A round window?'

'I think so.'

'I think it was as well. I think you were by London Bridge, not Blackfriars, and you answered the call of nature in Clink Street.'

'You do?' replied Philip. 'How so, inspector?'

'There's only one stone window in a brick wall anywhere in that neighbourhood, as far as I know,' said Alexander. 'The window you saw is what's left of the palace of the Bishops of Winchester. It used to stretch for hundreds of feet along the riverbank. Henry VIII met Catherine Howard in the park of the palace, it's said. Eventually it was demolished and the site became tenements and warehouses. When one of the warehouses burned down, the window came out into the open.'

Philip briefly sustained an operatic expression of admiring astonishment. 'Years I lived in London, and I never knew that. How do you know about that?'

'There's a sign by the wall,' said Alexander, but then Jane intervened to tell Philip about Alexander's walks.

Having opened another bottle of wine, Philip gave Jane a conspiratorial grin and left the room to fetch a book from upstairs. Putting his feet on the table, he declaimed: 'St Edmund the King. What's its date then? What's it look like?' Once Alexander had described that church in sufficient detail he shouted the name of another, as Mr Barrington used to throw out the names of battles and treaties and famous men. Flicking backwards and forwards through the book, Philip demanded an account of St Mary-le-Bow, St Lawrence Jewry, St Stephen Walbrook, St Mary Abchurch and many more, and Alexander duly described each façade and interior as he saw it in his mind, matching perfectly the picture on the page every time. When at last he tired of the game, Philip smiled with a bewilderment that now seemed genuine. He flopped a hand towards Jane. 'You know what I'm thinking?' he said.

And so, after much persuasion from Jane, it came about that Alexander and Philip and a dozen of Philip's students convened on the steps of St Paul's, on a Saturday morning in late March.

From the cathedral he took them down Ludgate Hill, along Fleet Street and into its tributary lanes. They continued along the Strand, and followed a circuit of Trafalgar Square. After a diversion through Admiralty Arch, Alexander led the group down Whitehall. At the Cenotaph one of the French boys snapped a bubble of chewing gum when Alexander pointed out the monument. 'Do you understand what this means?' Alexander demanded, but the boy chewed open-mouthed, looking up at the sky. 'It isn't just a lump of stone. It means something important,' Alexander insisted, and he made them see a column of the Cenotaph's dead and missing soldiers, marching in single file down the avenue of Whitehall, a column that would take two weeks to pass. 'Two whole weeks, marching all day and all night. And for the French people, and for the Russians, and for the people of Austria and Hungary, it was worse.' He told them about the silence that used to spread across the country at the eleventh hour of the eleventh day of the eleventh month. Using his father's words, he described a street at the stroke of eleven, and the silence that flowed into it as everyone stopped where they were standing and all traffic came to a halt, and for two minutes the city was as quiet as the sea.

'And now it's time to forget,' said the boy, but a girl with an ultramarine streak in her hair and a red tartan skirt called the boy an imbecile, and after the tour, when they were having a drink in a pub by St James's Park, she sat beside Alexander immediately and asked him so many questions about the places they had seen that he was still talking to her when Philip announced that it was time to get back to Brighton.

The following month Philip brought a second group up to London, and Monique came along again, to hear about the Inns of Court and Covent Garden and Soho, and it was Monique's enthusiasm, rather than her classmate's indifference, that Alexander talked about when he came to tell Sam and Liz what he had been doing.

'A good way to meet women,' Sam remarked, reverting to a theme he introduced every time Alexander visited them.

'She's a girl, Sam. A French girl. Now at home, with her French boyfriend, I should imagine.'

'Yes, but it's a good way to meet women, that line of work. With you in a position of authority and all. Women like that. Good looks and authority. Winning combination.'

'And you enjoyed it,' said Liz.

'Certainly.'

'A fact entirely unconnected to the attractiveness of Monique?' Sam enquired.

'Almost entirely.'

'I think it sounds interesting,' said Liz. 'I wish I'd come along. Learn a lot, I'm sure.'

'Could be a good sideline,' said Sam. 'Lot of demand, I'd say. Put an ad in the mags, I bet you'd get some takers.'

'You would,' said Liz. 'Get you out of that damned shop as well.'

He would take another of Philip's classes if he were asked, Alexander had decided, but Sam, without telling him, rang some of the hoteliers he knew through work and dictated a notice to them, which they brought to the attention of their guests. Then one evening he phoned Alexander to tell him that he knew of this family from Carlisle who were staying at a bed and breakfast in Gower Street with a couple of friends, and would pay a few quid for a personal tour, because they only had half a day to see it and didn't want to faff around with guidebooks because guidebooks were all the same and you spent all your time staring at the page instead of looking. 'I told them you knew your stuff, Mac,' Sam wheedled. 'They'll be disappointed if you're not available. Give it a go. You'll be great. You owe it to London.'

The first of the tour groups that Alexander would lead, sporadically, over the course of the next three years or more, gathered on a Saturday afternoon in July, in Paternoster Square. He welcomed Mr Sidaway and his wife Anne, and their daughter Julie, and their companions the Middletons, and preceded them into St Paul's. From the dome's upper gallery he identified the prominent buildings and traced the route they would be taking. In Watling Street he showed them where the Tower Royal had once stood, and introduced the subject of the Great Fire, in which the tower had been destroyed. In Queen Victoria Street, by the paltry remnants of the temple of Mithras, he evoked the dank green-walled room beneath the church of San Clemente in Rome, a city he had never seen, and described the carving of the slaughtered bull on its altar, flexing his arm to hold the animal's jaw as Mithras held it. They passed St Stephen Walbrook on their way to the Mansion House, where he conjured the avenue and canal that would have connected it to a piazza around St Paul's, had the city been rebuilt after the war as one team of architects had planned it. He summarised the history of the Mansion House and the Grocers' Hall and the Bank of England, where, he would remember telling them, plundered Spanish coins were put into circulation with the head of George III superimposed on the neck of the Spanish king.

'And that over there?' asked Mrs Sidaway.

'That's St Mary Woolnoth, designed by Nicholas Hawksmoor after the Great Fire. The first church to be built there was raised by the Saxons, on top of a Roman temple dedicated to Concord; Bank station was hollowed out below it, in the last three years of the nineteenth century. The interior is especially beautiful, but you will probably have to take my word for that, because I've never known it to be open on a Saturday. T. S. Eliot in one of his poems refers to the dead sound the clock makes when it strikes nine, but I'm taking his word for that, because I've never heard it.'

He looked towards the steps of Bank station, and he saw a flash that was the flash of Megan's hair, but the shock of it passed away in an instant, and what remained was a memory of contentment, a memory that was wholly pleasing. 'Over there is Princes Street,' he went on, 'where a strange object known as the London Curse was found in 1929. It's a piece of lead, inscribed in Latin: "Titus Egnatius Tyrannus is cursed".' Then he added, as if as an afterthought, '"and Publius Cicereius Felix is cursed"', and Julie laughed.

46. Roderick

Whenever they stopped, the fat man bustled to the front of the group, as if he had heard rumour of an accident and wanted to be sure of a good view of it. He wore a tight grey duffle coat and a grey woollen hat with a pompom on the top, and around his neck was wound, three times, a vermilion hand-knitted scarf. A newspaper protruded from one pocket of his coat and a notebook from the other, and in his right hand he carried a thick walking stick, with which he would occasionally knock the bandaging that bulged above the shoe of his right foot. He blinked twitchily while he listened, as though his eyes were being stung by smoke. It was at St Clement Danes that he began to take issue with his guide.

'Nobody is altogether sure,' said Alexander, 'how this church came by its name.' The noise of a pantechnicon obliged him to pause. The fat man grimaced with irritation, and his neck extended like a tortoise's from the coils of the scarf. 'It is said, however, that a Danish king by the name of Harold Harefoot was buried here, along with several of his compatriots. The original church appeared to survive the Great Fire, but not long after it was declared to be unsafe, and so was demolished. This replacement was mostly the work of Christopher Wren.'

'You'll find,' the fat man interrupted, 'that there's another explanation for the name.' Wincing, he gave his bandage a sharp tap. 'There used to be a church here for Danes with English wives. That was after Alfred had chased the Danes out. If you'd married an Englishwoman you could stay.'

'Is that so?' asked Alexander. 'I didn't know that.'

'I believe it is so. I'm not saying that your version isn't right. But there is another story.'

'I'm grateful to you, Mr –?'

'Roderick. Roderick Walton. Please, go on,' said the fat man, drawing a curlicue in the air with his stick.

'The steeple,' Alexander continued, stepping back to regard it, 'was raised in 1719, to a design by James Gibbs, who is best known as the architect of St-Martin-in-the-Fields, which we will be seeing shortly, after we've visited another Gibbs building.'

'St Mary,' said Roderick.

'Exactly. St Mary-le-Strand,' Alexander affirmed.

'St Mary what?' asked someone else.

'Le-Strand.'

'What's that about?' demanded a third member of the party. 'What's with the "le"?'

'You get English names like that. It's not all that uncommon. From the time of the Normans.'

'For instance?'

'Ashby-de-la-Zouche. Poulton-le-Fylde,' Alexander added. 'Anyway, we're getting ahead of ourselves. To return to St Clement, the church as you see it today is a reconstruction, because Wren's building was gutted by fire in the Blitz. It reopened in 1958 and was dedicated to the RAF and Allied air forces, who funded the restoration of the church. As we'll be seeing, the badges of some 750 squadrons and units are set into the floor.'

'Is anyone famous buried here, Mr MacIndoe?' enquired an American woman in a pristine belted trenchcoat.

'It's a rare characteristic of St Clement that there are no individual tombs inside the church.'

Roderick took one step forward and bounced his walking stick on its rubber ferrule, like a variety artiste finishing his act with a bit of panache. 'I think you'll find that Thomas Otway, the formerly famous playwright, was buried here.'

'What did he write?' asked the American woman.

'I couldn't tell you, madam, I am ashamed to say. But I think I would be right in saying that Bishop Berkeley is buried here too.'

'Who he?' asked the woman's husband, bemused by the way the tour was proceeding.

'A philosopher. Denied the existence of matter, as I understand it. The world is nothing but a collection of ideas that exist by the will of God, or something to that effect.'

'Oh,' said the woman.

'I may have misunderstood,' admitted Roderick.

'The graveyard,' Alexander intervened, 'was over there, where King's College now stands.'

'Samuel Johnson's not here?' asked the husband.

'No, I'm afraid not.'

'So what's the statue about?'

'It's here because Dr Johnson used to worship here, but he's not buried here.' Observing that Roderick was creeping towards the door, Alexander raised a hand. 'As I was saying, St Clement is today an air force memorial, yet one civilian is commemorated inside.' He looked at Roderick, whose blinking now became even more rapid. 'Sir Archibald Hector McIndoe, third President of the British Association of Plastic Surgeons, Vice-Chairman of the Royal College of Surgeons from 1957 to 1959, died 12th of April 1960. His skill in the treatment of burns earned the gratitude of the hundreds of airmen on whom he operated. Which is why there's a memorial to him here.'

'A relation of yours, Mr MacIndoe?' a woman with a satin headscarf slyly asked.

'Not as far as I'm aware. Sir Archibald McIndoe was a New Zealander by birth. Whereas I am a semi-Scottish Englishman.' Alexander stood aside to wave the group into the church. 'You'll find his name on the back of a chair, at the end of the right aisle. That's his memorial. On the same side there's a list of the rectors of St Clement. Look for the year 1843 and you'll come across the name of William Webb-Ellis, who is said to have picked up the ball and run with it during a soccer game at Rugby school, thereby creating the game that bears the school's name.' With Roderick beside him, Alexander followed the rest of the group through the outer doorway. 'And one last curiosity: on certain days the bells of this church play the tune of "Oranges and Lemons", as in the nursery rhyme: "Oranges and Lemons, say the bells of St Clement's."'

'Though this isn't the same St Clement's,' Roderick intervened.

'As I was about to say,' said Alexander.

'That's St Clement Eastcheap.'

'Quite. Where fruit from the Mediterranean was unloaded. Thus the rhyme.'

'Quite,' said Roderick, and he winked at Alexander as he took out

377

his notebook, as though the two of them had concluded a routine they had devised for the amusement of the others.

At St Mary-le-Strand it was not until Alexander had finished his introduction that Roderick spoke. 'You know about the column?' he asked. The woman with the headscarf looked disapprovingly at Roderick; an effort to suppress his disillusionment with Alexander was evident in the expression of the husband of the woman in the trenchcoat.

'I do not know about the column,' Alexander replied flatly.

'There was meant to be a huge great column here,' said Roderick, whisking his stick in the air as if to conjure the structure into being. 'With Queen Anne on the top. But she died, so they got a spire instead.'

Alexander was permitted to complete his speech about Somerset House without interruption. 'This is where the great architect Inigo Jones died, in 1652, and six years later Cromwell lay in state here, to the fury of many Londoners, who pelted the gate with rubbish that night,' he closed.

'First house in England to have parquet flooring,' appended Roderick, and he nodded at Alexander to indicate that he had finished his contribution. He remained quiet all the way down the Strand, except when they passed number 101, which he pointed out as the location of Ackermann's, the first London shop to be fully lit by gas, and at the Strand Palace Hotel, where, Roderick informed his companions, Edward Cross had displayed his celebrated menagerie, featuring a hippopotamus that had made a strong impression on Byron, who remarked on the creature's striking resemblance to the prime minister. By Charing Cross station he took out his notebook to paraphrase, it seemed, Alexander's aside on the subject of Coutts Bank, which Roderick trumped with an account of James Graham's Temple of Health, 'where clients could, on payment of a considerable fee, avail themselves of the "celestial bed", an item of furniture on which they were guaranteed, so Mr Graham claimed, to conceive a child without imperfection.' He gave a short, high-pitched, incredulous laugh, to which nobody responded.

The tour ended at the foot of Cleopatra's Needle. 'A peculiar assortment of objects was buried in the foundations of the obelisk,' Alexander told them, raising his voice against the traffic and the train that was crossing Hungerford Bridge. 'Newspapers, coins and a razor were placed in the foundations, as well as four Bibles and a guide to the railway services of Britain.' He paused to allow Roderick his intervention, but none was made. 'Also interred, in honour of the Egyptian queen whose beauty had conquered both Caesar and Antony, were photographs of a dozen Englishwomen who were held to be the loveliest in the country.'

Roderick made an addition to his book, holding it so close to his face that there was barely room for his pen between the page and his chin.

'And on that note,' Alexander concluded, as he always did, 'I must take my leave of you. Thank you for your company and your interest. I hope that you found the last two hours both instructive and pleasurable, and that those of you who are here on holiday continue to enjoy your stay in London. Should anyone wish to ask me any further questions, I'll gladly answer them as best I can.'

The group dispersed, having asked nothing more. Alexander watched one couple cross the road to the Underground station; the American woman and her husband and three others walked on towards Waterloo Bridge. The lightbulbs slung on poles along the riverbank were coming on; the river was the colour of roofing slates, and seemed motionless. Alexander looked for the moon, and noticed that Roderick, who had strolled off on his own in the Westminster direction, was coming back towards him.

With a gyration of his upraised stick Roderick hailed him. 'I wouldn't want you to think I lacked manners, Mr MacIndoe,' he shouted, and he removed his hat, uncovering a mat of margarine-coloured hair. 'Wanted to be sure that they'd gone. I fear I wasn't a hit with your clients, but dullards bring out the worst in me. My sincere apologies if I was ranklesome. Thank you,' he said, and he offered Alexander a perfectly white hand of fat, long and immaculately manicured fingers.

'Not at all,' Alexander replied.

Roderick replaced his hat as if to signify his satisfaction with the accord they had achieved.

'Pardon my asking,' Alexander resumed, seeing that Roderick did not intend to leave immediately, 'but why did you sign up for my tour?'

'Same as everyone else,' said Roderick, smiling benignly. 'Thought I might learn something.' He planted his stick in the angle of the pavement and the wall and leaned on it, in anticipation of another pleasing question.

'But you know more than I do, evidently.'

'I didn't know that beforehand, did I?'

'No, but you must have had a good idea.'

'And I did learn something. That you can't have a beard if you work at Coutts. Didn't know that.'

'Not much of a yield for two hours.'

'Better than most. Are you going that way?' Roderick enquired, pointing his stick at Northumberland Avenue, and Alexander, having no plan other than to return home, said that he was. 'So am I,' said Roderick. 'Do you mind if I walk with you?'

'No, of course,' Alexander replied. Lightly he took hold of Roderick's arm to steer him away from a mash of food in the gutter.

'I go on all of them, and I usually learn something. The thing about the Epstein figures, though. That wasn't quite right,' Roderick told him, like a friendly critic passing comment on an actor's performance. 'I read a letter in *The Times*, about ten years back. It wasn't because they were offended that they cut the willies off. It was because water and frost was collecting in the crevices, so the bits that stuck out were eroding away. Someone nearly got brained by a falling member. They had to be lopped off before they all fell off,' he stated seriously, and then, having glanced at Alexander as though to gauge whether a laugh were permissible, he chuckled into his scarf. 'You can use that next time,' he added.

'Thank you,' said Alexander.

Twenty yards on, Roderick put a hand on Alexander's sleeve to slow him down. 'May I offer you a piece of advice, Mr MacIndoe?' he enquired, and the tone of his question made Alexander look at the smooth white-skinned face and wonder what age Roderick was. He could have been thirty, or less, or forty, or older.

'Please.'

'You're not making the most of your resources, in my opinion. Your tour could be made a lot better.'

'Always room for improvement,' Alexander concurred. 'What might these resources be?'

'Oh come on, Mr MacIndoe,' Roderick chided. 'The voice is good, the delivery is good. Vivid, with an elegiac nuance. And of course you have a presence, an attractive manner. You're a very personable person.'

'Kind of you to say so.'

'But at the moment the medium is stronger than the message, if I can put it like that. With better material you could make quite an impact.'

'Mr Walton, I'm just a tour guide, that's all. I don't want to make quite an impact.'

'People are predisposed to like you, Mr MacIndoe. I saw that at once. They warm to you. There's a sort of rapport, immediately. You should make the most of that. Give them more human interest. Give them some stories.'

'I thought I did give them some stories.'

'Bits and pieces, Mr MacIndoe. Bits and pieces to fatten up the facts.'

'But the facts are what you like, no?'

'Yes, but I'm a special case. I'm an archivist,' said Roderick, as though confessing to a vice. 'Facts are meat and drink to me, but you need to lighten the diet for the general public. At the moment what you're giving them is a lecture, more or less. You should make it more intimate. Like you're taking them into your confidence. Give them stories. Funny stories, strange stories. Creepy stories.'

'Creepy?'

'Nothing succeeds like creepy. You'd be perfect at it. More than a passing resemblance to Christopher Lee, as I'm sure you've been told.'

'And I get these stories from where?'

'Well, you could go to libraries. Do some real research. Or –'

'Yes?' prompted Alexander, and now Roderick positioned himself in his path to stop him.

'Or from me.' He waved an arm like an impresario boasting of the magnificence of his theatre. 'I know a tale for every street of this city. Where we were a minute ago, for example. I can tell you a good one. You have a minute?' Roderick put a hand on Alexander's back and turned him so that they both faced the river. 'During the war, this was, soon after the new Waterloo Bridge had gone up. A policeman on the beat, crossing from the south side. Thick fog, naturally. A real pea-souper. He hears footsteps, running, then out of the fog comes this girl, very upset. He asks her what's up. "There's a girl down on the Embankment," she tells him. "Going to throw herself in." She grabs his arm, distraught. "Hurry. Please hurry." The constable follows her, down the steps, along the road. He sees this shadow in the fog, right by Cleopatra's Needle. He runs ahead, gets there in the nick of time. He pulls the girl off the wall. She falls into his arms. Her face is the face of the girl he followed from the bridge. He looks around. There's no one else there. Good, don't you think?'

'You believe stories like that?' asked Alexander.

'Good God, no. Would you?'

'No.'

'But that doesn't matter. Think of it as a folk tale. The soul of the city in wartime, that's what it's about. Despair and salvation, something like that. It's a good one, isn't it?'

'You made it up?'

'Certainly not,' Roderick denied blusteringly, in simulated indignation. He turned back to face Trafalgar Square, and tugged Alexander into motion again. 'Now, imagine what the story could be like if you told it. Nice voice, lugubrious face, but not too lugubrious. Dress you in black, that kind of image. Do the tours at night, goes without saying. What do you think?' Roderick asked him jauntily. 'You see what I'm proposing?'

'I'm not sure I do.'

'Yes you do,' Roderick encouraged. 'A sort of joint enterprise. I have hundreds and hundreds of stories up here,' he said, patting his forehead. 'Waterloo Bridge, for instance. I know dozens of stories about Waterloo Bridge alone. Do you know about the unfortunate death of the celebrated American diver, Mr Samuel Scott? Accidentally strangled himself on the old bridge, in front of a crowd of hundreds. Do you know that one?'

'A name unknown to me.'

'There you are. All these stories, and no audience. But with you –'

'So what's the plan? You write the script, and I deliver the lines?'

'Exactly,' replied Roderick, as if commending Alexander for an elegant formulation of a complex proposition. 'What do you think?'

'It's something to think about,' said Alexander.

'I love to ferret around in libraries, Mr MacIndoe. And I love to write. To compose little stories, vignettes, anecdotes. At home I have notebooks, dozens of them, full of scribblings, and it would be extremely rewarding for me to have a means of sharing my hoard. To have my notebooks brought to life, as it were. This arrangement would be mutually beneficial.'

Alexander looked towards Waterloo Bridge and considered what Roderick had proposed. 'I don't see why you need me, Mr Walton. Why not just do what I do?'

'Because, Mr MacIndoe, I am conscious, acutely conscious, that my physical aspect is not the most prepossessing, and that, furthermore, I have a manner that many find unattractive. I have tried to suppress my propensity for bumptiousness, but I am unable to do so. I am unable to diet and I am unable to ingratiate. I wish this were not so, because – may I be honest with you, Mr MacIndoe?' asked Roderick, straightening his back as if for inspection.

'Of course.'

'I thought so. You have a face that invites honesty. The fact is, I have few friends, Mr MacIndoe. Very few indeed. There. Vanity and a lack of company. My motives.'

'I don't know what to say.'

'Remuneration wouldn't be an issue. A small percentage of the revenue, say, or something along those lines. A nominal fee. Or no fee at all. Perhaps I could come along, make changes, improvements.'

'I'll need some time to think it over.'

'Of course. There's no hurry at all. Now, you mustn't think me rude but I must run. I have a film to attend. Italian horror film, title escapes me,' he gabbled. 'Very strong, I'm told.' Resting his foot on the frame of a shop window, he scribbled on a page and tore it out. 'They know no moderation, the Italians. Mediterranean gore not your sort of thing, I suppose?'

'Not really.'

'Never mind,' said Roderick quickly. 'This is my phone number.' He handed the page to Alexander and presented his notebook like an autograph album. 'If you'd be so good as to write your address, and I could send you a few pieces. No obligation. If I don't hear from you,

383

that's the end of it,' he promised, striking his stick on a strip of brass cladding, as though to ratify his oath. Backing away, he plucked the cap from his head again, as Alexander would remember, and his hair stuck up like comic horns.

47. The firemen's band

Something had happened at the end of the road and a queue of cars was forming. The small window above the central window of the bay was open, and a breeze made the net curtain sway, bringing exhaust fumes into the room, and the sound of laurel leaves in tremulous motion. A car horn blared two discordant notes at once. Someone swore. A bass beat became audible in the noise of the engines, and grew so loud that it made Alexander think of the din of the ack-ack guns on the Heath. A door was slammed.

Alexander's mother set her knife and fork on the rim of her plate, sighed, formed her fingers into a bridge, and turned her head to regard the traffic. Her eyelids sank, as though she were looking at the aftermath of a tiresome prank. 'This used to be a quiet street,' she remarked.

'It still is,' he replied. 'Relatively.'

'It's terrible,' said his mother.

'No, Mother. This isn't bad. It's quiet, normally.'

'Too many cars. Everybody owns a car nowadays.'

'Including me.'

'And nobody has any consideration for others. Listen to that.'

'It's bad,' Alexander agreed.

'He must be deaf,' said his mother. The top of a head appeared above the hedge of the neighbour's front garden, then a second head, and an exchange of shouts erupted. 'These people,' she murmured.

'We shouldn't have put the table here,' said Alexander.

'You'd still hear it,' said his mother.

'Yes, but,' Alexander began, but he did not continue.

'Have you done?' his mother asked, when the queue of cars had gone. Since the interruption she had not touched her meal.

'I'll take them through,' said Alexander.

'No, I'll do it.'

'Let me,' he insisted, and she released her plate. 'Shall I make you some tea?'

She pulled the curtain aside to look up and down the street, then let it fall back. She shook her head. 'Thank you,' she said. 'That would be nice.'

Alexander stacked the plates, taking care not to clash them, and carried them to the kitchen, past the door of the dining room, in which they no longer ate. He washed the dishes and pots, and filled the kettle, and went up to the bathroom, past the smallest bedroom, which now was empty. At the end of the landing the door was closed on the room that still contained his father's desk and books and journals. Half of his mother's house was dead, he told himself.

She was still at the table when he returned. With a flat hand she primped the crown of her hair as he put the tray down. 'Tea is served, madam,' he said. She looked at him keenly, as if she suspected his thoughts. 'Mother, have you considered selling this place?' he asked her.

'Why ever should I do that?'

'I'm not saying you should. But have you ever thought about it?'

'You're saying you think I should,' she said, and she turned her cup a few degrees.

'This house is so big, for one person.'

'For a little old lady,' she amended.

'For anyone.'

'I can cope, Alexander. I'm not senile.'

'But to maintain this place. It's difficult.'

'I'm comfortable. The bills get paid. Your father took care of me. A thrifty man, your father.'

'It's not the money I meant,' said Alexander.

'We could have moved to a bigger house, but he put security before everything. So we wouldn't want for anything after he'd gone. We were looked after. Both of us.'

'I know, Mother. I appreciate that.'

'This is our home,' she said.

'Yes, but living on your own. You don't need all this room.'

'I'll be the judge of what I need, thank you.' She pushed her cup towards him for it to be filled. 'Don't you worry about me,' she said, with emphasis on the final word.

At least once a week Alexander visited his mother. Month by month

386

the skin of dust thickened on his father's desk. The lettering on the spines of his father's books were erased by the action of the sunlight. In the smallest bedroom there was a smell of damp wool, and he would find catkins of hair and lint in the corners of the rooms in which his mother lived. She had a fall in the kitchen and for two months had to use a stick and had a thick strapping on her foot and shin. Still she refused to talk about leaving the house. Having seen her pause for breath on the stairs, or crouch painfully to reach the bolt on the back door, he would try again to persuade her. 'Don't make a fuss, Alexander,' she would say, or 'I don't need a nursemaid,' or 'Leave it be,' and then they would sit in the armchairs, on opposite sides of the fireplace, and read in silence.

Then, in December, Sam Saunders' son moved into a flat three streets away, and one evening Alexander suggested to his mother that he might bring Sam with him some time, and a couple of weeks later he did.

In the living room Sam and Alexander waited for his mother to come downstairs. 'Ready for judgement,' said Sam, buttoning the jacket of his best suit. He stood in the centre of the room, where Alexander had stood to be inspected when the two of them had come home together on leave.

Alexander's mother opened the door, and an expression of guarded curiosity arose in her eyes, giving her face a new vivaciousness. 'Hello, dear,' she said, affecting not to know that Sam was in her house solely in order to meet her.

'Mrs MacIndoe,' said Sam, bowing from the waist. 'You are looking splendid.'

'I am not, Sam. I am looking old. But thank you for lying. It's been a long time, hasn't it?'

'Best part of thirty years, Mrs MacIndoe.'

'Thirty years,' she wearily exhaled. She looked at him intently, as if in an effort to recall what she had thought of him thirty years ago. From a puckering beside her eyes it appeared that she had retrieved some memory that pleased her. Sam held out his hand. She took it, and Sam brought his other hand forward to enclose hers. 'You're not as plump as I remember,' she said.

'Very kind of you, Mrs MacIndoe,' Sam replied. 'I make an effort.'

'But every bit as charming.'

'Thank you.'

'It's a pity you didn't make a good impression on my husband.'

'Did I not?'

'You did not,' she chastised him. 'But it doesn't matter now.'

'I'm sorry,' said Sam.

'You're an insurance man?' asked Alexander's mother. She sat down in her chair, ushering Sam to the settee with a waft of her hand.

'An insurance man is what I am.'

'And your wife, she was Alexander's girlfriend for a while, wasn't she?'

'He stole her off me,' Alexander interjected.

'Not quite, Mrs MacIndoe,' said Sam.

'He did,' Alexander told his mother.

'Did you?' she asked Sam, apparently amused by the notion.

'No,' Sam stated ingenuously, with a hand on his chest.

'I have forgiven him,' Alexander countered. 'Shall I put the kettle on, as a sign of our accord?'

'Excellent idea,' said Sam.

'But he did steal her,' Alexander reiterated, going out to the kitchen.

When he came back his mother was sitting next to Sam, holding one side of the photograph he was showing her. 'Pretty girl,' she commented. 'She's pretty, isn't she, Alexander?' She raised the photograph of Robert's girlfriend towards him. 'Where is she from?' she asked Sam.

'London. Herne Hill.'

'But originally, where does her family come from?'

'From Grenada,' said Sam. Nodding to herself as she made connections in her mind, Alexander's mother pondered the photograph of Robert and Valerie. 'You ever been to the Caribbean, Mrs MacIndoe?' Sam asked her.

'People of my generation didn't do that sort of thing, dear,' she informed him. 'We never went abroad much.'

'You went to Malta,' Alexander reminded her.

'Yes,' she admitted. 'That was quite nice. And Madeira we went to. But it was a bit too hot for my husband, and we didn't realise there weren't any beaches till we got there. Swimming pools simply aren't the same thing at all.'

'Happy to leave the sea to the fishes, myself,' said Sam.

'Oh no,' she contradicted. 'A man for the sea and the hills was my husband.'

'But no banks on Ben Nevis.'

'And no lochs in London,' she responded, echoing Sam's regretful cadence. From the mantelpiece she took the photograph of herself and Alexander's father when they were young. 'Our honeymoon,' she explained. 'A weekend in Dorset.'

'Matching gaberdines,' Sam commented. 'Very beautiful. Very handsome,' observed Sam.

'I'm only twenty-one there,' she told him. 'In those days you looked thirty as soon as you left home.'

'So where did you meet, Mrs MacIndoe?' Sam asked abruptly, and to Alexander's surprise his mother received the question as though she had been asked about something impersonal, such as where she had bought her carpets.

'Here,' she said immediately. 'In London.'

'How did you meet him?' Sam went on.

'I threw myself at his feet,' she said plainly, and took a sip of her tea, as if to add its taste to the pleasure of the recollection.

'You did?' asked Alexander.

'Indeed,' she replied, with a laugh. 'I was shopping with my mother,' she explained to Sam, 'and I tripped on a paving stone, right outside Graham's bank, at the very moment he was coming out. I hurt my hand, and he took us inside so I could wash the cut. He went to the chemist's to get some lint and bandage for me. I remember the way he looked at my mother before he put the bandage on. Asking her permission to touch my hand, you see.'

'So that was it?' asked Sam. 'Love at first sight?'

'For my mother it was. She fell for him straight away. I thought he was a bit too smooth. Or I thought I did, but then I bumped into him again, outside the bank. He asked me how the hand was, wanted to know where I was going. For a moment I couldn't remember, and then I realised I was smitten.'

'What did you do?' asked Alexander.

'I told a fib. I said I was going to Seward's, the haberdasher's. And Graham asked if he could walk with me. So walked together, but I wasn't listening to anything he said because I was worrying what I'd do when I got to the shop. I bought a piece of blue satin ribbon. I took it out of my pocket that night, thinking it was funny that this was my first love token and I'd had to buy it for myself.'

'I've never heard this story,' Alexander said to Sam

'Flowers every Saturday he sent me, for a month,' she went on. 'Then he took me to the theatre, and in the interval he asked me to marry him. Always straight to the point with Graham. And his shoes were always so nicely polished. Like ink bottles, the toe caps were. A man who looks after his shoes will look after you, my mother said, and she was right.'

Alexander tried to imagine Nan Burnett uttering her motto about men's shoes. 'I've never heard any of this,' he said to his mother.

'Oh, I'm sure you have,' she said.

Several times in the course of the following year Sam came to the house with Alexander, and whenever they called she would tell them stories that he had never heard. She told them about her husband climbing a drainpipe in the blackout, to daub black paint on the window of a room in which a light had been left burning, and about her mother taking the mirror from her room when she was eight, to stop her becoming vain, and about her dancing on the pier in Brighton with a flighty girl called Joanie Holroyd, whom Alexander did not recognise as Mrs Beckwith until the story was nearly finished. They heard about the day that Alexander went missing and a policeman found him in a neighbour's coal shed, wrapped in his mother's housecoat, and the time he drew circles of castor oil on the front path, where the postman nearly broke his neck, and about the woman who kept chickens in her garden and sometimes gave Alexander a fresh egg, which he would carry back home and not surrender until the warmth had gone from it. Her hands became the child's sealed hands and her face assumed the child's determination, and as he looked at her hands Alexander wondered whether it was her intention to embarrass him, and why the stories she told about him were always from the years of his early childhood, and then it occurred to him that the boy she described was closer to her than he was now.

'Like this,' she said, and she frowned and her hands shook with tension, as if resisting an attempt to prise them apart.

'Greenwich chickens,' said Sam, shaking his head at the strangeness of it.

'It wasn't that unusual,' said Alexander's mother. 'Very handy when food was scarce.'

'I bet,' said Sam.

'I remember the rabbits,' said Alexander.

'That was a different house,' said his mother. 'The Dennises, you're thinking of. At number fifteen. They had the rabbits.'

'Really?'

'Definitely. The family that went to Canada right after the war. They threw open the hutches the day before they left. Rabbits all over the place.'

'And they were at number fifteen?'

'They were.'

'Let's have a look. Point it out to me.'

They went into the garden and stood on the platform of concrete, with the curtains of the dining room closed behind them. The sun was setting and rain would soon fall. The leaves of the neighbour's bamboo shivered.

'With the greenhouse,' his mother said, pointing to the fourth house from hers. 'That was the Dennises.'

'And the chicken woman?'

'She was where that greenhouse is,' she said to Sam. 'Next door was the carrot king. Grew the biggest carrots you ever saw in your life. Like torpedoes.'

'Dig for Victory,' quoted Sam.

'Ate them all by himself, mind you. Never shared a thing. A miserable man, he was. Name's gone clean out of my mind.'

'Mr Marley?' Alexander suggested. 'Mr Morley? Marley?'

'Marples, I think,' said his mother. 'And see there,' she said to Sam. 'The tree on the tilt? There's an air-raid shelter under that garden. The family that was in that house had a peculiar young man as a lodger. Every time the Luftwaffe came over he'd stand in the garden and shout at the planes. Encouraging them. "Come on, lads!" he'd yell, and then he'd jump into the shelter, just in case his lads were on target. Graham met him in the street once and punched his nose for him. Little Lord Haw-Haw my husband called him. Then he got killed by a bomb. He was in Woolworth's when the V2 hit it. They hardly found enough to bury.'

For a few seconds they stood on the rectangle of concrete, like actors who had forgotten whose turn it was to speak. A gust banged the kitchen door shut. Sam started at the noise, and muttered 'Bloody hell', holding his chest. 'Pardon the language,' he said, but Alexander's mother said nothing.

Alexander saw her look at the door, and then scan the wall, noting the cracked strips of mortar and the splitting paint of the windowframes. The linings of the dining room curtains were the colour of dishwater, and there were whorls of dirt on the glass. A look of submission came into her eyes for an instant. 'Come on,' she said, rubbing her arms.

And when they were sitting at the table that evening, as Alexander would remember, Sam told them about the work his son had begun on the bathroom of his flat, and Alexander's mother was scandalised by the expense of it.

'We used to wash in a cup of cold water,' remarked Alexander.

'It's easy to laugh now,' his mother said, and within a minute she was talking about the enamelled tub she would put in front of the fire for Alexander's bath on a Sunday evening, and how she would wrap him in a big blue towel that had a white thistle on it, which he used to hold in his fist as she dried him. One evening a brass band of firemen went up their street at bathtime, and she held Alexander up to the window, wrapped in his towel as tightly as a lamb in its fleece. He watched the trumpeters tramp past until the last one had gone, and when he couldn't hear the trumpets any more he cried his eyes out. 'He was inconsolable,' she said, looking out of the window as if the parade were passing by, and in that moment Alexander understood that when she told these stories she was preparing herself for the day when she would leave the house, and that every story told was like an object packed for her departure, or put aside to be left behind.

'But I was happy here,' he said to her. 'I had a happy childhood. Couldn't have been better.'

'We were all happy here, very happy, for quite a time,' she said, and she put one hand on Alexander's arm and one on Sam's.

'Now, now, Irene,' said Sam. 'No moping,' he scolded, touching her hand as though it were as fragile as a canary's head.

She looked at the street like someone proudly facing exile. 'I'm all right,' she said. 'I'll be all right. Alexander will miss this house more than I will. He gets too attached to things,' she said.

48. Goodnight Ralph

It's the wrong verb, Roderick was fond of saying. One might watch TV but one does not watch a film. You do not watch a book and you do not watch a film. Therefore the best time to go to the cinema is the afternoon, he would say, when one is alert and the environment is more conducive to close attention. And so it was usually a Saturday afternoon when Alexander and Roderick went to the cinema together, and it was on a Saturday afternoon in September, as Alexander would remember, that they walked along Orange Street on their way to see Herzog's *Nosferatu*, a film for which Roderick avowed a morbid liking, on account, he said, of the ghostly ship that glides into the harbour, with the dead helmsman lashed to the wheel.

'You know Isaac Newton's house used to be there?' Roderick asked, with a flick of his hand in the direction of the Westminster Reference Library. As was expected of him, Alexander confirmed that he did indeed remember this fact. 'And you know about the plan to encase the house in a monument?' Roderick continued.

'George Scharf's pyramid and globe, 1834,' Alexander responded.

'I'll take your word for the date,' said Roderick. He stopped, and his neck stretched out from his scarf as he smiled slyly at Alexander. 'But do you know of Etienne-Louis Boullée's memorial to Newton, the precursor of Mr Scharf's?' His eyebrows quivered, as if he were a comedian fooling with his straight man.

'I do not, you'll be glad to know,' replied Alexander, and he linked his hands behind his back to await that day's first item of instruction.

'Imagine a globe as wide as Leicester Square,' said Roderick, describing a circle above their heads with his hand. 'Bigger. Monsieur Boullée's drawings depict three tiers of conifers planted around the base of the globe, one above the other. The thing was to be so big that the tips of the lower trees wouldn't have reached the feet of those above them, and the tips of the highest wouldn't even reach the globe's equator. And the skin of the globe was to have hundreds of holes in it, so the sunlight would make the pattern of the night sky on the inside. Quite mad. Mad but heroic.' Roderick shook his head in consternation, as if seeing the monstrous sphere rising over Leicester Square. 'I found a picture of it in there,' he then said, seizing Alexander's arm. 'I'll show you. We've got time, haven't we? Five minutes.' He tightened his scarf and led Alexander through the door of the library.

In the threshold of the reading room Roderick paused to scrutinise the other users. At the largest table a young man was gazing at the ceiling while his forefinger pressed a page as if to hold in place the word that had given him his thought. Opposite him, a shaven-headed man transcribed addresses from half a dozen telephone directories, with the fervent demeanour of someone on the trail of a conspiracy. Surrounded by open books, the library's other user, a man in a black corduroy suit with a beard as profuse as a Greek Orthodox priest's, was writing on a single sheet of paper with an inch-long stub of pencil, as the fingers of his left hand ran quickly up and down the columns of print. Roderick smiled approvingly, then crossed the room. Passing along a stack, he stroked the spines of the books as though feeling for a secret catch in a wall. His hand stopped. 'Here,' he said, hooking a heavy volume from the shelf. Eagerly he turned the pages until he came to the image of Boullée's colossal sphere. 'Astonishing, isn't it?' he marvelled, presenting the picture.

Alexander regarded the minuscule human figures that stood in the dusk of the monument, under the simulated stars, and for a second, though the scene was absurd, he experienced a taste of wonderment, a taste that was the same as he had experienced as a boy when looking at the Martian cities in his comics, where cars sped through tubes that were as clear and straight as thermometers and the atmosphere was cold and smelled of ink.

'Look at this,' said Roderick, tapping Alexander's elbow. He was watching the bearded man, who was carrying one of his books up to the counter. The bearded man advanced very slowly, with the book open on his hands, as if bearing a platter. He proffered it to the librarian who had emerged from the office behind the counter and spoke to her, meekly, indicating something on one of the pages. The librarian – a woman in her early thirties, taut and slim as a long-distance runner, with dark hair that was parted severely down the right and cut perfectly straight at the level of her jaw – glanced at the bearded man, and at the book, and at the man again. Her eyebrows lifted so subtly that no other part of her face seemed involved in the expression, and then her wide thin lips parted to utter a word. The bearded man swivelled the book to examine the sentence underneath his finger. With a discomfited smile, he turned the page towards the librarian once more, and seemed to repeat his question. The librarian bent forward to inspect the book again, and seemed to give the same reply. She straightened, in a movement that was hydraulically gradual and steady. The bearded man watched her open a box of index cards, and returned to his table. 'Poor woman,' said Roderick. 'Every week she has to go through this performance. Always pestering her, that one. He pretends he needs help to read the footnotes.'

'Got short shrift from her,' commented Alexander.

'He always does, but it makes no difference. He will not be deterred. He is in love.'

'I see.' Grimly the bearded man put the book back on his table. The librarian was writing on a card, winding and unwinding a lock of hair while she wrote. Her demeanour suggested that she might be writing a report on the irksome incident that had just occurred. 'You're sure?' asked Alexander.

'Quite sure,' replied Roderick. 'So am I. In love, that is. With her.'

'You what?'

'Why ever not? Do you mean to imply that you detect some flaw in my dear Lady Disdain?' demanded Roderick.

'Good name.'

'Thank you. She's German. Her name's Cornelia. Cornelia Biehl,' said Roderick, admiringly. 'I saw it on an envelope.'

'You've spoken to her?'

Roderick closed the book, held it at arm's length as though bidding it goodbye, and restored it to its shelf. 'I have. She helped me with an enquiry.'

'And?'

'And nothing. I tried to flirt with her, but she didn't notice. Which was not a little humiliating, as you can imagine. But exciting as well. A woman with no time for flirting. Superb.'

'But you haven't spoken to her again?'

'I can't,' complained Roderick, huddling against the shelves as if for shelter. 'I'd make a mess of it. I'd be like him with his small print. An obvious pretext. Ridiculous.' He peered around the stack at the bearded man; Cornelia rose from her seat and went into the office. 'We'd better get going,' he said, and he hurried across the room before Cornelia could return.

Not until *Nosferatu* was over did they talk about Cornelia again. Still in his seat, Roderick clutched at his chest in emulation of the vampire's convulsion of longing and misery, and gasped, as if with his final breath: 'I confess.' Clawing at Alexander's arm, he smiled ecstatically at the blank screen.

'You confess?'

'I have a plan, Mr MacIndoe,' croaked Roderick. 'Will you help me? Please.' He sucked his cheeks to make them sink, and rolled his eyes pathetically. 'I am a worthless creature, Mr MacIndoe. I am a shrinking, creeping, worthless, pitiful thing,' he mourned. 'But you, Mr MacIndoe. You –' he wheedled, and he extended a crooked forefinger towards Alexander's chest, like Nosferatu transfixed by a spot of blood on the skin of his guest.

'Explain yourself, Roderick,' said Alexander, putting on his coat.

Roderick helped him with a sleeve, and continued in his own voice. 'I would like you to help me with Cornelia,' he said to Alexander's back, as they shuffled along the row. 'I think I could succeed, eventually, but it's the bridgehead that's the difficulty. Once I get in close,' he said, crouching and curving his arms like a boxer in a grapple, 'I think I can acquit myself well. But it's that first step. The lineaments of desire. You have them, but I do not. This is the problem we must circumvent.' He stooped to pick a half-full bucket of popcorn from the floor and held it between his fingertips. 'Live like pigs, some people,' he grumbled, glaring at the bucket rather than meet Alexander's gaze.

'And your plan?' asked Alexander, opening the door to the foyer.

Roderick crushed the piece of litter into a bin and wiped his fingers with a handkerchief, one by one, considering Alexander's question. 'It took one phrase for me to fall for Cornelia. "Let me go and look for you," she said, and that was it. From those seven words, from the way she said them, I felt I knew her. I felt I could tell how she takes life. You think that's absurd, don't you?' he asked, flinching at the sunlight.

'Not at all.'

'But of course I've done some research as well, to be sure. I've watched her. I've taken note of what she reads. Last week,' he confided, 'she was reading Macaulay. Can you believe it? Macaulay. Nobody reads Macaulay any more,' he said, dazed by his good fortune.

'How long has she been under observation?'

'Months. Many months,' he admitted, with a smile of compassion for his quarry. 'We have another shared interest, Cornelia and I,' he went on. 'Cinema,' he said, smacking his lips. 'She reads the reviews in all the papers. Every one of them. We have the same tastes, I know it. With your assistance, who knows what may happen? But without your assistance, Alexander, I fear she may never come to appreciate my vibrant personality,' said Roderick, and he pressed his palms to his cheeks like a politician laying hands on a baby's face.

'What's the part you have in mind for me?'

'Well,' Roderick replied, with a framing gesture of his hands, as if his plan were a physical object that he was setting straight, 'we have a common ground, as I say. We have to meet in a cinema, in circumstances conducive to conversation. Now, *Les Enfants du Paradis* is coming up soon, and I'd wager it's Cornelia's kind of film. So, what I propose is that you and I go to see it, and we give Cornelia a ticket to make sure she goes too. I mean you give her the ticket. If you offer it, she'll take it, I'm convinced. Say you bought it for a friend who now has some other engagement.'

'Two tickets,' said Alexander. 'You have to give her two tickets. One ticket is as bad as the footnote subterfuge.'

'You're right,' replied Roderick delightedly. 'One ticket would be obvious.'

'But if you give her two it looks as if you're assuming she has a boyfriend to bring. Which is a possibility you should be prepared for.'

'Of course.'

'Are you prepared?' asked Alexander, placing a hand solicitously on Roderick's shoulder.

'I am,' asserted Roderick nobly. 'So you'll be my Trojan horse?'

'Make sure you buy two pairs, far apart. Not a block of four.'

'Right you are,' replied Roderick, and they set off for Wilton Row, to meet that evening's group in the pub where a subaltern was once flogged to death for cheating at cards, and where the sword on the wall had been seen to move and inexplicable footfalls had been heard upstairs, most often in September.

In preparation for his conversation with Cornelia, Alexander returned to the library on the following Saturday and spent half an hour with a randomly chosen volume of the *Encyclopaedia Britannica*, at a desk that Cornelia could see whenever she looked up from her catalogues. Two weeks later he returned and sat at the same desk, where he simulated concentration on an electoral register and silently rehearsed what he might say to her. On the third visit, having waited for a moment when he could speak to Cornelia without being overheard, he walked purposefully past the counter, stopped at the door as if arrested by an inspiration, and approached her. 'Excuse me,' he began, reaching into his jacket for the envelope, 'I couldn't help noticing –' and his voice sounded thick and insincere. 'I don't know if you'd be interested –' he said, standing where the bearded man had stood, and being regarded by the face that had regarded the bearded man.

'I'm sorry?' said Cornelia.

'If they are of no use to you, perhaps you might know somebody –?' said Alexander, leaving the rest of the sentence unsaid. He took the tickets from the envelope and pushed them towards Cornelia's hand. 'I don't need them now,' he explained. 'I'd only throw them away. I can't get a refund, you see. So someone should make use of them.'

Cornelia read the tickets, then turned her scrutiny to Alexander. 'Thank you,' she said, but she did not touch the tickets, and still had not touched them when Alexander looked back through the panes of the door.

As the lights went down in the cinema, Cornelia's silhouette moved across the picture. She sat half a dozen rows in front of Roderick and Alexander, and she was on her own. Rod stared fixedly at the screen throughout the film, but when Jean-Louis Barrault cried 'Garance!' as his lover fled, Roderick gripped Alexander's arm and allowed himself to look towards Cornelia. Her shoulders rose and fell, once. 'You speak first,' whispered Roderick, but Cornelia hurried away, leaving by the exit at the front. 'Garance!' Roderick echoed feebly.

'I hadn't thought of that,' said Alexander.

'Soderini moltissimo,' Roderick swore. 'What now?'

Roderick refused to visit the library until the issue was settled, one way or the other, and so Alexander went back on the following Saturday, though neither of them had any notion as to how an introduction might now be brought about. Cornelia smiled at him when he walked in, and thanked him for the tickets as he left, and that was all. Two weeks later he said hello as she passed his desk carrying a pile of magazines, and she smiled, no more warmly than she had smiled before, and Alexander smiled at the bearded man, who scowled at him, as if he took him for a rival. 'The rush hour,' he joked to Cornelia on the way out. She surveyed the room, counting the seven readers, and nodded, removing a card from her index file.

Then, on a Saturday afternoon in November, Alexander and Roderick came out of the National Film Theatre and saw Cornelia browsing at one of the bookstalls under Waterloo Bridge. 'This is it. Now or never,' Roderick asserted. 'Go on, Alexander, friend of mine. Get over there. Say something to her. You have an excuse.'

'And what are you going to do?'

'I'll loiter,' said Roderick. 'Be charming,' he urged, giving Alexander a smack on the shoulder.

Cornelia stood at the end of a long trestle table, checking the index of a huge paperback. Nonchalantly scanning the upturned spines, as though he were a man who could spot an interesting title in the merest fraction of a second, Alexander moved along the other side of the table, keeping Cornelia at the border of his vision. She was still leafing through the book when he reached the point directly opposite her. He waited for her to notice that he was there, and at last Cornelia raised her eyes. She looked at him exactly as she would have looked at him had he been standing at her counter in the library.

'Hello,' he said.

'Hello,' said Cornelia.

'Hello,' he said again. 'This is a coincidence.'

'It is,' said Cornelia.

'Did you see the film?' asked Alexander.

'Which film is it you mean?' she asked.

'Here,' he said, and he waved at the doorway of the National Film Theatre, where Roderick was no longer standing.

'No,' said Cornelia. Tucking the book back into its row, she looked at Alexander with perfect neutrality. 'Was it good?'

'I enjoyed it.'

'That's good,' said Cornelia. She looked at Alexander's face and then at the book he was holding, which seemed to amuse her, as if it were a price tag left unwittingly on a sleeve. 'Are you going to buy that?' she asked.

Alexander glanced at the book he had lifted from the table. It was the second volume of the collected correspondence of two people whose names meant nothing to him. 'I very much doubt it,' he smiled.

'I did not think so,' said Cornelia, and she watched him put it down.

Over Cornelia's shoulder, Alexander saw Roderick raise a magazine to his face then slide it aside. She was about to leave, and he said: 'Cornelia, you remember those tickets, for the film –'

'Excuse me?'

'Those tickets that I gave you, for the film. In fact they were from a friend of mine who likes you, and I was wondering if you would –'

'You know my name?'

'I beg your pardon?'

'My name. You know my name. How do you know it?'

'It was on a letter.'

'A letter? Where?'

'By the phone. In the library.'

'I see,' she said.

'I have a friend who –'

'A friend,' Cornelia repeated.

'Yes.'

'I see.' She paused, and her gaze ran meanderingly over the rows of books. 'Who is your friend?' she asked, not looking at him.

'His name is Roderick.'

'Roderick,' she said, making each syllable distinct. 'Roderick,' she pondered, as though assessing his veracity by the sound of the word.

'That's right.'

401

'I don't think so,' she told him, smiling a stern apology.

'You don't think so?'

'No.'

'Forgive me, but I don't understand.'

'I don't think so,' said Cornelia, watching the train that was crossing Hungerford Bridge. 'Roderick. No, I don't think so.'

'I'm sorry?'

'There is not any friend named Roderick, I think.'

'Believe me –'

'Your friend named Roderick. It is you, yes?'

'No,' insisted Alexander, 'I really do have a friend.' Ten yards behind Cornelia, Roderick was counting coins into the palm of a stall-holder. 'Over there,' Alexander nodded.

Reluctantly Cornelia turned around. With a straight arm she pointed at Roderick, as if pointing the way to someone who had asked for directions in the street. 'Is that your friend?'

'He is,' said Alexander. 'That's Roderick,' and as his name was pronounced Roderick grinned at Alexander and held aloft the magazine he had bought, like a trophy. Alexander acknowledged him with a look that told him not to join them yet.

'I know him,' said Cornelia. 'He has been in the library.'

'He has.'

'He's weird.'

'He's a little unusual,' Alexander concurred.

'A bookworm,' said Cornelia, making it sound like the name given to a member of some disreputable organisation.

'Among other things. A filmworm as well.'

'What is the matter with him?'

'What do you mean?'

'Why does he make you speak to me? He can speak. He has spoken to me before.'

'He's bashful.'

'That is stupid. He is not a boy. How old is he?'

'I don't know, exactly.'

'He is your friend and you don't know how old he is?'

'About thirty-three, thirty-four.'

'I am thirty-three. He is older,' she decided, again looking straight at Roderick, who had now banished himself to the farthest stall. 'And you are older than him,' she said.

'Yes, I am,' said Alexander.

'Why are you friends?'

'I don't know. But I can tell you how we came to be friends,' he offered. Cornelia smiled like someone agreeing a price, and Alexander told her about Roderick's appearance outside the church of St Clement Danes and their walk along the Strand. He had not quite reached Cleopatra's Needle when Roderick, having removed his scarf and stuffed it into his carrier bag, strode up to Alexander.

'May I interrupt?' he enquired, with plausible casualness. 'Roderick,' he informed Cornelia, offering a businesslike handshake.

'Cornelia,' said Cornelia, accepting it.

'Cornelia,' replied Roderick graciously, pronouncing the word like a connoisseur of names.

'Which I think you know,' said Cornelia.

'Indeed,' admitted Roderick instantly, with a compromised smile. He pulled the handles of the bag apart and took out the old magazine he had bought. 'Look at this,' he said, opening the magazine at what appeared to be a cityscape of smog and shadows and sooty roofs. Like a waiter presenting an expensive menu, he put the magazine into Alexander's hands, and Alexander recognised, in the background, the Dome of Discovery, gleaming like an oily hubcap.

'You see?' said Roderick to Cornelia. 'It's here.' He touched the roof of the Festival Hall in the photograph, then gestured at the building behind them.

Alexander looked at the shrouded figures who stood as stiff as mummies on the colourless pavements, between the colourless buildings and the colourless river, and the picture seemed as bleak as an X-ray. 'I remember it,' he told Cornelia.

'You remember it?' she replied, and her eyes widened slightly.

'And if Alexander says he remembers it, he remembers it,' said Roderick.

'It was like a funfair. But better.'

'Someone told me the Skylon was made into ashtrays,' said Roderick.

'The what?' asked Cornelia.

'That thing,' Roderick explained, putting a fingertip on the photograph, close to Cornelia's thumb. 'And look,' he said, turning the page. 'Look at these adverts. Aren't they something?' A man in a brown suit stood proudly facing a woman who clasped her hands in delight beside their new car, which shone with the same light as had shone on the door of the Bovis stove.

'I can't believe you remember much,' said Cornelia to Alexander. 'You must have been so small.'

'Not much,' he agreed. 'Some pictures. A train. Bits and pieces.'

'It was winter?' she asked, turning back to the picture of the Festival site.

'No. It was summer. It looks like winter there, but it was summer.'

'English summer,' added Roderick.

Cornelia leafed back and forth through the magazine, but nothing detained her attention, and then Big Ben struck. 'I must go,' she said, passing the magazine back to Roderick. 'My film is beginning soon,' she explained.

'*La Strada*?' asked Roderick. 'You're going to *La Strada*?'

'No,' said Cornelia, '*Batman*.'

'*Batman*? Remarkable. So am I,' he exclaimed, clapping a hand to his brow.

'I think you are not.'

'I think you are correct,' said Roderick, cartoonishly slumping his shoulders in defeat.

Cornelia looked at him quizzically for a moment and then laughed so loudly it was as though she had just understood a complicated joke, and Roderick stared at her as though her laughter were an unsuspected skill.

'I shall leave you,' said Alexander, raising his hands towards their shoulders, simultaneously, in a stalled embrace. Panic passed across Roderick's eyes, and Cornelia produced a smile that was like a quotation of her workaday smile at the library counter.

'See you soon,' said Roderick.

Alexander crossed Hungerford Bridge, heading for the Coliseum, where he would meet another group, perhaps without Roderick, and he would recount the history of the building and tell them about the party of theatregoers who in 1918 saw a friend taking his seat at precisely the moment he was killed in France. At the Theatre Royal they would stand under the colonnades where his mother sang to him and the two girls were repelled by the face of Sidney Dixon, and he would retell Roderick's tales about the Man in Grey, who appeared in the Upper Circle before the premieres of *Oklahoma!* and *South Pacific* and *The King and I* and *My Fair Lady*, wearing a tricorne hat, a riding cloak and a sword. They would pass Covent Garden tube station, where Jack Hayden, a ticket inspector, saw the ghost of William Terriss, the manager of the Adelphi theatre, more than forty times, half a century after the embittered Richard Prince stabbed Terriss to death. At the Haymarket he would recite the story of John Buckstone, manager of that theatre until 1879, who in 1949 was perhaps seen by Donald Sinden, who saw a man in Ralph Richardson's dressing room and said goodnight to him, thinking it was Richardson, before realising that Richardson was still on the stage. In the middle of the bridge Alexander stopped and, having checked that nobody was near, called 'Goodnight Ralph,' under his breath. He could not see Roderick or Cornelia by the bookstalls. 'Goodnight Ralph,' he repeated, with a more cheerful inflection.

49. 5 November

Half a dozen years later, Alexander would find that this year had left fewer traces than many of the years of his childhood, but he would remember one afternoon in May, soon after Roderick had started his new job and moved to Lewes with Cornelia.

He was standing alongside Sam in the foundations of the conservatory. Sitting on a sack of sand, Sam raised the binoculars he had stolen on the day they were demobbed, and surveyed the school playing field, where a charity fête was being held. 'Wife located,' he reported. 'Range one hundred and fifty yards. Has engaged the enemy.' He pointed towards the tennis courts, where Liz and Mrs Stannard, their new neighbour, were talking beside a stall of cakes. 'Subject of incontinent dog yet to be broached, I'd guess,' said Sam, and he turned at the hip to scan the area between the courts and the school buildings. 'Aha,' he murmured, in the voice of an upper-class officer discovering something of interest in the terrain, then took a drag of his cigarette. The binoculars were directed at a table where a woman in jeans and a rugby shirt was distributing beakers of orange squash to a team of children. 'Sylvia Quinlan,' said Sam, with an appreciative smile. 'Lives down the road. Recent arrival,' he added, and put the cigarette to his lips again.

'Yes, Sam. You've mentioned her before,' said Alexander.

'School secretary. Divorced a couple of years back. No children.'

'Yes, Sam. You told me before.' ·

'Forty-three, forty-four, thereabouts. A youthful forty-four.'

'Yes, Sam. You've told me.'

'Nice woman.'

'Yes.'

'Very nice woman indeed,' said Sam, passing the binoculars.

'I'm sure she is,' said Alexander, looking at Sylvia Quinlan. Most of her face was obscured by her bobbed auburn hair.

'Attractive, don't you think?'

'Undoubtedly,' said Alexander. He lowered the binoculars, but Sam tipped them back, like a drunkard encouraging a companion to drink. Obediently he observed Sylvia Quinlan's pleasant smile, her attractive profile, her suntanned skin. 'Seems most congenial,' he commented.

Crushing the cigarette with a heel, Sam snatched the binoculars. 'Al, are you going to carry that bloody torch for ever?' he demanded. 'Life goes on, mate.'

'Indeed it does,' Alexander replied.

'I mean, time is passing.'

'I'm not carrying a torch, Sam.'

'Could have fooled me.'

'I'm just not on the look-out, that's all.'

Sam trained the binoculars on Sylvia Quinlan again. 'Have to do it for you, you cussed bugger. Fetch us a beer.'

When the conservatory was completed, Sam and Liz invited some friends for drinks one evening. Helping Liz in the kitchen, Alexander heard Matthew Stimpson arrive, and a couple of other guests a few minutes later. Sam had put the portable TV beside the draining board, so he could keep up with events at the Olympics as he ferried things from the kitchen to the garden. Alexander stopped for a moment to watch a heat of the men's two hundred metres, and as the runners crossed the line Sam appeared in the doorway, with Sylvia Quinlan. 'That wasn't a race,' Sam declared. 'That was chemical warfare.' He scooped a couple of dishes from the table. 'Al, this is Sylvia, who works at the school, the one out the back. Sylvia, this is Alexander, my longest surviving friend.' Sam nudged Liz towards the door and the two of them stepped out, leaving Sylvia, who looked at Alexander as though they were in a lift that had come to a halt between floors.

'You enjoy the athletics?' asked Sylvia, attending to the strap of her watch.

'I do,' he replied. 'Do you?'

'Not really. The Americans always win, don't they?'

'The sprints, usually.'

'Makes it dull, I think,' said Sylvia. 'They should handicap them, like horses. Put weights on their backs.' She looked at the plates that were left on the table and then she smiled, as if they reminded her of something amusing. 'You've known Sam how long?' she asked.

'More than thirty years,' he replied, returning to the sink.

She looked at him as though she were working out the consequences of what he had told her. Her fingernails stroked the skin of her throat. 'How about you?'

'About two weeks,' she said, and she smiled again, in the same way. 'I've known Liz longer.'

'Oh,' said Alexander. 'How long?'

'About two and a half weeks.' Her gaze moved to the closed door and her eyes narrowed with suspicion. 'He's matchmaking, isn't he?'

'I'm sure he is.'

For a few seconds more she stroked her throat, and then she took a tumbler from the table and filled it at the tap. 'I've half a mind to be annoyed,' she said. 'How about you?'

They went to see a film in Lewisham. That was soon after Hurricane Andrew had struck Florida, as he would remember, because she made some remark about her brother, whose name was Andrew and who had lived in Miami for a while. One evening she was meeting some former colleagues up in the West End, and she and Alexander went to the cinema at Marble Arch in the afternoon. A couple of weeks later they had a meal at an Italian restaurant in Frith Street, an evening of which he would recall nothing more vividly than her spoon going round and round the cup for a very long time, like a ball in a roulette wheel, as she stirred the sugar in her coffee. This must have been in late October, he would deduce, because he told her about Roderick and Cornelia and that he was going down to Lewes for the fireworks on 5 November. She said she had heard about the Lewes bonfires and would like to see them, but the following day she phoned him at the shop. 'It's not a good idea, is it?' she said. 'We don't really have anything to say to each other, do we?' she explained, before he could agree with her.

He had planned to stay with Roderick and Cornelia on the night of the fifth, and to visit Jane and Philip the next day, but then Jane said they were coming out to Lewes, and he arranged to meet them on the Cliffe bridge. The parades had already commenced by the time they arrived. Alexander introduced the two couples to each other, but so many people were crowded near them it was impossible to be heard without shouting. In single file they walked up the hill towards the war memorial, where Roderick, pointing back towards the hill that rose behind the bridge, tried to tell Philip and Jane the story of the Lewes avalanche. It was the worst avalanche ever to occur in England, he told them. 'Later, big boy,' said Cornelia, hunching her shoulders against the crush. Behind her, a gigantic papier-mâché head lurched up the slope. They carried on, walking in step with a brass band and half a dozen men in Viking costume, one of whom, Alexander realised, was the inspector who had checked his ticket at the station. The procession led them to a field where there was a bonfire so large they had to screen their faces from its heat, though they were fifty feet from the flames. Fireworks louder than mortars exploded from the far edge of the field and lit the chalk cliff with a continuous blossoming of immense, star-white chrysanthemums. 'What a waste,' groaned Philip. He counted in time to a succession of salvoes: 'Fifty quid; one hundred; one hundred and fifty; two hundred.' Alexander, looking away from the lights in the sky, met the gaze of Jane, who mimicked his elated face then smiled as she shook her head, as though she found him incorrigible.

There was almost no conversation between the four of them, and they would never be together again. When the display was over, Alexander accompanied Jane and Philip back to the station, then wandered up the High Street alone. He would remember the oily air, and the bottles and scorched rags and half-burned lengths of timber in the road, and the tiny green flare that dribbled over the rooftops from someone's back garden, and the canopy of smoke above the church at the top of the rise, like the graveyard fog in an old horror film. And he would remember the young couple who trudged towards him up the centre of a steep street, passing a bottle of cider back and forth. He watched them turn out of the street, each leaning on the other, and when they had gone, he would remember, the sound of breathing came out of the darkness at the end of the unlit driveway by which he was standing, and he stared into the darkness and saw a stable door.

50. Irene

Alexander closed the car door softly and looked down the brick-paved road. It was a Saturday afternoon, but in the cul-de-sac where his mother lived it was a perpetual Sunday. The loudest sound was the low-pitched creaking of the entrance billboard, on which an elderly couple with marble-white teeth smiled in the doorway of their ideal home. Every window in the cul-de-sac was closed, and nothing moved in any of them. The woman who lived in the house on the corner was raking leaves away from the tall yellow asters on the edge of the lawn. Cakes of broken asphalt were heaped in the gutter, left there by the contractors who were laying gas pipes under the pavement. The asphalt gleamed like licorice, and a cat lay curled at the feet of the pot-bellied plaster nymph that stood on the little rise of grass by the parking bay. Trying to cast off his torpor, he waited for a minute, watching the flecks of rain gather on the windscreen, and then he went inside.

Mrs Bingham, wearing a camelhair coat and a bonnet that looked like a fawn carnation, was leaving his mother's flat. 'It's your son, Irene,' she called into the hallway, from which a smell of hand-lotion and vegetable soup escaped. She gave Alexander a flinching smile. 'She's got a job for you,' she said. 'You're in the nick of time.'

Alexander's mother stood by the living room window, on a sheet of thick translucent plastic, glaring at a brown velour armchair. 'Alexander,' she greeted him, as though he were the building's janitor, 'will you look at this thing?' She let him kiss her cheek before continuing her complaint. 'What's the point of it, if it weighs half a ton? How's an old biddy like me supposed to move it?'

'I'll move it for you,' said Alexander. 'Where do you want it?'

'Look,' she said, and with her stick she stabbed a corner of the seat. Making a faint hiss, the cushion rose gradually, tipping forward as it rose. 'Helps you get up, you see? Gives you a lift. But the wheels are stiff and it's too heavy.'

410

'Leave it to me, Mother.'

'Ethel helped me get the wrapping off, and that nearly killed us.'

'Where would you like it to go?'

She leaned on her stick with both hands and surveyed the room, as if considering the problem for the first time. 'I think I like it where it is,' she decided. 'It's everything else that's wrong now. Can't see the TV from here, but if you move the TV the stereo will have to go there and if that goes there we'll have to move that table.'

'Not an insuperable problem,' Alexander assured her, putting a hand on her back. He could feel the ridge of her shoulderblade through her cardigan.

'I should have kept the old chair,' she argued with herself. 'Never used it, but at least it didn't take over the place. Don't know what I was thinking of.'

'We'll sort it out. You park yourself on your throne and I'll bring you a cup of tea. Half an hour and we'll be done.'

'If I drink any more tea I'll drown.'

'Well, I'll make myself one, and then you can direct operations.'

'Never known anyone drink tea like Ethel. Must have tea in her veins, that woman.' She whacked the plastic sheet with her stick as Alexander went towards the kitchen door. 'Can you get rid of this rubbish first?' she asked.

He rolled up the sheet and took it down to the bins, where bundles of undelivered phone directories were piled against the wall. A curtain trembled in the window with the team of china shire horses on its sill. Like a pre-echo on a record, he heard himself ask the question he asked his mother when he returned: 'So how was your week, Mother?'

She replied, as she did so often: 'It passed.'

'No incidents?'

'Sam dropped by. Is that an incident?'

'That's nice of him,' said Alexander, hauling the coffee table out of the place where the stereo was to go.

'His daughter's having a baby, he said.'

'He told me. Good news.'

'Is it?'

'Of course it is.'

'I suppose so. I never met the girl.'

'It's good news,' said Alexander.

For a while she watched him, and then she remarked, with a sadness that did not seem genuine: 'Odd the way it turns out.'

'What's odd?' asked Alexander, though he knew what she would say.

'There's you a bachelor and there's Sam a grandfather,' she replied.

'That's the way it is, all right,' said Alexander. Lying on his back, he glanced at his mother through the loops of wiring. She was looking at the ceiling, as though someone had asked for her opinion of the colour it had been painted. 'Been out since I saw you?' he asked.

'Bridge club outing on Tuesday,' she said.

'Oh yes?'

'Went to see a show, eight of us. Up in town.'

'Well, that's an incident. What was it?'

'*Phantom of the Opera.*'

'And?'

'And what?'

'And how was it?'

'Ghastly,' she said, in a voice replete with tedium. 'Wouldn't have got away with it in my time.'

'This is your time, Mother.'

'It was rubbish, anyway.'

'No good tunes?'

'None. Singers who couldn't act to save their lives. Couldn't sing, come to that. I could do better, even now. The chandelier was the best thing in it. Thirty pounds each the tickets cost us.'

'That's a lot.'

'Robbery. And everybody loved it. Even Ethel. Terrible.'

'They don't all have your ear, Mother.'

'A killjoy, I am. That's what Violet Kennedy called me. Violet Kennedy, of all people. The grumpiest old bat you ever met.'

'Violet always makes me think of that misprint Dad found in the paper: "The mayoress was prevented with a bouquet by her sister, Violent." Remember that?'

'Because we're all decrepit they think we should agree about everything. As if you all think the same the minute you get a pension. People you'd have had nothing in common with forty years ago. All we have in common is that we're still alive.'

412

'Where would you like this?' he asked, touching the tall, narrow table on which her photographs were arrayed. 'I'll have to put a speaker here, otherwise they won't be far enough apart. You won't get the stereo effect.'

'Yes, Alexander, I understand. It's the arms and legs that have gone, not the brain. Not entirely.' She inspected the room in which she lived, and it seemed as if nothing in the new arrangement was to her liking. 'Put it there,' she instructed him, with an imprecise wave of her stick. 'Somewhere there,' she said, and she closed her eyes and settled back in her chair. A rueful half-smile appeared briefly. 'I'm sorry, Alexander,' she said, without opening her eyes. 'An afternoon with Ethel tires me out. She's a good soul, but I have to do all the talking. Leaves me like a flag with no wind in it. She doesn't have much to say. But she's a good soul. Like you,' she said, in a voice that declined into a tone of affection overlaid by disappointment with her own life and with his, a disappointment that would prevail, he knew, as their conversation wandered across the subjects across which it always wandered. It was a pity that nothing came of Jane, she might remark, or a pity that Megan turned out the way she did. It was a shame he had never found someone. He could have had his pick, with his looks, if he'd only made an effort. Nothing ever happened to the widow and her bachelor son. They were just waiting, she would say, and he would not contradict her, though it was not true. 'But what about you, Alexander?' she asked. 'What's new with you? Any excitement?'

'The same old drudgery from day to day,' he replied cheerily. She opened one eye and regarded him critically. 'No news,' he confessed with a smile. Sitting on the floor, having matched each plug to its socket, he looked around, at the things his mother had kept and brought to this barren room: the vase that used to stand on the mantelpiece, the clock that used to be in his parents' room, the square of lace that Nan Burnett had made when she was a girl. He looked at his mother, and then he thought of something he could do. 'It's your birthday soon,' he said.

'Not that soon,' she said.

'Soon enough. I'm taking you out, for a birthday meal. In advance.'

'What are you talking about, Alexander?'

'I shall brook no argument,' he said. 'Sam recommended a place, a new restaurant in Blackheath. You like fish still?'

'Yes, but –'

'Eight o'clock?'

'Alexander –'

'Is seven-thirty better? May I use the phone?'

'Alexander,' she said again, but more to register her surprise than to protest.

The restaurant was in a converted factory, two streets from where his mother had worked in the later years of the war. At the entrance their coats were taken and hung in what had been a goods lift, and then they were led up a staircase like a fire escape to the dining room, where the floor was waxed oak, like a ballroom. They were shown to a table underneath the slim steel railing of the mezzanine. Silver-painted pipes and ducts traversed the ceiling, running parallel to deep black girders with rivets the size of tennis balls. On the opposite wall hung a large circular clock with roman numerals and spear-shaped hands, of the sort that used to be found in railway stations. At an adjacent table a young man and a young woman were each talking into a phone. Alexander saw his mother glance uneasily at them. 'I'm the oldest person here,' she remarked. 'I'm the oldest person who's ever been here.'

'And I'm the second oldest.'

'They'll refuse to serve me,' she said, but she was shifting excitedly in her chair, and when the black-clad waiter slotted a menu into her hands and enquired if she would like a drink before her meal, she asked without any hesitation for a dry Martini and made scandalised eyes at Alexander. She uttered quiet exclamations of disbelief as she scanned the menu, which she moved back and forth, as though her incredulity were making it difficult to read. 'Are you sure about this, Alexander?' she asked. 'It's a lot of money for fish and chips,' she said, before ordering the grilled ribeye with sauce Béarnaise and potatoes. When her dish arrived she prodded it, tentatively, with the tip of her knife.

'Don't play with your food, Mother,' Alexander chastised her. 'I won't bring you again if you don't behave.' She detached a flake of flesh and raised it cautiously to her mouth. 'Is it good?'

'Nothing tastes as good as it used to.'

'Same with me, dear. But we're not going to send it back because our tongues are clapped out, are we? Does it taste good, all things considered?'

'It does. But it's very expensive.'

'Good grief,' he growled. 'Stop fretting, Mother. Just enjoy it. The present hour alone is man's.'

She swallowed her water with a gulp. 'The what?'

'The present hour alone is man's,' he repeated.

'That's rather deep, Alexander,' she commented, frowning at him accusingly.

'It's not me, that's why. Dr Johnson.'

She took another piece of fish and nodded as she tasted it, as if the taste were an interesting idea. 'And since when have you been reading Dr Johnson?'

'I haven't. It's a titbit from Roderick. He found it. From a poem Dr Johnson wrote.'

'And why did Roderick imagine this might interest you?'

'Because, Mama,' he joked, 'it was written in Greenwich Park, and the poem's called "Irene". That's why.'

She looked at him and patted his hand. 'A strange boy,' she said, but she smiled as if she had been flattered. And at the end of the meal she took his hand again and said: 'That was marvellous, Alexander. Dreadfully expensive, but marvellous. Thank you.' She made him lower his head so she could kiss him on the forehead, and as they left the restaurant she hooked her arm under his and rested her hand on his forearm, as she used to do with Mrs Beckwith, he remembered, when they walked through the park.

'Goodnight, madam,' said the man at the door. 'Goodnight, sir.'

'Goodnight to you,' she said, and she glanced at Alexander, copying the man's supercilious smirk.

On the way back she asked him to drive past the old house. The front garden was now an expanse of gravel, with a single Japanese maple in a vast half-barrel in its centre. White cloth blinds hung in all the windows. A spotlight illuminated a new white door. They looked at each other but said nothing. His mother gazed at the house again, as if it were the grave of someone she could no longer remember precisely. 'That'll do,' she said, and they drove away.

Alexander made a pot of tea and they listened to records for an hour. They listened to the Ella Fitzgerald album he had bought when she moved into the flat, and to Frank Sinatra and Lena Horne and Nat King Cole. They recalled the afternoons when she would come into his shop to listen to the new releases, and together they sang part of some of the songs she had liked. Around midnight she fell asleep, and when she awoke Alexander put his jacket on.

'It was good of you to come,' she said.

'Not at all.'

'The dutiful son.'

'Not a duty, Mother. A pleasure.'

In front of the hallway mirror she embraced him. 'Look at that,' she said, turning his face towards her reflection. 'And look at you. You'll be an old man soon.'

'Indeed,' said Alexander. 'Goodnight. Lock up.'

The metal cowls of the streetlamps were chattering in the wind, he would remember, and plastic bags and scraps of paper were swirling in the amber light of the cul-de-sac. He would remember stopping the car and opening the window to hear the wind in the trees of Greenwich Park. The foliage surged like a wave on a night sea. It was nearly two o'clock. At some moment between then and nine o'clock, when Mrs Bingham called to see her, his mother died.

51. Be like the dead

As his secretary held the door open Mr Tully looked up from the four perfectly parallel piles of documents that were on his desk. 'Mr MacIndoe,' the secretary announced, her voice softened by sympathy for the client, or perhaps for her employer.

Placing his left hand on one pile and his right hand on another, Mr Tully pushed himself up like a tired swimmer from a pool. 'Mr Mac-Indoe. Gavin Tully,' he said, giving Alexander a grimacing smile that seemed to acknowledge a shared misfortune. Mr Tully wore a three-piece suit of the same tone of brown as his desk, and horn-rimmed glasses of the type Alexander's father had worn thirty years ago. Finely combed and oiled, and divided by a lard-white parting, his hair resembled the open pages of a book of black paper. He was about forty years of age, but it was as if he were impersonating a man of sixty. 'Tea, coffee?' he enquired, in a voice that was almost fey. Alexander declined. 'Thank you, Veronica,' said Mr Tully, and the secretary left them alone, closing the door as gently as a mother leaving her infant to sleep.

Mr Tully motioned Alexander towards the armchair that faced his desk; the leather quilting wheezed as Alexander sat on it. After giving two sharp pulls to the hem of his waistcoat and adjusting the cuff of each shirtsleeve so that slivers of identical width were on show, Mr Tully brought his hands together, fingertip to fingertip. In the warmest terms he recalled Alexander's mother, and his father, and then, grazing his lips with his praying hands, Mr Tully regarded the papers. 'Yes,' he mused, prolonging the vowel equivocally. Arched as if to play a chord, a hand sprang across the papers, touching each stack.

'Which brings us to the complications,' said Alexander.

'Yes,' said Mr Tully. 'Yes, it does.' His gaze travelled across the bookshelves behind Alexander and seemed to see the subject of their discussion looming there.

'You said that there are things that are not as they should be.'

'Yes,' Mr Tully agreed. 'Yes, that is the case, I regret to say.' He drew a long breath and leaned forward, supporting his chin on his thumbs. 'Some of your father's investments hit a patch of rough water in the eighties,' he went on, like a detective establishing the facts of the case before revealing his thoughts. 'This you know, of course.'

'Yes,' Alexander replied.

'Yes,' echoed Mr Tully. 'It could have happened to anybody. Such things happen to a lot of people, of course. It's all a gamble. You never know.'

'Of course.'

'And some sectors of the portfolio your father had assembled did not fare particularly well afterwards. After his death. There was a degree of underperformance.'

'Indeed.'

'It's a salutary tale, that someone with your father's experience, his expertise, should have sustained such significant losses.'

'It is,' Alexander consented.

'It is,' said Mr Tully. He eased back into his chair and a look of extreme solemnity came into his eyes, as though he were a physician who could no longer delay imparting his fatal diagnosis. 'It is apparent, Mr MacIndoe, that your mother, after your father's decease, made a number of decisions that proved to be detrimental, highly detrimental, to her interests, and now, of course, regrettably, to yours. Some of these reversals can be attributed to bad luck, as I say. Very bad luck.' He took a letter from the top of one pile and laid it on Alexander's side of the desk, pinning it with a forefinger that was pressed onto the rubric of Lloyds of London. 'The insurance market is a perilous enterprise, by its very nature, and perhaps your mother was not properly apprised of the risks of this venture before making her commitment to it.' Mr Tully plucked the letter away, as if to remove a noxious object from under Alexander's nose. 'I should advise you, Mr MacIndoe, that there are liabilities here that will consume a substantial portion of your mother's estate. A substantial portion,' he repeated, and his eyes tightened with empathetic grief. 'What we should discuss at some point, Mr MacIndoe, perhaps now, is the quite extraordinarily bad advice that your mother was consistently given by Mr –' he lifted a dozen pages as if raising a stone that might be covering something

418

repellent – 'Ibbotson,' he read. 'The Barlow Clowes affair,' he continued, letting the pages fall. 'A calamity, as you know. Perhaps another mistake on Mr Ibbotson's part. We all make mistakes. But what I suspect is becoming apparent, Mr MacIndoe, is that we may be looking at a case of something rather worse than incompetence. Your mother's affairs are somewhat entangled. We have a not inconsiderable amount of work still to do. Certain anomalies, however, have come to light. Let me explain.' Mr Tully took hold of a tranche of papers and carried it round to Alexander.

Having heard the lengthy explanation, Alexander agreed that Mr Tully should proceed in the way he had outlined, and thanked him for his efforts, and left the solicitors' offices having in no way betrayed his bewilderment. Of neither his father's misfortunes nor his mother's had he known anything. Walking home, he recalled conversations with his parents, searching for clues that he had missed, but could find none that were not clues solely in retrospect. That evening he went into the room in which he had stored the things he had saved from his mother's flat, and for an hour or more he sat amid the cases, raising memories that brought no resolution. There could be no resolution, he knew. He could never know why his mother and father had both kept him in ignorance of things that Mr Tully had reasonably assumed he had known, yet as he turned the pages of the photograph albums and was struck again and again by the gaze of his parents, he felt that he had failed them. Often, in the succeeding weeks, a confusion of guilt and incomprehension would seep into his mind when he was in the flat, like an emanation of the room. From this period of his life he would remember nothing of any substance, except for the day that he would come to see as the day his life again began to change.

It was the fourth time he had driven down to Lewes to stay with Roderick and Cornelia since the birth of Maximilian. Roderick opened the door and handed the boy to him straight away, as though passing a parcel to a courier who was late. 'He's been on tenterhooks,' said Roderick, stroking the cheek of the somnolent baby. A skim of pink plaster was drying on the walls of the hall and a carpet of polythene sheets extended back to the kitchen, where Cornelia was filling the washing machine. 'Come in,' said Roderick, pushing the door shut before Alexander was clear of it. 'Come and see this. A mighty acquisition.' Alexander waved to Cornelia and followed Roderick into the front room, where a tea-chest stood amid tussocks of straw and shredded paper. 'An entire set of Pevsner in there,' Roderick told him, pointing proudly at the tea-chest. 'An entire set, in good condition, for less than the price of a few days' plastering. Incredible bargain.' He withdrew a book and riffled its pages over Maximilian's head in benediction, causing a small draught of mildewed air. 'Your patrimony, Max,' he smiled, swinging the book like a censer.

Cornelia came into the room, pulling one of Roderick's sweaters over her head. 'What are you doing, you strange man?' she demanded, putting out a hand to receive the book, which she put back in the tea-chest firmly. 'Hello, Alexander. You'll stay tonight?' she asked, brushing the dust off her fingers.

'Do not mistake that for a question,' Roderick warned. 'Acceptance of hospitality is compulsory.'

Already Cornelia's hands were around Alexander's waist, tying the straps of the pouch. 'We shop,' she told him.

With Cornelia on one side of him and Roderick on the other, as though forming an escort, they walked down the hill and past the waterless outdoor pool, where a young man wearing headphones was shoving a slurry of decomposed leaves along the blue concrete floor. 'The oldest public pool in the country,' observed Roderick, in a tone like that of an estate agent with a prevaricating buyer. The young man stopped at the bottom of the slope, under the diving board, and leaned on the handle of his broom as if inviting them to commend the work he had done. 'Who is that?' Roderick asked.

'One of the Barretts. Paul, I think,' said Cornelia.

'Ah,' said Roderick, nodding with satisfaction. He looked at Alexander and smiled, in a manner that again made Alexander think of a salesman. 'A sizeable clan,' he added.

'Six boys,' Cornelia explained, but she said it to Roderick, as though following a script they had devised for Alexander's benefit.

At the apex of the footbridge they stopped to watch a scarlet kayak pass under them. Roderick removed his glasses and stooped to inspect his son. 'Asleep,' he reported to Cornelia, and winked approvingly at Alexander. The kayak was approaching the road bridge, on which a queue of traffic from the supermarket had formed. 'Busy,' Roderick remarked, and he looked from Cornelia to Maximilian to Alexander, making a proposition that Cornelia immediately understood.

'Why don't we leave you here?' she said. 'You and Max can sit in the sun for a while and we'll come back for you. We'll only be thirty minutes.'

'Maximum,' Roderick assured him. 'Make yourself comfortable,' he said, offering the riverbank.

Another kayak soon slid around the bend of the river; the fibreglass of its hull had faded to the colour of rosewater, and the rower was digging at the silted water like a tunneller as he rode the current. A supermarket trolley lay askew in a bed of caramel mud, with gouts of spinach-green mulch caught in the mesh of its basket. Alexander glimpsed the dark back of something that scampered across an islet of matted grass, beneath the lip of the opposite bank. From somewhere upstream came the tolling of a church bell; downstream the saws in the timber yard yelped and groaned. Under the branches of a nearby willow there was a translucent blue box that glowed in a spill of sunlight when a gust moved the leaves of the willow aside. The blue light swelled and faded and swelled in the discarded box, like a sign that was meaningless. A perfume like bitter almonds, carried by the breeze, awoke a sentence that seemed to belong with it: 'Be like the dead and you shall be saved.' The words were Mr Barrington's, he eventually recalled; he tried to picture him, and Mr Barrington's face appeared and disappeared, like a shape glimpsed in a quickly moving cloud.

Cornelia came back without Roderick. 'He has gone to buy wine,' she explained. 'But he will buy some books. I know him. He is a deranged person.' She placed the carrier bags on the embankment and sat down beside him. For a minute she gazed at the river, and then Maximilian stirred. Cornelia looked at Alexander as though he had said something to her that she suspected was a lie. 'How are you, Alexander?' she asked abruptly.

'I'm fine,' he said.

'How are you, Alexander?' she asked again, with precisely the same intonation.

'I'm fine, really.'

'I think that is not true,' Cornelia said. She lifted Maximilian from the pouch and kissed the top of the baby's head as she looked at Alexander, as if to oblige Alexander to speak with greater candour.

'I'm OK,' he insisted. 'Things are different.'

'Of course. It is hard. You liked your mother,' she said, offering a finger for Maximilian to grasp. 'It was hard for me, and I did not like my mother very much and she did not like me.' She smiled at Maximilian, making big eyes for him.

'Why didn't you like her?' asked Alexander.

'I did not like her because she did not like me and she did not like me because I did not like her. I don't know. It doesn't matter. She has been dead for many years, and we are talking about you. I think you are not fine. I think there are other things. Shall I tell you what I think?'

'I think you're going to,' said Alexander, but Cornelia did not smile.

'It is your life that is wrong,' she asserted, smoothing Maximilian's hair as though to ease the shock of her statement.

'My life?'

'Yes.'

'That's serious,' he laughed, but he felt like someone beginning to recognise the accuracy of a caricature of himself.

'To me it is obvious. It has always been obvious. You are not truly a shopkeeper, Alexander. It is not a bad thing, to be a shopkeeper. We need to buy things. But you must have money in your heart to do it. You do not have money in your heart, and so I think you are in the wrong life. You do not have the soul of a shopkeeper. Roderick thinks the same, but he would not tell you. I am more honest than Roderick,' she said, and she jutted out her lower lip, in truculent apology for this fault. Repositioning Maximilian in her lap, she added: 'A shop is not a poetic thing, but there is something poetical in you. I believe so.' Cornelia narrowed her eyes enigmatically, like a fortune teller, and smiled.

Alexander looked away, embarrassed at being so mistakenly described. 'I never thought of Roderick as a diplomat,' he replied.

'He is English. But you are changing the subject again. The subject is you.'

'And my uncommercial soul.'

'Alexander, do not make fun. I am giving you advice because I care for you. But if you do not want my advice –'

'No, please. I do,' he said.

For a moment Cornelia stared into his eyes, as if to gauge his honesty. 'To me it is obvious,' she repeated, less forcefully. 'What is it you are doing with your life? You are working in a shop. Why are you working in your shop? Is it a tradition in your family?' she demanded.

'I wouldn't say that.'

'Can you say you like your work?'

'More than most people, I suspect. Work is work. It has its good days. And I'm my own boss.'

'How long have you been in your shop?'

'It's the only place I've ever worked.'

'No,' Cornelia gasped. Catching her breath, she placed a hand on her chest. 'No. This cannot be true.'

'It is true.'

'No. That is a tragedy.'

'Cornelia, it is not a tragedy. Sleeping every night in a shop doorway might be a tragedy. Running a shop is not. You might think it's boring, but I'm satisfied.'

'I don't believe you,' she responded.

'It's true.'

She made wide eyes at Maximilian again, as if encouraging him to share her incredulity. 'You should leave your shop,' she said emphatically. 'Leave it. Leave London. That's what I think.'

'And become a gentleman of leisure?'

'Alexander, you are being silly. You know what you should do. It is obvious.'

'To you, evidently.'

'To anyone.' Crossing her hands on Maximilian's chest, Cornelia closed her eyes in an attitude of meditation, with a smile that seemed to signify her confidence that enlightenment would quickly come to Alexander. After a minute she opened her eyes and blinked at him.

'Well?'

'Oh, Alexander,' she sighed. 'It is so very obvious.' Her right hand drew a semicircle in the air and uncurled to indicate the lawn on the opposite bank. 'Look. A big garden. And next door? Another big garden. And next to that? Another one. You think that people with gardens like these have the time to look after them? Of course not. Not all of them. It's a lot of work. Too much work for a lot of people. Some are too busy, some are not strong enough. They need help, and they will pay for it. Not much, but do you need much?' she asked, and Alexander agreed that he did not. 'No, you don't. You are – what is the word? – frugal.' Alexander regarded the garden on the other side of the water and Cornelia watched him, as though awaiting his opinion of something she had created. 'Why do you do all the work in our garden? It is not only because we are friends, is it? No. It is what gives you pleasure, isn't it?'

'It is.'

'There are so many big gardens here, I think you could pick and choose. I'll prove it,' she said, getting to her feet. 'There is nobody to stay for, is there? You have friends, but there is nobody more than a friend?' she asked, in the manner of a clerk taking details for a form.

'No.'

'Well then,' she smiled, and gave a soft clap. 'Roderick would be happy if you were here. And Max.' She started to untie the pouch, picking at the knots in the small of Alexander's back. 'And me,' she added.

As they walked through the town, digressing down roads to peer over fences at gardens that Cornelia presented to him as if making a gift of them, Alexander imagined the rooms of his flat, and already they seemed like rooms he had left some years before. And the following night, before returning home, he drove past the shop and parked within sight of it. He turned off the engine but did not get out. For more than an hour he sat in the car, staring indifferently at the black glass and at the letters of his name. He had started to work there in 1957, he told himself. He counted the years, and felt that he should be appalled, but was not. Cornelia misunderstood, he thought, and then it seemed that Cornelia did not misunderstand. He contradicted himself again and again, and it was like a broken switch flipped on and off, on and off.

52. The father

It was almost half a year after the conversation with Cornelia that Philip and Jane moved into the house that Philip had bought with the money he had been left in his father's will. On the evening of the day they went to view it, Jane phoned Alexander. It was an enormous house, in a Victorian crescent, she told him, and there was a flat in the basement, which they would let out, sooner or later. She had discussed it with Philip. He had no objection to taking Alexander as a tenant, none at all, she assured him.

On a Sunday afternoon in January, soon after contracts had been exchanged, Alexander went with Philip and Jane to look at the house. Setting out from the study in the loft, Philip conducted Alexander through the building, pointing out the floors that would be relaid, the windows that were to be replaced, the walls that would be ripped down. 'This has potential,' he stated, looking out of a back window at the cracked concrete terrace, from which a flight of concrete steps descended to a garden of rain-flattened grass and unkempt rhododendrons, and then he noticed, in a corner of the room, a small pool of water on the floorboards. While Philip investigated the damage, Jane took Alexander down to the flat.

Each of the rooms in the basement was small, and the room at the front was so dark that they had to switch a lamp on, but the dull light off the sodden lawn put a tinge on the walls of the kitchen that was as soothing as moss, and the air held a refreshing perfume of mint and wet brick. Rainwater falling into a clear glass jar on the outside sill of the kitchen window made a sound like a xylophone note, and outside, on the small square patio, there stood a bucket-sized terracotta pot that held nothing but soil. The soil was black and deliquescent, as lustrous as the skin of a seal. Looking out of the window, for an instant he was not certain whether that year's Easter had passed or not, and it was then that Jane said: 'You could stay here until you find somewhere else.'

Philip's footfalls crossed the ceiling. 'Are you sure about this?' asked Alexander.

She looked at him as if she might decide to take offence at his question. 'Of course,' she said. 'Are you?'

'About the flat?' he replied.

'About everything. About leaving London.'

'Yes,' he said, and he felt, for the first time, that he was.

They went back upstairs. 'When a man is tired of London, he has finally seen sense,' said Philip, and he shook his hand in congratulation. 'You'll be expected to do the garden, you understand,' he added, peering at a patch of discoloured plaster above Alexander's head.

Mr Ibbotson, it turned out, was culpable of nothing more than being, as Gavin Tully put it, luckless, ill-informed and inappropriately confident. As if to make amends for having raised his client's expectations with talk of criminality and prosecution, Mr Tully applied himself vigorously to the transfer of the lease and all the attendant legalities, and by the end of April the shop belonged to Charlie Williamson and the overdraft had been cleared. Alexander went to live in Brighton.

The advertisements he placed in local newspapers and shop windows in Brighton and Lewes brought work as quickly as Cornelia and Jane had predicted. Within the month he was making a herb garden for Mrs Webb in Kingston, whose recommendation led to work for her neighbour, Mr Siviter, for whom he built an oak belvedere in an alcove of roses and night-scented stock. Before he had finished at Mr Siviter's he was called by Mr Sorley in Ditchling and Mrs Nicolson in Robertsbridge, both acquaintances of Mrs Webb, with gardens that Alexander was to tend, once or twice a week, for several years. By the summer every weekday was occupied.

He replanted and maintained the garden for Jane and Philip, with whom he spent little more time than he did with Roderick and Cornelia. Every couple of weeks or so they would invite him upstairs for a drink or occasionally a meal, generally in the company of other guests. Philip was always affable, in a manner that seemed not insincere but nonetheless often implied a degree of effort, as a man might behave with a distant relative of his wife. Although Philip sometimes drank more than Jane seemed to think was sensible, their evenings were pleasant and were soon forgotten. But then there was the day in September, when Sam and Liz were visiting.

In the middle of the afternoon, soon after the three of them had returned from the shops, Jane knocked on the back door and asked them if they'd like to join the barbecue that she and Philip were having that night in the garden, with a few of the students from Philip's school. Six were expected, but only four arrived: a Portuguese lawyer called Rosana; a Finnish engineer named Esa; Claudia, a film student from Modena; and Matteo, her boyfriend, who worked for Alfa Romeo.

'Every boy should have an Alfa, once in his life,' Philip told everyone, putting an arm around Matteo's shoulders. 'Not more than once, though. Ever had an Alfa, Alex? No? I had one. Bought it as soon as I could afford a car. Lovely thing. Sexy as a snake. Sweetest engine you ever heard. But the stuff wrapped around it was junk. Bag of rust inside a year. The engine costs £10,000, the bodywork's free. That's what they used to say, isn't it?' he smiled, and left them before either of them could say anything.

Having learned from Jane that Alexander's family came from Scotland, Matteo asked if he had ever seen the Dolomites, and on being told that he had not, described for Alexander, with an ingenuous ardour, the precipitous terrain around the mountain village where he was born and his parents still lived. You could walk in the mountains along paths that were marked for many kilometres, but in places the paths were so difficult that there were iron ladders in the stone that you had to use, he explained, and he acted out a clamber on a steep rock as he looked over Alexander's shoulder at Claudia, who was following Esa and Rosana on a tour of the garden, while Philip cooked the food and drank from a glass that never seemed less than half-full, and Jane talked to Sam and Liz, whom she had last seen at the funeral of Alexander's mother.

They sat on white plastic chairs ranged around a table on the lawn. Esa told a circuitous story about a corrupt architect back home, which nobody appeared to follow through all its digressions except Rosana, who seemed to decide quite early in the narration that she should take the responsibility of understanding it. Sam stared at the leaves of the beech tree, to stop himself from laughing, Alexander could tell. Liz

427

alternately took small sips of her wine and smiled at Jane or Matteo or Claudia. No longer sober, Philip went back to the grill to bring second helpings, and Claudia followed to help him. When everyone at the table had been served, she stayed with Philip for a moment. In a low voice she said something to him, and Alexander heard Philip reply: 'Ask. Go on. You never know. Ask.' Looking at Alexander, Claudia shrugged.

To break the silence that followed the demise of Esa's story, Matteo told an anecdote about some arms deal he had heard about, in which each party had somehow ended up bribing the other. There was another silence, then Philip remarked to Rosana: 'You know about Claudia's film?' Bolting a mouthful of pasta, Rosana mumbled that she did not. 'Claudia's going to make a film, over the summer,' Philip told the group. 'Most of it, anyway. That's the idea, isn't it?' he asked Claudia, who leaned forward to take her glass from the table.

'A little film,' said Claudia diffidently, swiping her hair from her brow. 'Video film.'

'With some of her friends. A Pasolini kind of project. Amateurs for maximum authenticity.'

'And minimum cost,' added Claudia.

'A sort of fable,' said Philip. 'Shall I tell them the story?'

'If you like,' said Claudia, to Philip and then to the others.

'Correct me if I go wrong,' said Philip. 'It's set somewhere in Italy, in the third quarter of the last century. The heroine is Chiara, daughter of a lawyer. A beauty. To be played by Claudia's friend, Elena.'

'Eliane.'

'Eliane. She's being courted by a young man, Domenico. All of a sudden his interest wanes. She has no idea why. Eventually she discovers what Domenico had found out – that she is not her parents' daughter but a foundling. Her natural father was one of Garibaldi's Thousand, but he is dead now. The mother is God knows where.'

'But she finds her,' Claudia interrupted.

'Eventually she finds her. She's living in a religious community out in the countryside. A back to basics kind of outfit. Very hair-shirt. The leader of this community is an example to them all. Fifty licks of the lash at dawn, then a breakfast of grass and grit. Lives in a stone cell.'

428

'I've got it,' Sam butted in. 'The holy man turns out to be the girl's father.'

'Exactly,' said Philip, raising his glass to Sam. 'The mother was ravished by him, then abandoned the consequent child and withdrew from society in shame. But this isn't clear at first.'

'And he was never a hero, of course,' said Esa.

'Oh no. He was a hero. A big hero and a big sinner.'

'How does it end?' asked Rosana, out of politeness rather than interest it seemed.

'The daughter hears her mother's story, and after a bit of nifty deduction, and the revelation of an incriminating scar on the holy man's neck, she works out that the poor woman has unwittingly become an acolyte of the man who abused her. The girl denounces her father, who is seen walking off into the rain.'

'This is why we can make this in England,' Claudia intervened. 'The rain.'

'So the girl returns to the town, where Domenico, chastened by the heroine's love for her mother, comes to his senses and marries her.'

'An uplifting story,' Sam remarked.

'Very,' said Liz, fastening the buttons of her cardigan.

Philip replenished Liz's glass and offered the bottle to Esa. 'The coda,' he resumed. 'The preacher in exile. He lives in a cave, gets a reputation as a saint. Villagers come to him for guidance. He speaks to them through a chink in the rock. Tells them he is a terrible sinner who should be left to rot. One day a woman hikes up the mountain, bringing her blind daughter. In a frenzy he rushes out of his cave, clutching the rock he uses to beat his chest all day long, and he smacks the child across the head with it. Woman flees, bearing the unconscious girl. Hermit dies. But then we see, at the same moment as the old man expires, the blind child asking its mother to move a candle closer. How's that? What pathos, eh?' Philip shouted, swigging the last of his wine. 'And Mr MacIndoe –' he prompted, waving the tongs at Claudia.

'Perhaps you could be the father?' Claudia asked Alexander. 'If I make the film, would you be him?'

'I don't think it's something –'

'Non-speaking role, virtually,' Philip broke in. 'All you have to do is look as if the end of the world is nigh.'

'You have such a face,' said Claudia.

'Thank you, but –'

'I don't see Alex as a soldier,' said Liz, at which Jane shook her head in agreement.

'You have seen Alex as a soldier,' Sam reminded her. 'Not an Oscar-winning performance, I admit.'

'You would be perfect,' Claudia persisted. 'If you had a beard, it would be an El Greco face.'

'Go on,' Philip goaded. 'You'd be great.'

'I couldn't.'

'Why not? You've been in showbiz before. He used to be a singer, in a pop group,' Philip told Claudia, who looked admiringly at Alexander.

'We were terrible.'

'Your voice is very nice,' pleaded Claudia.

'I couldn't, really –'

'Please,' said Claudia.

'Please,' echoed Philip.

'I can't,' said Alexander, offering the bottle to Rosana, who declined.

Claudia's film remained the subject for a few minutes more, and when Alexander went into the house to fetch some candles and a jug of water Claudia followed him, and asked him again if he would help her. She stood in the doorway of the kitchen with her arms limp by her sides, in a posture of meekness. He was sorry, but he could not, Alexander told her; he put a jug in her hands and turned to fill another. Perhaps he could think about it some more, she suggested, and she carried the jug away. From the kitchen window Alexander observed her cross the lawn, watched by Matteo and by Philip, who tilted his head at her quizzically as she approached. She was talking about the cathedral in Modena when Alexander put the jug on the table. It was where the idea for her story had come to her, she explained. She saw a young woman with her mother, praying, and it was the way the young woman glanced at her mother, when her mother's eyes were closed in prayer, that inspired her, she said, looking at Alexander as though this detail might persuade him of her integrity.

The conversation slumped, and then Philip picked up a newspaper that had been left on the grass. 'We should check the personals,' he told Esa.

'Why?' Esa asked, seemingly responding to the edge of malice in Philip's voice.

'Because I happen to know that Katherine – you know Katherine? Room six?'

'She is horrible,' Esa asserted.

'Philip,' said Jane, reaching for the newspaper.

'What, my love?'

'Put it down.'

'Katherine, I happen to know,' Philip went on, raising his voice, 'has placed an advertisement in today's issue, and I was wondering if we could find it, that's all.'

'Don't, Philip,' said Jane. 'It's not kind.'

'That would be a serviceable description of the fragrant Katherine,' Philip retorted, and he began to read. '"Diehard romantic, bloodied but not beaten, ready for more punishment." Could be. "Gold-digger seeks sugardaddy." Nope. "Bored? Wanna f asterisk asterisk k? Send pic – this might be our lucky day." Too brazen. Not our Katie.'

'That's enough,' said Jane, taking the corkscrew from Alexander. 'Claudia, could you pass that bottle?'

Bringing the page into focus, Philip continued: '"Female bla 35 bla bla attractive bla bla bla fine wines, books, travel bla bla bla bla companionship bla bla bla bla bla love." Might be, might be. By the way, Jane, did I tell you the rumour about Katie and Kennedy? Mr Kennedy, our principal,' he explained to Sam.

'We don't want to hear.'

'Yes, we do. I think we do,' Philip responded, looking questioningly at Claudia and Matteo. 'Everyone likes a bit of gossip.'

'Not everyone,' said Jane, inclining her head to Liz. 'Particularly about people they don't know.'

'It's a good story, I promise. Skulduggery, duplicity and a spice of romance.' Grinning, he rubbed his hands together as if massaging oil into his skin. 'We could put it to the vote. Anyone not want to hear an exemplary tale of office politics?'

'For God's sake, Philip,' Jane objected.

'For God's sake what?'

'Enough.'

Alexander raised a hand. Liz and Sam followed, and then Rosana, shrinkingly, looking at Alexander as though for permission.

'That would appear to be a clear majority,' said Jane, receiving from Philip an affronted glare that slid onto Alexander's face and became a hard smile.

'It really was a funny story,' Philip told him. 'Lessons to be learned from it. Ah well. You'll never know now,' he said, and he smiled to himself as if he thought he had in some way defeated Alexander.

'We should get going soon,' said Liz, and Rosana looked at her watch.

But they all stayed in the garden for another half-hour, until all the wine had gone, and then Jane called a taxi for the inebriated Esa, who was escorted up the path by Matteo, with Rosana and Claudia and Philip in single file behind them. Liz and Sam were ready to leave when Philip came back, but he insisted on making coffee for them and was tripping up the steps before they could get out of their seats. 'I'm sorry,' said Jane dejectedly. 'He's worried about work. About losing his job. Half of them are going to have to go.'

'No security anywhere any more,' Sam commiserated. 'You're over the hill at fifty.'

'Sam thought he was for the chop last year, didn't you?' said Liz, putting a hand on his knee.

'I did. Pushed aside by a pimply youth the moment your back's turned. But I'm a dirty fighter. More than a match for the pimples. For a few more years, anyway. You two are all right, though,' Sam said, nodding at Jane and Alexander. 'No whippersnappers to worry about in your line of work.'

'We die in the saddle,' Alexander agreed, and Jane looked away from the house to smile at Sam.

A quarter of an hour later, as Philip still had not reappeared, Jane went inside. She returned straight away, to report that Philip was asleep. She offered to make them coffee, if they didn't mind a short wait. Sam and Liz thanked her but said it was a long drive and it was getting late. They collected their coats from Alexander's flat and he walked with them to the road.

Alexander helped Jane carry the glasses and bottles and plates up

432

into the kitchen. Philip lay on the settee, on his back, with his arms thrown upwards, his right leg bent on the cushions and his left heel dug into the folds of the rug. He looked, Jane said, as if he were pretending to have been gunned down. Alexander ran the water into the bowl. In the garden, the light of the guttering candles gave the white plastic chairs the sheen of alabaster. 'Guess what I came across the other day?' said Jane, standing behind him. 'That picture of us in Edinburgh. By the castle. We looked good.' She took a plate from him. 'The clothes are shocking though,' she said after a silence, and then there was another pause. 'Worst thing is,' she continued, 'I look at the picture and then I look at myself in the mirror, and what I think I should see is the face in the picture. But the face in the mirror isn't me. It's like I'm looking through my face. You wouldn't know what that's like.'

'I would,' he said.

Slowly she gave the plate a last wipe. 'No, Alexander. You wouldn't,' she said, incontrovertibly, and he did not contradict her. Neither of them spoke again for several minutes, until Jane asked: 'What did you think of the film?'

'A bit impractical, I'd say.'

'A bit nonsensical,' she said.

'Quite.'

'You wouldn't do it, would you?'

'Of course not.'

'Making a fool of yourself with a gang of students.'

'Exactly. It won't happen.'

Jane looked out at the empty chairs. 'They've always been happy, haven't they?' she asked after an extended silence, as if a realisation had surfaced in her mind.

'Who?'

'Sam and Liz.'

'I think they probably have.'

'They're nice,' said Jane. 'I always liked them.' She went into the living room to put a cushion underneath Philip's head. She sat down in an armchair, and closed her eyes. Alexander ran another bowl of water to wash the glasses. When that job was done he went out into the garden to blow out the candles.

53. Creeping Jesus

Early in the morning Alexander walked along the seafront to the marina, as he often did on a Saturday. The tide had been high the previous night, leaving a belt of pebbles and seaweed rags and plastic bottles on the path below the cliff, and shallow pools that shone like sheets of aluminium foil in the cold sunlight. At the harbour he sat on a wall for a while, as was his habit. He listened to the thuds of the hulls and the chittering of the cables against the masts, sounds that reminded him of mornings on holiday when he was a boy, when he would go outside before his parents were awake to stand in the lane, listening to the sounds of the animals and machinery in the surrounding farms. A man in a yellow jacket emerged onto the deck of a boat and knelt beside a spool of rope; the engine coughed and a roll of smoke appeared over the lane of oily water between the wharves. Alexander watched the boat move out to the harbour mouth, and then he walked back. The newsagents' shops were opening as he passed through the centre of town.

He did some paperwork on the patio outside his kitchen. Late in the morning an old RAF plane with fresh roundels and crisp green camouflage flew low overhead, and the noise brought Jane out onto the terrace. Turning to follow the plane over the rooftops, she noticed Alexander at his table. 'Thought it was an earthquake,' she commented, and she went indoors without saying anything more. Half an hour later she reappeared, to invite him upstairs for some lunch. Philip was at a conference for the day, she said, so he could come up whenever he liked.

There was a shower of rain around midday, and when it was over Jane put two chairs on the terrace, facing the garden. They ate from trays, watching the droplets glinting within the rhododendron bushes as they fell from leaf to leaf and made them bob. She asked him, as if she were addressing an uncle, if he could remember the bombers in the war, and he told her about the plates shaking on the sideboard,

434

and putting his hand on a steel bar in the cellar of his house to feel it vibrate like a pipe through which water was running.

Shortly after Alexander returned to his flat he heard music from upstairs. The orchestra continued for a while and then stopped, in a manner that did not sound like an ending. For several minutes he waited for the music to start again, but it did not. He put down the book he had been reading and went into the bedroom. Through the window he saw Jane. She was standing at the end of the garden, staring at the ground underneath a rhododendron. Folding her arms, she seemed to contemplate the thing she saw. She turned a quarter-circle, but then the impulse to act appeared to leave her, and she lowered her head. Ticks of rain were accumulating on the window, yet she stayed where she was, staring at the ground. Alexander went out into the garden. She looked up at him as he approached, and smiled wanly. When he asked her what was wrong she did not answer, but bowed her head once more, directing her gaze at a patch of soil. Alexander spoke her name, and she raised a hand towards him and blindly her fingers brushed his arm. 'Jane?' he repeated. She raised her face into the drizzle, and then she led him into the house.

She took him into the living room, where the television was on, but with the sound turned off. A horse race was in progress. 'Sit down,' she requested, patting the seat of the leather armchair, beside which, on a folded newspaper, sat a cold cup of coffee. 'Here's something,' Jane said, lifting a video cassette from the top of the television. Expressionless, she held the cassette between her fingertips and twirled it. She held it towards Alexander, showing the label, on which a word was written in turquoise ink.

'I can't read it,' said Alexander.

'Neither can I,' she replied. 'It was in there,' she said, pointing to a sports bag that lay open near the door. 'The bag wasn't there. The bag was under the stairs. I had to read the meter, and there it was,' she explained. 'A few things in there could do with a wash, I thought, so I dragged the bag out, and found this.' She grasped the cassette and shook it at him. 'A strange place to file a video, I thought. Strange handwriting. It aroused my curiosity. And I found myself watching it, like an idiot.' She posted the cassette into the player and sat on the settee to watch it.

The racehorses vanished and were replaced by the figure of Alexander, pushing an empty wheelbarrow across the lawn. He watched himself cross the grass, moving into and out of focus. The door of the shed opened and he stepped forward into blackness. Instantly the image flared and then settled, like the surface of a pond becoming calm after the impact of a stone. Now he was stooping to inspect the blue asters, which in the film were purple.

'I don't get it,' he told her.

'You will,' said Jane. 'Give it a bit longer.'

By the Zebra carnations he stopped and gazed upwards. The camera tracked his gaze to the sky, found nothing of interest, and returned to Alexander's face.

'I look like a half-wit,' he commented. A wry smile, directed at the screen, was Jane's only reply. He concentrated on the television, wondering what was the intended object of his concentration. 'When was this?' he asked.

'I have no idea, Alex,' she replied, raising a finger discreetly to the eye he could not see. 'Some time last year.'

Alexander's face, swelling to fill the picture, blurred and ceased to be a face. Then he was back at the door of the shed, oiling the blades of the shears. 'I still don't get it,' he said again.

'Oh, Alex,' she rebuked him tearfully. 'Think for a second. Look. It's obvious.' She took aim with the remote control and pressed the pause button. Marooned mid-stride on a lawn of luminescent grass, the figure of Alexander shuddered in a deluge of white needles. 'Ask yourself: where was the camera?' She set the figure walking again, then froze it. 'Couldn't have been on this floor, could it? The angle's not right. Couldn't have been from here,' she said. 'Now, who do you think was pointing a camera at you, from upstairs? Why would they be upstairs, do you imagine?' she asked, and now there was vindictiveness in her voice. 'Wouldn't be Philip, would it?'

'I don't know,' said Alexander, bemused.

'You don't know? Why, for God's sake, would he want to do that?'

'I don't know. Why would –'

'Well, it wasn't Philip, Alex. It wasn't Philip,' she repeated, and listlessly she sat back.

Without looking at the screen she pressed another button. The film wound forward rapidly. Four or five people hurried with puppet-like steps along a path; like puppets they collapsed onto a pair of benches below a tree, and then they were gone, and heads were jerking up and down in a room that had a blackboard in it. 'Got it now?' Jane asked. In the background a door opened and all the people in the room were drawn out through it, as if by suction. A sloping roofline appeared and what seemed to be an enormous angel, against a clear sky. Looking at Alexander, Jane waved the remote control and the film slowed down. He looked at the striped façade of an old church, with a portico in deep shadow. 'I don't know where this is, exactly,' commented Jane, 'but I can guess the country.' The camera focused on a young man who was sitting on the ground outside the portico, removing a shoe. 'Here we are,' sighed Jane. The camera moved closer; the young man looked up and reached towards it, laughing. The picture went dark, and then an expanse of pink material appeared, above a triangle of dark skin, and then Claudia's face slipped into the picture. She puckered her lips at the lens. 'Well, what do you think of that?' asked Jane, freezing the film. Claudia's mouth vibrated on the screen; Jane put her face close to it and smiled admiringly. 'No, but she is beautiful,' she remarked, and she punched the player with a single knuckle. The machine screeched and ejected the cassette. She clasped it to her chest like a prayer book, and closed her eyes in an attitude of mourning. 'This is disappointing,' was all she said. 'This is very, very, very disappointing.'

Alexander helped her to her feet and sat beside her and took the cassette from her hand. Only then did she open her eyes. She looked at the wall in front of them as if it were a window through which something of little interest could be seen. 'Did you suspect? That evening she was here?' she asked him casually, after a prolonged silence.

'No.'

'Neither did I,' she said. 'Neither did I.' She put a hand lightly on his arm and peered again at the wall. 'You never can tell, can you? Can't trust anyone,' she said, as though recalling some advice that she had forgotten. 'Except you, of course. I shouldn't have given up so easily,' she said, but in the same disengaged voice.

'What will you do?' he asked.

She picked up his hand and kissed the back of it. 'Don't know,' she

437

said. 'I suppose, past fifty, it's sensible to forgive. It's the pragmatic thing to do, isn't it, at our age? If you haven't got the nerve to be on your own. I'm not as tough as you. I don't want to be on my own. But you'd forgive, wouldn't you?'

'I don't know. I doubt it.'

'I think you would. I know you would. But my instinct is not to,' she stated, and she seemed to be cheered by her own words. 'My instinct is to cut his kidneys out.' She kissed Alexander's hand again, stood up and strode into the kitchen. She returned with a pair of scissors held dagger-like at chest height. 'Pass me that,' she said, holding out a hand to receive the cassette. With the scissors she hooked a loop of tape, and then she pulled at it and continued to pull until the entire length of film lay coiled in her lap. 'I'll fall to bits soon,' she said, as if informing him of an unimportant decision she had taken. 'I'll come and see you then, if I may?' She fed the tape into the jaws of the scissors.

Alexander was watching the nine o'clock news when he became aware of Philip's voice, monotonous like the noise of a grinding machine in the distance. Jane's replies, if there were replies, were inaudible, until footsteps crossed the room quickly and heavily, making the ceiling shake. 'Yes,' Philip shouted. 'Yes, yes, yes,' he protested, and then Jane was talking over him. There was the sound of what might have been an overturned chair hitting the floor, and a cry from Jane. Stealthily Alexander opened the back door and crept across the broad corridor of light that traversed the grass. From behind a screen of leaves he saw Philip fling his arms wide, as though to invite a blow to the chest, then turn his hands inwards at his heart, in self-accusation or denial. Listening to Jane, Philip chewed at a thumbnail. He threw his arms up again, shouted, and took a stand at the window, with his fists on his hips. He turned his head to speak back into the room, and as he did so he pushed the French windows violently, as if he intended to break the hinges. 'Can you hear everything?' he yelled into the garden. 'Getting it all, I hope? I'll keep the door open. Wouldn't want you to miss anything.' He scraped a flowerpot across the terrace to pin the French windows back. 'Creeping fucking Jesus,' Alexander heard him mutter as he went back inside.

Two days later, in the evening, Jane came down to Alexander's flat.

'The battle continues,' she reported, as though she were keeping a promise to tell him what had happened. 'We're in separate rooms,' she said, blowing the steam from the coffee he handed to her. 'Separate rooms, separate meals, separate schedules.'

'Has he gone out?' asked Alexander.

'No,' she said blithely. 'He's upstairs, in his study. Stewing. Composing his next speech.' She looked out at the garden, and from her unfinished smile he understood that she would not leave Philip.

That summer, on midweek evenings, Alexander came to expect the clang of her sandals on the iron spiral staircase that connected the terrace to the alcove by his back door. For an hour or more he would listen as she repeated the arguments that had occurred since she had last talked to him. Week after week, recounting conversations and disagreements that became more convoluted with every visit, she described her gradual reconciliation.

'He's sulking,' she said to him.

'Why's that?'

'He's making out he thinks I'm having an affair. Spaniel eyes when I leave the house to see the lover in the basement.'

'He doesn't believe that?'

'Of course he doesn't. He's trying hard, but he can't make himself believe it.'

'Hardly surprising.'

'But he really is jealous. Which makes him feel better, in a way. Making some sort of reparation for adultery.' She was holding an orange, and she peered at him over its horizon. 'Of course we could have an affair now, and we'd get away with it. A perfect double-bluff,' she smiled, and the humiliation of her betrayal was in her eyes.

'He looks right through me,' said Alexander. 'If he can't get away first. Dives into the car when he sees me coming up the path, or jumps back into the house. He can't stand me, can he?'

'You're a witness to the crime, Alex.'

'Yes, but it's more than that.'

'Perhaps,' she conceded. 'He thinks you're an under-achiever, and there are few things worse in Philip's world,' she said, picking up her cardigan. They took a stroll around the garden, arm in arm. 'Of course, Alex, none of this would have happened if you'd married me,' she

439

whispered, and she looked at him intensely, confusedly, as though momentarily she might have meant what she said. Then he saw her glance over his shoulder before she kissed him, like a child thanking a relative for a gift, and he saw that Philip was watching them from the living room.

54. Flat 3

Alexander was working at the Wilsons' house, up by the school, the day after he told Jane that he would be leaving. Soon after six o'clock, on his way home, he stopped in the centre of the village to buy some milk and the evening edition of the local newspaper. As he entered the newsagent's shop, the assistant was pinning advertisement cards onto the board in the window, and one of these was for a one-bedroomed flat in a street near the crest of the hill. From the telephone box by the car park Alexander rang the landlord, Mr Adams, who arranged to meet him an hour later, outside the house. It was a white-washed semi-detached house, with carmine windowframes and the number of the house in carmine wooden numerals, like the numerals on the side of a fishing boat, above a carmine door. To the right of the front steps a steep and narrow flight, barred by a small iron gate, descended to the door of the basement flat, which was fronted by a rockery that almost touched the glass of its window. When Alexander arrived, Mr Adams was sitting on the ground, holding a small plastic pot in one hand and in the other a slender brush, which he was dabbing onto the spring of the gate. Mr Adams was Alexander's age, but stout and bald, and he wore an old blue tracksuit with the letters CCCP across the shoulders and a pair of thick-soled trainers that were speckled with plaster and paint of various colours. 'Be with you in a second,' said Mr Adams, inserting the brush into the spring. 'You're the chap who rang?' he asked, withdrawing the brush and dipping it in the pot.

'Mr MacIndoe, yes.'

Mr Adams glanced at Alexander's boots. 'You're not a student,' he remarked, as if Alexander had claimed to be one when he phoned.

'No, I'm not,' replied Alexander.

'Students of all ages nowadays, mind you. Not like when we were youngsters,' said Mr Adams.

'Indeed.'

'But you're not a student.'

'No,' said Alexander.

Mr Adams rocked an inch one way and then an inch the other, as though he were being jostled on a bench. 'So what is your line of work? Something agricultural, I'd guess.'

'I'm a gardener. I have my own business.'

'You have your own business but not your own home?'

'That's right.'

'Local man?'

'I'm from London.'

'Thought so. Solvent, are you?'

'I am. I prefer to rent,' Alexander explained.

'Seventy pounds a week. Is that within your range?'

'It is,' said Alexander. 'That seems very reasonable.'

'I'm a very reasonable man,' said Mr Adams, making jabbing motions with the brush. 'It's semi-furnished. Bills extra. Gas heating and hot water, radiators throughout. Gas cooker. TV aerial point, but you'll need your own TV. One month's deposit. I won't have pets.'

'Neither will I,' said Alexander.

Mr Adams looked at Alexander's face for the first time. Placing the pot on a step, he dug a hand into his tracksuit and held a fat bunch of keys over his shoulder for Alexander to take. No two keys were of the same type, and each was marked with a dot of paint. 'Top of the stairs, flat 3. Yellow's the front door, green's the door to the flat. Take your boots off before you go in, would you? Don't want mud all over the carpet. I'll be with you in five.'

The staircase was bare and the colour of creosote, and the runnels of paint on the door of Flat 3 looked like a sweat of milk. Against one wall of the front room a low bed had been set, with a mattress that was still wrapped in polythene. By the window there was an old armchair, its sagging seat bolstered with a couple of brown velvet cushions. A flimsy white wardrobe with turquoise handles stood at the far end, by a matching chest of drawers. A square table with corkscrew legs occupied the centre of the room; a single dining chair was tucked under it. The thin brown carpet had risen into ridges that resembled a net of veins, and the wallpaper had been repainted so many times that a narrow band of half a dozen different colours ran around the switches and above the skirting boards. It was so quiet that Alexander could hear the chimes of a clock in the flat below.

Mr Adams grunted as he put his toolbox down in the hall. 'Have you seen the kitchen?' he asked, and he beckoned Alexander into a room that was panelled with varnished boards, like a mountain chalet, and contained a small refrigerator, a cooker that had not recently been cleaned, one cupboard, a table topped with green Formica, and one green plastic chair. 'You might appreciate the view,' said Mr Adams, looking out of the window at the neighbours' overgrown gardens. 'Better out the front, though,' he added, putting out a hand to receive the keys.

The windowframe knocked in the wind as they regarded the sea. 'Does you good, they say,' Mr Adams remarked. 'Contemplating the waves. For myself, it makes me a bit low after a while. All that action. Up and down, up and down, all day and all night, day in, day out. But a lot of people like it.'

'I like it,' said Alexander.

'You'll find it's a quiet house. Not much traffic. They keep themselves to themselves next door. Been there fifty years, thereabouts. The Tomlins. Retired, they are. They go on holiday a lot. To Majorca. Spend more time in Majorca than here. Ever been to Majorca, Mr MacIndoe?'

'I haven't.'

'Nor me,' admitted Mr Adams, frowning at the window. 'Excuse me a second, will you?' he said, and he went over to the toolbox, from which he took a box of matches. He struck a match, extinguished it, bit it with dentures that were as bright as toothpaste, and slotted the halves between the windowframes to stop the knocking. 'Went to Marbella a couple of years back. The wife's idea. I didn't much care for it. Been to Marbella yourself?'

'I haven't. I've been in that area, but not actually to Marbella.'

Mr Adams prodded the windowframe with a forefinger, and seemed to find his handiwork adequate to the situation. 'You've got a lovely girl downstairs,' he resumed. 'Been there a year now. Theo's her name. At the university. You'll hardly know she's there. And in the basement you've got Colin. He works at the Newhaven docks. Does a lot of night shifts. The basement doesn't get a lot of light, so it's right up

443

his street. Nice young man. You'll not see him from one week to the next.'

'Would you mind if I redecorated?' asked Alexander. 'A lick of paint. Nothing extravagant. White emulsion.'

Mr Adams looked around the room, as if to root out the defect that had provoked Alexander's question. His gaze came to rest on the rash of tarnished drawing pins that covered the wall above the bed. 'Can't see any reason why not. So you're interested?'

'It's exactly right,' said Alexander. 'I can supply a reference from my present landlady. And from my previous landlord.'

With his hands pushed deep into the pockets of his tracksuit, Mr Adams inspected the room, as if he were the prospective tenant. 'I don't think that will be necessary, Mr MacIndoe,' he decided. 'But perhaps you should take a look around again, to be sure.'

'I'm sure,' said Alexander, taking his chequebook from his jacket. He wrote a cheque for one month's rent and his deposit, and a week later he moved into Flat 3, where he was to live for the rest of his life.

One evening each week, most weeks, he would drive over to Lewes to eat with Roderick and Cornelia. Once a month, most months, he would take the train to London to spend a Sunday with Sam and Liz. In the summer they sometimes went to Kew or Richmond or Hampton Court, but usually they wandered around the West End, where they would go for lunch in a café or a pub, and browse in the shops, and perhaps see a film in the late afternoon. Occasionally he would meet Jane in the teashop by her clinic. Philip was rarely mentioned, and nothing from their past was ever discussed, except on the day she told him that Sidney Dixon had died. He had died the year before. Her father had only heard a couple of weeks ago, she told him, and she put a hand on his and immediately withdrew it. Sidney had married, it turned out. His wife ran a jewellery shop, and was a lot younger. In his will he left half his savings to her; the other half he left to the hospital in East Grinstead, where Sir Archibald McIndoe had worked.

Alexander worked from eight or nine to five or six o'clock each day, from Monday to Friday, sometimes on a Saturday, when necessary on a Sunday as well. In the evening, if he was not visiting Roderick and Cornelia, he might go to the cinema, or watch a film on video, or read

444

a book about history or the natural world. He went to bed at eleven o'clock, as a rule. He would lie in bed, listening to the murmur of voices in the flat below, or Theo's music, or the beat of her fingers on the keyboard of her computer. Nobody came to the flat, except Theo, who once in a while dropped in for a cup of tea, and Mr Adams, who called on the first Wednesday of every month to collect the rent, and stayed sometimes for an hour or so, to play a few games of draughts or backgammon.

He lived this way, contentedly, for more than two years.

55. Carpe Mañana

Shortly after seven o'clock on a mild September evening the doorbell rang. Laying down his knife and fork, Alexander leaned out through the open window and saw a young woman with dyed black hair, scrutinising a postcard or a photograph. She pushed back a sleeve of her top to look at her watch, then pressed the button again. Having posted the picture into a pouch on the thigh of her trousers, she stepped back and looked up before Alexander could withdraw. She waved at him. 'Mr MacIndoe?' she called, in a voice that was keen and pleasant.

'Yes?' he replied.

She took another step backwards, onto the pavement, and her smile broadened as she gazed at him. 'Mr MacIndoe, could I have a word? I'm not selling and I'm not conducting an opinion poll or anything like that. A couple of minutes of your time?' Alexander noticed that she was wearing silver trainers. She looked down at her feet, then up at him. 'I really won't keep you long,' she promised. 'But it's a personal matter.'

When he opened the door she was standing with one foot on the step and one on the pavement, with her arms folded and her head tilted interrogatively.

'Thank you,' she said. 'I hope this isn't an inconvenient moment.'

'Not at all,' Alexander replied.

She stayed where she was for a few seconds, looking at him with assertive dark grey eyes. 'You don't know who I am, do you?' she said.

'I'm afraid I don't.'

'We've met before, but a long time ago. A very long time,' she smiled, and stood upright before him on the step, with her hands behind her back, offering him a last opportunity to solve the mystery of her.

'I'm sorry,' said Alexander.

'You don't remember.'

'I don't.'

'That's OK. Neither do I. But I know we met once.' She held out her hand. 'I'm Esmé,' she said. 'Esmé Clarke. Shaun's daughter.'

'Good Lord,' said Alexander, and Esmé smiled again, as if receiving a compliment. 'Oxford Street.'

'Apparently. You remember?' Esmé asked, theatrically incredulous.

'Yes, I do,' he told her, and he recalled the child kneeling in the aisle between shelves of toys, but he could not see a face that in any way resembled this young woman's.

'You bought me a present,' said Esmé, and then she added, 'so Megan says.' She looked at him directly, awaiting a reaction to Megan's name. Seeing none, she said: 'Can I come in?'

His body felt encumbered as he climbed the stairs, as though he were raising his limbs through water. 'How did you find me?' he asked at the door of his flat.

'That really wasn't difficult,' said Esmé, surveying the hall. 'She told me where your shop was. I went there, and found it had gone, but I spoke to the manager of the shop that's there now. He was very helpful.'

'Charlie,' Alexander said, pointing the way to the front room.

'I didn't get his name. He gave me an address down here. I'm in Brighton for the week, so I went along a couple of days back and got your address from a very impolite man, who seemed to think there was something funny about being asked where you were.'

'Philip.'

'Whoever.' The fluttering curtain caught her attention, and then she noticed the unfinished meal on the table. 'Oh, I'm sorry. I can come back.'

'No,' said Alexander, directing her to the armchair. 'Do sit down. I'd finished, pretty well.' He returned to the chair at the table and pushed the plate away. 'So you're in touch with Megan,' he said, and his tongue felt clumsy on the word.

'We were never out of touch, not totally. She sent me a card every year, on my birthday, without fail.'

'But you've spoken to her as well, evidently. You've seen her.'

'I have,' she confirmed, and she smiled to transmit to Alexander the pleasure of her conversations with Megan. 'Many times, in the last year,' she continued, tantalisingly, but Alexander did not say anything. 'Shall I explain?' she asked.

'It's why you're here. Please.'

'You sure? You don't seem too thrilled by this.'

'Thrilled is probably not the way to put it.'

'I've thrown you a bit.'

'That's closer, I'd say.'

'I'm sorry. I would have phoned first, but I couldn't find a number. Don't you have a phone?'

'I have a phone,' he said, nodding towards the table in the corner.

'But you're not in the book.'

'I'm not in the book, no.'

Esmé looked at the table, at the telephone and the books piled by it. She looked at the room in its entirety, and seemed to be considering how she could describe his flat without making it sound depressing.

'Please,' said Alexander. 'Go on.'

She looked out of the window, regaining her resolve from the sight of the sky. 'Well,' she resumed, 'to cut it short, I had a bad time a couple of years back. A very bad time,' she said, shaking her head at the memory of it. 'I'd come out of a bad relationship, with a guy who really messed me around. My mother had taken off. Disappeared to some commune somewhere. For the fifth or sixth time. Attention span of a gnat. Should I be telling you this?' she wondered. Alexander replied with a noncommittal gesture of his open hands. 'So she'd gone, and my father was smashed all day, and I'd been ill for months. Washed out all the time. Then I hit thirty, and I didn't know what I was doing with my life. I had a crisis. You're meant to know what you're doing by then, aren't you? Thirty is when you've got to know yourself.'

'So I believe.'

'Well, I didn't. I had no idea who I was, where I was going. Not a clue. I'd lost the plot in a major way, and there was nobody I could turn to. And then it came to me: I knew I had to see Megan again. It was so obvious. I'd loved her when I was a kid. More than my mother. I'd loved my mother, but I'd really loved Megan. She'd been such an influence on me,' she told him, but something in Alexander's demeanour made her stop. 'You think I'm babbling, don't you?'

'Please, continue.'

'You wanted me to explain,' Esmé objected, glancing out of the window again.

'I do.'

'I'm just telling you what happened. I'm sorry if it sounds ridiculous to you, but that's how it was.'

'It doesn't sound ridiculous. Carry on.'

For a few seconds she worried at the zip of her top. 'I knew I had to see her,' she went on. 'She'd cared about me when she lived with my father, and I knew she still cared, in some way. She'd stayed in touch. She didn't have to, but she did. She hadn't seen me for years, so she'd be able to see me clearly, because she was coming from outside. But she was close as well. I knew I could talk to her. It made sense. You see that?'

'Go on.'

'So I wrote to her. We met up, and we got along brilliantly, right from the start. Right from the re-start.'

'And she solved your crisis?'

'She helped, yes,' said Esmé sharply. 'A lot. She gave me some good advice. But more important than that, she's become a real friend. The more I've got to know her, the closer we've become. She's a strong character. Such a strong character. Someone you can measure yourself against. It's great, knowing her again. It really is great.'

'I'm glad,' said Alexander.

'I've learned a lot about her. About you and her,' said Esmé, bending forward in the chair and knitting her fingers.

'And what have you learned?'

'That Megan loved you, and that she was never happier than when she was with you.'

'That doesn't sound like something Megan would say.'

'She mentions you whenever we get together. In some way or other you always get brought in. She talks about her father and she talks about you. She's told me everything.'

'Everything, eh?' he smiled.

'A lot. Enough.'

'Enough for what.'

'Enough to know what should happen now.'

'So you've come on a mission to turn back the years?' said Alexander, glancing out of the window. 'To reunite what has been put asunder?'

'If you like,' she said, but then suddenly she lost patience with him and smacked a palm on an arm of the chair. 'Why are you being like this?' she protested. She glared at the wall and took a deep breath. 'Sorry. I know why you're like this. You're angry with her. Of course you are.'

'I'm not angry with her, Esmé. There's no reason to be angry. There never was a reason to be angry. You don't understand.'

'I do understand. I've seen her, and I know what she wants.'

'Better than she does herself?' Alexander responded, and he fixed his gaze on her eyes, preventing her from interrupting. 'Esmé, I didn't vanish. It didn't require the services of Interpol to track me down. You found me easily enough, and Megan could have done the same if she'd wanted. Thank you for your concern, and I'm glad you've made a friend. But you should leave this alone.'

'Of course she wasn't going to come after you,' Esmé argued. 'Not in the circumstances. It's obvious why she wouldn't.'

'It's obvious that –'

'When I saw her again it was like finding the missing piece of a puzzle. And that's what it would be like with you two. Each of you is the other's missing piece. You were made for each other, I know you were.'

'Please. Listen to yourself. That sounds like something from local radio.'

'I don't care how it sounds, Alexander. You were made for each other. You shouldn't be apart.'

'Nobody is made for anybody, Esmé. You might live well with somebody for a while. For a long time, even. But there's no such thing as the perfect match. Not unless one person's forcing the other to fit.'

'I don't agree.'

'Life isn't a jigsaw puzzle, Esmé.'

'So what is it then?'

He paused, turning to look down at the street. 'A flood,' he said, and laughed quietly.

Esmé was chewing at a corner of her lip when he turned back. 'She'd love to see you again,' she said. 'I know she would.'

'Let me ask you a question, Esmé. I am assuming that Megan knows nothing about your visit. Am I right?'

'I said I'd like to meet you.'

'But you didn't say you were going to play the detective.'

'I'm not playing at anything.'

'You didn't say you had a plan.'

'Not in so many words. But she didn't order me not to do anything.'

'I see,' said Alexander. He took hold of the plate and stood up.

'Can I take your number?' asked Esmé, getting to her feet.

'I'd rather not,' said Alexander.

'In that case, I'm going to give you mine,' she said. From one pocket she took a steel-covered notebook in which a postcard was lodged, and from another she took a tiny pen. 'I'm going to give you hers as well,' she stated, writing on the card. 'And her address. She's not far away. She's been there for more than ten years now, and she's not likely to be leaving any time soon,' she said.

He looked at the card and saw Megan's address. It was only five or six miles from where they used to live, and as he read the address he experienced, fleetingly, a sensation of loss, as if a moment from the day she left had slipped into the present.

'You can read my writing?'

'Oh yes,' he replied.

Standing at the window, Esmé stretched her back, like a dancer limbering up, and smiled at him. 'The story of your life is the story of you and Megan. That's what I think, and I think you suspect I'm right. You'll regret it if you don't get in touch. You know you will. If you don't do it you'll end up like that,' she joked, pointing up the road, where an old man was hobbling alongside a scruffy terrier. 'Is that what you want to be like?'

'I don't know what he's like and neither do you. He could be the happiest man in Sussex.'

'I doubt it,' she said.

'So do I,' admitted Alexander.

She turned the postcard over in his hand. On the front was a cartoon of a deserted square, with a church and a cactus at one end and a waterless fountain at the other; against the basin of the fountain a hunched man was asleep under a sombrero. On his T-shirt was written: 'Carpe Mañana'.

'Very humorous,' he said.

'I thought it was funny,' said Esmé, and now there was a warmth in her eyes.

'I'd be grateful if you told Megan nothing about this.'

'Why not?'

'I need time to think it over. There's nothing to be gained by forcing things any further, is there? So don't file a report, please.'

She looked at him, drumming her fingers on her upper lip. 'OK. I won't say a word,' she said.

Seated at the window, Alexander watched Esmé get into her car. She inspected her face in the rear-view mirror, and seemed satisfied with what she had done. From the glove compartment she took a phone; she punched in a number, listened, and tossed the phone onto the passenger seat. Her fingers rippled on the steering wheel; she checked the time, then drove away.

Alexander read the address on the card and he felt almost nothing, but that night he could not sleep, and he found himself dragging from underneath his bed a suitcase that he had not opened since he had moved into the flat. He tipped the contents of the suitcase onto the floor and opened the wallet of photographs that lay on top of the pile. A picture of Liz with her hair dyed blonde was the first he removed, and then came Nan Burnett, and Megan holding Mr Beckwith's hand to her head like a beret, and himself and Sam sitting on the tailgate of an army lorry, and himself and his parents and Megan and Mrs Beckwith at Praa, and Jane in Princes Street. He pushed the photograph albums away, to sift through the other things that he had kept: a watercolour of the Theatre Royal that Sid Dixon had painted, and a Jubilee Medal from Sid Dixon's shop; half a dozen copies of *Melody Maker*; a bookmark with a drawing of the Bellevue Hotel on it; a button embossed with a pair of wings; a flyer for The Park Rangers; a pale mauve cinema ticket and a spent flashbulb; a card from Edwin Coleman that still smelled of sandalwood; Sam's business card and a business card for MacIndoe's and a third for The Videocentre; a ticket for the bullring in Ronda; a postcard of the amphitheatre at Epidavros, and another from Fatima; a bundle of school reports; the order of service for the funeral of Mrs Joan Beckwith; a programme for Bonfire Night in Lewes; a small cassette with Megan's voice on it; pictures of Tollund Man, and Perón's return to Buenos Aires, and himself in Carnaby Street; an envelope containing a key from the Beckwiths' house, a key from the flat in which he and Megan had lived, and a nail from the Doodlebug House; leaflets from the churches of St Mary Abchurch and St Clement Danes; a paper hat that he had worn on VJ day; a shirt that had once been black-blue.

One by one he examined the scraps of almost six decades, waiting for each to release its memories, and memories arose from every object, propagating other memories in profusion. He saw his mother running beside the hedges with her arms aloft, and looking at him over the kitchen table with a maroon scarf knotted on the top of her head, and scrubbing at a window with a ball of newspaper, and holding out the hem of her gingham dress, and smiling into an empty copper pot, and her face below a beam of light in which there were swirls of cigarette smoke. He saw his father at his desk, with a spot of light on each lens of his glasses, and laughing at *A Night at the Opera*, and standing in the wind, lost in thought, on the hill near Pitlochry. He saw Megan in her blue-checked pinafore, and sitting on a sparkling step, and walking through the park with Mr Beckwith, and sulking in the Doodlebug House, and he saw her white foot resting on his hand, as the rain came through the awning of Sid Dixon's shop. He saw Megan descending the steps of Bank station, and facing the moonlit wall of a light well, and hitching his white cotton shirt onto her shoulders, and bubbles running over her throat, and pearls of water on her scarlet mittens. He remembered kissing her by the church. He remembered the tins of food in perfect rows in Mr Beckwith's kitchen, and the glimpse of Mrs Beckwith's breast, and the puddle of bird's-foot trefoil, and the sun on the rocks of Rinsey Head, and Megan's hairclip on Mr Beckwith's muddy palm, and Mrs Beckwith dead. He remembered Sam at the dinner table in his parents' house, and embracing him by a basket of geraniums that the landlord's daughter had watered, and smoothing his tie by the house with the green tarmac drive. He remembered Liz putting her face to the big radio, and Liz's short violet dress, and her grass-green buckle, and her father with a glass of sherry in each hand. He remembered Jane crossing her bedroom, naked, and her lips whispering as she kissed him, and walking between gravestones in Edinburgh. He saw Mr Barrington with his book and the jar of copper sulphate, Mr Greening in his paisley cravat, Sid Dixon turning a soup tureen in his white-gloved hands, Esmé with a plum-coloured elephant that had yellow eyes, and Pen Hollander's purple hair. He saw Roderick bouncing his walking stick outside the church, Mr Owen turning a ball on a circle of blue paint, Roy Draper holding his severed finger, a woman with a cerise headscarf sitting in a car, a man in a black corduroy suit carrying a book to Cornelia, and Sir Archibald McIndoe's pinstriped sleeve. He saw the barrage balloons in the smoky sky and the feet of Mr Fitchie, and Sister Martha's fingernails and Mr Harvey's fingernails, and Douglas Nesbit sitting enthroned on the settee, showing his teeth. He remembered a tiny green flare against a night sky, mustard-yellow lichen on thick grey planks, a steel wall covered with a slime of salt, streetlamps chattering in the wind that stirred the trees in Greenwich Park, a woman in a turquoise woollen bonnet, the sound of bells by the Panthéon, the doctor's room with the sticky red seats, a kayak with a pale pink hull, a mauve and pink sunburst on a quilt, and the crack of the door of his father's study. He saw a half-moon in a flow of starling-coloured cloud, a fragment of glass on the driveway of the scout hut, the silky ash on the joists of the Doodlebug House, the till in the grocer's, a frog under the rhododendron in Nan Burnett's garden, and rain on the silver roof of the Dome of Discovery. He saw the flakes of white paint on the window of Sid Dixon's shop, a pub with black doors and windowframes, a bright red hosepipe that leaked water, strings of bunting slung over trestle tables, a boy making a megaphone of his hands to shout across an empty valley, and the birthmark between Lily's breasts. He saw Gareth Jones and Eric Mullins, and Mrs Pardoe, and Mrs Darling and Mrs Evans, and Harold Stevens and Geoff Darby, Lionel Griffiths and John Halloran, Jimmy Murrell and Mrs Murrell, and Mr Gardiner. He saw Mrs Solomon, Mr Owen, Mick Radford and Dave Gordon and Billy Barton, Ronald Prentice, Court-ney Wilson and Gisbert, and dozens of other ghosts, as clearly as he saw, in the weakening darkness, the reflection of himself in the mirror at the end of his room. He allocated the things and places and the people he remembered to their years, and accounted for every year of his life, beginning with the cold February morning in 1944 that arose from a postcard of the Virgin Mary in a blazing sun. Year by year he completed his life, but what he made was not a story. The years were no more than labels on his memories, which were all present in the same place, and he was the place in which they existed, in a state of equanimity that was the sum of them. He had become a theatre of memories, a reef of memories, Alexander told himself. He desired nothing. He remembered Jane's bedroom, and Megan's face freckled with salt and with the shadows of raindrops. He dropped the card into the case. Seeing buds of condensation on the wall of the shop, a piece of orange vine on a fragment of china, three letters on a table, a saddle like brass in fierce sunlight, he fell into sleep.

56. Sea lavender

Alexander MacIndoe lay in bed, watching the shapes that were cast on the ceiling, shapes as faint as a few days' dust on white paint. The clouds that he could see were no bolder than the shadows on the ceiling. For many minutes all he could hear was the ticking of his watch, then the noise of a passing car wiped through the room. There was a sound like an axe striking soft wood, which was the sound of a dog barking down on the beach, he realised. A peal of gulls burst over his roof and fell swiftly behind the houses.

He took a shower, put on the black suit and white shirt he often wore on Sundays, and went to the kitchen to make his plate of toast and mug of tea. Across the gardens, the curtains were closed on every bedroom window. The fences were dark with the rain that had fallen in the night, and cast no shadows on the lawns. A crimson dress had been left hanging on a washing line. A large red plastic ball was in the pond of the garden with the bush of yellow roses. Nothing moved, except a thrush that took flight from the frame of the children's swing.

He sat at the table to review what he would be doing in the coming week and compile a list of things he would have to buy at the nursery that afternoon. When he looked out of the window again, he saw that a part of the sky was in motion, like a spill of milk seeping through white cotton. The leaves of the cherry tree quivered. One curtain had been drawn back.

From the box in the hall he fetched the tools that had to be cleaned and oiled. He worked until eight o'clock and then put on his coat to go out to Mr Kidwell's shop. At the front door he felt a breeze that smelled of seaweed and wet shingle. On the paving stones, squares of silvery water trembled within borders of dry grey concrete. Mr Kidwell was washing the salt from his windows; Alexander took his newspaper from the untouched pile behind the counter and put his coins in the till. They talked on the step of the shop, looking out at the scuffed surface of the sea, until another customer arrived. A boy carrying a fishing rod crossed the road; he wore vast green rubber boots, which thumped like a slack drum with each footfall.

Alexander made a second mug of tea and carried it to the armchair by the window. Having read the front page, he put the newspaper down and gazed at the sea. One morning, after a storm, his father went to look at the sea at Portobello, and the water looked, his father had said, as if a rasp had been rubbed backwards and forwards on a sheet of tin. And Alexander went with Jane to Portobello on a hot and stagnant afternoon, and the sea looked like a vast plain of raw clay; she stood in the water, holding her skirt up, and threw her sunglasses for him to catch. He opened the newspaper. At ten o'clock Roderick rang.

There were three people ahead of Esmé Clark in the queue. 'Make your mind up time,' she said, taking a credit card from her wallet. 'We'll just about catch it.'

Megan Beckwith looked at the station clock. It was almost eleven. She had made up her mind, but now, thinking of Alexander MacIndoe, what she recalled was the windy, empty platform of Bank station. She had left before the train came in, and gone back up to the street, where Alexander was no longer to be seen, and what she felt now was a weak reprise of the bleakness she had felt then, and the elation of being free.

Raising her eyebrows, Esmé fluttered the card at Megan. 'You're on board, yes?' She checked her watch and snarled at the back of the head of the woman at the ticket office counter, who was poring over a timetable that had separated into two pieces as she unfolded it.

'I don't know,' said Megan. Her fingers, she realised, were undoing the buttons of her raincoat, as if she were entering someone's house. The minute hand of the clock edged backwards a fraction before springing forward and halting midway across the hour's final segment.

'This is ridiculous,' said Esmé. 'You've had months of dithering. Let's go. You can finally decide on the way there.' A clerk at a neighbouring counter rapped the glass partition with a coin, summoning Esmé. She turned to Megan. 'Well?'

Crouched under backpacks, a dozen teenagers in identical blue nylon jackets scuttled towards the platform for the Brighton train. 'Go on,' said Megan.

457

'Good,' said Esmé, and she asked for two tickets.

'I'm sorry.'

'Don't worry. Let's see what happens. You can spend the day on the pier if you decide to back out. I'll only be gone a couple of hours.'

'I'm a bit too old for funfairs.'

'Whatever. You can get some sea air, if nothing else. Have a day out.'

'Yes.'

Esmé signed the counterfoil and gave Megan a frown. 'I think you should knock on his door.'

'We'll see.'

'What harm can it do? He wanted to keep seeing you. You told me that yourself.'

'That was years ago. He doesn't now, it seems.'

'Pride, that's all.'

'Ah,' said Megan. 'I see. Male pride.'

'It'll be OK,' said Esmé. 'He said it was up to you. He does want to see you. I know he does.' She put a ticket in Megan's hand.

'He might not be there.'

'And tomorrow I might get hit by a bus,' said Esmé, taking Megan's bag from her shoulder.

When he opened the door to Cornelia, he saw Roderick standing on the verge with Maximilian, by the open boot of the car. Maximilian was wearing the shirt that Alexander had bought him for Christmas, and his football boots, which he was pressing repeatedly into a patch of mud. Like a man signalling from a shipwreck, Roderick waved to Alexander with wide sweeps of his arm.

'Not an easy morning,' explained Cornelia. 'The child is misbehaving. You may not want to stay with us for very long.'

'He's excited about the party, I expect,' suggested Alexander.

'I don't know what it is. It might be that,' said Cornelia, adjusting the slide in her hair. 'We thought we'd go to the café by the bookshop. Ist das in Ordnung?'

'Ja. Natürlich.'

'Sehr gut,' approved Cornelia, and she tucked a hand under his arm

458

as they waited for a cyclist to go by. 'You can't walk with those!' Cornelia shouted across the road. 'Put your proper shoes on.'

Roderick lifted a pair of shoes from the car and dangled them like bait in front of Maximilian. Obediently the boy took the shoes, but instead of putting them on he stared at the ground, studying the imprints he had made with his studs. Alexander stood beside Maximilian and looked down at the neat pattern of pits in the rubbery mud.

'Hello, Max,' said Alexander. Maximilian smiled at him, but did not reply.

'You can't walk with those boots,' said Cornelia, bending down to remove them.

'I can,' said Maximilian, taking a step backwards.

'You'll wear them out.'

'I won't.'

'Maximilian. You are not going to the café with these boots on your feet. They won't allow you inside like this. You wouldn't like it if someone tramped through your bedroom with muddy boots on, would you? Put your shoes on.'

'I'll carry them,' said Maximilian, hugging the shoes to his chest.

'You will put them on.'

'No.'

'Put them on.'

'No.'

'Mayday, Mayday,' muttered Roderick from the corner of his mouth.

'Maximilian, you will put your shoes on.'

'When we get there.'

'You'll wear them out. They're not meant for pavements. You wear them on grass. Not on stones.'

'I'll walk lightly.'

'If you damage them we'll never buy you another pair.'

Maximilian held his father's hand and tugged it like a bell pull. 'Put the shoes on, Max,' said Roderick, as if they were both conceding defeat, and Maximilian laboriously removed the boots.

'Where's the party, Max?' asked Alexander. The boy surrendered the boots to his father and said nothing.

'Your friend Neil, isn't it?' said Roderick, helping his son to tie the laces of his shoes. 'The offspring of Tory cannibals,' he explained to

459

Alexander. 'Wee Neil doesn't have pocket money, he has a pension.'

'Neil is a nice boy,' said Cornelia.

'Neil doesn't stand a chance,' replied Roderick. 'Boarding school, university, management training, marriage, promotion, children, directorship, golf, freemasons, adultery, divorce, alcoholism, bitterness, misery, death. Predestination of his class.'

'Nonsense,' asserted Cornelia, correcting a lock of Maximilian's hair. 'He's a nice boy.'

They descended the hill, with Cornelia leading and Alexander following Roderick and Maximilian, who walked hand in hand until Maximilian stopped so suddenly that Roderick's grip was broken. On the other side of the road there was a house that had no front. Colonnades of rusting jacks supported the beams of the roof and the ceiling of the lower storey, from which a lamp still hung. It was a broad flat dish of frosted green glass, of a type that had been in fashion many years ago. A swell of sunlight, moving into an angle of the opened bedroom, revealed a rectangle of golden green wallpaper, embossed with gold diagonals. In a corner, beside a low pyramid of rubble, stood a stool with a seat of white nylon fur and four tapering black legs.

'How did they live with that paper?' Roderick wondered.

Maximilian's gaze explored the gutted house, moving systematically from room to room. Cornelia, ten yards ahead, tapped at her wrist. The sunlight shrank from the house, and Maximilian reached for Alexander's hand.

As the train went into the tunnel Megan looked at her face on the pane of greasy glass, and in the same instant her eye perceived the shine of the steel of the windowframe, and the smell of dust from the seats became a taste at the back of her tongue. A memory touched her like a rill of cold water. It was the memory of a room that she was leaving, and she was unhappy. Now she saw the room: it was in Ronda, and she was looking from the dusty corridor into the room, where the bed frame was raw steel, and Alexander was closing their suitcase.

'You all right?' asked Esmé, putting her magazine down.

'Yes. Twinge in my back,' Megan replied. The sun struck her eyes and the room in Ronda was erased. 'What do you think?' she asked, pointing to the magazine.

460

'I don't know. Some of it's not bad. Some of it's good. But there's a lot of crap in here. A lot of drool. I can't write drool. You write this kind of stuff with a penis dipped in ink.'

Megan laughed, then checked the seats behind her to make sure no one had overheard. 'Read me a bit.'

'You don't want to hear this.'

'I do. I want to know what drool sounds like.'

'Blather, drivel, drivel, "a straight-to-video college-kids-in-peril lech-fest that ringfenced Fliss with a bevy of D-cup babes whose futures, I think it's safe to say, lie in the world of one-hander websites." You don't want to hear this, do you? "A written-by-autopilot saga of cross-generational hatchet-burying, *Autumn Leaves* was a tsunami of syrup that left no survivors – apart from Fliss, who somehow created the illusion that there was a lot more to little Amy than met the eye. And what met the eye was pretty damn good, because Fliss looks better in gingham than most girls do in skin. Then came highbrow kudos with *Scarlet and Black*, with Fliss sensational as top-drawer totty Mathilde de la Mole." Is this entertaining? I don't think this is entertaining. Do you think this is entertaining?' She held out the magazine to display a picture of Fliss Reynaud lying naked on a surfboard.

'I'm out of touch. She seems like a nice girl.'

'Sometimes out of touch is best.'

'Ah,' said Megan, nodding with mock sagacity.

'Now don't you start that again,' said Esmé. She flapped the magazine to make Megan look away from the fields. 'You should see him. It'd be stupid not to see him. Totally stupid.'

'You're right,' said Megan to the glass.

'Of course I'm right,' said Esmé, writing a note in the margin of the magazine. 'I'm always right.'

From the café they walked to the seafront, where Cornelia took Maximilian into Mr Kidwell's shop to buy him an ice cream and a comic. Roderick and Alexander continued down the ramp to the path behind the beach.

'So how's work?' asked Alexander.

'Ho hum,' said Roderick, shielding his eyes to watch a waterskier

461

turn and crash. 'I'm thinking of setting up a film club. A couple of people at work are interested. We have a projector.'

'One projector?'

'That's all the true cinéaste requires. We shall, of course, inaugurate our first season with a *Nosferatu* double bill. If we get it off the ground.'

'What are the chances?'

'Hundred to one against, I'd say,' Roderick replied immediately. He sat on a low wall and rested his hands on the curve of his belly. 'I must do some exercise,' he sighed, and he smiled indolently at the sea. 'Have to lift some heavy books after eating.'

Alexander sat down beside him. 'You seem a little – preoccupied,' he commented.

'I'm all right,' Roderick replied, inviting a response that did not come. 'The boy's been a problem lately. There's tension in the house.'

'Things seemed fine at lunch.'

'A lull. There have been rows of the most tremendous intensity. Cups rattling on the table. Racial stereotypes have been bandied about. There have been tears.'

'Brought about by –?'

'The behaviour of the boy, the schooling of the boy, the attire of the boy, the TV allowance, hair length, general attitude. A panoply of discord. We are not getting on.'

'Temporarily.'

'I'm sure. But recently I've found myself envying you, in your second-floor cave.'

'Don't be foolish, Roderick. There's nothing to envy. You have a good life. We both have a good life.'

'That's true,' said Roderick, and he looked at his hands as if he had chosen them and was considering whether they suited him. 'She wanted me to talk to you,' he said, noticing that Cornelia and Maximilian were approaching. 'About the way things are, at the moment.'

'Really?'

'Really.'

'I can't imagine why. I don't know anything. Not about being a parent.'

'No, but confession helps.'

'Not much of a confession,' said Alexander.

'There's more, father,' Roderick laughed.

They watched the waterskier rise from the water, raising a quill of spray, then sink, as if into something viscous.

On the station forecourt Esmé checked the map. 'Do I get a cab or do I walk?' she asked herself, but before she could decide her phone rang. 'Hi,' she laughed into the phone, moving away and raising a hand to Megan in apology.

Megan surveyed the station building and the broad street that stretched in front of them, aware that both had looked different when she had last been in Brighton, but unable to picture what she had seen then. Trying to work out when that visit had been, she recalled seeing *Atlantic City* with Alexander in the afternoon, because the rain was so heavy, and afterwards walking along the windswept pier, which was as bleak as the boardwalk in the film. Alexander had been wearing his grey coat, she seemed to remember. Boys with scarlet hair were kicking a can against the doors of the shops underneath the esplanade. She asked herself what year this would have been, though she knew that the question was of no importance, and still did not know what she would do when Esmé had gone.

'I'll walk,' declared Esmé. 'We're ahead of schedule.'

'Which way do you have to go?' asked Megan.

'Straight ahead, then left at the Clock Tower is quickest.'

'I'll come with you that far.'

'Aren't you taking a cab?'

'No.'

'OK,' Esmé replied, giving Megan a penetrating look. 'You're back-sliding, aren't you?'

'No. I just don't like taking taxis.'

'You're backsliding,' said Esmé, with a cynic's grin.

'Esmé, please. Respect your elders. Enough.'

'OK. Easy.'

They walked in silence to the Clock Tower, where they parted, having arranged to meet at the station at seven o'clock. Megan watched Esmé disappear into the crowds on North Street. There was a Bond Street somewhere in that direction, she told herself, and a Regent Street as well. Kensington Gardens was in that area too. Churchill

Square was around the corner, where Alexander had bought her a pen to replace the one that was in the bag that was stolen. She recalled the way he had sidestepped into the shop and plucked at her sleeve, and then she stopped herself and hurried down West Street, as if to walk away from the distraction of what she remembered. The buildings ended and the sea's horizon filled her vision. She had not decided what to do, but she took from her bag the card on which Esmé had written Alexander's address, and she turned left for the bus station.

'This is unusual,' Alexander remarked to none of them in particular, and he went over to the foot of the cliff and cupped a hand around a clump of mauve plants. 'It doesn't look like much, but it's very rare,' he said to Maximilian. 'It's called Rottingdean sea lavender, and this is the only place in all of England where you'll find it. It's originally from Sicily, which is a part of Italy. People planted it in their gardens, but it escaped.'

'How do flowers escape?' asked Maximilian.

'On the wind. The wind blows the seeds about, and now it grows on the cliffs. And that up there,' he went on, 'is another type of sea lavender. This is the only place in the east of England where that kind grows. There are lots of different kinds and they are all related to a plant called thrift, which is also known as ladies' cushions, or cliff clover.'

'You're pitching it a bit high, I think,' said Roderick. 'He's only five years old.'

Alexander bent the stems gently, to bring the flowers closer to the boy's face.

'We shouldn't tarry,' said Roderick. 'Neil's dad probably imposes a fine on latecomers.'

Maximilian stood on his toes to peer at the sea lavender. 'Can you see, Max?' Alexander asked him, and the boy nodded.

'Back to the car,' said Cornelia, putting a hand on her son's shoulder. 'You don't want to miss any of the games, do you?'

At the foot of the ramp Alexander shook hands with Roderick. 'I'll stay down here for a while,' he told him, and then he shook hands with Maximilian. 'Enjoy the party,' he said. Maximilian turned away.

'It's going to rain,' Cornelia observed to Alexander, and she kissed him on the cheek.

When the rain began, Alexander sheltered in a bus stop by the golf course. He looked up at the island of basalt-coloured cloud, at its fringe of surf-coloured vapour, and waited for it to pass.

Through the window of Alexander's flat Megan saw a paper lightshade and a segment of ceiling and a section of cornice and a door that led to other rooms in which Alexander lived. Finding herself on the point of crying, she returned to the end of the street, where she took from her bag the letter she had written to him. She read his name over and over again, and she remembered the appearance of his name on the order of service. As he read at the lectern it was as though the congregation had become invisible to him. She recalled the repulsive vicar. 'Eternal peace is his,' he told her, complacently, as if giving himself credit for the destination of her father's soul. 'He's not asleep,' she said, 'he's dead.' Mr Harvey shook her hand with a hand that was cold and hard, and then Alexander was by the trees, gesturing to her, and later she sat beside Alexander on the hill, until dusk, barely speaking.

Rain began to fall from a single vast cloud that covered the whole town. Across the road a fat man was holding open the rear door of a car, and a thin woman was shouting at a boy who was looking into the car as though he suspected that he was being lured into a trap. Megan rang the doorbell once and waited. There was no reply. She did not ring again but posted the letter quickly, and immediately wished she had not, and sat down on the step. She raised her umbrella. She remembered her mother standing beside her father in the garden, and putting her arm around his shoulders as she cut a rose and pushed its stem into a buttonhole of his shirt.

Within ten minutes the rain became a haze that was warm and brilliant, and swirled in eddies behind the moving cars. The tarmac gleamed through wisps of steam, as though it had been newly poured. Steam rose in flame shapes from the hoods of the traffic lights. Alexander ambled through the town, taking detours down roads in which he had worked. He passed the Marwicks' house, where he had planted a hornbeam hedge and raised a trellis of clematis and honeysuckle. He passed Mrs Barker's house, where he had made an enclave of blue aconites and hydrangeas and delphiniums, and the Wilsons' garden, where the Californian poppies were in bloom. At Mr Harper's house he saw Mr Harper's daughter sweeping the brick pavement between the herb beds. He thought of something else that he needed to buy at the nursery. Startled by the lateness of the hour, he turned down the alleyway that led back towards his street.

From the corner of his street he saw a woman sitting on the front step of his house, holding an umbrella across her knees. She was wearing a black beret and red raincoat, and she stood up and waved at him when she saw him. A moment before his hand raised itself, he realised who she was.

Megan saw Alexander raise his hand like someone who had been gone for an hour, but he did not smile as he came closer. She stood up slowly, and ran a hand over the buttons of her coat as he approached. A couple of yards away from her he halted; he said nothing; his eyes traced a frame around her. 'Alexander?' she said. He looked at her eyes and seemed to flinch. 'You didn't recognise me, did you?'

'Not at first,' he said.

'I've spread a little,' said Megan, patting a hip. His dull gaze fell to her hip then rose to a place in the region of her shoulder. 'But I recognised you at once. A touch of grey,' said Megan, and she stopped the hand that had begun to move towards him.

'This is a surprise,' he said at last, but there was no surprise in his voice. It was as though he were merely putting a name to something.

'I'll go, if you want,' she said. 'Say the word and I'll go back.'

'No,' he said. 'So she told you?' he asked. 'Esmé?'

'Yes. Of course she told me. Why on earth wouldn't she, after tracking you down? Or did you think I wouldn't do anything, once she'd told me?'

'I don't know, Meg. It's possible.' He looked at the keys in his hand, as if he could not comprehend why he should possess such things.

'Do you want me to go?' she asked him.

Ruefully he surveyed the sky above his street. 'No, I don't want you to go,' he said, yet his expression did not change when his gaze returned to her.

'I know this must be strange,' said Megan. 'Arriving unannounced.'

'No. No,' he replied, but the sentence that he seemed to be commencing remained unspoken.

'I did write to you.'

'I never got anything.'

'No, you wouldn't have,' she smiled. 'I only put it through the door an hour ago.'

'Hm,' said Alexander, as if he had not listened to her reply. He stepped past her and opened the door. 'Come in,' he said.

Megan looked up at the windows of his flat again. Everything was white and looked as fragile as an eggshell. 'Let's go for a walk instead,' she suggested. 'I've been sitting down all day.'

He stooped to pick the letter from the mat, and held it towards her without even reading his name on the envelope. 'Or do you think I should open it?' he asked, keeping hold of the letter.

'It's not a masterpiece,' said Megan. 'Open it if you want. There's nothing in it I won't tell you now.'

He relinquished the letter. 'I have to do something,' he said. 'I won't be a minute.'

The front door closed on her. Folding the letter in half, into quarters, she considered leaving before Alexander returned, but she was still on the step when his shadow appeared on the stippled glass panel of the door. She crammed the letter into a pocket and busied herself with the sleeve of her umbrella.

'Down to the waterfront?' Alexander proposed.

'So you can push me in?' she replied, but again it was as though he had not heard. Like a steward at the end of a long day, he half-raised an arm to show the way they should go. 'You've been here how long?' Megan asked as they left his street.

'In this flat? A couple of years or so.'

'You're gardening?'

'I'm a gardener.'

'That makes sense. And you're happy?'

'It's satisfying,' he said, in a way that imposed silence on her. By the frontless house he asked: 'And you're still teaching?'

'For one more year. Then I retire.'

'You enjoy it still?'

467

'It's satisfying,' she responded, with a half-smile that he was intended to notice, and did.

Alexander glanced at the house. 'And you never did get married,' he said, with the intonation of a compliment.

'No, I never did. There goes our Megan; she never married. Do you know when I heard that? When I was twenty. That nosy old prune who lived over the road. Remember her?'

'Mrs Harley? Mrs Hartson?'

'Hartson,' she confirmed, tentatively. 'You didn't either? Get married?'

'No,' said Alexander.

'A lady friend?'

'None,' he replied, and there was a tightening of his lips that might have signified amusement. 'So, Esmé's back in your life?'

'She is.'

'Quite a character.'

'A dynamo,' she agreed. 'What our Esmé wants, our Esmé gets. As a rule.'

'I'm sure.' They passed Mr Kidwell's shop and went down the ramp to the shore. 'I still see Sam and Liz from time to time. You remember Sam and Liz?'

'Good grief, Eck. Of course I remember Sam and Liz. It's not that long ago.'

'Their boy's married now,' said Alexander, ignoring her exasperation. 'Clare has a girl.' The flank of a distant ferry, hit by the sun, shone like a stump of chalk; behind it, and as far as they could see to east and west, clouds the colour of flint were rising. 'And Jane Nesbit lives not far from here,' he added.

With her foot Megan pushed a large pebble aside. 'Eck?' she asked. 'You'll stay in touch? With me, I mean.'

'What do you think?' Alexander replied, and he put his hands in his pockets and went over to the foot of the cliff. He perused the cliff-face as though he were reading it. 'Come and look at this,' he said.

She stood beside him. 'I really don't know,' she said. 'Will you?'

'See those?' he asked, aiming a finger at an outcrop of mauve flowers. 'This is the only place in England you'll find them.'

468

'Is that so?'

'It is so.'

'Is this the same flower?' asked Megan, indicating a plant that sprang from a crack of the footpath.

'No, it's not. It's ordinary thrift. Otherwise known as cliff clover, or sea pink, or ladies' cushions.'

'Not rare then, this one?'

'Not rare at all.'

She plucked a sprig of thrift and put it in the buttonhole of her coat. They walked on.

All Fourth Estate books are available from
your local bookshop

Or visit the Fourth Estate website at:

www.4thestate.com